The Savannah Stories

Bad Blood

The Savannah Stories

Bad Blood

J.L. Lemon

ISBN-13: 978-0-9909589-7-0

Published 2020

To Dad

I wish you could see yourself through my eyes.

You stand taller than a mountain,

You are stronger than Hercules,

You have the heart of a lion

(and that heart is made of gold),

And you have the soul of an angel.

You are and always will be my hero, mentor, guardian,

best friend - my whole world.

I love you more than words can say.

To Mom

I still miss you and love you dearly.

Family ties mean that no matter how much you might want to run from your family, you can't.

Unknown

The day began normally enough. Savannah went about her sergeant's duties, first getting updates from her detectives on their cases then completing time sheets, signing overtime slips, and following up on background investigations.

The morning took an odd turn at ten after nine. She'd settled at her desk armed with reading glasses, a pen and bottle of Tylenol on the side (the latter to cure the inevitable headache inspired by status reports and evaluations) when she heard Josh Hunter, her captain, quarreling with someone in his office next door. The stranger's strong, deep voice never rose to an alarming level that demanded intervention but it held a ring of authority that refused argument. She puckered in places that made her cringe. Debated over closing her door. If the zone commander (which it very well could've been) was that upset, she wanted out of the line of fire since he'd walk right past her little office to leave.

She found herself leaning toward the wall hoping to catch a few key words, just enough to discern the gist of disagreement. It didn't work. She felt sorry for her captain. Josh Hunter was a nice guy who held his temper in check with recalcitrant officers, detectives (and new sergeants such as herself) unless they committed one of cardinal sins of police work.

The two men parted ways on a tense note. Zone commander, had to be. Savannah reached for the Tylenol until hearing the rhythmic sound of dress shoes marching down the hall – toward her office. She abandoned the Tylenol, figuring nothing past morphine might ease the pain once the commander finished with her because if the higher ups were unhappy with the captain they weren't exactly thrilled with his subordinates either.

She collected the small bundle of papers and tried to look very busy scouring stats but was too nervous to notice any of them.

The dress shoes entered her peripheral vision. The long, purposeful strides continued past. She breathed a sigh of relief. At least she'd go home with her ass in tact and not have it handed to her.

Then the stride stopped. *Spoke too soon, didn't you?* The silent berating continued even as the shoes stepped to her doorway then stopped. Zone commanders never waited, not when they had a burr under their saddles (as Ennis, her Texan husband, would say). Angry senior officers sometimes knocked (as an insignificant courtesy) then barged right in.

"My God," the voice that reamed out Josh Hunter softened with amazement, "It always amazes me how much you look like her."

Confused, Savannah glanced up from the printout. The man arguing with Josh stood about six feet, had a full head of neatly styled silver hair and what she assessed as a wistful expression. His general physique touted a man in his sixties that kept in shape and maybe still lifted a fair share of weights. He wore an expensive black tailored suit, white shirt and fancy gray striped tie. Not a zone commander but someone with class, money and moxie who didn't mind verbally kicking a cop's ass – or kick ass in the business world. Lee Morgan was notorious for his business acumen and it was rumored he ruined stubborn competition who refused to bend to his will.

She herself had no intention of getting an ass-kicking from a member of the Forbes Top 20. She liked her ass just the way it was, thank you. She removed her glasses with a smile, "Mr. Morgan, it's nice to see you again. It's been a while."

He'd looked enraptured when he stepped in the office. He'd done this every time they ever met which wasn't often. The moment her hand clasped the soft warmth of his, he covered her hand with his free one. "Honestly, it's been too long." He held her hand a beat longer, "Every year you favor Charlene more. Such a beautiful woman."

"Yes, she was."

Lee chuckled, "I was talking about you. You both remind me of dark-haired Rita Hayworth."

Savannah blushed. Of the two daughters, her older sister Georgia heavily favored Charlene but Savannah accepted the compliment anyway.

The last time she'd seen Lee Morgan was at her last commendation ceremony. She'd met him when she was very young. Charlene took her and Georgia to his palatial home in Augusta where the butler and cook lavished the children in attention. Over the years Morgan treated her high school golf team to an expensive lunch every year to celebrate winning the state championship. Since then he'd attended every one of her commendation ceremonies. He really was community oriented, it seemed, by his presence at local functions and his well-publicized philanthropy.

Lee noticed her nameplate, "I see you've earned a promotion to sergeant. Well done, my dear, well done. I know Charlene is proud of you and so am I." He continued in a nostalgic, almost melancholy tone, "When we were dating, she wanted a daughter that favored her and she got one."

Yes, her name is Georgia – wait. "*Dating?* You and Mama?"

"Oh yes, we grew quite close too. Even discussed eloping at one point."

Savannah barely caught her jaw from slinging open. Her mother? Not only dating Lee Morgan but she entertained eloping with him too? Talk about a newsflash.

He waved off his comment, "But that was a lifetime ago. She fell in love with Robert and married him instead. Last time I saw Charlene was in the hospital before she passed away."

"You stayed in touch all those years?" Amazing. Did Lee Morgan pine for a lost love for decades? And why hadn't her mother ever mentioned dating him, much less their plans to *elope?*

"On and off, yes. She was a lady far too special to forget or let go of entirely. Do you remember the first time we met? You were four. Charlene brought you and your sister Georgia along to visit me. My cook made a cake for the occasion. You ate until you were so full you fell asleep in your sister's lap. I'll keep that memory with me forever. Charlene apologized for your voracious appetite but I thought it was charming how you curled up in Georgia's lap. And here you are grown and with a successful career. How time flies."

Oh, yes, she remembered the trip. Mr. Morgan had been a most courteous host to his younger guests, providing food and a "friend" to show them around the mansion. The chubby fellow in a black suit very much like a penguin spoke in a British accent which Savannah thought was very enchanting. He led her and Georgia to rooms filled with fine art and delicate things behind glass. She specifically recalled hinged ornate jeweled Fabergé eggs, their contents a mystery until the butler opened one to reveal a finely detailed gold carriage. Savannah called it Cinderella's carriage. There were so many delicate, beautiful things she'd have to stay for weeks to see them all. She put words to her thoughts, "Oh yes, I remember that visit. You were very kind to me and Georgia, letting us explore your home and yes, that cake was amazing."

He appeared impressed, "Mrs. Gardner still has the recipe. Perhaps you could visit and see if it's as delicious as you recall. I know Charlene would be pleased you did." His blue eyes roamed the room. They settled on her framed commendations hanging on the wall. He finally pointed to a current photo on Savannah's desk. One of her, Ennis and the kids taken on her birthday, "What a lovely family. The oldest girl looks like you did at that age, right down to the dimples."

Lily was five and yes, she inherited several of Savannah's traits, including her dimples.

For some reason conversation came easy with Lee Morgan. Too easy, maybe, but the man's interest felt genuine like a friend wanting to catch up. Never one to miss a chance bragging about her husband and kids, she rounded the desk and put a name with each face, "That's my husband Ennis. He's a detective here. He's gone right now or I'd introduce you. Then this ball of fire is Lily, next to her is Anna and our latest little bundle is Daniel."

Chuckling, Morgan pointed to Lily, "This one is your mirror image. They're all handsome children and your husband... Ennis? He loves you very much, I can see that as clear as your love for him." He reached in his suit coat and handed her his card, "I'd like you to come by my house this week whenever you have a chance. Give me a call and we'll set up a time."

"Not to be rude but what's this regarding?" *Because if it involves your argument with my captain, don't expect me to help. I worked too hard for those sergeant's stripes to lose 'em.*

Lee Morgan appeared anything but offended. He'd dealt with bigger fish than an old flame's nosy kid. "Reminiscing and possibly some business."

What sort of "business" could a multimillionaire want with a cop? The possibilities depressed her. Whatever it was, it might fatten their bank account but it would suck precious time away from her family – if she agreed to this "business" he mentioned. Lucky for her she'd learned years ago how to say no to rich people but she'd call Morgan and set up the meeting anyway. As he said, Charlene would be pleased she did.

She scanned the tan card with black writing. The man didn't waste money on flair, that was certain. At the top it simply read "Morgan". The company was a conglomerate like Berkshire Hathaway so nothing else need be said, she supposed. Below the company name and emblem was his name and number. "I'll look over my schedule and give you call this evening."

They parted with friendly handshakes and smiles but once Lee Morgan drove off in his black Mercedes, Savannah made a beeline for her captain's office. "What did Lee Morgan want?"

The mention of the name thinned Josh Hunter's mouth, drew his brow tightly together. In the last hour he'd aged ten years. He slumped back in his chair heaving a sigh of warning, "I hope you're not here to argue on his behalf. I heard you two getting chummy."

She reined in her resentment, "Chummy? To ease your mind we're only acquaintances. According to him, he and my mother were an item before Daddy came along. Now, does that vet me enough to learn what your tiff entailed?"

Hunter apologized. Her explanation performed wonders, however, because his nice looking, normally semi-line free features returned. "He claims he's in danger because of that book being released next week. He's afraid of repercussions probably because of his questionable business practices."

She slanted him a skeptical frown.

He defended his statement, "He's a successful businessman but he didn't get that way just wining and dining clients. He put his foot on the owners' necks and – oh, nevermind. You like him for some reason so I'll be quiet."

"Wait. What book?"

"You live in a cave now? Everyone's heard about his son's book. Even my wife wants a copy."

"What book?" she asked again.

"*Bad Blood*. Apparently his boy wrote a scathing warts and all account of the Morgan family. Nothing you'd want on Ancestry.com, if you know what I mean. The family had injunctions and lawsuits going for a year or more to stop the publisher. The injunctions ended last week. Before you ask, Morgan never told me why, exactly, the son is out to destroy the family name but he fears repercussions from the book when it's released."

The fear of repercussions didn't surprise her. The part about his son did. "He has four boys, right? Which one wrote it?"

"Tucker."

Oh. Him. "He's been in plenty of trouble in the past."

"Not according to our records."

"Okay, he's been in a lot of trouble in Augusta. I'm sure the family had it swept under the rug though."

Hunter's brow shot up, "You do realize you're accusing your cousin of a crime. He was the sheriff back then."

"Bobby wasn't corrupt. He couldn't buck the system and if the system says let it slide, he just didn't grease the way down. He was like you. Stuck in the middle of a political circus."

"Well, I know my roll in this drama and I told Morgan *repeatedly* I couldn't officially assign officers to play bodyguard while he stays in the city. I suggested he find a personal security guard for protection."

Dread dropped like a rock in Savannah's gut, "Great. I think I know who tops that list."

2

Savannah decided like medicine, the meeting with Lee Morgan should be taken quickly and while she held her nose. She spent the two hour trip to Augusta finessing reasons why providing private security held no allure for her, no matter the amount of money. Yes, the extra cash would help the children's future college tuition (she expected that argument) and perhaps she and Ennis could allot a little chunk to renovating the main bathroom or building a backyard deck, two dreams they'd had since they moved in. But the sacrifice of time weighed heavier to her. She prized the few hours she spent with her husband and babies far too much to give them up.

She required no directions to the Morgan residence outside Augusta since she'd grown up admiring the palace her whole life. The miniature Versailles – that was her description of it – rose on the horizon as she drove along the highway. And it stuck out like a glorious, extravagant thumb.

Savannah stopped at the end of the quarter mile driveway to the house. A sense of déjà vu struck her but not because she remembered coming here so long ago. As a child, a visit to the grand mansion was a wonderful, unexpected treat. The sheer size of the place and opulence overwhelmed her. Crystal chandeliers bigger than their dining table at home. Marble fireplaces. The most majestic staircase she'd seen in her life swept from the first floor to the second story, the curved railing spreading wide like arms waiting to enfold a giant. The view from the upper story both thrilled and intimidated her back then. But today, this visit to the Morgan mansion made her edgy. Lee used her mother (and their supposed relationship) to lure her there, probably on the pretext of hiring her for bodyguard duty. Not such a fairytale visit.

A mighty ornamental black iron fence surrounded the estate, cutting it off from the rest of society. A brick security guard house and a two large iron gates crowned the entrance. Two men were on duty. A portly, balding fellow in his mid-fifties manned the security cameras while a younger, more ship-shape man in his late twenties exited the small building. Ex-military, she guessed, judging by his gait and ultra well-groomed appearance. She rolled down the Charger's window as he approached with a clipboard, "Name?"

"Savannah Prince Rutherford." It was best to use all those names in case Mr. Morgan forgot her married one. Something told her, however, that Mr. Morgan forgot nothing about anyone.

A quick stroke of the pen on Mr. Squared Away's clipboard verified her appointment. He stepped back, turned toward his partner in the guardhouse and gave him a curt nod. The gates began opening.

"Drive through, please," Squared Away said. "Enjoy your visit."

Driving through was easy. Enjoying the visit? Well, she'd see about that. First thing she had to do was figure out where to park her Dodge so it didn't lower the property value. She pulled into the circular drive and parked facing the massive, wide open forecourt.

Savannah chose a dressier pantsuit for the occasion. Nothing too flashy (because she owned nothing falling into that category) and nothing too drab (God forbid Morgan think Charlene and R.J. raised a frump).

She appraised the house up close before exiting the car. A shiver shook along her spine at the sheer fortune these people possessed. To actually own such a grand mansion and a battalion of employees to help run it. Dear God, she felt so out of place here.

The ten limestone porch steps added a degree of exercise to the visitor's day. She already tended to her husband, two girls and baby boy before embarking on the two hour drive. In her opinion, she really didn't need any more exercise.

A gentleman in his late fifties opened the door. His attire consisted of black trousers, white shirt and black tie and he had friendly features despite his lack of a smile. She'd seen butlers in her career. Lately they were younger – and one even female – and a couple strayed from conventional formal wear. This guy did not. His dress shoes sparkled, gloves stark white, and not one gray hair on his head dared stray out of place.

A thread of insecurity wound through her. *I should've worn a dress. I'm leaving the impression of a magazine salesperson.* "Savannah –" she cleared the frog that suddenly lodged in her throat and tried again. "Savannah Rutherford to see Lee Morgan."

Impassive as every other butler she encountered, he stepped aside, swept his gloved hand in a flourish toward the entry with a stiff, British, "This way, madam."

In her line of work the name "madam" fell far short of favorable but his accent explained it all. British preferred madam while Americans opted for ma'am. She stepped into her own fairytale fantasy where the floors were shining marble, the sunlit foyer reached to the second story ceiling and the enormous crystal chandelier above her sparkled with finely cut prisms and diamond-like pendants. Only the décor changed since her visit thirty-something years ago. Dark bronze and cream wood furnishings replaced a more feminine floral interior.

She followed Jeeves to the living room (or great room or whatever highfalutin folk called it). He stopped at an antique chair that looked like it cost half her annual salary. Everything around her tweaked her uneasiness again, especially Jeeves's clipped, "If you will be seated, madam, I will let Mr. Morgan know you are here."

"No need, Spencer," a familiar voice entered the room. Savannah breathed a bit easier now.

Morgan greeted her, shook her hand and motioned her to sit.

"Drinks, sir?" Spencer stood aside while Morgan chose a chair close to his guest.

Lee must have sensed her anxiety and answered with a down-to-earth, "I've asked Mrs. Gardner to bring milk and a treat for us. She remembers Mrs. Rutherford when she was referred to as Little Miss."

She'd forgotten that. The reminder flashed a picture of a very elderly man dressed as Spencer was. He'd been a joy, like a jovial grandfather leading his granddaughters around a fairgrounds to take in all the sights while Lee escorted Charlene off to another part of the house. Savannah and Georgia saw them once when the butler escorted them past a doorway. They'd been sitting on a couch together in (if Savannah recalled correctly) a serious conversation, not the lighthearted banter their mother shared with the staff. When Savannah began asking for her mama, Mrs. Gardner magically appeared, armed with her chocolate cake and a large glass of milk. The lady had been much younger back then but no less friendly than the butler. Savannah remembered it tickled the lady when she asked for another slice of cake – and a second glass of milk.

"*Milk*, sir?" Spencer's face looked like Anna's when her mama mentioned broccoli or cauliflower casserole for supper. The stoic expression returned so fast Savannah wondered if her mind played tricks on her. "My apologies, sir. I'll have Mrs. Gardner serve the *treat* and *milk* in the dining room."

Hint, hint, Mr. Morgan. Spencer ain't too keen on the company you're keeping today.

"No, here is fine." Lee stood, straightened his polo shirt then approached his butler. Morgan did not seem happy. He spoke to Spencer in a whisper. Their brief confab ended when Spencer glanced at her then uttered, "My sincerest apologies, sir. It will not happen again."

Morgan dismissed Spencer for other duties. A contrite half-smile crossed his lips when he returned to his seat, "I apologize for Spencer's outburst. He's a little *too* British at times."

"Is this Little Miss?" a Scottish brogue inquired.

Savannah turned toward the voice. A plump elderly lady entered the room holding a silver tray with two glasses of milk and two saucers. On one sat a slender piece of chocolate cake and on the other, a piece three inches wide. Beneath the wrinkles and slightly hunched back, Savannah semi-recognized the woman who resembled Flora from

Sleeping Beauty. Way back when she'd had a kind face, voice and demeanor and hadn't changed one bit. This was Mrs. Gardner.

The woman's face broke into a smile reminding Savannah of her grandmother's, "Indeed it is. I could spot this pretty face in a crowd of a million, I could. I remember when you visited years ago, curled up tight as a kitten in your sister's lap, you were. It's a pleasure to see you again and *oh my*, you so very much favor your mother!"

The blood rushed to Savannah's cheeks, "Thank you, Mrs. Gardner. It's good to see you too."

"Heavens, and you sound like her too!" She flinched as if she'd spoken out of turn. "Well, from what I can recall of her voice, that is."

How did this woman, a cook for this rich businessman, remember Charlene's voice? Her mother hadn't made a habit of dropping by as far as she knew. Savannah thanked her again. It spurred the older woman on, "Such a sweet lady she was and I've no doubt you're just as fine a lady. Now, this is the same recipe I used when you were a wee tyke. Whatever's left over I'm to send the rest of it home for you and your family," Mrs. Gardner carefully placed the tray on the table.

"That's very kind of you, ma'am," Savannah replied, "They'll enjoy it as much as I will."

"If you need anything, tell Mr. Morgan and I'll be right out."

They had a few more exchanges before the older woman waddled back to the kitchen.

Lee handed Savannah a saucer then took one for himself, "You've made her day. She loved to visit with your mother when she dropped by."

Yeah, about that. "How often did Mama drop by?"

"Not often enough, believe me." He nodded to her saucer.

She obliged by taking a bite of cake and had to curb a moan of pleasure. Mrs. Gardner's cake transported her to a time when she and Georgia roamed the halls of this elegant mansion, escorted by a kind older man who showed the children finery only royalty could afford and meeting their cordial host – Mr. Morgan, their mama called him – who encouraged the girls to indulge in the rich, delicious desserts.

"Absolutely scrumptious," she moaned after the first bite of cake. "Ennis and the girls will love this. Thank you and before I leave I must thank Mrs. Gardner too."

He'd taken one bite of his cake and set it aside. "Certainly. In fact, I'd hoped to give you a tour of the house and grounds after we conduct our business, if that would be acceptable with you."

After a swallow of milk, she placed her saucer on the tray. Good as the cake was this peculiar meeting set off inner alarms. He could hire any off duty officer for protection without lavishing them in an elaborate overture. Why did he butter her up with cake and milk, references to her mother and dusty memories? "Sure. So what business are we conducting?"

"I admit seeing you the other day stirred fond feelings of Charlene. She was a good woman, a strong one…"

As Morgan went on about her mother, Savannah distanced herself from the talk. If she allowed herself to feel too deeply or extend the conversation too long, she'd descend into a bottomless depression. Her best defense against this was to mentally review the next day's paperwork waiting on her desk.

"…I'm hoping you'll consider signing on as security when I'm in Atlanta. I realize your schedule is hectic what with your job, Ennis and the children but I'd feel safer with someone I know."

She wanted to let him down easy. "Mr. Morgan, I don't–"

"Please call me Lee and before you turn me down, my plan is to make you Chief Security Officer in Atlanta. You'd help vet your fellow officers and choose the most capable candidates." He reached in his suit jacket, handed her what looked like a folded check. It was. "This would be your salary."

She steeled herself for the amount. If the multimillionaire truly feared repercussions from Tucker's book, money was no object. Savannah unfolded the check. The breath left her body. A weird heaviness settled in her fingers as if she held every dollar the check represented. In the span of seconds images raced through her mind. Bathroom renovation, a backyard deck, a new Ram for Ennis, even a chunk of Lily's college was covered. "Mr. Morgan – Lee, I'm not only flattered, I'm floored by this number." And all the zeros at the end…

"In a perfect world, you'd say yes right here, right now but you have a family to consider and I assume you want Ennis's input on the offer."

Still stunned, she could only nod.

"May I make one more proposition you can discuss with your husband?"

Another nod. *You can't accept this, Savannah. You love being a cop.* Then the other voice took over, the one specializing in guilt. *But don't be selfish.   Your family can use this money.   Imagine the possibilities…*

He handed her a second check but placed his hand on hers, "Before you look at the check, my other offer is this: Come to work for me full-time.   You'd be based in Atlanta, Chief Security Officer there, but you'd need to be flexible enough to work here in Augusta on certain occasions." He removed his hand.

Had he noticed the tremor in her hands? If so he never let on. Savannah opened the check. The ability to speak abandoned her. Her tongue lay dead and dry in her mouth while her brain attempted to absorb the number.   It was too large.   Too many numbers to comprehend. Could this amount fit into hers and Ennis's meager bank account without it reading "Tilt"?

"That's your annual salary," he said with a smile in his voice.

Meanwhile the lump between her ears chugged away, finding reasons to accept without Ennis's approval. It counted off the prospects the way a game show host announced the contestant's potential prizes. A renovated bathroom, new deck, brand new Ram, private schools for the kids and last but not least, cha-ching, buh-bye mortgage, Lily's college is paid for in record time and Anna's is way ahead of schedule. *How can you lose?*

The tremble in her hands worsened.   The other side of the argument hit her square between the eyes. *Lee Morgan heads the company now but what happens when his kids take control? I'll be canned and then what? I'll be too old to return to law enforcement past mall security. Sounds like fun. Not.*

Lee's warm hands wrapped around held her unsteady ones. He gave them a gentle squeeze, "Stop over-thinking. Talk it over with Ennis and get back to me. It's a big life change, I realize that." Subdued delight lilted in his voice, "But just imagine the things you could do for the two of you and your children."

3

An hour and a half and four bookstores later Savannah plunked down twenty-five dollars plus tax for "Bad Blood", the hottest must-have read on the New York Times Best Seller List and Amazon.

She managed to grab the last copy (misplaced on a separate display) five seconds before an eagle-eyed twenty-something woman honed in on it. The woman followed Savannah to the checkout pleading with her to hand over the book as if her life depended on having it. Savannah repeatedly declined to do so since she'd claimed the book fair and square.

With the woman at her heels like a yipping Chihuahua, Savannah never felt more relieved to see a checkout. She picked up the pace after a man joined the two's trek once seeing the book under the detective's arm. Before that he been hunkered over the customer service desk, hand shoved through his hair and explaining to the clerk that his wife would serve him liver and onions for a week if he missed bringing home a copy of Tucker Morgan's book – then he spied Savannah toting hers to the register.

If not for her older sister, Savannah wouldn't have battled society for the four hundred fifty page tome but according to Georgia, "It's not only based on the Morgans but it's so engrossing you won't set it down!"

Now who could refuse that? Not a police sergeant ready to yank her hair out from caring for hers and Ennis's new addition. Their brand new baby boy kept Mama so busy when he peed, pooped, ate and various other things, well, one might think there was no time to read. One would be wrong. She was desperate for diversity.

The clerk tucked the receipt inside the thick book and thanked Savannah for the purchase. At the door, Eagle Eye blocked her exit, "I'll pay you forty bucks for the book." She pulled the green from her purse to prove she meant business.

"I'm sorry but no. Have you tried the bookst–"

"Look," the woman's voice developed an edge, "I waited a year for that book. I've been to every store from Midtown to Sandy Springs to Duluth for that thing. This place is my last hope. Fifty bucks, how's that?"

"Ma'am, I'm not selling the book. They'll get another shipment in soon I'm sure."

"Excuse me, but that's a copy of *Bad Blood*, isn't it?"

Savannah sighed, turned. Now Mr. Liver & Onions joined the party. The annoyed woman across from her nodded, "But she's selling it to me. Sixty dollars, right?" She rifled her handbag until digging out another twenty.

"Seventy. No, seventy-five. I can't eat liver and onions for a solid week. Have mercy on me, please."

The woman's laserlike vision zeroed in on Savannah's wedding ring – something her own left hand lacked. "You're married and got kids, right? Here's enough money to take them to Six Flags. *Just let me have the book.*"

Savannah's frustration mounted, "What is the big deal over this book?"

By then both greedily leered at the book the way Gollum stared at his "Precious".

The woman's jaw plummeted, "You haven't heard? The Morgans converged across the city buying up copies–"

"And," Mr. Liver and Onions added, "they're still trying to stop the publisher, even after they lost the lawsuit. Amazon sold out early this morning, every store in the city is sold out and I'm desperate. How about eighty-five bucks? Sound good?"

"Is there a problem?" A man approached the threesome. The nametag pinned to his blue dress shirt read "Manager" beneath the name Doug. He addressed the two empty-handed customers, "If you don't keep your voices down and leave this lady alone I'll have to call the police."

 "That won't be necessary," Savannah said, retrieving her police ID from her purse. "I'm a sergeant with APD."

"I apologize for this inconvenience, Sergeant. Thank you for your purchase." In the nicest way possible, Doug told the others, "If you folks will follow me, I'll check in the back for extra copies."

Savannah could tell the "extra copies" were a fib. But eagerness to own the book drove the two to trail behind him, jockeying for first position and the mother reminding Mr. L&O that she arrived first.

Savannah hurried to her car, locked herself in before someone else accosted her about buying the book. Before the two angry, still empty-handed customers exited the store, she left for home. On the way she called Georgia, "You neglected to tell me I should wear body armor to buy this thing. It's practically a war out here." Then proceeded to relay her experience at the store. "I felt like a Brinks guard walking into a hold-up."

Georgia's earlier enthusiasm waned, "You're lucky to have found a copy. Apparently, the Morgans spent the morning collecting every copy they could and Lee Morgan filed another lawsuit against Tucker's publisher."

Savannah pulled into her driveway. The girls were in Katherine's yard playing while the neighbor cradled Daniel in her arms. Lily and Anna waved at their mother who waved back then they ran to meet her. "Again? What's in this book they're trying to hide?" she asked Georgia while shifting into park and killing the engine.

"Don't know but you and I are about to find out. People are bombarding Tucker on social media wanting to know where they can buy a copy. Right now the few copies are available on eBay and are selling for over two hundred dollars."

Savannah appraised the thick book in the passenger seat. Funny, it didn't look like a car payment but if she waited long enough, selling it might cover a month if they were lucky. Still, "Georgia, is this book really that good or is it just a bloated edition of the National Enquirer?"

"It's scandalous, yes, but Tucker should know all the juicy secrets, right? Remember Mama and Daddy telling us those stories? So far, Tucker confirmed some of those rumors."

"You mean the rumors of Lee having people murdered to get his way?"

"Well, not those but he does say Lee put plenty of people in the poorhouse when they refused to cooperate with him. Tucker portrayed him as a real jerk when he was younger."

No wonder he and Mama never got married, Savannah thought.

Now she regarded the book in a different light. She recalled stories bandied about, especially by their father R.J. who regaled family dinners with Morgan antics he'd heard at the bar. The tales left his kids spellbound and their mother silent as he recited juicy, outrageous, and sometimes disgraceful tales that no one thought possible in modest, wholesome Augusta, Georgia. No matter the outrageous stories, Savannah reveled in memories of roaming the beautiful house with six or seven bedrooms and just as many baths. She recalled how friendly the butler, maid and cook were. She remembered fantasizing about living there, attending balls and dances, meeting her Prince Charming and being the princess swept off her feet. That happened to rich people. Lots of wonderful things happened to rich people, she'd thought at the time, especially those as nice as Mr. Morgan. So when her daddy told unthinkable stories of a "heartless cur who couldn't care less about the little guy", it confused her. Mr. Morgan hadn't looked or sounded intimidating or ruthless as her father claimed, at least not with her.

Staring at the book in the seat beside her, Savannah shook her head. The Morgans were silly for reacting as they had. Better to leave the book alone than draw all the attention to it by suing everyone involved and scooping up the few available copies. That only validated the stories inside.

Lily knocked on the driver window. Anna did the same. Savannah signed off with Georgia, promising to dive into the book ASAP. Which meant after she settled in the kids, fixed supper, helped Lily with her golf lessons and a few other things. She tucked the book under her arm and climbed out of the car.

Katherine Collins met her at the porch, Daniel's diaper bag slung over her shoulder and the baby sweetly sleeping in her arms. Dressed in forest green slacks and floral pullover and her shoulder length auburn hair draped stylishly past her shoulders, Mrs. Collins always presented the picture of perfection. Not a day since the Rutherfords moved in had Savannah seen Katherine in anything shabbier than slightly faded designer slacks and top – for gardening duty.

Katherine zeroed in on the book, "You found one."

"The last one in the surrounding area, I guess. Two people tried buying it off me. They'd have probably mugged me for it if the store manager hadn't intervened."

Katherine's porcelain skin flushed with excitement, "Give me details on the good parts."

O O O

"Daddy finally gave permission for us to work on the attic." Georgia sounded happier than a kid in a candy store.

Savannah figured she called to discuss Tucker's book. Instead she discovered her sister volunteered her to help troll a musty, hot attic – and for what? The attic only held Christmas decorations, Seth's baseball cards and comics and a bunch of stuff no one probably wanted anymore. Even so, ever since their mother died, R.J. forbade anyone to enter the attic, much less rummage its contents. To ensure they stayed out he installed a padlock on the door and no one except their daddy knew why.

Savannah lacked her sister's enthusiasm, allowing a flat *Yay* to slip out before asking, "How'd you get him to take the padlock off the sacred door? He's guarded that room like it's Fort Knox."

"This morning I asked if I could squirrel around for a piece or two of furniture Mama stored."

Not answering my question, sis. "Again, how did you get him to agree?"

Silence ensued. *She bribed him, that's how.* Georgia tiptoed into it, "Well… I kinda promised we'd eat lunch with him."

Savannah shrugged, "Seems cheap enough. When do we–"

"And supper."

She sighed. *Yeah, right. Cheap enough until you read the fine print, Savannah.* She rolled her eyes. "Any other details you're holding back? We're not staying the night because I've got a passel of kids and a reluctant husband that already hates spending one minute with Daddy."

"No. Lunch and supper, that's all, I promise. He wanted," she cleared her throat uneasily now, "just the two of us. Said it would be like old times."

"That's what I'm afraid of, Georgia. Old times. The longer we're together the more apt we are to fight, you know that. And with Daddy, fighting comes with fists or belts."

"It's one day, Savannah. We can do this. Just ignore him when he gets upset. Excuse yourself if you have to. Now tell me how far along you are in *Bad Blood.*"

"Page twenty-six. Lily's golf lessons took longer and Daniel was fussy when I got home."

"Isn't it engrossing?" She tittered like a little girl privy to a secret.

Oh definitely, she agreed. Engrossing. If a person hadn't been offered employment by a Morgan it would've been the perfect word. Otherwise they looked just loony enough Savannah feared their crazy might jump on her like fleas. The book jacket alone promised Hollywood-worthy drama. Tucker Morgan's forward left no bones about it. His ancestors were poor Irish immigrants that settled in the hills of Kentucky, made a still and a fine living out of making moonshine. They clawed their way up the success ladder, crushing their competition and even killing them in some instances. No one was off-limits, not even law enforcement.

Tucker mentioned rampant sexual indiscretions by the men and their wives who demanded the best of everything as payment for those indiscretions. Tucker alluded to a sibling no one mentioned because of Lee's overactive sexual appetite. By the time Savannah mowed through the forward she felt not only woozy but uncertain about accepting Lee's offer. Yes, yes, the book was written with malice aforethought. How much of it was actually true? But Tucker knew the consequences of publishing such a tell-all or even a slightly embellished account – or he should have. He was swimming in lawsuits by now. Lee's lawsuit may have been dismissed but it didn't keep other people mentioned in the book from suing him.

"It feels a little close to home since we've been to the Morgan Palace, doesn't it?" Georgia asked.

You have no idea. "Yeah. So why were we even there?"

"Mama used to work for Lee. I guess they were still friends."

Savannah's eyes bugged, "I'm sorry, *what* did you say?"

"I forgot what she did. Part-time secretary or something. It involved paperwork, that's all I remember. She'd bring me along some days. I was only a small child but I felt like a queen in that huge house. Their butler was very kind. Kept me entertained and served me chocolate milk the few times I was there."

"Why in the world would Mama have worked for the Morgans?"

"She wanted extra money, I do recall that. Daddy was always so tight with their money. She enjoyed splurging on an extravagance once in a while for herself but mostly me and Seth. She loved buying me dresses and he was always into sports at school and needing equipment."

Savannah really needed to sit down so she did. Talk about surprises. The week was full of them. "How long did she work there?"

Georgia paused. Savannah heard the wheels turning back almost forty years or so. Her older sister stretched the words as if still mulling over the time, "About a year I think. We'd have to ask Daddy."

"That's all? A year?"

"Well remember, hon. You came along about that time. Mama had her hands full with her pregnancy. You weren't an easy baby on her."

Savannah sneered at the phone, "Thanks."

"Sorry. I suppose between the job, the pregnancy and keeping her own house it all became too much because she avoided getting out during that time. She was sick a lot."

"Georgia…" Please stop.

"Hon, I'm only explaining what happened, at least from what I remember. She took to her bed for months, not getting up except for necessities. Seth and I had to fix supper a lot of nights. Just sandwiches and easy stuff. Even Daddy pitched in."

Picturing her father in a brightly colored apron cooking anything past boiled water brought a humorous smile to her face.

"Lee kept checking on her, though. He'd call during the day but she never felt like talking so I'd chat with him. Seems as though they became friends in that time she worked for him."

She guessed Georgia had no clue about their previous relationship. She might tell her about that when they sweated their asses off in the attic looking for furniture. "Did I tell you Lee Morgan was at the station the other day?"

"No, what did he want? Another restraining order against Tucker? I'd think a lawyer was a more appropriate need."

"He wanted personal police protection against the book's fall-out. Josh about had a cow. Morgan wasn't happy but before he left, he saw me, we chatted and he gave me his card. He wanted a meeting."

Georgia gasped. "A meeting? What about? What did he want, Savannah?"

"He offered me a job."

4

Georgia's Tahoe rolled up in the empty driveway. She and Savannah drove the two hours to Augusta expecting to see their father's pickup parked in the drive or on the curb. It wasn't. Georgia seemed disappointed. Savannah was not. "Daddy said he'd be here," the elder sibling lamented.

Savannah checked her watch. Ten fifteen. R.J. started early that morning and if they swung by the bar four blocks away, his antiquated Chevy would probably be parked cattycorner in the lot. "He'll be here soon enough. Let's get busy while he's gone." She reached to the floorboard for her purse. When she climbed out she grabbed her travel mug of extra strong coffee.

She'd much rather have stayed home and changed her son's muddy diapers than face her drunken father at any point during that day. Even Ennis considered it a great trade off to stay home with the kids on his day off rather than spend the day with R.J. Prince.

Georgia collected her things and they headed to the door. "Dane's supposed to join us. He didn't feel comfortable leaving us alone with Daddy."

"Good for Dane." That was the best news of the day. Sorting out an attic was hard enough without having to watch their backs.

"Have you given Lee Morgan an answer yet?"

"No. I owe him one soon though. It's very tempting especially with the salary and the fact I could work from Atlanta. I'd hate to move back here even for that kind of money."

Georgia overlooked the last remark. She knew living in the same city as their father would be a nightmare. "Sounds like he really wants you because there are plenty of private security companies available to him."

"I think it actually revolves around Mama." She decided against telling her sister about the romance between Lee and Charlene. The kids' hard-working daddy won her heart, not the rich boy living outside of town. All she would say was, "He really liked her."

A nostalgic smile crossed Georgia's Rita Hayworth features, "Well, she was an extremely likeable lady." She keyed the lock, opened the door and immediately gasped at the living room's disarray.

Why, Savannah did not know. "It always looks like a storm blew through. Why are you freaking out?"

Dirty plates, liquor bottles and glasses covered their mother's coffee table. R.J. made a TV tray out of the once beautiful cherrywood piece. Half thrown back blankets covered the couch. Several wrinkled and previously worn white t-shirts and khakis slung over the two wingback chairs. Their daddy hadn't slept in his own bed since their mama died and deemed the living room his new bedroom.

Georgia sniffed the air. Yes, the place smelled stale. A heavy tinge of old Johnnie Walker hung in a sour, invisible fog around them. What had her sister expected? Lilac arrangements and Glade commercials? Hardly.

Georgia plucked a white t-shirt from the wingback but Savannah took it, threw it back. "We're not maids today, sis. We'll tidy up our bathroom first." She saw Georgia start to object and lifted a hand in a stop gesture, "And we'll tackle the kitchen and downstairs bathroom if we're not too tired. Just calm down. This is status quo for the house and you know it."

Since he barely used the upstairs, it needed only a quick sprucing up. Savannah saw her sister fretting over the rest of the house but knew cleaning it *and* rummaging a hot, musty attic would sap the last of her energy to zero.

Georgia set her purse down, marched to the living room window and opened it. Maybe now, Savannah thought, she'll be halfway satisfied.

"Open the kitchen window. Let's get some fresh air in here."

Halfway satisfied? Who was she kidding? They'd clean the whole house by nightfall. Savannah's purse joined her sister's, her shoulders slumping as she trudged off to follow orders.

They spent most of an hour on the upstairs. R.J. hadn't returned from his usual haunt by then so they turned their attention to the walk-in attic. Unlike his bedroom, their father deemed that room off-limits, not just to himself but the children as well. Savannah recalled a rather nasty argument when Seth wanted his son Dylan to have his old comic book collection and went in search of it. R.J. stormed upstairs, physically tossed Seth out of the attic and into the hall then blockaded the door with a threat to knock Seth into "next year" if he disobeyed him. Only

Georgia pried the reason out of him. *Your mama's things are in there. I don't want 'em disturbed...*

Savannah watched her sister unlock and remove the padlock their daddy installed years ago. Georgia grasped the doorknob to the attic then paused. Because of R.J.'s protests over the years, the process felt ceremonial and exciting. They'd finally see inside the sacred room. *This must be how archaeologists felt when they discovered the Valley of Kings...*

Georgia took a deep breath, "Ready?"

Savannah shrugged, "Why not?"

The door swung open, rested against the stop. Both sisters winced and stepped back at the heat billowing out and enveloping them in blast furnace temperatures. So far it was the hottest fall on record and the attic felt more like summertime. Savannah winced at the thought of the next few hours trolling around boxes and furniture, pouring sweat and waiting until nighttime to get a long, cleansing shower. "He couldn't have agreed to this last spring when the place wasn't a kiln?"

She propped the door open to Georgia's halfhearted protest, "Daddy will get mad if you leave it open."

"So he'd rather find us dead in here?"

Georgia opted not to argue. She flipped the switch, bathing the large space in subdued light. They both stood in amazement and for Savannah, a fair amount of horror. Cardboard boxes ranged in size from two feet long and a half a foot high to over three feet square. Furniture had also been stored at the back like puzzle pieces. Their old baby crib that saw her parents through three kids. An old wooden rocker once belonging to Grandpa Prince. End tables and an antique hutch of Grandma Culberson's. Dust covered toys sat atop boxes. And that was just the unboxed stuff visible from the door.

Savannah blew out a breath, "My God."

"It'll be a chore but we can do it." Georgia always sounded so damn cheery when it came to work.

"Georgia, vacuuming is a chore. This," she searched for the right words. "This is insurmountable."

They slowly ventured in, surveying what they could without disturbing anything. Georgia pointed to a box labeled *Seth's Comic Books/Baseball Cards*. Savannah whispered, "Let me grab those and stuff 'em in your car. Seth will be so happy to finally get them."

"We'll take them but let's see what else is up here first."

They passed another box marked *Records,* another read *Old Newspapers/Magazines* and three more, these a bit smaller than the others and stacked atop each other. On the bottom box Charlene had written in black marker *Seth's Baby Clothes, Georgia's Baby Clothes* on the middle one and *Savannah's Baby Clothes* on the top one. "Oh dear Lord," Savannah groaned. "They saved our baby clothes."

Georgia turned to her sister with humorous, "And you haven't saved one thing of Lily's or Anna's over the years?"

Savannah flushed, "Oh, shut up."

As they progressed toward the back of the room, more stacked boxes lined the walls along the sloped roofline, these bearing different titles all in Charlene's neat print. Yearbooks, Wedding Dress, R.J.'s Tackle Box/Fishing Magazines, Christmas Decorations… "I'm tired now," Savannah confessed. "Just looking at all this stuff is exhausting." She drew her arm across her forehead. The stuffy attic held heat better than an oven. "Since we've entered Hell's Half Acre, wanna give me a head's up on what one or two items you're searching for?"

With annoying grace, Georgia stepped over and around furniture and a lamp that had fallen across the pathway. She stopped at (of course) the attic's far end. Savannah followed her trail, though not as gracefully as Georgia had. She squinted in the dim light to see what inspired this impromptu trip to Augusta. The object stood three feet high, had dusty wooden slats held together (probably) by the spider webs crisscrossing them. The wooden panels on each end still showed a happy frolicking cartoon lamb but its white wool coat yellowed after so many years. An idiot could have figured out Georgia's fascination with their old crib. "Georgia, are you–"

"Yes!" Her excitement exploded into the room's silence.

Sweat be damned, she thought, grabbing her older sister in a hug and offering congratulations. Locked in the embrace, their giddy laughter filled the musty space. Words failed Savannah because Georgia and Dane tried for years to have babies only to meet with disappointing results. She settled for, "I'm overjoyed, sis. This is the best news ever. How long have you known?"

"Three weeks. Keeping this from you has driven me crazy."

"How did you swear Dane to secrecy?"

She proudly announced, "Told him no more football or Dr. Pepper if he let it slip to anyone, including Ennis. I just wanted time to adjust and to realize it's really true."

"What's all the shoutin'?" R.J. yelled from the attic doorway.

"Nothing, Daddy," they lied in unison then stifled another laugh – barely.

He grumbled then slurred, "Ya better stay away from Mama's things. I'll tear ya in half if ya mess with 'em."

They answered *Yes, Daddy* together as well. Sliding her hand across the rail then shaking the dust off, Savannah appraised the old crib through different eyes. After forty years, it needed serious help but Dane, like Ennis, was handy at such projects. Once restored, Georgia's baby would occupy the crib that saw the Prince family through three children. *Georgia's baby...* Savannah could hardly believe it.

Georgia looked it over, as usual seeing past its nicks and scrapes to see its future glory returned once again. "I want this crib. The three of us grew up with it and I've always wanted it for my child. Dane said he'd work on it if you and Seth agree."

"You're kidding. Why would we argue about this after what you've been through?"

"Thanks, hon. I knew you'd be okay with it." She eased her hand along a railing. She withdrew into a brief contemplative silence then, "Seems like a dream. We've tried so long for a child I'm nearly too scared to hope."

Savannah hugged her from behind, held her sister close for a long moment, "You've got us to help you through this. Anything you need just let us know. You'll be a terrific mama, Georgia. This baby is blessed to have you and Dane for parents."

Georgia patted her sister's hand, thanked her. Savannah heard her walking a fragile tightrope of emotion. Georgia cracked a joke to help fight back tears, "Dane's already bought a baseball glove, just in case it's a boy."

"Girls can throw a mean fastball too."

Georgia laughed, "So true." She checked her watch, "Speaking of Dane, I wonder where he is."

"Probably crowing to Ennis about the baby."

"I know tradition says not to tell anyone during the first trimester but I've been busting to tell you both. You've been so supportive during our struggles to conceive."

Before Savannah replied, Georgia pointed past her sister's shoulder, "Look."

She did. Their mother labeled every box in the attic – except half a dozen. In red marker, those were written in their daddy's utilitarian, slightly shaky penmanship. He gave their contents general names such as *Charlene's things*, *Charlene's clothes* or just plain *Charlene's stuff.*

She and Georgia visually roved the boxes in reverent silence as if they'd stumbled on the Prince family's Holy Grail and assessed the risk of approaching it. Finally Georgia dared to speak, "Do we?"

Wary at the prospect of mining those oh-so-tempting memories, Savannah listened for their father. No sounds on the stairway or upstairs in general. "If Daddy catches us…"

"This may be our only chance to look. We'll take turns guarding the door. You take the first shift."

Savannah went to the doorway. So far so good. Tape ripped from one box top. Cardboard flaps scraped against each other. Georgia worked fast opening one box then another. Silence fell over the room. Savannah counted twenty full seconds before hearing clothes being rustled aside. She wiped her brow with her forearm again, more from nervousness than heat. If their daddy caught them rummaging Charlene's things, they would go home sore and bruised.

Georgia gave an update, "Just clothes in this one."

A beating for trolling their mother's clothes. Not exactly what Savannah had in mind that day. Those boxes were the sole reason their daddy forbade them from crossing the attic threshold in the first place – and here they were diving into them. With Georgia's pregnancy news, Savannah vowed to take the blame and the brunt of R.J.'s temper. Having her sister miscarry from abuse or stress would polish Savannah off.

Her heart tripped in her chest, breath caught in her throat. Were those footsteps on the stairs? She debated over warning Georgia, and telling her to close the boxes and forget it. Tense moments crept by. No heavy footfalls tromping up the stairs. She released the breath, long and low. Dear God, she'd pass out from fright before Georgia finished snooping.

Sheets of newspaper rattled. Her sister was unwrapping fragile treasures, oohing and ahhing over them. "Hurry up. I wanna see too," Savannah pressed.

"I'm leaving them for you to see," Georgia assured. She noisily tore into the next box as though sensing their limited time.

A sound downstairs clenched Savannah's stomach. She cocked an ear, her hearing so acute she could probably hear two blocks away. The noise turned out to be R.J. jerking a drawer open. He rattled silverware, closed the drawer. He was fixing his lunch.

Savannah propped against the doorjamb, willing her heart to calm down. What started as leisure spelunking expedition for a crib turned into trying to avoid an explosion. Now she knew how the bomb squad felt on a call. "*Georgia, hurry.*"

"Come here."

Yeah right. "I'm busy saving our asses from annihilation right now but thanks all the same."

"I mean it. *Get over here.*"

Muttering a curse, she hurried over then stopped once eyeing the object Georgia point to. A box bearing the benign label *Charlene's stuff* held several old leather-bound books. Georgia opened one. The first page was self-explanatory. Their mama kept journals and by the looks of some of them, they were older than Savannah. Georgia proved it by showing her one marked a couple of years before their parents married. Charlene would have still been a teenager. "I wonder if she kept journaling after we were born," Savannah mumbled. It would have surprised her if Charlene had time to write. The woman stayed busy twenty-four seven. The only time Savannah saw her sit down was in church, to read her Bible, to eat or when she was ill.

Georgia already dug down in the box. The answer was yes, Charlene wrote a journal every year. They settled on the book dated before Charlene and R.J. married. She opened the cover. An earlier yet familiar style of their mother's beautiful script filled the pages. Savannah tried to keep an ear tuned to the door in case R.J. barged up the stairs.

But the words on the page seemed determined to draw her in, much the way they captivated Georgia. It felt both like an invasion of privacy and a rare peek inside the window of their mother's innermost thoughts.

Georgia tapped a phrase their mother wrote in a hectic manner – Savannah recognized the stiffer lines and letters. Charlene was upset when she wrote the entry. *Some sisters I've got. Neither approve of R.J. and parrot Mama and Papa. They're not genial toward him in the least. They ignored him at Thanksgiving and refused to speak to him. Katherine brags like her husband hung the moon. R.J. works for a living, a good honest job. He's nothing like that brown-nose Katherine married, thank goodness…*

Georgia sat the book aside, chose another dated when she was six. Judging by the month, Charlene would have been popping with Savannah. The two sisters stood shoulder to shoulder reading the hurried cursive. The scribbled words told Savannah that their mother was damn angry when she wrote the entry. *It's Easter. They all know something's wrong, including Mama and Papa. Of course they blame R.J. for all our problems but they don't know the half of what we've been through and never will. I will go to my grave without telling another soul. The holiday has gone as usual, tense and unpleasant and at times hateful. None of them will talk to R.J. and Katherine and Emma also treated Seth and Georgia like lepers. I plan to skip the reunion in July. The baby will be born in June anyway. They can treat me however they like and R.J. holds his own against them but they will <u>never</u> treat my children that way again.*

Georgia clapped the book shut, startling Savannah. One look at her sister told the younger sibling to tread lightly then she asked, "Do you remember that?"

She replied with pursed lips and a stern nod. The book went on top of the others in the box. "I do, unfortunately. I wondered why Daddy sat outside in the cold. I stayed out there with him for a while until he told me to go inside before I caught a chill. You know, Daddy wasn't always…" her voice trailed off as if she caught herself before blurting a no-no. Then it seemed she retreated into a moment of melancholy. "He was sweet when he wanted to be," Georgia continued. "He always had a bad temper and he drank, yes, and hit us on occasion but it worsened after…" she stopped again.

Savannah had a good idea what was next, "After I was born?"

Georgia quickly shook her head, "No, not really."

Your face says otherwise, sis.

"Okay, maybe after Mama got pregnant. But when he was around Mama's family he was at his worst. You remember what happened every holiday we shared with them, don't you?"

"Yes. We got the shit beat out of us for blinking too loudly. Georgia, I know they didn't want a third kid, especially six years after you, but why did Daddy's temper get worse because of me?"

"I don't know."

"What the hell's keeping you two, anyway?" R.J. demanded from the attic door. "Thought you was needin' somethin' specific." Heavy footsteps creaked along the floor. He was coming inside.

Ice water pumped through Savannah's heart. She had to stop him before he realized they'd been trolling in forbidden boxes. She pointed to Georgia then the box, whispering, "Close it up." Then calmly ambled to the door, "There's a lot of things up here, Daddy. We have to move some stuff to find what we're looking for."

Even at his age, R.J. Prince's stature and strength impressed anyone who met him. He was no man to quarrel with, much less pick a fight with. The foolish folks who'd did found themselves flat on the ground. His shoulders and arms bore testament to his career in construction work. From top to bottom he still held his own if need be. That's why Savannah panicked inside when he stepped around her and headed directly for Georgia. She'd protect her pregnant sister at all costs.

"What're ya lookin' for?" he asked his oldest daughter. "I'll help then we can eat lunch after we find it."

Georgia stayed composed as Georgia always did, "That's okay, Daddy. We need a break anyway." She met him halfway to the door, safely away from their obvious snooping. A kiss on the cheek inspired a smile from him.

Savannah kissed his other cheek. It amazed her how it brightened his mood. He proudly announced, "I went to the store for bread, bologna, peanut butter and ham. Take yer pick. Tonight we'll eat whatever's left over."

"How about a hamburger?" Savannah suggested. "It's been a while since we ate hamburgers together."

"Ya mean from that burger joint on Broad Street?" he asked.

"The one and only."

A rare toothy grin spread across their father's face and he slung a heavy arm across her shoulders, "My baby's a genius."

5

After lunch, Savannah and Georgia found some alone time together to sort more boxes. Charlene carefully packed mementos from their childhood, preserving them for the future. That was their mother. So meticulous and methodical. They dug through old toys and dolls placed with care and plenty of room so as not to crowd the contents.

They ran across a box containing the three children's old drawings and schoolwork. Each stack lay neat and flat and in their own folder labeled with either "Seth", "Georgia" or "Savannah". Being the youngest child, Savannah's folder lay atop the others.

Savannah grabbed the one bearing her name, amazed that, "Mama kept a math test of mine. Of course this was the only one I probably made a 98 on too." She aced elementary school spelling and geography tests (with grades of A+, thank you very much) and an English test that had an A with the word "Excellent" written beneath in the teacher's red pen.

Georgia laughed. She had opened a second parcel of her sister's work and read through two pages so far. "This is so cute. You were around nine or ten, weren't you?" She handed them to Savannah who skimmed over the first page. A blush darkened her complexion. Oh God. Chester Chipmunk. The rodent dapperly dressed in a fedora and green plaid jacket.

Georgia chuckled, "We had a second writer in the family. You know, I remember that chipmunk. Drove Daddy nuts and Mama kept chasing after it with a broom."

In an attempt to emulate her talented high school age sister, Savannah tried her hand at creative writing. In neat, loopy cursive she penned a few stories about talking animals. Chester Chipmunk's adventure in the Prince backyard nibbling away at flowers and flower bulbs and digging a home, another regarding Chester's lonely love life and his search for Mrs. Chester and two other stories, these last adventures taking place in downtown Augusta. He visited a baseball game, took rides on the buses and accidentally rafted aimlessly down the Savannah River without an oar. Chester was sly, spry and managed to outfox the master of the Prince house – a big, burly man with broad shoulders, bulging muscles and a short fierce temper. She'd modeled the aggrieved mother/flower planter after Charlene and the hassled father after R.J. who'd relentlessly chased their chipmunk.

All together the four complete stories spanned fifty pages front and back. She would read it later, in private, before going to bed. That way, she'd go to sleep laughing instead of kvetching about her aching back. "You can't call this writing," she rattled the pages.

"I call it potential. You should try your hand at it again." Georgia nudged her, "In fact, you should read that to Lily and Anna. They'd love it."

"Georgia," she whined, "I want my children to love and respect me, not commit me to the nuthouse the first chance they get. It's awful."

"Not what I read. For your age it was pretty good. A little polish, a little re-write, add more animals and stories and you might have a children's book of your own there. Think about it."

She gave a noncommittal shrugging nod.

"*Seriously* consider it, Savannah. It's a good start." Georgia wasn't smiling or laughing now.

Thirty minutes later, the doorbell rang. They heard R.J. talking with Dane. It sounded pleasant enough, probably since Dane came bearing gifts of hamburgers and fries for supper. "Hello the house!" Dane called from the stairway. "R.J. said you're busy trolling up here. Y'all about ready for supper?"

o   o   o

Stuffed full of double decker, juicy hamburgers and homemade fries from "the joint on Broad Street", the foursome leaned back in their chairs to digest. R.J. sat his Coke aside in favor of a glass of Johnnie Walker. The ladies settled on their Cokes and Dane his trusty Dr. Pepper. Savannah couldn't remember a more peaceful, nice time with her father. Earlier Georgia told their father about her pregnancy so that contributed to the lack of fussing at supper. The only fussing their daddy allowed himself was telling Georgia to sit down while they served the meal. Even he realized the struggle she and Dane suffered for those years trying to have a child.

"What'd ya pack up to take home?" R.J. asked the three.

Savannah answered for her sister, "The crib and some childhood toys and schoolwork of ours. And Seth's comic books and baseball cards."

He nodded, lifted the scotch for a healthy swallow, "You leave your mama's things alone?"

"Yep," Dane blurted before giving Savannah a chance.

She'd planned to say the same thing but he beat her to it. No, they hadn't left Charlene's "things" alone. After loading the crib, schoolwork and Seth's things, she and Dane carried the two heavy boxes of journals to the Tahoe while Georgia chatted with R.J. in the kitchen. In the back of the car they found the blanket Georgia brought to cover the crib for transport. Savannah and Dane opted to cover the journals instead.

They'd gone back upstairs long enough to shift items around and fill the gap left by the missing boxes.

"Good," R.J. refilled his glass.

The three exchanged a covert glance, the implication clear – we're toast if he finds out the truth.

Georgia watched him put the bottle back on the table. "Daddy, Savannah had a job offer. It'll pay quite bit more than being a detective."

He indulged in a sip of scotch, "That right? Anything's better than you being a cop. Out there with the rapists and murderers. Never made sense to me or yer mama. So what's the job and where?" The glass clunked to the table, "Yer not movin', are ya? That why Georgia mentioned the job? Because you wouldn't?"

Savannah tried to calm him down, "No one's moving, Daddy. It does pay a lot more than I make now though."

"If ya ain't gonna be movin', then you'd be stupid not to take it. What's the job?"

"Chief Security Officer. Well, I think he meant working my way toward it. I'd start out helping vet new employees and security officers."

R.J. swirled the scotch in the glass, mulling over the description. "Must be a big operation. Pays good and ya stay here. Why haven't ya hired on yet?"

"Daddy," Georgia jumped in, "what do you know about Lee Morgan?"

He slammed the scotch down. The liquid sloshed over the sides as he bolted to his feet, "That who this bigshot is?"

The others pressed back in their chairs but Savannah was who he aimed the question at. He gripped the sides of the table, trembling with the sudden, explosive rage she'd lived with since childhood. Over the years R.J.'s hair turned silver and his wrinkles he had deepened but his body remained strong and imposing and the scorching temper still held plenty of fire. Enough that even into their forties his children feared him.

R.J. leaned toward Savannah, "You stay away from that bastard. Ya hear me?"

She took a chance asking the one question most people would. "Why? Daddy, it's more money than I make in a–"

"*You hear me?*" He drew closer until she smelled the scotch on his breath. "Stay away from him."

Dane came to his feet, "R.J., don't get in her face."

Their father's icy blue eyes pinned his youngest, "If I hear you've been near that son of a bitch, I'll come after ya, girl. I'll make ya regret defying me. Do ya hear me, Savannah Charlene? Do I make myself clear?"

Her fight or flight instinct kicked in but she literally sat trapped, her back against the wall and her father blocking the easiest avenue of escape and Dane's empty chair cutting off the other.

"Daddy," Georgia said in a gentle tone, "what's wrong with her accepting the job?"

"Stay outta this, Georgia," R.J. warned.

When Savannah didn't immediately answer, his fist doubled, "I'll ask one last time. Do I make myself clear?"

Her vision dropped to the fist cocked to strike. Her back twinged in remembrance of those beatings. "Yessir. Perfectly clear."

o o o

Dane blew out a breath, "Well, *that* was tense."

He and Georgia arrived home at eight that night. Once Savannah capitulated, R.J. took off for the bar he frequented, at least that's what the three left behind assumed. So they packed up and left but not before Georgia left a note on the table with the old standby *something came up and we had to leave.* He'd call and rail at them in a drunken rage if she didn't. Georgia dropped Savannah off at home. They spent most of the two hour trip in silence. Georgia attempted light conversation but received very little in response. When the bright lights of Atlanta's suburbs heralded the way home, she pressed the accelerator a shade further, hitting the Perimeter's on-ramp ten miles per hour over the speed limit. Dane closed the distance behind the Tahoe with his Silverado. They all just wanted to get home.

Ten miles from Savannah's house, Georgia had broached the subject, "I'll give him a day or two to cool off then I'll call him and ask what his grudge is against Morgan. He just reacted, that's all. You know how he is."

A glance in the passenger's seat revealed a woman who perfected brooding as well as R.J. perfected lashing out. In the soft glow of the passing streetlights, however, Georgia saw defeat in her sister's posture. Their hopes for an enjoyable visit with their daddy had gone straight to hell because of one name. Savannah's gaze had stayed straight ahead on the road, "Don't get involved, Georgia. You don't need the stress. This is my problem and I'll sort it out. Like Daddy said, just stay out of it."

Once home, Georgia relaxed when Dane wrapped her in his arms, kissed her. She returned the embrace and laid her head against his chest, "Poor Savannah. She was so excited about that job too. I think she was considering it and what a blessing it would've been to have her out of harm's way for once. Daddy screwed the whole thing up."

"She can still take the job. She's forty-one years old, not sixteen. It's a dream deal. It's more money, she can have steadier hours and spend more time at home. They could try for that vacation to Hawaii they've always wanted."

How wonderful if her sister and Ennis finally planned the honeymoon they never had. How nice to have enough money to consider private school for the girls or having enough in the bank to do more than dream about Hawaii. They were all nice thoughts but, "She won't disappoint Daddy."

"He's easy to disappoint."

Georgia agreed, "He's been that way all my life." She hesitated then finished, "Well, nearly all my life. Until Savannah was born he wasn't but after that, *whew...*"

"Does he resent her for some reason? I know she's six years younger than you so she had to be a surprise."

Georgia eased from the embrace, trekked into the bedroom to change into her nightgown. "I don't really know. Growing up she suffered the brunt of his beatings. Seth and I suffered our share but nothing compared to hers. Sure she was headstrong and unruly but what child isn't to a degree? She never deserved how he treated her, no matter whether they planned for her or not."

Dane shucked his jeans and shirt, tossed both into the clothes hamper. He caught Georgia naked and hugged her from behind. A large warm hand pressed to her belly. He placed a soft kiss to her nape, murmuring, "I can't wait for our baby. I hope you're having twins," he smiled against her ear, "no, triplets."

"Someone's a wishful thinker. You should have seen Savannah's face when I told her. For a moment I saw that little girl I used to know, the one that beamed on her birthdays and Christmas and always sought my approval for anything she did. Too bad Daddy never gave her his."

Dane eased his hand up to her breast for a gentle squeeze. Her eyes closed on a sigh. His other hand traveled down, down, down...

Her eyes snapped open, "Did you unload the journals too?"

"Lady, I'm trying to get you in the mood here. Why are you resisting?"

She repeated her question then, "I have an idea."

Crestfallen, he replied, "I had one too but mine got usurped by a bunch of books."

"No, no. We'll get back to this. But did you–"

"Yes, darlin', I unloaded the journals after I unloaded the crib. The box is in the garage."

"I'm going to dig through them and see if Mama wrote during the time she worked for Lee Morgan. Maybe it might shed light on whatever Morgan did to Daddy."

O O O

The next morning after breakfast she and Dane went to the garage. The box was a two foot tall rectangular shape and chock full of journals of different styles from small notebook to leather-bound. The further down they dug, the quality of journals reduced from leather-bound down to the more basic spiral notebook.

Georgia, being Georgia, liked things organized. She and Dane removed the books two at a time, checked the dates then placed them aside in sequential order.

Dane stared at the collection in amazement, "Now I know where your proclivity to write came from. Was she born with a pen in her hand?"

Overwhelmed at the treasure trove of handwritten memories, Georgia could only shake her head, "I never knew she kept journals." And she wanted to spend the day reading them too. It would be like a visit with her mother again, cooking Christmas supper and sharing birthdays or shooting the breeze about everyday things. Glancing through one book, she noticed her mother noted an evening "with the girls", just her and her two daughters on the front porch one summer evening in the shade of the magnolia tree, drinking lemonade and eating moon pies together.

Charlene made use of the entire book, writing on every page, whether a long entry or a short paragraph. How far back did they go?

Dane ran a hand though his hair, sighing, "Are you looking for a particular year?"

The question realigned her goal. She'd completely forgotten the reason for trolling into Charlene's innermost thoughts. She felt a little guilty about it too – but not guilty enough to stop. "The year before Savannah was born and probably the year of her birth too."

For R.J. to lose his composure over one name, Georgia felt confident Lee Morgan had done something personal to inflame R.J.'s rage. Their daddy made a living in construction and at one time owned his own business. Something happened that he sold the business and found a job with the competition. Georgia always figured it cost too much to keep both a family and business so he opted to let one go. She recalled R.J. doing well in his venture, building homes in the newer area of Augusta and bringing home enough money for gifts for his wife and, at the time, two children. According to the internet (she did a little research since she couldn't sleep well) Lee Morgan used his family's fortune and got into shipping. By Georgia's calculations, it occurred years after R.J. built his successful construction business. Thanks to his name and the family fortune, Lee's business flourished so quickly he began gobbling up smaller companies until Morgan Industries became a conglomerate. At the same time, R.J.'s construction business began a long stretch of struggling and decline.

"Here," Dane handed her a journal with a blue cover. "The year she was born. And..." he dug in again, brought out another and checked the dates, "the year before."

Georgia gathered them to her breast as if they were gold. "I hope these have some answers in them. Let's go inside and start reading."

They brewed coffee to sustain their journey into the past. Perched at the kitchen's marble topped island, they delved into Charlene's perspective of her life decades earlier – Dane took the journal before Savannah's conception when Charlene worked for Morgan. Georgia cracked open the journal containing the tail end of her mother's last pregnancy.

The two read in silence until Dane's brow shot up, "Found the part when Morgan hired your ma. According to her he made her one of his secretaries for, and I quote, 'an embarrassing amount of money. I can't wait to see Georgia's face light up when she sees that dress she's wanted for a month. She will look like an angel.'"

Georgia could see her mother paying for that beautiful green dress her little girl spied in the store window. She remembered begging Charlene for the pretty dress. Her mother always took a moment to window shop at the upscale clothing store but never bought anything for herself, however to Georgia's pining for the green dress, she'd answered, "We'll see."

Tears glistened in Georgia's eyes at the memory of that pretty green dress and at Charlene's delight when she presented it to her.

She dabbed her tears.   Revisiting the past was a bad idea. Charlene would never see her grandchild growing in Georgia's belly. Never hold or spoil the baby like all good grandparents did.   Surely the same thoughts plagued Savannah when Lily, Anna and Daniel were conceived but it didn't ease the pain Georgia felt now.

She closed the journal, "I'll let you read them and give me the CliffsNotes version."

By his expression he understood perfectly.   While he read in silence she busied herself measuring flour, sugar, cinnamon and other ingredients for a coffee cake.   Savannah called her the Nervous Baker. Stress caused an increase in pies, cakes or in this case, coffee cake.   The family (and neighbors) judged her stress level by how many desserts she made and shared.   She earmarked the coffee cake for her and Dane but would slice up a good portion for their elderly, widowered neighbor.

It wasn't nerves but dark nostalgia that clouded her mood. Yearning for the old days when she and her mother – and sometimes Savannah – gathered in the kitchen to cook.   The days she could pick up the phone and spend an hour chatting over little things with Charlene or simply reminiscing about her mama's childhood.

"Morgan and your ma got along pretty well," Dane's voice snapped her from the memories.   "She must have enjoyed working for him. Easygoing, good sense of humor."

Georgia kept working but kept a cautious eye toward her husband. A third of the way through the journal she asked, "Nothing about Daddy or any interaction between him and Morgan?"

"Nope, nothing yet." He methodically read through it but used his finger as a bookmark.

Thirty minutes later a spicy cinnamon aroma hung in the air. The kitchen clock ticked away seconds. Pages turned with regularity. Georgia took time from cleaning countertops to check the coffee cake's progress, pleased with how it looked and smelled. Dane read half of the book by then. She saw his jaw start to clench. "What's wrong?"

He lifted his index finger to hold her off but Georgia wasn't stupid. Her husband rarely exhibited his temper. The tight jaw and frowning features tweaked her curiosity. He'd found something important.

"Honeybun…"

Dane normally called her *darlin'*. He used *Honeybun* in private. The switch in pet name along with his troubled features gave her pause, "What did you find?"

"How important is this, really? It's already wearing on you since you hit the baking routine."

She tried not to take offense. "We'll eat it or I can run it next door to Paul."

"Georgia, maybe your daddy was right. Leave it alone and let's forget about it."

Why did go philosophical all of a sudden? She repeated her

question. He rubbed his forehead, "I don't usually tell you what to do but since you're pregnant and it took us forever to get that way, can we, for the sake of the child, let this go? Nothing's worth tempting fate and if you read these you'll get depressed because you miss your ma."

Nice try, hon. "Savannah and I didn't risk life and limb for those journals just to ignore them. Yes, it's difficult to read them but we wanted to." She reached for the book.

He swung it behind his back, shaking his head, "Please, darlin', it's important to me."

"Reading them is important to *me*." She held her hand out, waiting.

The standoff lasted another minute. Georgia's patience hit its end, "*Dane.*"

Lips pursed, he slowly presented it to her. She heard him mumbling under his breath. Yes, she was stubborn. Not as stubborn as Savannah but she held her own. Georgia opened the book, fanned the pages, "The place with the gap?"

"Two pages ahead of it she mentions quitting the job," was the tense sigh. "And the considerable sum she was paid upon leaving."

Georgia backtracked two pages and began reading. Dane pushed a bar chair against her backside, "Sit down."

At the bottom of the page, she did. The subject her mother wrote about stole the strength from every muscle in her body. "What? Is this..." she swallowed hard. "She's saying Lee Morgan–"

"Put it down, Georgia."

"He..." she continued reading the second page. "He didn't...

How *could* he… *How dare he…*"

"Georgia," Dane grabbed for the book but she was faster, jerking it from his reach. She turned the page to see a brief paragraph that picked up a few months after the gap. She dug deep to shore up her courage and endure the shocking conclusion. *Three months have passed. I'm still trying to make sense of why it happened. Why me? Lee's request that I work late. Him offering me a glass of wine. The fuzzy, muddled feeling when I woke up. Then it all came back to me. He'd offered me a ride home, said I wasn't fit to drive because I was tipsy. I told him no, I'd be fine. I couldn't have R.J. see Lee drop me off. He'd go mad. The money still infuriates me. That staggering wad of bills he slipped into my hand before I left. With it I could buy our kids practically anything their hearts desire. I've hidden it though, so R.J. won't come across it by accident. I should give it to charity. It's dirty money. But we need the cash with R.J.'s business struggling the way it is. But I feel like a high dollar whore whether I keep the money or not.*

I can still feel his hands on me. The fingers digging into my wrists. I can feel him inside me… The word no means nothing to men like Lee. They find a way to silence their victims. He thinks money will keep me quiet. He's right about one thing. I can't go to the police. R.J. would find out. I'd have to testify. And Lee would win because rich, influential people never lose. I'd be humiliated and vilified because the Morgans are Augusta. Lord, I never asked for this and I need guidance. What do I do? How can I live with what Lee did because now I'm pregnant…

6

Savannah glanced between her mother's journals and Tucker Morgan's *Bad Blood.* The stores couldn't keep one on the shelves and the other would get her ass kicked if her daddy noticed them missing from the attic. One exposed Morgan family secrets to the point Lee went to the police for protection. The other revealed her mother's innermost thoughts, her history, a facet of her personality that no one read except her. There was no comparison. Savannah picked up the journal and began reading.

I couldn't believe it was my sister speaking. Her viciousness at such a traumatic time in our lives. But it <u>was</u> Katherine and she managed to sink to a new low when she demanded, "I want everything I've ever given you packed up and left on the porch. Do you hear me, Charlene? Everything."

Savannah closed the book. Maybe these journals weren't such a great idea after all. Those brief lines written in her mother's elegant cursive threw her back to a time when anger ruled Savannah. The mere mention of Aunt Katherine or Aunt Emma stoked a hatred so black she barely stayed civil around them.

She remembered her mother massaging her temple, the fingertips digging hard into tense muscles until she winced. How had this all

turned so backward, Charlene asked her baby girl. Grandma Culberson
wasn't even buried yet and war had been declared on the youngest
Culberson sister.

Fifteen-year-old Savannah hadn't had an answer. In a low
menacing voice her aunt ordered Charlene to gather up Christmas gifts,
birthday gifts and "hand-me-downs" (as Katherine called used items
given to her siblings), box them up and set it all on the front porch for
the world to see. "And I want it all on the porch by 8:00 tonight. I'll
pick it up then," Savannah remembered her saying, "*8:00 tonight. Is that
clear?*" Katherine hadn't given Charlene a chance to answer before
hanging up on her.

Savannah hated to tell her arrogant aunt but she never really gave
much to Charlene in the first place.

"Katherine, you're overreacting," Charlene replied.

"Am I?" the voice dared her to argue. "Apparently you don't
want Emma or me a part of this funeral. If we're not a part of it, we're
not a part of the family."

"Oh, for heaven's sake. You're my sisters. Of course you're part
of Mama's funeral. I–"

"You already picked out the casket!"

Now that was a low blow – and untrue. Charlene mentioned her
preference, that was all, but since Katherine and Emma discovered
Grandma Culberson left Charlene executrix of her estate, the two made
their youngest sister's life insufferable.

Savannah stepped back when her mama's usually slow temper
flared to scalding, "As I recall you and Emma had most of the services

planned out before I got there. The funeral director said you arrived twenty minutes early. Now *who* was left out again?"

"We were out and about early. Emma needed a dress for the funeral. The funeral home seemed a natural stop on the way to the mall. We only put in our suggestions for the casket, songs and eulogy."

Savannah put a hand to her mother's shaking one, "Please calm down, Mama. She's always going to–"

"While you were writing a check!?" Charlene practically shouted at her sister.

Katherine turned her nose up, "Don't worry, Charlene. Once you got there we would have divvied the bill into thirds. You'd have your part in it. But as you reminded us peons, you are the executrix of Mama's estate. I guess that means whatever *you* want, you get..."

Savannah stared at the journal. Touched it. Dared to open it and glance down the page she started.

My head hasn't stopped hurting since Mama was diagnosed with cancer a year ago. My life – our lives – have turned upside down in those long, painful months. I've dedicated what time I have to caring for Mama while trying to present a semi-normal existence to my own family. I worry about Seth being in the army. Stationed overseas in such a hostile country, God only knows if I'll see my son alive again. I worry about Georgia who moved to an apartment in Atlanta. It's such a big city and not safe for a beautiful woman living alone. Then there's my baby girl. I probably worry most about her. Savannah's fifteen and so full of life and so determined to prove herself. She's improved her grades and excels at golf. I pray the colleges take notice. She's got a God-given talent for the game and the enthusiasm to carry it into a profession. But she's got such a temper, especially around Katherine and Emma. She tries so hard to defend me but she reminds me of R.J. so much at times it scares me. For a child conceived under such painful circumstances, she's been such a blessing to me. She and Georgia help out where they can, cleaning house, cooking meals, taking over Mama's care when possible. I couldn't manage without the...

"'For a child conceived under such painful circumstances'?" Savannah whispered aloud. "What did she mean?" *Well, I won't find out for a while since Georgia has the earlier journals.* Once she finished reading those earlier journals her sister would want to trade with Savannah. She decided to keep reading and picked up where she left off. Her vision immediately gravitated to Lee Morgan's name. *Katherine and Emma bowed up when Lee walked into the funeral home. Besides my sisters, he was the last person I wanted to see. I suppose his arrival was fortuitous as Savannah had just squared off with Emma and Katherine about Mama's arrangements and their treatment of me.*

Lee's presence temporarily silenced our argument. He addressed Savannah first asking how she was doing and if she needed anything. She looked confused as to why he was there. After all she'd only seen him once or twice in her life and had no clue of our past together. To her credit she treated him kindly for a man she may not have remembered from so long ago.

He approached me next (like an old, dear friend) and offered his help. That angered my sisters to no end.

Katherine stepped closer to Savannah, stabbed a finger at her,

"You need a good whipping, young lady. You shouldn't treat your elders this way and get away with it."

My ever undaunted baby girl stared directly at her aunt replying, "Then my elders oughta act like adults, not vultures."

Katherine raised her hand to slap her. Savannah anticipated it and reached to grab her hand but Lee beat her to it. "Hit this girl and you'll answer to me, Katherine. She's defending her mother as well she should…"

Savannah closed the journal, remembering back to the time. Remembered Lee defending her. She'd been appreciative to him and apologized for him seeing the family – including herself – at their worst.

That was enough walking down memory lane for one day so she delved into someone else's dirty laundry for a change.

She switched to reading Tucker Morgan's *Bad Blood*. If she didn't try to keep some pace with Georgia, her sister might finish her copy and blab all the juicy parts without meaning to.

The next chapter started out benign enough with Tucker detailing Lee's killer instinct in business, swallowing up small companies like a human Pac-Man. He enjoyed highlighting his father's ruthlessness in the professional world. Then he switched horses, telling the story of Lee and four-year-old Preston driving home one day when he came upon a little girl walking down Walton Way, a main thoroughfare in Augusta.

The child couldn't have been more than six as she trudged down the sidewalk, shoulders hunched. She's too close to traffic, Lee said, and why was the child walking a busy street alone when she should be in school?

He pulled the Mercedes to the curb amid the honking horns of protesting drivers and Preston's whining to go home.

Lee told the boy to be quiet. He knew this girl and refused to let her wander the streets alone. He rolled down the window and called to the child who'd already shifted away from the car pulling alongside her. She stopped when he called her by name but refused to approach the car.

"What are you doing out here?" Lee asked. "Shouldn't you be in school?"

She started walking with a slower gait and he noticed she favored her right leg. Lee kept pace but asked Preston if she looked like she was limping.

Preston huffed out, "Who cares? Can we go home now?"

Lee tried again, "Savannah, you know me. I'm Lee Morgan, Charlene's friend. You've been to my house before. You remember my collection of Fabergé eggs? Your favorite was the one with the carriage inside. And I know you remember Mrs. Gardner's chocolate cake."

Savannah paused. Looked at Lee again. Now she approached. He leaned across Preston sitting in the passenger seat, "Why aren't you in school, sweetheart?"

"Nurse sent me home."

"What's wrong?"

"My back hurts."

"How did you hurt your back?"

"I made Daddy mad again."

"Great," Preston crossed his arms. "We'll never get home now."

Lee snapped at his son to shut up.

At this point Savannah glanced up from the book. She remembered that day. How could she have forgotten that encounter with Lee Morgan? He was a kind man to her and in those days kind men were rare in her life. She started reading again.

"Your mother doesn't know the school sent you home, does she?"

She shook her head, "They called but she wasn't home."

"And they let you walk out?"

She shied from his rising anger, probably afraid he'd somehow blame her the way her father always did. "I left when no one was looking," she said. "I don't feel good. I just wanted to go home."

"Have you got a key to your house?"

"Yessir."

"Climb in, sweetie. I'll take you home."

Fear filled her eyes, shook her head, "If Daddy sees me in a strange car, he'll get mad again."

"He won't see me, I promise. Let me take you home so you can rest."

According to Tucker's book, Lee watched her get in the back seat and cringe as she adjusted to a more comfortable yet awkward position. Tucker stressed how furious Lee was at the girl's father and, in private, threatened to "do something about him".

For a kid not even born yet, Tucker captured her feelings perfectly. She had been scared Lee might place blame on her for leaving the school early. How was Tucker privy to the incident anyway? Had Lee recounted it at some point and Tucker took notes? Writers were strange ducks. Georgia jotted notes all the time for her books, even when conversing with someone else.

O   O   O

The phone rang while she busied herself cleaning house. Ennis had to work that day so she planned to spruce up the place and maybe, just maybe, read a few more pages of Tucker Morgan's book. If the children let her of course. Over the years she'd learned the fastest land animal wasn't a cheetah but a toddler, especially after that toddler was asked what was in their mouth. She also discovered two surefire ways to draw a kid's attention. Trying reading a book comprised of words longer than two syllables or trying to go to the bathroom alone.

The girls' contribution to house cleaning amounted to picking up their toys – or trying to. Savannah noticed the productivity nosedived once they got in a spat over a stuffed elephant that somehow got christened Howie. Mama straightened out the confusion, "Anna, sweetheart, that's not Howie. That's Lily's Heffalump. Howie's in your toy box."

Savannah began dusting Lily's room. She'd done three rooms when her cell phone rang. She asked Anna to bring it to her. Her daughter did more than that. She answered the call. If it was work calling, she thought, what a surprise they got. A four-year-old answering her mama's phone. *I'm Anna. Who are you?* A pause then *one moment, pleeeze.*

Savannah smiled at the last comment's professional flare.

Anna marched in, proud as ever, and offered the cell phone to her, "I answered it."

"I heard. So who is it, Nosy Rosy? Work, Mrs. Porter or Daddy?"

"Wee Mogan."

She took the phone, thanked Anna and answered it, "Yes, Mr. Morgan."

A small chuckle floated from the phone, "What a delightful girl you have. Very bubbly and polite. I'd love to meet your children sometime. Mrs. Gardner would be in seventh heaven to bake them her chocolate cake anything else their hearts desire."

"We can arrange a time, sure. What did you need?" She shooed Anna away from Lily's toy box. She'd grabbed the elephant again, "Anna, please put Lily's Heffalump back." Then returned to Lee, "I'm sorry. They're a handful today."

He laughed once more, "I remember those days. Hard to find any personal time, isn't it? You realize that if you accept my job offer it covers child care too. In your case your children would only be a few walls apart and looked after by vetted professionals. That's one of the perks of working here. Before you say anything, I'm just giving you information, that's all."

"I love my kids but they enjoy their time away from their helicopter mother and frankly I enjoy that time too. Is there something you needed?"

"Am I imposing too much to ask for a brief meeting? Obviously you're busy so if another day is more suitable we can reschedule it."

"I don't have any other day. This is my day off unless I'm called back to work for some reason. What's the meeting about?"

"I've had an employment packet assembled for you. It includes disclosure forms, your duties, salary, benefits and extras. I want you to have a full picture of what your future holds if you join us. And since I caught you on a busy day, I'll send it via messenger so you'll have time to look it over tonight. If you're interested, drop by the lab for drug testing tomorrow."

Wow, that's fast. "Tomorrow? What's the rush?"

"I want you on board ASAP," he chuckled, "*before* you have a chance to think too hard about it."

"Even though I've never headed up a security team in my life? This is mighty deep water you want me to dive into. One massive screw-up and you'll want me out and if you don't, your boys sure will."

"You let me worry about the boys. And you strike me as a bright woman who can learn the ropes in record time. You already have law enforcement training so some time with my existing Chief Security Officer is all you need. Expect the packet this afternoon and remember, tomorrow drop by for the drug test."

7

Savannah's phone rang at precisely nine the next morning. She checked Caller ID, saw the name Morgan and clicked on. She was surprised to hear a different voice other than Lee's.

"Ms. Prince, this is Preston Morgan, Lee Morgan's son. I realize you're at work but I'm hoping you can spare a moment to meet at my office. My schedule's tight today so how about in an hour?"

Apparently all Morgans moves at a lightning pace. First Lee pushed for the drug test, now Preston pressured her into a quick spur-of-the-moment meeting. "Sure, I can drop by."

"Good. I'm assuming you know where the Morgan Tower is?"

"Yes, it's been years ago but I've been there before." Years ago. Yeah. Try when she still wore a uniform and patrolled the area with her FTO Riley Murphy.

"Feel free to park in the building's parking garage. I'll give them your name. See you in an hour."

Now why would Preston want a powwow with her? Likely to question his father's sanity for pursing her for a job she knew beans about.

She left at nine thirty to allow for traffic. Savannah stopped at the lowered barrier blocking off access to the parking garage. Two stern-faced armed guards in crisply ironed uniforms stood in the guard station, one for incoming, the other for outgoing cars. If she accepted Lee's offer, would these behemoth obvious ex-soldiers be under her command as well? And how would they cotton to a female former police sergeant ordering them around?

The guard stepped out holding a clipboard, "Name and appointment time."

"Detective Sergeant Savannah Prince. Ten o'clock with Preston Morgan." She omitted the Rutherford to avoid confusion.

He checked his watch, wrote something on the clipboard, jotted down her license plate number then lifted the barrier.

Savannah's brow rose. Was she meeting a businessman or the President of the United States? The only things missing were a strip search and a vehicle scan for bombs.

Savannah cleared the first line of defense, now for the second. She took the elevator up to the reception area. The doors opened to sheer opulence. Rich, wood-grain walls trimmed in gold accents surrounded her and gave the place a warm, welcoming feel. Marbled tiled floors shined with a perfect polish. She made her way to the reception desk. The glass-topped mahogany desk stretched about ten feet in length with two suit-clad twenty-something men manning it. A flash of her badge gained her entrance through the metal detectors – after the first twenty-something jotted down the department name and badge number.

She took the elevator which had the same wood and gold décor as the reception area. Its interior could house twelve people with sufficient elbow room and managed to quiet her claustrophobia a degree but not entirely. She took that time throwing on her mental armor for the meeting. She expected to hear from "the children" sooner and being second in command under Lee, it figured Preston made the call.

The elevator opened to smaller reception area with dark paneling and beige carpet. Landscape paintings adorned the walls and four leather chairs and matching couch waited to cradle backsides that made more in a day than she did in a year.

Savannah approached another, smaller glass-topped mahogany reception desk. A slim, attractive woman in her late twenties sat behind the desk. Between the black skirt suit, red lipstick and hair pulled back in a severe bun, she looked more like a dominatrix than a secretary.

She provided the woman with her name and appointed time. Two mouse clicks later and the woman appeared surprised (if surprised meant one scarcely raised brow) to see Savannah's name on the schedule. She buzzed Preston's office

As she had downstairs, Savannah felt completely out of place. Rich people weren't her thing. Her dress style never measured up as evidenced by the sideways glances from the doorman, downstairs desk dudes and this woman.

Dominatrix met her gaze. Yep. The woman missed her calling. When she said *Mr. Morgan will see you now*, Savannah halfway expected her to brandish a whip to move the detective along. Preston's secretary added, "Third door on the left. He's got an important meeting after yours so please make it brief."

"He called me so I'd say the ball's in his court." The people in that building assumed her time wasn't as important as theirs because, well, because she wasn't one of them, she supposed. Savannah knocked on the door.

A resounding baritone called her to come in. Preston's office looked exactly what she expected from a Fortune 500 executive. Large, imposing oak desk, comfy leather chair, a fully stocked bar and two elegant hardwood guest chairs that promised comfort during her visit. Renaissance paintings hung on the dark paneled walls. A luxurious thick beige carpet covered the floor. Opulence to the nth degree.

The lavish surroundings chafed her but not nearly as much as seeing not one Morgan but two in the room. Preston and Ethan. Armani graced Preston's late thirties physique while considerably younger Ethan opted for tan Dockers and navy blue polo shirt. Ethan, if she remembered correctly, fell in line behind Preston in the birth order, followed by Tucker then the baby Grady. Both older brothers favored however Preston inherited the lion's share of Lee's looks while Ethan bore a resemblance to their mother with lighter hair and dark eyes. Both men rose from their seats and Savannah stopped to address Preston, "I thought this was a private meeting between us, Mr. Morgan."

"My brother insisted on his presence. This is family business and he has every right to be here."

Why did that whole comment sound as pompous as he looked?

Ethan was the first to greet her with his name and a warm, firm handshake, "Sergeant, it's good to meet you. I'm just hanging around to annoy my brother. Hope you don't mind too much."

Preston already looked exasperated by his brother's presence, "Sit down, Ethan. You're wasting time." He shook Savannah's hand, formally introduced them both. He buttoned his gray suit jacket, smoothed his maroon designer tie while offering her a seat, "I'm sure you're busy so we'll get down to business."

Ethan reclaimed the leather chair beside hers. He turned it a degree to face her instead of his brother. Preston waited for him to adjust the chair to his satisfaction then continued, "My brothers and I are aware of the offer our father tendered to you."

"The CSO job here in Atlanta." She wanted to prevent any miscommunication.

Preston seemed a tad insulted as if her mentioning it questioned his intelligence, "Yes. We are also aware of the 'salary' attached to that proposal. We would like to present our own offer –"

"Don't be condescending, Press," Ethan interrupted. "First, you put this thing together without conferring with me, Tucker or Grady. And secondly, the sergeant is probably smarter than you think. She *is* a detective, after all."

Now she felt ambushed. The two played the old good cop/bad cop routine on her. And Ethan was right. She was smarter than Preston gave her credit.

The man behind the desk stared daggers at his younger brother, "Don't you have a tee time to get to?"

Ethan didn't respond so Preston moved things along, "Ms. Prince, I'm tendering *my own* offer to you." He reached in his suit coat. A checkbook came out. His hand wrote in hurried strokes with the pen. He chicken-scratched his signature at the bottom much like her doctor signed his prescriptions. Riiip... Preston extended the check to her, pen still in hand, his "offer" tucked between his index and middle fingers. She saw his vision flick to the clock. He wanted this concluded fast apparently.

She stayed put, "I don't understand. I haven't accepted or declined the job so why throw this at me?"

He dropped all pretense now, "My father may want you but I don't and I want you to decline his offer and go away. Here's your check."

Savannah's eyes narrowed. Her hands grasped the armrests, "I'm sorry you have such a low opinion of me. For your information, I don't accept payoffs."

"Oh," he sounded surprised but sneered as he said, "so you're not like your mother, is that it?"

Ethan sobered, "Press, don't..."

Savannah rose to her feet, unable to comprehend why he would attack a woman he never met. "What did you say?" Her voice held in unspoken threat. One that warned him to tread carefully or else. She might be an upstanding cop but even upstanding cops had their limits. Her family was that limit. No one sullied the good name of Charlene Prince. No one.

Ethan's happy-go-lucky mood disappeared as he whispered a warning to his older brother. You're skating on thin ice, she heard him say.

Preston bulled ahead, "I said 'so you're not like your mother'. Out for a big payday, so to speak."

"Explain that comment," she stepped against his desk, moved aside his hand holding the check, "And be careful the words you use. I may be a cop but I'm her daughter first and foremost."

"There's nothing to explain. During her employment your mother lured my father into an affair. My father finally came to his senses and gave her a considerable amount of money to leave quietly. That's what this," he waggled the check, "is for. To make her daughter go away and thus avoiding dredging up anymore of the Morgan sordid past."

Ethan's shoulders slumped. He shook his head, "Mrs. Rutherford, I must apologize for my brother's behavior—"

"You're calling my mother a whore?" Her voice scarcely expressed the rage boiling inside her. Her fingers grasped the edge of the heavy wood desk as she debated over upending it on top of him.

Preston didn't seem to notice or care, "What else do you call a woman who won't keep her knees closed?"

The words struck her like a backhand. She never considered herself vengeful and hadn't, as far as she remembered, misused her authority as a cop. But good old Preston Morgan had her vowing to reconsider a few of those dirty little tricks available to police officers. And if she ran dry on ideas John Mathis stockpiled plenty in his many years on the job.

"Our brother wrote a four hundred page anthology of secrets and lies about this family," Preston's vision momentarily cut to Ethan, "and I'm the only one bailing water. So before my father drills another hole in this boat, I'm plugging it today." He waved the check at her, "Take it, leave and don't even think about coming back for more."

Savannah saw the amount written on the check. She nearly swallowed her tongue – but instead of cashing it she yearned to wad it up and shove it down the bastard's throat.

She didn't trust herself to speak. She stared at the man dragging her mama's name through the mud with filthy outright lies. *You'd best not change lanes without signaling, buddy. I'm gonna have your license plate on a list and anytime you cut a corner of the Georgia traffic laws, you're getting pulled over.*

Ethan noticed the subtle change in her posture, "Press, you really should apologize and Mrs. Rutherford, understand that Preston's views are his own. I don't condone his actions or words."

She heard him but she was far from finished with Mr. Preston Asshole Morgan. "My mother was a God-fearing Christian who treasured her marriage vows and her family. You, Mr. Morgan, have plenty of *bailing* to do with that juicy book Tucker wrote. It's sold out locally, number three at Amazon and listed as a New York Times bestseller. I strongly advise you to concentrate on keeping your head above water, *so to speak,* and leave my mother's memory alone." She buttoned her jacket, straightened her shoulders. She felt fairly sure that, "Lee has no clue what you're doing, does he? Throwing money at me while throwing crap on my mama's memory."

"No," Preston's hand remained extended, waiting for her to pluck the check from it. Waited for her to fall for the lure of easy money. Didn't everyone want money? Didn't everyone dream of those life-changing amounts? Sure, but not when it was a payoff and most of all, not when it cost her mother's reputation. Savannah refused to sacrifice her mother's memory for cash and that appeared to flummox Preston Morgan who added a postscript, "And don't try going upstairs to see my father. He's in New York." Now he sighed. The fun of ripping her late mother's character apart faded. Now he was bored, "Take. The. Money."

He just kept adding fuel to the burning rage inside her. "I have his cell phone number." How's *that*, you sanctimonious sack of shit? "Maybe he'd like to hear how you've slandered my mother and tried to pay me off."

Preston's laugh emerged dry and cynical, "Ms. Prince, do that and I'll have a chat with the chief of police. You won't like the results."

"And before your call hits the cell tower, I can have the fire department here for an impromptu inspection just to shut down your business for the day, maybe two, and if you cut a left turn too sharp, I'll have your Porsche pulled over."

"Oh," Ethan's tone lilted, "she *does* sound like a Morgan, doesn't she, Press?"

"What does that mean?" she snapped at him.

Ethan backed off, hands lifted in surrender, "I'm not poking at you. He is."

And the poking (which felt more like skewering) was about to end. "Good day, Mr. Morgan." She nodded to Ethan, "And to you, Mr. Morgan."

"I dunno, Press. She's met you toe to toe in this bout. Better than our brothers ever have."

"Shut up, Ethan," Preston demanded.

Savannah's eyes flashed the same message to the "good cop" of the two. She didn't need some smartass winding either of them tighter than they already were.

As she opened the door, Preston dangled the carrot one final time, "Ms. Prince, you walk out now and the deal is off."

Without looking back she said, "You know what you can do with that deal too. And my name is *Sergeant* Savannah Prince Rutherford."

With a determined stride she stormed down the hall to the elevators. Approaching the reception area she noticed half a dozen men and women in suits sitting and waiting for their meeting with Preston Morgan. Hers and Morgan's raised voices kept the small crowd captivated until she walked in. Still, as she marched into the reception area only a few bothered to glance away. Even Preston's secretary gaping mug broke with stoic tradition. Savannah gave her a curt nod as she passed by, "That fast enough for you?"

Savannah stewed from Preston's office to the parking garage Mr. Pretentious insisted she use. The beginnings of tears welled. She hadn't expected a grand acceptance by the Almighty Morgan clan but she hadn't anticipated such outright venom and the insult of a payoff. She wanted out of there while solemnly vowing never to step foot on Morgan property again.

The tears disappeared by the time the elevator door to the parking garage slid back. A second elevator dinged, signaling the impending arrival of more suckers dumb enough to visit Morgan's business monolith. She hurried to her Charger.

"Mrs. Rutherford!" A man's voice echoed through the parking garage. Ethan.

He hadn't seen her yet – and she hadn't intended to change that either. She keyed the lock, opened the door.

"Savannah! Hold up a sec!"

Shit. He spotted her. "I'm not interested in your brother's offer," she said in case he too suffered the throes of a massive ego trip.

The man's speed told her he was no stranger to running or bobbing and weaving through parked cars. She waited for him but didn't wait long. Heaving a few heavy breaths he shook his head, smiling, "You're one fast lady."

She nearly bowed up. *Fast?* What the hell did he mean by *fast?* After Preston called Charlene a whore, she put nothing past these people.

Ethan overlooked her frown, "I ran like the wind to catch you but you'd already caught the elevator." He leaned on his knees to catch his breath – or so it seemed. Savannah recognized the move as a stalling tactic. A chance for her to calm down and for him to organize his spiel.

For the record, "You wasted your effort. I'll never take his money."

"That's his answer to everything. This book fiasco has him bouncing off the walls and trying to put out fires he thinks are starting."

"I was never a spark. I don't believe for a minute my mother slept with any man except my father. If disparaging people or their relatives is how Morgans handle things, I want no part of that job."

Ethan's nonchalant spirit waned, "And that's your choice but listen, Dad was really fond of your mother and I've heard him say he considers you a daughter."

"Why's that? We've met only a few times. Golf tournaments and commendation ceremonies and those were to show he's active in the community."

Ethan smoothed a hand along the blue Charger's roof, "I think it's more than that. You certainly impressed him over the years. Personally I like you too. You've got the grit Dad said you had and I'll bet when people aren't questioning your mother's marriage vows you've got a good sense of humor. You and I could have a good friendship if you'd let us."

"What's your game, Ethan? Between this and that crap upstairs this whole meeting doesn't make sense."

"The only game I have is golf, if that counts, and considering your high school successes, I figure you still enjoy it too. Tucker's so bitter about life for whatever reason, Grady's immersed himself in his work and we've both seen Press at his best – or worst as the case may be. My brother and I are too different to get along. You, on the other hand, are a mystery. One I'd like to know better."

She wasn't convinced. If Ethan switched from good cop to good, *accepting* son, she needed to be careful. Because despite her convictions, he might be playing her just to keep his daddy happy about the CSO job. "Better how?"

"Well, we know you're far too smart and scrupulous to accept bribes which speaks well for your character and our police department. I love to golf and I remember how good you were in high school. Care to join me for a round sometime?"

Oh yes. Golf still held a special place in her heart. Her clubs rarely saw the light of day anymore with her family and the job. It sounded exquisite. Perhaps too exquisite.

He sweetened the deal, "Ever played Augusta National?"

She snorted, "Yeah, right."

"Would you like to play Augusta National?"

"Is water wet?"

His shoulders visibly relaxed, "It would be a fine opportunity to get acquainted, agreed?"

"Agreed." If he wasn't playing her for a fool, that was. But Augusta National? She spent her whole life driving past the course, pining, *yearning* for a chance to play the course. He'd whetted her appetite (which he fully intended to do) so now what?

"Oh my," he leaned against the car, "this *is* a struggle for you, isn't it? Am I being genuine or am I manipulating you, right? I can assure you I am well-intentioned. My father means a great deal to me and since meeting with you he's been on top of the world. If he thinks Savannah Prince Rutherford is worth knowing, so do I." He waggled his brow, "Who knows? You might actually like me."

She continued debating over his real motives and what to do. Ethan waited then laid another reason on her, "Listen, wouldn't your mother be happy you played the most famous course in the world? Well, next to St. Andrews, of course."

He sounded genuine but, to her, rich folk made their living by putting on airs and saying the right things. "What are your feelings about my mother?"

"I think people are fallible. I believe they can get lonely or be driven to do things they normally wouldn't, not that those circumstances apply to her. People make their decisions and apparently she and Dad shared a past none of us are privy to. Unlike my brother, I try not to judge."

His psychology and social skills far outweighed his brother's but that little ping at the back of her brain cautioned her to be careful. "You're right, people are fallible but I guarantee Mama wouldn't sleep around."

Ethan shrugged it off, "Press can be a jerk. He's a whiz at business, hard as stone, but if it's a personal issue, he reverts to a child. Temper, words and general unpleasantness. So Mrs. Rutherford, fancy a round of golf at the best course this side of St. Andrews? They serve a mean pimento cheese sandwich – or literally anything you might want."

What the hell, she decided. If it all went to shit, at least she'd still have the memory. "Sure, why not?"

He stuck out his hand, "Shake on it. Then it's a done deal."

Savannah wrapped her hand around his. It felt warm and confident. Ethan slipped a card from his slacks, jotted down another number below his office one, "My cell number. Call me with your schedule and we'll work something out on a day and tee times."

"I will. Do you need my cell number?"

He pulled his phone from his belt, waggled it, "Got it. Courtesy of Dad."

8

"For once Pops was right. You should have left Mama's things alone."

Georgia pursed her lips. Seth's lecture pricked her ire. The last thing she needed was to hear *I told you so.* She called him for advice, insisted they met in private so he drove to her house. She stated the obvious, "Well, we didn't leave them alone so now what do we do? I don't want to tell her what happened with Mama and Lee Morgan and I sure don't want her to finding out she might not be Daddy's—"

"The way Pops has treated her over the years it's like he already knew."

"Seth." Her frustration mounted at her older brother. Did he complicate things on purpose? "*Savannah* doesn't know, that's the point."

He traced the rim of his coffee cup, "Did you read ahead to see if Mama was positive the pregnancy came from the attack? Before you think about destroying Savannah, let's get the facts first."

She wanted help, not antagonism. Seth not only looked like their father, he acted like him sometimes too. She bowed up with a curt, "I'm not trying to destroy anyone." She shook the leatherbound, two hundred page grenade at him, "But she wants to read these journals too. She'll read the same thing I did. Then what?"

Seth's blue eyes met her green ones. As if he sobered to what she said, he ditched the sarcasm, "Hide it from her. Tell her there wasn't a volume for those years."

"Won't that look strange? Mama wrote a journal every year and suddenly Savannah's conception and birth are conspicuously missing?"

Seth leaned back, sighing, "Georgia, you can't prove that she's Morgan's kid, not without DNA and I don't see Lee or Pops willing to donate a sample, do you? This is a can of snakes, not worms, sis. You tell anyone and all hell is gonna break loose."

"He's right," was all Dane said. He readjusted Daniel in his arms while feeding the baby then compared two photos Georgia sat side by side. One was Savannah's high school graduation picture and the other was Charlene and R.J.'s wedding photo. He asked Georgia, "What makes you think she's not R.J.'s?"

"It's not that I don't think she's Daddy's. It's just difficult to tell."

"No, it's not. She's got blue eyes, he's got blue eyes."

Georgia brought up the Morgan homepage on her iPad. She zoomed in on Lee Morgan's portrait, "So does Lee."

Seth crossed his arms, his frustration mounting, "Doesn't mean she's his kid."

Dane compared Savannah and R.J. again, "Her nose and R.J.'s are similar."

Georgia pointed to Lee, "Same basic shape."

Dane pooh-poohed the idea, "His is wider. She's got a cute nose."

Georgia sort of smiled, "It is cute."

He tried again, "She's got R.J.'s chin."

And again her brow lifted, "They're about the same but—"

Seth threw up his hands, "You're just determined she's Morgan's kid, aren't you?" Seth's voice carried enough Daniel gave his uncle a look. Uncle Seth toned it down, "She inherited plenty from Pops, including that hellacious temper and, I'm sorry to say, the alcoholic gene. She's Pop's kid, Georgia. For all our sakes, leave it at that."

o   o   o

"Just who do you think you are?" a woman barked from Savannah's office doorway.

The woman – correction – women (there were two) converged on her desk like freight trains dressed in Prada and Vera Wang. Looking fresh from a Paris catwalk, the two trophy wives wearing diamond wedding rings the size of satellite TV dishes, towered over the detective until she rose from her seat and removed her glasses. She stood a good three to four inches taller even without high heels. "Can I help you?" *Out the door, perhaps?*

"You can leave my husband alone. No," the loudmouth thrust a finger at her, "you can leave the entire Morgan family alone."

"Stay away or you'll be sorry," the second one echoed. It reminded Savannah of a child's threat.

Savannah did not back down, "How about telling me exactly which Morgans you are before you try bullying me?"

The brazen one dressed in red stared her squarely in the eyes, "Lydia Morgan, Preston's wife, and I don't bully. I get things done. You're abusing your authority," she sneered at the nameplate on the desk, "*Sergeant*, and I intend to put you in your place."

"And I'm Tucker's wife Sabrina," Lydia's companion piped up, "and you'd better not try that trick with him."

"What trick–"

"I know who you are," Lydia cut her off, "and you'd better forget any ideas of getting rich off this family."

What... the... hell was she yammering about? She opened her mouth to ask when Lydia jumped down her throat again, this time with a wicked smile, "Oh yes, I know all about your mother's indiscretions and the fact Preston offered you money to go away. I'm offering you something more valuable. Continued employment. I'll have you booted out of here faster than your mother grabbed that *severance* check."

Savannah's hackles rose. She rounded the desk. Sabrina tugged at Lydia's arm muttering *let's go*. Lydia refused to move. Savannah stared down at her, scarcely able to contain her rage, "I suggest you leave right now, lady. You say one more word about my mother–"

"What's going on in here?"

She retained solid eye contact with Lydia. "Mrs. Preston Morgan is putting me on notice," she told Josh. "Apparently I can lose my job because I went to see him after *he* demanded to meet with *me* yesterday."

"Ma'am, I'm Captain Josh Hunter. Let's go into my office and discuss your issues with Sergeant Prince."

Savannah heard Sabrina gulp.

"No," Lydia replied in a clipped fashion, "I've made my point with her." She aboutfaced and marched past him, out the door and, Savannah assumed, out of the building. With Sabrina trying to catch up.

"What the hell just happened here?" Josh demanded.

She glared at the empty hallway, "I don't know exactly, but you saved her a bloody nose. No one disparages my mother and gets away with it. I don't care who they are."

o   o   o

At 10:15, Josh Hunter leaned in her office, "Savannah, with me now."

Why did he sound like she'd stepped on his last nerve? She'd been ambushed by Lydia and Sabrina bright and early that morning so he hopefully didn't hold her responsible for the confrontation.

She dropped the phone in its cradle and went to see her boss. She was surprised to see another person in the room. A man in a black suit and a gold badge clipped to his belt. He was the size of a defensive tackle with a stern, imposing presence that put her on edge.

She nodded a greeting to both then asked Josh, "What's up?"

Dread. That was the sour note in her captain's voice. He reluctantly introduced the defensive tackle as Captain Tony Banks from Internal Affairs.

Her gut clenched. The bowels threatened to turn liquid. Barely a full year passed with her sergeant's promotion and trouble came knocking. Had Lydia made good on her threat to sever her employment? Could she? Whatever Savannah faced she'd do it with dignity.

Josh took the lead, "Did you by any chance threaten Preston Morgan? Something to the degree of–"

"According to him," the captain butted in while referring to his notes, "you threatened to have him stopped for cutting a left turn too sharply."

Lying was out of the question since Preston's brother would vouch for him. Incredulous, she asked, "He threatened to call the chief of police if I merely called his father."

"Why would you call his father?"

Savannah gathered from Banks's tone he didn't give a shit why. This meeting was a dog and pony show for Josh's sake and Preston's way of flexing his political muscle. Plus, how could she phrase "he accused my mother of being a whore" in a more palatable way? "It was personal and I'd rather not say."

"Savannah," Hunter urged her to spill the beans, "if you don't explain yourself, you'll be suspended."

What!? "But he can insult my family and no one bats an eyelash? Well, how stupid am I? *Of course* he can because he's a Morgan." *Careful*, a little voice in her head warned. *The guy you're practically yelling at can force you to the unemployment line in a heartbeat.* She tried to dial down her ire, "It's not like I dialed up the patrol division and said pull Preston Morgan over if he slams his Porsche's door too hard. C'mon, I didn't call them at all. Ask around."

"Sergeant, he *was* given a citation for cutting a turn too close. Explain that."

"Maybe he's a lousy driver. I only know I did nothing wrong."

Banks didn't care. "Five days suspension. You know the routine."

Savannah stared, incredulous, at Josh Hunter while sliding the .38 from her holster and unloading it. "Good to know the Morgans have friends in the department. I'll be sure not to jaywalk or cut a turn too close on the way home." She placed the gun and badge on Hunter's desk, not in the Internal Affairs lackey's waiting hand.

"You have only yourself to blame, Sergeant," Banks accused. "I hope you learn your lesson about threatening citizens."

She was halfway out the door when she turned to respond, "I didn't exactly pull my gun on him and all I've learned is who's on his payroll."

"*Ten* days suspension," Preston's lackey amended.

Whatever. "I'll bring my off duty gun to Captain Hunter later." She seethed as she stormed down the hall to Ennis's office, "Report to Hunter. He's in charge now."

A puzzled Ennis glanced up from the computer, "Why? What happened?"

"I've been suspended," was all she said.

O O O

"Thank you for meeting me," Ethan opened the restaurant's door for her. Savannah stepped inside the ritzy Signature Room, an astronomically expensive three star Michelin establishment known for exceptional cuisine, prompt, courteous service and week long waits for reservations –

that was unless your name happened to be Morgan. Ethan apparently had George Clooney's clout. When he spoke, the Signature Room listened – and found a table for him.

Despite Ethan's casual wear, the ultra upscale atmosphere intimidated Savannah, making her feel terribly underdressed for the spur-of-the-moment meeting. J.C. Penney pantsuits failed to measure up to Saks Fifth Avenue but her inferiority complex could also have something to do with being temporarily unemployed.

"Well, it's not as if I have a job right now." Bitterness threaded her voice despite her efforts to hide it.

"I apologize for Preston. He can be petty at times."

"The suspension goes on my record and I have a family to support so could you tell him to back off before I'm fired?"

"I'll do what I can to talk sense into him," Ethan replied as the maître d' nodded a greeting to him and retrieved two menus. He escorted them through the busy main dining room to a secluded table in the back. Ethan seated her then took the chair across from her.

"I can assure you I never followed through on that threat."

"It's not just the threat that upset him. Tucker's book exposed uncomfortable aspects about our family."

The waiter approached for their order. Ethan held him off by saying, "Drinks first, John. I'll have a scotch on the rocks and my lady friend will have…"

"Club soda please."

The waiter hesitated a half second to see if she pulled a joke. Ethan nodded to him, "Club soda it is." John the waiter appraised her with a slightly raised brow before walking off. First JC Penney, now her choice of drink. Nothing measured up. She gave a mental eye roll. She could never fit into the rich world.

Ethan volunteered an amused, "You're allowed to drink, you know. They serve whatever you like."

She shook her head. "What else has Preston's back up? Can't just be my empty threat and Tucker's book. Your family's weathered gossip and hearsay for years."

He flinched, "Yeah, but this is different. More people are involved, including your mother."

Savannah bowed up, "Not you too."

He lifted his hands signifying surrender the way he had in Preston's office, "Whoa. I'm not accusing your mother of anything."

She pursed her lips when the waiter delivered their drinks. Good thing she went cheap because this meeting was headed for a premature end. She started to say something once the waiter left but Ethan beat her to it, "Apparently you don't know what happened. Not surprising, I guess. It was a long time ago."

"What are you talking about?"

He eyed the club soda, "Sure you wouldn't prefer something more substantial?"

She declined so he reached in his back pocket and unfolded a full size sheet of paper. After a slug of scotch he presented it to her, "This is a copy of the severance check Dad gave your mother."

Savannah retrieved her glasses from her purse and slid them on. Her jaw slackened at the number written on the check. What kind of job did Charlene have anyway?

Another waiter approached holding a tray of sliders. He sat a small plate in front of Savannah then one for Ethan and placed the selection of sliders on the table. "Your usual appetizer, Mr. Morgan."

Savannah kind of smiled, "Sliders? Here?" She expected caviar, shrimp pâté or crab cakes with gold leaf.

Ethan claimed one each of bacon and beef. "Your choice of beef, bacon or turkey. They're delicious. Try one."

She chose a bacon, "So why such a large severance check?"

He took a healthy bite of his bacon slider, swiped his mouth with the linen napkin, then wolfed down the bite as if he'd been starving for a week. For some reason he reminded her of a blue collar Bubba who didn't give a hang who approved of his down-home ways, even in a hoity toity restaurant. He spoke around the mouthful, "Like I said, he liked her a lot."

She bit off a small piece, chewed and was surprisingly impressed, "These are good."

"Bacon, caramelized onions, pickle, and melted Gruyere cheese. Heaven, aren't they?"

Especially on an empty stomach. They hit the spot and told him so. She returned to the check dated several months before she was born. Charlene always said Savannah was a hard baby to carry and to deliver so it stood to reason why she resigned when she did. The baby was giving her fits. Counting it out, Savannah estimated her mother was three months pregnant when Lee wrote the check.

Ethan continued nibbling, this time grabbing another beef slider.

He again spoke around his mouthful, "Did your mother ever mention my dad?"

She shook her head, "The first time I realized they knew each other was when Mama brought me and my sister to the mansion in Augusta. Why?"

He hesitated. Slowly chewed then awkwardly swallowed. The food hung in his throat and he chased it with water then scotch. With an uneasy tone, he said, "Turns out Dad and Charlene did have an affair. Dad really cared for her, he told me that himself. The check was his way of helping her out financially."

Savannah's first instinct was to get up and leave. It didn't take long for Ethan to drink the Morgan Kool-Aid, did it? These people couldn't tell the truth if their lives depended on it, she fumed. The notion her mother slept around on her daddy was preposterous.

She removed her glasses. Time to set this man straight on one thing and do it eye to eye. "My mama would never violate her marriage vows. Period."

"I'm afraid she did. She got pregnant and kept the child." Ethan lowered his voice, "You are that child. That's why Preston tried to pay you off. According to Dad, you are our sister."

"That's utter nonsense," she rose to her feet, pushed the chair in its rightful place. What a waste of time. She met Ethan expecting decent conversation and a halfway edible meal. She got lies and microscopic sandwiches.

Ethan sighed, reached in his pocket again. This time he withdrew a small folded piece of aged paper. "I understand your anger,

Savannah, but before you leave, read this."

She plucked it from his hand, shook out her glasses and while giving him the evil eye, slid them on. With utmost indignation she dedicated the time due such ridiculous accusations. In short, she spent two seconds scanning the handwritten note. Then she slowed down. This was her mother's handwriting. Charlene's normally neat, flamboyant script appeared hurried and shaky. Savannah read her mother's words dated (at the top) several months before Savannah's birth. *Lee, we need to talk. I'm pregnant. R.J. can never know what happened or see me with you. Meet me at the lower level of Riverwalk at nine in the morning.*

Her muscles went weak. The letter robbed her breath. She swore she felt her heart break. *I'm pregnant. R.J. can never know what happened...* The letter, written by her mother, still failed to add up to *she had an affair* yet there it was in black and white. *I'm pregnant. R.J. can never know...*

Ethan got up when she stabilized herself on the back of her chair. He put an arm around her and guided her to sit. Without argument, she did. He waved the waiter over while telling her, "I think you need that drink now."

Stay outta yer mama's things. I don't want 'em disturbed. R.J.'s warning raced back with a double edge to each word. Had he simply been territorial or had he learned of the affair and knew the boxes contained proof? Savannah stared at the words, trying to make sense of them. Trying to absorb their meaning. The letter suddenly felt heavy or perhaps the weight of those words made it feel that way. She couldn't be the product of an affair, she told herself. But she held in her hand evidence something happened between Charlene and Lee and for some reason, her mother believed Savannah was his. Too much. It was all too much to deal with, at least sober. "Whiskey, neat," she said. "Make it a double."

9

Before meeting with Ethan she called Ennis to pick up the kids. With everyone safe and happy at home, she certainly refused to rain on their good moods. Once she fortified herself (and gave the news time to sink in), then she'd go home.

Savannah dropped by a hole-in-the-wall bar The Golden Parrot for a couple of drinks. The dimly-lit establishment had half a dozen small tables, a TV, restroom, shelves lined with every hair of the dog a person could ask for and a guy to serve them. She spotted Uncle Jack right off – but was willing to slum it with another brand if need be. Tonight she wanted, *needed*, relief from the memory of her mother's letter to Lee.

A couple of drinks turned into another one for good measure. Then another. Again she signaled the bartender for a refill. She watched as he poured the beautiful clear amber liquid in the glass, marveling at how Uncle Jack's magic juice softened the news of her newfound bastard status. Uncle Jack *could* perform miracles so why had she given it up so long ago? She'd remedy that once the shock wore off. One trip to the package store and she'd stock up on a bottle or three. *No one better judge me, either. No lecturing, yelling or interventions. They know who their fathers are – and have known it all their lives.*

She swallowed the whiskey in one gulp. Stinging warmth burned down her throat and landed in small, soothing embers in her stomach. Oh yes, her body sighed. Like coming in from the cold to sit by a nice cozy fire.

She called for a refill then checked her watch. Three hours passed since the floor dropped out of her life. Charlene's note sent Savannah into a tailspin only Uncle Jack slowed to a manageable descent. Now she felt numb as she reviewed hers and Ethan's conversation after that first slug of whiskey. Oh sure, "Dad" loved the idea of having a daughter. This according to Ethan who hadn't been a twinkling in his rich daddy's eye until Savannah turned five years old.

Lee seemed genial enough at their last meeting. Perhaps a little pushy, definitely a shade too eager for her to accept his job. His face brightened as he recalled the visit from way back. Yeah, she grumbled to herself, the one where he spent twenty minutes with his "daughter" and an hour with that "daughter's" mama. What had he and Charlene discussed? Visitation rights? Financial support for the little bastard child?

She threw back the drink, signaled the bartender again. The fellow in jeans and white t-shirt (the latter advertised The Golden Parrot) looked like a refugee from a Grateful Dead concert. Long beard, fat mustache and a waistline to match. Tattoos of naked women graced each hairy forearm with the name Vivian emblazoned beneath the figure on his left. Savannah wondered if Vivian realized Mr. Golden or Mr. Parrot or whatever his name was carried her likeness on his arm.

He stood in front of Savannah, hand around the neck of her

favorite uncle's specialty. He did not pour. "Listen, sweetheart, you're tossing those back like water. Take a breather, go home and wear it off."

She pulled out the money to pay her tab plus the extra shot she waited for, "Listen, Mr. Parrot, I want one more drink. I've had an incredibly crappy day."

"You're gonna have an incredibly crappy tomorrow too if you keep knockin' 'em back. I'll call a cab for you right quick."

"I don't want a cab. I want another drink." She slapped an additional ten dollar bill on the bar, "This should cover the drinks and your trouble."

He leaned closer, whispering, "Lady, if I make a call, I'd rather it be for a cab or to your husband to come get you. Not to the cops because you drove outta here drunk."

"Well, you're in luck, Mr. Parrot. I am the cops." She slid the cash across to him, "One more drink and I'll call my husband." There was always tomorrow for a trip to the package store.

Parrot's vision narrowed. He extended his hand palm up, "Car keys first, Officer."

What? Did she look like an *officer*? No sirree, she held a coveted title. A real bona fide rank – a boss's rank – and she worked her ass off for it too, thank you very much. "Sergeant, if you please, sir," she heard the words slurring together. Oh, so what? It wasn't every day a person's parentage ripped from under them.

"Sergeant," he tapped the bar, "keys. Right here."

Aggravation sparked in her voice, "If I were a man, would you treat me this way? Do you hate women or cops or both?"

Parrot sat the bottle aside, making it clear Uncle Jack's tap just dried up. "No, Sergeant. I don't hate women or cops and I don't care if Jesus was sitting where you are. I'd ask for His keys too. Now how about I get you a ride home?"

Well, if that's the way he played, she'd take her toys and go… to the package store. Then where? She couldn't very well go home in this condition, not unless she enjoyed Ennis and the troops ganging up on her. Ah, she'd deal with that later.

Savannah gathered her purse and suit jacket, "I'm taking a walk."

"*Keys.*" He sounded way too big for his britches for a bartender, especially when he leveled the same threat with a sterner tone, "I don't want to sic the cops on one of their own but I will."

He would too, according to his expression. "Shoulda called this place the Golden Nag," she grumbled while digging into her purse until fisting the keyring. A small angel dangled from the Charger's ignition key. Before handing it over she leveled a warning of her own, "These and my car better be in pristine condition when I come back for them. The name is Savannah Rutherford."

"They'll be fine, Sergeant Rutherford," he assured.

O O O

Savannah muttered all manner of insults as she she walked in the hot Atlanta evening. Sweat squeezed from her pores the second she stepped out of the bar's air conditioning. Parrot thought she was stumbling drunk. Well, she thought grimly, not *stumbling* exactly but not fit to drive either. In the end, visions of her husband and children made her cough up the keys, not the tyrant behind the counter. She didn't want her family burdened with a funeral. It would be rude to leave the kids motherless and leave her darling hubby alone to raise three kids. Plus they were all four so adorable. They loved her and she loved them back.

The sun dipped behind the skyline, bathing the area in residual light but the lingering heat baked the city until early morning and even then it took very little to break a sweat.

Crowds thinned out around shops and cafés by that time of evening. Buckhead made a special effort for the out-of-towners. Establishment owners and employees were friendlier (except one Nazi bartender at the Golden Nag that was) and tourists held VIP status in most places. The area certainly wasn't crime free but better than other parts of the city that would send tourists screaming back home and banning the name of Atlanta from their vernacular.

She approached a grouping of people – more tourists – and held her elbow closer to her waist to protect her gun. She tightened her hand around her purse strap as she ambled along. She was drunk, not stupid.

Laughter from a comedy club spilled into the street. Passing a café, children greedily finished off their desserts, scraping silverware on plates. Families everywhere. Walking the sidewalks. Eating. Talking. Holding hands, carrying children, enjoying life.

Savannah kept walking toward a small nearby park. She'd hang out there a while and gather her thoughts away from noise and people.

O O O

Ennis hadn't heard from Savannah in hours. He'd picked up the kids after work when she called to tell him she was meeting Ethan Morgan. She shut off her phone for the meeting and not turned it on since. He considered adding yet another message to her voicemail then decided to contact the last person he thought had contact with her. Ethan Morgan.

By that time most places prepared to close for the day. By a parent's clock, it approached time to tuck kids into bed. He'd ordered pizza for supper, fed and changed Daniel, all while wondering where she was and why she hadn't called or come home. Savannah never shirked her responsibilities, especially since having kids.

If need be he'd call their neighbors Edward and Katherine Collins to babysit while he tracked down his wife. He refused to bother Georgia. Since learning of her pregnancy the family treated her like a china doll and for good reason. She and Dane tried forever for a child and no way in hell would he jeopardize it by telling her that her sister was MIA.

He called Morgan's office anyway and left a message for Ethan explaining who he was and why he needed to speak with him ASAP.

Ten long, excruciating minutes passed when Ennis's cell phone rang. "We met for appetizers and drinks at Signature Room," Ethan told him. "After that we parted ways."

Her last known location. Signature Room. The meeting with Ethan didn't unsettle him. What did – "Drinks?" he repeated, hoping Ethan meant tea, Cokes, that sort of thing. Surely that's what Ethan meant. Please let that be what he meant, Ennis prayed.

Ethan found amusement in the question, "Yeah, you know.

Scotch, bourbon. Hey, I need to apologize to her too. When you see her ask her to call, will you?"

"Why would you need to apologize?"

"I kinda slammed her with some heavy news. Not the sort of thing anyone would expect."

"What news?"

"She'll tell you if she wants you to know. Listen, gotta run. Please tell her to call me, okay? Thanks."

Ennis clicked off, unable to fit the puzzle pieces together. *Scotch, bourbon... Slammed her with heavy news... Not the sort of thing anyone would expect...* If Savannah resorted to drinking again, the news wasn't heavy, it was devastating.

O   O   O

Savannah walked to Sunnybrook Park, a natural, underdeveloped park in Buckhead's Garden Hills community. The 2.4 acre "pocket" park provided a quiet, peaceful atmosphere enhanced by centuries old beeches and oaks. The low-key park was just what she needed for peace and quiet while ruminating over her new bastard status.

She sighed when her bottom hit the park bench's metal seat then winced when it clashed against her tailbone. She'd walked for blocks and blocks until her legs ached and fatigue sank to the bone. Weariness clouded her mind in numb disbelief. The rug and her paternity had been yanked from under her so how did a person find their balance again after hearing that news? More booze, that's how, but since a jerk bartender stole her car keys, her only option was suffer.

Savannah leaned back, turning her gaze to the moon. What a difference a few hours made, she thought. The whole idea that she was Lee's child made her want to laugh and cry. Truthfully she'd rather stay a Prince. R.J. used his fists and his sharp tongue to get a point across but he was her daddy, not Lee Morgan. At least she assumed he was. Until that afternoon, she was sure of it.

Savannah powered up her phone. She rubbed her forehead, amazed at the, "Five messages? Really, Ennis?" She listened to each message in case disaster befell her home life. Nope, just him wanting to know where she was. Then a message from Ethan apologizing for "upsetting her". Upsetting her? Try "nuking" her. Not only had he and his family tainted Charlene's memory, they'd stripped Savannah of the only father she'd known, mean as he was sometimes.

She tilted her watch to the street lamp. Her kids needed their mother no matter what shape she was in. At least the children wouldn't put her through an endless interrogation of where she'd been. They'd just be happy to see her.

Before dialing her Ennis, she braced herself for the onslaught. Once he heard her thick molasses speech, he would thank God she was okay then his voice would wind down to disappointment. From there she'd endure his sidelong glances for months to see if she'd indulged again. Then he'd begin regular searches though cabinets, closets and anywhere else a person could stash a bottle. But first thing tomorrow when she sobered up and after the brutal hangover faded a degree, a cascade of lectures would crank up. First Ennis then by morning

Georgia, Seth and probably God Himself would lecture her. She'd pay threefold for those drinks. Once with money, two with endless scoldings and sermons from family and finally the punishing hangover awaiting her.

o   o   o

"She said near the entrance to Sunnybrook Park," he told Seth. He'd called Savannah's older brother after speaking with her. The truth came harder than swallowing is aunt's chicken spaghetti. Something sent Savannah into a tailspin, he told Seth, and she was drinking again.

Ennis asked Katherine Collins to babysit while he and Seth picked up Savannah. Ennis's wife exhausted her blue streak while describing the bartender who commandeered her keys "like the damn Gestapo". She bulled ahead using more colorful language he hadn't heard from her lips since her last bender years ago. Oh Lord, he rubbed his forehead, he dreaded that night and the next day. "She mentioned Lee Morgan. Something about way back when then said she'd never fit in and never want to. She's been thinking about his job offer but–"

"It's not about the job offer," Seth grumbled. He'd brooded in the passenger seat since Ennis picked him up. He stared straight ahead, jaw set so Ennis assumed he ignored him and opted instead to brood. It surprised him when Seth began explaining the fact Lee Morgan believed Savannah was his child.

"You mean Charlene had an affair with Morgan?"

"No, I never said that," he replied with clipped finality.

Seth was never one to elaborate. It frustrated anyone who knew him, including Ennis, "If there's a chance Savannah is Morgan's daughter, those two had to, well, you know—"

"Ennis, drop it. Georgia's already flipping out. I want that baby born and her getting upset isn't helping. If she finds out Savannah's hitting the bottle again, she'll go ballistic." He turned to face Ennis. "Do not tell her about tonight."

When Ennis glanced over, he puckered in uncomfortable places. Light from streetlamps and oncoming traffic illuminated a younger version of R.J. Prince. His scowling expression promised swift and violent retribution if Georgia lost her baby due to Ennis's loose lips. All Ennis could do was say, "You got it."

But Seth wasn't finished. "I'll keep Savannah at my place tonight and take tomorrow off to get her back on her feet. Tell the girls she had to work late or that she wasn't feeling well, whatever you think'll fly with them. And, for God's sakes, don't tell your boss the truth."

"I'm not stupid, Seth." He would have argued about who took care of Savannah except she possessed a hell of a temper when she drank. If their kids witnessed her in that shape, Ennis wasn't sure his wife could live with herself.

He made a turn onto Brentwood Drive, the street adjoining the park. Both men began searching for people on park benches. Ennis slowed the Ram but opted to park instead, saying it was too dark to see. They traveled another hundred yards when Seth pointed at a bench between two large-trunked trees, "There she is."

Ennis glanced in the direction he indicated. Framed by the two trees and arching canopies sat a lone hunched figure, elbows on knees, head hanging low. *That* was Savannah? The person sitting there looked utterly defeated, nothing like his headstrong, confident wife.

He and Seth hurried to her. She sat stone still on the metal bench, not a sound around them except the whispering breeze rattling brittle leaves.

"Babe, we're here," Ennis announced softly to avoid startling her.

With a long, weighty sigh, she pushed herself upright, a task looking and sounding like the most laborious thing she'd ever done, "We?" She tilted her face up to see Ennis and Seth standing in front of her. Confusion gave way to emotion upon seeing her brother.

The two shared a rare tender moment that had Ennis battling his own tears. Seth eased beside her, took her hand in his, "My baby sis. It's been a horrible day for you."

She sniffed back more tears, "You knew?"

He squeezed her to him, "I just found out about it too."

"At least," she replied, "we know why Daddy – I'm sorry – *R.J.* beat the shit outta me so often. I guess having to raise another man's child set wrong with him."

"Van, Georgia and I have the same scars, you know that."

"Not as many as I do. Georgia told me he changed when I was born. Became more violent. I guess we know why now."

"You don't know the whole story about Mama and Lee and you're not in any condition to hear it either."

Seth's last comment tweaked Ennis's curiosity. The whole story. He made a note to meet with Dane. Maybe he could shed light on this situation.

"My whole life has been a lie. Daddy's not my daddy, you and Georgia are my half-siblings, at least not full blood." Her voice quivered, "Not like I thought."

Ennis heard her heartbreak. Nothing gave her more pleasure than bragging on her Army Ranger brother and famous author sister. They still were her siblings but he understood her sentiment. She felt part of the genetic bond disappear. Now it clung by half its strength.

Seth gently squeezed her hand, "Savannah, you are our sister, no matter the DNA. Those Morgan kids have no clue about you. They don't know your love for peach pie, the reason you grow lilies and hydrangeas in your garden or why you hate Cocoa Puffs."

That caught her by surprise. Yes, only certain family members understood she ate herself silly on Cocoa Puffs during her pregnancy with Lily. She couldn't stand the cereal – but Lily adored it. "You know why I grow those flowers?" she asked as a tear slid down her cheek.

Ennis couldn't believe his eyes. Drinking normally transformed his wife into an aggressive, sometimes hateful person ready to duke it out with anyone. This time it had the opposite effect on her. It softened her personality to the point she seemed almost childlike.

Seth thumbed her tear away with an amused smile, "Yeah, kid, I do. Mama would be proud of your garden too. And as for being half-siblings, that's bullshit. Georgia and I can read your moods, halfway predict what you'll say and do. We pretty much know what makes you laugh, cry or get angry. *You are our sister.*"

Savannah's hold on her emotional control weakened. She leaned against him, put her head on his shoulder. Ennis welled up at the sight. Never in his married life had he seen Seth and Savannah share such a poignant moment.

"C'mon, Van," Seth said as he and Ennis helped her to her feet. "You're coming home with me."

She curled both arms around Ennis, holding on as if he was her only bouy in the ocean of chaos, "Thank you for coming after me." Her trembling lips pressed to his. Right now the last thing he could be was angry with her for drinking. The news rocked her back on her heels. Peeled back her confidence to reveal the vulnerable side to a woman with a steel backbone and iron will. She reminded him of a lost little girl desperately searching for her way home. "We'll make it, babe. We're all here to help you."

With an arm wrapped around her waist to steady her, Seth assured, "It'll be okay."

Seth and Savannah sat in the back seat. She leaned against him, still sniffing back tears. Seth slid his arm across her shoulders and hugged her close. He repeated, "It'll be okay, sis."

They started out for Seth's house. On the way, Ennis glanced in the rear-view mirror. As he drove, light from streetlamps cast a fleeting glow upon the siblings. Seth with his arm around her and Savannah struggling to dry tears. The older brother reached over, took her hand in his.

10

Ennis hung up from lying to their boss. He told Josh that Savannah had a touch of food poisoning. It wasn't a total lie considering whiskey was ingestible and for people like Savannah, drinking was a form of poisoning, at least in his opinion.

He took a vacation day to take care of the kids while Seth brought Savannah back to the land of the living. He finished feeding Daniel when his phone rang. It was Georgia. "Ennis, we need to watch Savannah. We can't stop her from seeing this and I guarantee it will drive her to drink again."

He decided playing dumb was his best defense for now, "What are you talking about?"

"She's still reading Tucker's book, right? What page is she on?"

He never kept track of her reading. Only the title, not her progress. "I have no clue where she is. She hasn't had time to read lately."

Georgia's voice weighed down with dread. "Get the book, thumb to the photo section."

He opened the book laying on the end table beside Savannah's recliner. The first photo showed an old black and white photo of Lee Morgan and his siblings with their parents. "What am I looking for?"

Ennis asked Georgia. "All I see are Morgans standing in front of a mansion the size of Miami."

"Flip through the photos. I won't need to tell you when to stop."

He hated statements like that. It always meant big trouble. He dutifully turned the page. Lee Morgan's growing up years. Then another. The beginning of Lee's rise to the top. Another page showed his wedding. Ennis restrained a sigh. Capital "B" Boring. No wonder Savannah hadn't made a serious effort to read this rag. He turned another page. His children. He flipped again, seeing each son highlighted with a then and now picture and a brief description of their place in the birth order. Yep, he thought, this is a snore-fest.

One more page. His heart stopped. His breath caught. "What the hell…" he whispered.

"You found it," Georgia stated the obvious.

Oh, he found it alright. He stared at the familiar face smiling back at him. There were a couple of photos dedicated to that one page alone. The first was a school picture of a girl about five years old. Even at that young age, soft, loose waves draped past her shoulders but her golden brown tresses hadn't taken on the darker chestnut tones it had now. These days that child's photo could easily be mistaken for Lily. But this particular grinning child grew into the beautiful woman that eventually became his wife. Her gap-toothed smile made Ennis curious if the photographer cracked a joke before snapping the picture.

He forced his vision away from the adorable dimpled smile to the caption below. *The One No One Talks About. Savannah. The firstborn and the result of an affair with her mother Charlene.*

Ennis dropped into Savannah's recliner like his ass was made of lead. He gave the photo below the school picture a look. Georgia waited patiently on the phone.

The second picture was a newspaper clipping from the Augusta Chronicle during Savannah's high school golfing days. Its bold headline read *The Augusta Bomber Strikes Again.* It listed her first and last name but Tucker had the surname blurred out. As if that will prevent readers from making the connection, Ennis fumed.

With one hand propped on a golf club (the driver and reason for the nickname) and the other holding a trophy, Savannah's proud smile said it all. *I'm on my way and nothing can stop me.* Except something did. Her mother's cancer diagnosis. That's when Savannah found booze.

The caption read: *The Morgan patriarch kept track of his daughter's success on the golf course and later her career as a police officer.*

Now Ennis developed a headache. "Shit," he mumbled.

"It gets worse," Georgia forewarned.

How could this possibly get any worse? Savannah wouldn't only be shocked at this revelation, she'd be outraged that her mother's reputation had been besmirched and her own private hell regarding her paternity exposed to the world. Anyone reading that rag would take the words as gospel – after all, Lee's son wrote it, a person who sat at the supper table every night, a boy who could have overheard things or uncovered dark, juicy secrets over the years. Why wouldn't it be true, they'd say. "Lay it on me," he told his sister-in-law.

"Lee Morgan raped our mother. Mama wrote it in her journal.

Savannah supposedly is the result of that attack."

The air left his lungs. He inadvertently dropped the book in the floor. His mind went blank but for one word. Rape. Savannah's mother suffered the worst indignity a woman could possibly bear and she still kept the baby and raised her into a fine woman. His biggest issue right now though – did R.J. know about all this?

"Ennis? Are you there?"

Georgia's voice broke his daze, "Yeah, yeah I'm here. Does your daddy know about the attack and the pregnancy?"

"I couldn't say. He forbade us from trolling into Mama's things. Maybe he does know but I'm not asking."

Dear God, he wanted to burn the damn book, throw it away, anything to prevent Savannah from reading it. God only knew what was in there and she'd already promised the book to their neighbor Katherine Collins. The whole world would soon be privy to what Ennis just learned, except in the book Charlene willingly slept with Lee, she'd not been raped.

Ennis rubbed his temple, wondering if this could get any worse. Well, he resigned to himself, at least he knew the reason she jumped off the wagon and dove headfirst into Whiskey Lake yesterday. Or did she even know about the rape yet? Yes, as a matter of fact, this *could* get worse. Much, much worse, actually. "What am I supposed to do? I can't keep her from reading it and she's giving it to Katherine when she's finished."

"I don't know, Ennis. I really don't. Just watch her, I guess. That's all we can do. Try to minimize how much she drinks because I don't think we can stop her, not after this."

"I'll do what I can. Georgia, don't let this affect the baby. You and Dane have waited too long for this, don't jeopardize the baby."

"I won't. I've already had a lecture, well, several actually, from Dane. He wants me to stop reading the book."

"Sounds like good advice."

Daniel started crying in the crib. "I gotta go. Daniel's probably muddy again. Please take it easy, Georgia. Savannah and I are really looking forward to spoiling our new niece or nephew."

He heard a smile in her voice, "I'll be careful, Ennis. Don't worry."

Daniel peed his diaper so changing him didn't take quite as long. He expected Savannah home in a few hours but wasn't sure how good a shape she'd be in. The night before she looked pretty plowed. No doubt she felt not just plowed but plowed over by a 747 that morning.

Still, he understood her devastation. The book was out there. People were reading it. Clamoring for it. Paying exorbitant prices on auction sites for a copy. It was a matter of time before the questions began. The looks and stares to see a resemblance between her and Morgan. And the gibes at work. Some cops would tease her relentlessly once they or their wives read the book. Last night's binge could be the beginning of a meltdown depending on how merciless society treated her. Because in a town the size of Augusta it wouldn't take long for the connection to be made. Her friends from high school, Charlene's friends and acquaintances as well as Georgia's and Seth's would piece it together in a heartbeat. In a moment of folly Ennis only prayed R.J. never found out about the reference but sometimes men at a bar had the loosest tongues of all.

He rubbed his temple again then headed for the medicine cabinet for an aspirin. Oh, yes. It *would* get much, much worse.

O   O   O

In the early morning hours, Savannah heard movement. Footsteps. The floor creaking. In the back of her mind, she questioned the noise. She and Ennis lived in a house with a concrete foundation and the last time she looked, concrete did not creak.

Her eyes opened to slits. Good. No bright lights. But... where the hell was she? She oriented herself in the muted moonlight filtering through the curtains. She was not only on the wrong side of the bed but the furniture was all different and the door was offset to her right, not her left. Everything's backwards just like my life, she groaned in the silence. It took a few more seconds to recognize her surroundings. Seth and Leah's guest room. That explained the backward arrangement, the maple furniture and extra soft bed that felt more like a cloud than a mattress. Her vision passed across her purse on the nightstand along with a glass of water and what appeared to be two aspirin. The last thing she remembered before passing out again was Seth, Ennis and Leah all saying it would be alright.

Nausea woke her before sunrise. Her head threatened to explode and her coordination skills consisted of breathing and wildly flailing against the covers before she ruined Leah's handmade quilt. She managed to sit up after a frustrating struggle then proceeded to bang the water glass with her hand until liquid sloshed onto the wood table. Saved the quilt, ruined the antique table, she berated herself. Nice, Savannah.

She stretched the sheet over and hurriedly mopped up the mess and in the process brushed the aspirins in the floor. She felt as graceful as a bull in a china shop. And the tremble in her hands made things worse.

Her brain fired to life with an urgency only a hungover person or someone suffering food poisoning could appreciate. It strung together two words that sent her stumbling for the door. *Bathroom now.*

Minutes passed. Savannah kneeled at the toilet, one hand cradling her forehead, the other her stomach as if the former might split open and the latter might be ejected with the next heave. Oh dear God how foolish had she been?

She barely finished the thought when another wretch barreled full-force up her throat like a freight train. *Shee-yet,* she managed to groan before all hell broke loose. Both hands gripped the porcelain with hopes of stability. The wave of sickness tied her gut in a knot and stripped her throat with acid. The sour taste coated her tongue. Why, oh why, had she resorted to drinking? The pulsing thing between her ears reviewed the previous day. Oh. She was the bastard of the family, *that's* why she went off the rails. That's also why R.J. beat the shit out of her in her youth. He knew.

The most unbelievable aspect of the revelation was their mother. An affair? The woman who *lived* the Ten Commandments, who graced the church in good health or bad, broke her marriage vows? Vows made in the presence of the Lord she worshipped every minute of the day with every breath she took and every beat of her heart? None of it made sense and frankly Savannah lacked the fortitude to ferret out the whys, at least for now. Fact was, the whys died with Charlene.

Another heave steamrolled her, this one so deep and powerful it temporarily sucked the strength from her, forced her to prop back against the tile wall. What a mess this week had been, she thought. Seth's favorite term began with "cluster" and ended with a word that earned Lily a stern talking to when she'd uttered it the first time.

A good while passed when she felt stable enough physically and emotionally to clean up and face her brother – or half-brother as was the case. She finger brushed her teeth and rinsed her mouth out with some Scope that packed quite a minty punch for her current condition. While washing her face it occurred to her that she went from two total, one hundred percent blood siblings down to none. They were all "half" this and "half" that. Despite that, the fact remained that neither Ethan, Preston, Tucker nor Grady would have cared enough to drag her sorry ass to their home to sleep off her binge. No. Seth had and if given the chance Georgia would have too. Staring at her pale, sickly reflection in the mirror she thanked the brother who loved her enough to drag her drunken butt to his house so she could wear off her hangover away from the kids.

Stairs acted more like an obstacle course for a hungover individual. She had to dredge the memories from her drinking days to recall how to descend stairs without falling and killing herself. Then she remembered there were no hints, shortcuts or memories. It all relied on a steady grip and pure luck. Each step presented a challenge. She once imagined Olympic games for drunks. The first event would be climbing and descending stairs – before and after a binge.

Savannah took her time easing down the stairs until stopping a few steps from the bottom.

"You can't stop her from taking Morgan's offer," Leah said.

"She said she already turned him down," Seth answered. "Once she finds out the truth, she'll be damn glad she did too."

"You're not telling her. She needs time to recover from the fact she might not be R.J.'s."

Savannah's cell phone rang. Why was it in the kitchen? She mentally shrugged, thinking she'd dropped it while stumbling up the stairs or something.

Seth mumbled. Leah cautioned him not to answer the call. He did anyway, "Stop calling my sister. I don't care how much money your family has, you screw around with Savannah again and you'll deal with me and her husband."

Why was her brother answering her phone? Or screening her calls or whatever he was doing? She eased toward the kitchen (God, being sneaky with a hangover was as graceful as a roller skating elephant) then stopped short of the kitchen door.

"Feel better now?" Leah asked her husband. "You do realize poking sticks at the Morgans might make things worse for her. Look what Preston did. She's already suspended for uttering an empty threat and for wounding his pride."

"That family is poison. The whole world knows it and after what Lee did to Mama, I'm not about to let them sink their talons into

Savannah. We don't know anything about Ethan Morgan. That invite to Augusta National could be a lure. He's not stupid. He knows she loves golf and probably realizes how much she's wanted to play there all these years."

"Ethan might not be anything like his father. How would you feel if people assumed you acted just like R.J.?"

"She wants to golf with that bastard at Augusta National, fine, but me or Ennis will be there too. Lee Morgan destroyed Mama when he raped her. His son isn't getting a chance to do – well, whatever illegal, immoral act he's got planned for my sister."

The world collapsed around Savannah. Lee Morgan raped her mother. What's more, Savannah was the product of that violent union. Her knees gave, sending her rear painfully to the stair behind her. She gripped the baluster because the dizziness returned. What happened between her mama and Lee was worse than an affair. It was *rape*. And she'd been the result. Her whole life she'd been a constant reminder of that incident and her mama's pain.

The urge to puke toyed with her. She temporarily swallowed it back, "Now I know why Daddy hates Lee Morgan. And me for that matter. It's hard for him to love a child born from a rape."

Feet scrambled from the kitchen. In seconds both Leah and Seth were in front of her. Seth eased beside her, put an arm around her. He sounded simultaneously mortified and contrite, "Van, I'm sorry you heard–"

She fought against his hold. Seeing her hand race to her mouth, he stood and pressed against the wall to let her through. She bolted for the downstairs bathroom. On the way she heard her brother repeat, "I'm so sorry."

11

Mathis waited for Savannah to ease into the passenger seat of his detective sedan before warning, "Ennis told the boss you're sick so stay on your side of the car and don't breathe in my direction. I don't want your crap."

She slanted him a dirty look, "It's not contagious, John."

He shifted into drive then wrinkled his nose, "Geez, did you go toe to toe with a whole fraternity on downing shots?"

"I've had a bad week." She gripped the armrest as he turned a corner a bit too fast for her.

"Must be a hell of a week if you're drinking." He wheeled onto the main thoroughfare – one notorious for its potholes – and sped up to just above the speed limit. "Have anything to do with your suspension?"

Savannah rubbed her forehead. Her hand slipped and nearly poked her in the eye when he slammed into a pothole. "It's related to it, yes."

"Where's your car?" Bump. Another hole.

"The Golden Nag – *Parrot.* The Golden Parrot." The car rattled through a bigger, wider pothole that tested her patience and stomach. "Mathis, stop hitting potholes. Move to the other lane where it's smoother."

"What's happened? Why are you on the sauce again?"

She snapped around to him then settled down when her head throbbed and triggered a dizzy wave of sickness.

Mathis answered her scowl, "Hey, I remember the bad old days too. You nearly got suspended for drinking on the job."

"Thanks for the cozy reminder."

"Prince, how long have we known each other?"

"Long enough to know to stay out of each other's business."

"Not for nothin' kid, but if I gotta answer to a higher being at work, I'd rather it be you, not some snot-nosed, go-gettin' youngster that barks orders like a tyrant."

So many compliments in one sentence, she sneered to herself. So far she gleaned she was old and lacked ambition. Of course hangovers sensitized a person to light, sound, movement, food, drink, people's words – pretty much everything in life. On the bright side, at least, in his opinion, she wasn't snot-nosed. She'd take that as a high compliment since he possessed a library of colorful, scathing derogatory descriptors that he saved for his most annoying people.

"Oh boy," he sighed, rounding another corner, "I can tell I stepped in it again. Look, I meant it as a compliment. I just don't want to lose you as a boss *or* a friend so take my advice for whatever it's worth. This thing that's got you drinking again? If you can, get rid of it. If you can't, step away from it. You got a good life, Savannah. Don't screw it up." He pulled to the curb in front of her Charger, "We're here. You want me to go get your keys?"

Shame overwhelmed her. First she drank herself stupid. Then

she called Mathis for a ride and bitched him out for offering common sense advice. Some way to treat a friend. "No, I made this mess, I'll clean it up." She patted his hand, "Thanks for the advice, John. I heard you and I appreciate the fact you care about me."

Mathis squirmed. They usually never got touchy-feely with their words – or any respect. They communicated in their own way, his mostly with sarcasm and her shooting back one for one. But they always seemed to understand each other until today when he felt comfortable enough adopting an older brother role. It made sense. They'd known each other since her rookie days and the man was ten years her senior. He shrugged a shoulder, "Just tryin' to help."

"You're a good friend. I don't want to lose you either." She eased out of the car, thanked him again, and went to collect her keys.

O   O   O

Trying to prepare lunch was like tackling calculus during a rock concert. The thought of food made her gag and the mental capacity it took to process the steps ended up tying her brain into a painful knot as it elbowed her skull with every heartbeat.

For God's sake, it's mac and cheese, she berated herself. The girls clamored around her when she got home. The neighbor, Katherine Collins, looked after the kids until Savannah arrived then brought the brood over. After seeing Savannah's condition, Katherine offered to fix lunch and feed Daniel. Embarrassed yet again for going on a spree (and the world finding out about it), she declined then thanked Katherine for her kindness and apologized for the inconvenience, blaming the hangover on a celebration that went too far and too long. *I can only use that excuse once or she'll know the truth. You're a drunk like your daddy...* Her daddy. R.J. or Lee. Who's DNA created the idiot fighting the hangover and dealing semi-successfully with three excited (and uncommonly loud) children?

Who the hell cared right now? Everything from her toes to her hair hurt. She carefully rubbed her face to try and focus her mind better. Lily helped her clear the lunch dishes which she appreciated since Daniel's feeding time approached. Before he cranked up a chorus of crying – that noise guaranteed to finish her off – she would feed him then wash dishes.

Her cell phone rang. She hoped it wasn't Ennis checking on the progress of her hangover because her comprehension and speaking skills still hadn't quite balanced out yet. The Caller ID, however, read "UNKNOWN CALLER". She sat the phone down. It rang until going to voicemail. She'd check it later. Telemarketers didn't need her money. *She* did since a herd of Morgans ganged up on her and had her suspended.

It rang again. This time she answered it because the noise lanced her brain like a flaming spear.

"Hope you enjoy your time off. Threaten my husband again and you'll be fired."

Ah yes. The cherry on her crappy day. Lydia Morgan. She wouldn't take time to spar with the smug, rich bitch, not today. "Lose this number and quick," she hung up.

Lily had been gathering bowls and silverware and bringing them to the sink. Savannah noticed she kept staring at her. Yes, normally she was livelier and more conversational with her children but after that phone call, a twisting push came from her stomach as if it warned *one word and you'll hurl*. Savannah wanted to tell Lydia she, Preston, Sabrina and the others fought an imaginary battle. She wanted nothing to do with the Morgans, particularly after meeting them.

"You didn't eat anything," Lily said. "Are you okay?"

The word "eat" inspired a small heave. Not even close, kid. She pressed her lips tight and swallowed back the urge, "Yeah, honey, just not feeling real good right now."

"Are you sick? Aunt Leah can help."

"Not this time she can't. I'll be alright, don't worry." What a lie. Wearing off the nausea and pounding headache was simple. The suffering her mama endured then mentally reliving it every day while carrying the results of that rape for nine months – now that took an extraordinary woman. A woman who never resorted to alcohol to cope.

Savannah thumbed away a tear. She heard Lily and Anna setting up a tea party in Anna's room. Their upbeat interaction fed their mother's sadness. At that age she'd worried about missing Sesame Street on TV or not charming the money out of Charlene for ice cream when the truck jingled down the street playing "Pop Goes the Weasel". She never questioned whether the man walking through the door smelling of scotch and sweat after a day building houses was her biological father. She knew to make herself scarce if he'd had a bad day. She knew Georgia liked to take her to the nearby park when their daddy came home angry.

She knew on particularly bad days Seth took her looking for an elusive stray cat that they never seemed to find. But she *knew* who her daddy was. Or thought she did.

The doorbell rang once, twice then three more times. The impatient visitor then repeatedly banged on the front door.

The girls ran into the living room only to have Savannah shoo them back. The visitor was about to suffer the wrath of a woman itching to tear into somebody – and she didn't want her daughters to see it.

She yanked open the door, already in the process of laying into the rude visitor, "Lay off the–"

That was as far as she got before she caught a whiff of Old Spice mixed with scotch – then a battering ram sank into her gut. She stumbled back as R.J. stepped inside and advanced on her, his fist cocked for another punch. She heard Lily gasp then follow with a horrified *Grandpa*. Savannah strained to draw enough air to warn the girls, "Go back to your rooms," before R.J.'s sledgehammer of a fist crashed against her temple. The blow knocked her sideways and she fell to the floor hard on her side.

R.J.'s hand fisted in the neck of her blouse and hoisted her upright. "I told ya to leave yer mama's things alone. Ya opened all the boxes, *stole* some of 'em," he shook her hard. "They're my property, not yers. What's worse, ya dragged yer sister into lying for ya. Where are they, Savannah? Where's my property?"

"Daddy, listen to me, plea–"

"You listen to *me*, girl," R.J. rolled his fist, "I want my property. If you ain't got it, Georgia does. I'm headin' over there after I finish with you."

Protect Georgia and her baby... "I'm responsible for this, not Georgia."

The fist sank so deep in her stomach it stole her breath and strength. Savannah went to her hands and knees and puked. Pain paralyzed her. From the corner of her eye she saw Lily and Anna peeking into the living room. Savannah waved them back hoping to keep them out of harm's way because when on a rampage, R.J. mowed through anyone within sight.

Today however he centered on the object of his rage. Savannah. She heard sound of leather zipping through belt loops. He gripped the buckle tight in his fist, "Ya lied and ya stole from me." He swung back. Savannah reverted back to childhood, curling up against the lashes before the first blow landed. "Daddy, I'm sorry." The belt caught her outreached palm, laying a strip of fire in its wake. She trapped a whimper behind clamped lips, wishing her equilibrium return enough for her to fight back. He swung the belt unmercifully as if backhanding her with it. She'd forgotten just how damn painful it felt until now. "Daddy, stop! Just stop–"

Another lash struck across her back making her arch against the pain. The man's power verged on superhuman. She'd not seen him this enraged in years. Nothing she said stopped him – or caused him to hesitate. She had to wait out his temper and pray for minimal damage.

A hail of lashings rained down on her. Each strike felt like he hit her with a hot branding iron. Her wrists and arms took the brunt as she tried unsuccessfully to deflect each attack. He swung over and over until tears streamed down her face. Until she pleaded. But she refused to do one thing: Promise to return the journals. Her outright refusal to return "what she'd stolen" was met with mounting rage and escalation of his vicious attack.

Her arms burned and stung. Her stomach teetered on convulsing inside her from the punches or purging the pain by throwing up. She curled up, praying for God to exhaust R.J.'s anger soon. If she waited out his attack, it might prevent him from confronting Georgia. She'd never forgive herself if something happened her sister or the baby.

O O O

The door slammed. He'd gone. Finally. Savannah looked at the clock on the mantle. Ten short minutes from doorbell to departure. That's all it took. Ten short minutes to the rest of the world, a near eternity to the victim of R.J.'s temper.

An odd distant whining rang in her ears. In days of old the sound stayed high-pitched and steady like a power saw cutting wood. This time the droning rise and fall refused to abate and gradually grew louder as she lay there.

Crying roused from the nursery. When R.J. slammed the door, it woke Daniel. How the child slept through the shouting she'd never understand. Now he awoke with a vengeance and here she was flat of her back.

She lost count of the lashings. She only remembered she bit her tongue trying to subdue the urge to curse and cry out. Protesting in any way provoked a worse beating, she'd learned that as a child.

R.J. played no favorites in where he struck her. The stinging stretched from her throat and neck down her arms and across her back and chest. He'd been crazy with rage when she told him no, she wouldn't return the journals. In retrospect, she questioned the intelligence of that decision.

His attack, the ensuing pain and her lingering hangover headache tipped her queasiness over the edge causing her to heave on the entry floor. He'd left shortly after that, vowing to teach Georgia a lesson about stealing as well.

Savannah pushed herself to a sitting position. Touched her throat that still stung and began aching after the drubbing. "Lily, bring me the phone quick." She hated for the girls to see her, to see the small mess on the entry, but she had to warn Georgia about the storm called R.J. Prince coming her way. And she only had a few minutes. Georgia lived a short ten minutes away in Sandy Springs. Just a hop, skip and a jump considering R.J. drove faster than a bat out of hell. Once she alerted Georgia, she could tend to Daniel – if she could shake off the lightheadedness.

Lily emerged from her bedroom holding the telephone, her blue eyes wide as saucers. "Mama," was the timid inquiry, "are you okay?"

She stroked her daughter's hair with a shaky hand, "I will be, sweetie." At least the droning whine stopped. She was grateful.

"I don't like Grandpa." A statement spoken with outright conviction.

Savannah winced at the ache in her stomach, "Right now neither do I." She reached for the phone but drew back when the doorbell chimed again. Had he come back?

Lily charged for the door and received a harsh scolding for disobeying her mother's orders to stay back. The youngster pulled it open, assuring her mama, "I called the police."

Oh crap. Savannah held a hand to her gut. This day just kept getting better. What would she tell the cops? *My daddy, who it turns out is not my biological daddy, barged in and beat the shit out of me? A cop getting her block knocked off by her father. Perfect.*

Two Dunwoody police officers stepped in. One older and seasoned, the other probably a year on the job. The older cop was built like a Mack truck, the younger one tall and willowy. Both had their hands on their holstered guns.

Lily boldly looked up at the officers towering over her and took charge, "Grandpa came in and started hitting Mama. She needs help."

Well, why tell the cops anything since her daughter pretty much summed up the embarrassing situation?

Daniel wailed from the bedroom. She needed to tend to him. Testing her balance, she tried pushing to her knees but fell flat of her ass again.

While Mack Truck spoke with Lily, Willow Tree approached Savannah, "Ma'am, do you need an ambulance?"

"No, just a little help to stand. Thanks." She groaned then swayed a bit once back on her feet. She rubbed her forehead. The pain was incredible. "My father's on his way to my sister's house in Sandy Springs. Can you have their department send a car to her place? I was about to warn her when you showed up. Her name is Georgia Rutherford and she's pregnant so it's imperative they get there before he does." She gave him Georgia's address then a description of R.J.'s pickup and the license plate number.

He relayed the information while steadying Savannah with a hand around her arm. His gentle grasp hurt, since she'd used that arm to shield her head with. R.J. nearly bloodied the arm in his rage. She tugged at his hold, wanting to go to Daniel. Her son was scared and upset too.

Officer Mack Truck held a hand up to stop her, "I'll go after the baby, ma'am." For such an imposing figure he turned warm and sweet when asking Lily, "Can you take me to the baby?"

She ran ahead of him and pointed down the hall, "He's in here." The two disappeared, chatting with each other as they went.

Willow Tree's name was Sims according to his uniform. He guided Savannah to her recliner and urged her to sit. Anna ran from the hallway straight to her mama who patted the seat beside her. Sims hoisted her up and the girl glued herself to Savannah's side and started sucking her thumb. By then Officer Mack and Lily emerged with Daniel. He (Officer Olson she learned from his nametag) laid the baby in Savannah's waiting arms. "I understand you're a sergeant with APD," he said.

She nodded then began shushing her son's ear-splitting cries. With the revelation of her occupation, both cops seemed to view their victim in a different light. Mostly surprise. Yes, even police officers have nuts in their family, she wanted to say.

Savannah motioned to Lily for the phone. Daniel's crying temporarily softened enough if she listened close and spoke loud, she could tell Georgia trouble was headed her way. Dane answered and she forewarned him of R.J.'s wrath and reinforced it by saying the cops were on the way.

When she ended the call, Sims informed her, "A patrol unit pulled your father over for speeding two miles from here. They arrested him for assaulting a police officer. Apparently he socked one of them in the nose."

Horrible as it seemed, she thanked God R.J. punched the cop. Now the onus was off her to keep him behind bars that day.

"Are you pressing charges for what he did to you?" Olson asked.

Savannah realized how it would look. She'd heard it thousands of times as a uniform cop. The police arrive at a domestic abuse call, see the bruises, tears and frightened kids – then the victim refuses to file a complaint. She spent her days in uniform feeling like a hypocrite, pushing abuse victims to press charges when she herself refused to file against her own daddy for his actions. But today she didn't care how it looked or sounded. Her life was complete chaos and if R.J. found out she filed charges against him, Ennis might as well book a hospital room for her the next day.

"I know how this looks, guys, but no. I have enough to deal with right now."

The young one countered, "But Sergeant, if you don't..."

"Save it, Sims," his partner instructed. "She knows the risks."

Frantic footfalls pounded the sidewalk outside. The screen door flew open and banged against the stop. Ennis charged in.

"He's my husband," she told the two officers who'd thought seriously about drawing their weapons. To Ennis she warned, "Watch your step," then pointed to the puke on the entry floor.

"Daddy!" Lily ran into his arms. He scooped her up held her while trying to catch his breath. He stopped breathing altogether upon sight of Savannah, "Dear God, look at you. What the hell happened?"

She was confused. "How did you know anything happened?"

"I was on my way to interview a witness and thought I'd drop by to check on you. Now *what happened?*"

She explained the situation while watching his expression transforming into a mask of rage. Ennis looked to the cops, "He in custody?"

They nodded. "Good," he said with a ring of vindication. "About time he paid for everything he's done to her."

"He assaulted our officers when they pulled him over for speeding. They're pressing charges." Olson clarified with a nod to Savannah, "Your wife declined to."

"What?" Without saying so, Ennis questioned her sanity. To remove all doubt he asked, "Have you lost your mind? Look at yourself. He deserves jail time, babe. He's deserved it for years."

"Don't you think my life is crappy enough without having Daddy declare war on me? He did this because he thinks I stole Mama's journals. What would he do if I filed charges on him? He will make bail and he will come after me. I was hoping to delay you cashing in my life insurance policy for oh, say, another thirty, forty years."

12

Once the cops left, Ennis cleaned up the mess in the entry, wondering whether she needed a trip to the emergency room. She assured him it was part hangover, part surprise and shock of R.J.'s attack and yes, pain and dizziness. Unless he hired a team of wrestlers to haul her ass to the hospital, she said, she was staying home. Later he heated soup for supper and while the girls wolfed theirs down, he and Savannah barely touched theirs.

Afterward he called the Dunwoody police station to learn R.J. still resided in jail with not much hope of bail that evening. Neither Savannah nor Georgia offered the money and Ennis knew damn well Seth wouldn't.

Savannah felt better knowing they were safe from another ambush, she said and opted to change into her pajamas and lounge for the evening. Her stomach showed an outline of R.J.'s fist. A red mark brightened her temple but nothing stood out like the well-defined stripes on her arms and neck. R.J. hit her so hard with the belt it left red, slightly less defined stripes on her back. The whole experience hurt and humiliated her, especially since Lily and Anna witnessed the beating.

Ennis settled Savannah in her recliner with a good, noncontroversial mystery novel and cup of cocoa then grabbed a jacket and took off for the local police station. He planned to teach that old man a thing or two – well, as much as he could being separated by cell's the bars.

The cops stuck R.J. in the furthest cell from humanity to muffle his ranting. Officer Sims spotted him marching toward the jail and stopped him, "Sir, your wife needs to press charges." He tossed an uneasy glance in the direction of the cells, "He's foamed at the mouth since they brought him in. He blames her for stealing from him and for having him arrested."

Ennis appreciated the warning, he told Sims, but the decision was hers. Sims walked away shaking his head. No, Ennis hadn't agreed with her decision either. As it turned out, R.J. still blamed her for everything including the arrest. A chill crawled up his back at the thought of his father-in-law making bail and his resulting wrath...

The instant R.J. laid eyes on Ennis, he jumped to his feet, his rage renewed, "You tell my daughter to return Charlene's diaries. They ain't no business of hers. She had no right to take 'em."

"I'm not telling her anything, old man. You stepped over a line today." He hoped R.J. read the violence in his eyes. He approached the cell, lowered his voice so only Savannah's father heard him, "Steer clear of my family because next time I see you, you're taking a ride in an ambulance."

R.J. stalked to the door, met him face to face, "Set that badge aside, boy, and I'll show ya who's taking that ride. Savannah stole those books. She better get 'em back to me quick." His fingers wrapped around the bars, strangling them in his fists, "I was just warmin' up on her today. She don't want a next time."

"There won't be a next time. You're not touching Savannah again. By the way, she's not responsible for your arrest. You are. When you hit that cop, he charged you with assault on a peace officer. Savannah should have pressed charges too but for some reason she cares about you."

"She's got a hell of a way of showin' it. Defyin' me, stealin' from me then lyin' to me. I want those books!"

"Why? She already knows the truth. She found out what Lee Morgan did to Charlene."

The color drained from R.J.'s cheeks. Ennis had him on the ropes, he assumed, and went in for the knockout, "She also knows Charlene got pregnant by him too. That's the reason you beat her the hardest all these years – because she wasn't yours."

R.J. stared back at him. The man possessed a dangerous temper anyway but that steady, unblinking stare could make Superman shiver. Ennis held his ground both physically and visually. The old man wouldn't win this battle.

R.J. struck faster than a rattlesnake. In one split second his hand shot out, fisted Ennis's shirt and jerked him against the bars. Ennis scarcely missed smashing his nose but his cheek took the brunt of the attack.

"Now that I got ya up close and personal, boy, ya better listen. That kid is mine, through and through, birth to death. She just gets too big for her britches and needs a reminder what happens when she screws up. She had no right, *no reason*, to violate her mama's privacy. When

Charlene died those books became mine. Ya bring those books back tonight because when I get outta this cage, I'm going home to burn 'em all."

O O O

"He can stick that idea where the sun doesn't shine."

Ennis anticipated a heated reaction – in fact it was rather mild compared to his mind's vision – but her volume and tone still stung.

Savannah fumed ever since she found out he'd gone to the jail, a move he now regretted. In spades. He floundered to find the right thing to say. "He coulda been blustering."

By her incredulous stare, he understood his communication skills severely lacked. He'd nearly convinced himself he'd dropped a few points on IQ then recognized she was just damn mad and humiliated about the whole day and nothing anyone said would calm her down.

"Daddy doesn't bluster, Ennis, you know that. If he gets his hands on those journals, he *will* burn them but he's *not* getting his hands on them. I'll rent a storage unit for them to keep them safe if I have to." She vowed, "I'll be damned if he's destroying the very last of Mama's existence. Those journals are priceless and Georgia and I are keeping them."

Not surprisingly she parroted Georgia's views on the subject. The journals were sacred and staying with them, not stored away for the precious words to be forgotten. When he called Georgia to update her on the jail visit with R.J., she'd also insisted Savannah and the kids stay with her and Dane for protection. He knew Savannah's answer but promised to tell his wife anyway. He cleared his throat, "I told Georgia about his threat and she and Dane want you and the kids to stay with them until he cools off."

It took a second to process. To his astonishment, she broke into laughter. "So they're gonna house us until I retire, is that it? Because Daddy still nurses grudges older than Father Time."

Ennis found no humor, especially after seeing the aftermath of R.J.'s abuse all over her.

Savannah seemed to hear his thoughts. Her mood sobered, "No one's staying with them. Georgia doesn't need the stress. If the kids need a safe place, I'm sure Seth will keep them but Daddy's not driving me from my own home and he's not getting those journals back. I'll protect them with my life."

Ennis flinched on that last sentence, "Just don't let them *cost* you your life."

13

Lee Morgan refused to take a hint. He'd called both her cell and home number. She ignored every one. What did her new daddy want anyway? Brunch at Bacchanalia or to swap stock tips? The little stock she and Ennis owned failed to compare with a financial giant whose worth amounted to the gross national product of a small nation. Morgan could go to hell and his sons could too.

In her haste and anger the day she was suspended, she'd left behind a couple of personal items so she drove to the station to sneak in, pick them up and sneak out again. The moment she stepped inside, she wished she hadn't shown up. The catching area brimmed with uniforms preparing for their shift. Many of them turned to her. Others leaned against the desk sergeant's kiosk sporting smug, knowing smiles.

"Whoa," the desk sergeant exclaimed at the sight of her. "Did you win or lose that fight?"

She kept walking. She was in enough trouble on and off the job. Piling on more wasn't in her plans.

"Sorry to hear about your suspension," he added said but he didn't sound one bit sorry. It was merely an opening for his officers to chuckle which they did. "Must be a hard life finding out you're related to a millionaire and his son's got it in for you."

Savannah noticed Major Hoffman, the zone commander, glanced up from his computer. He'd transferred to Zone 2 a few months earlier and seemed like a fair boss and easy to get along with. Hoffman heard the sergeant's taunt and resulting subdued laughter. She stopped and shook her head, "I don't have time or energy for this, Sweeney."

"Seriously, how'd you piss off baby brother enough for him to get you booted?"

More laughs. She just stood there. Since Sweeney replaced Sergeant Bailey (a kinder, gentler soul, at least toward her), her life at the station consisted of dodging barbs or not-so-veiled teasing. Privately she referred to him as Sergeant Sweeney Todd, but instead of dispatching his victims with a straight razor, this guy used his finely honed tongue to finish people off. Everyone suffered his bad attitude, not just Savannah, but today the target landed on her and the more he prodded, the tougher it was to control her temper.

Savannah started toward her office, "I'm just here to grab a couple of things, not get harangued."

"My wife got Tucker Morgan's book. Look what she found."

Savannah turned. He waved a photocopy of her pictures in Tucker's book and handed it to one of the uniforms. Yes, she saw those and the captions earlier when Ennis pointed them out. What could she do about it? Nothing.

While the page passed from officer to officer, she braced for an onslaught of verbal harassment.

"*The One No One Talks About*," he taunted. "You were a cute kid, dimples and all. I never realized you were that good at golf. *The*

Augusta Bomber. Impressive."

The last uniform handed the page back to Sweeney who tacked it on the bulletin board. "We'll just keep this here so everyone knows we have a celebrity in our fold. Your badge shouldn't be gold, Sergeant, it should be platinum."

The uniforms chuckled uneasily after viewing her expression. She said nothing but again, started toward her office.

"You and Daddy gonna knock a few balls around and see whose handicap is lower?"

More laughter. This only inflated his ego. She nearly said *I'd love to knock a few balls around – if you'd step from behind that desk* but let her scowl say it for her. It didn't back Sweeney down but the uniforms sure clammed up. As it turned out, intuition must have warned her to keep mum because Major Hoffman stood in his office doorway.

"Sergeant Sweeney," the major's gruff reprimand brought every cop in the room to attention. No one dared to speak, cough or breathe. The major stepped into the crowded room, hands on his hips and armed with a piercing stare that drilled into the mouthy desk sergeant, "I'm still waiting on those reports that are two days late. I want them in one hour – and no typos this time. The rest of you earn your paycheck or you may find yourself without one." He marched to the bulletin board and ripped the photocopied page down, "If I see this or anything relating to Tucker Morgan's rag or *anything* I could construe as derogatory toward Sergeant Prince on that board again, I'll make sure the culprit is transferred to airport duty. Understood?"

In unison the masses barked an emphatic, "*Yes, sir.*"

"Do I need to remind you what that board is used for?"

He focused on Sweeney but they all, including Savannah, answered, "*No, sir.*"

"Good. Let's get back to work." He zeroed in on Savannah but his tone softened a shade, "That includes you, Sergeant Prince. You're reinstated as of this morning. If you need to go home and make the appropriate arrangements for your family, do so. See me when you return. I'll have your gun and shield waiting."

Like the others in the room, Savannah was speechless. They glanced at her then whispered among themselves. She heard bets being made whether Lee Morgan exercised his influence to get her back on the job.

Major Hoffman's authoritative voice returned, "And if I hear any gossip or references to anything other than police work, someone's walking a foot patrol until I say they're not. Get busy." He nodded to Savannah and again in a little softer tone said, "Get back here ASAP, Sergeant."

"Yessir. Thank you, sir." She aboutfaced and headed for the door.

When she returned, Major Hoffman handed back her gun and badge – and some advice. "I know you're taking a lot of guff about that book but you handled it well out there." He looked at the desk sergeant, "Certain individuals won't let you forget it either."

"No sir, certain individuals won't." A wave of self-consciousness reddened her face when she saw his vision roam her visible wounds. She tried hiding the marks on her throat with makeup. It worked to a degree.

He centered on her throat then dropped to her hands and wrists. "Everything okay at home?"

It took more than makeup to disguise the marks on her extremities. Starting at her hands, R.J.'s tirade stood out in red slashes all the way to her elbows. The worst were located on the underside of her forearms and upper arms and they burned like Satan's tail whipped her, especially when anything touched them. She'd worn her suit jacket to hide the majority of wounds (Lord, they ached when the fabric touched them) but Hoffman saw enough to concern him. By his phrasing he seemed to accuse Ennis of the attack. Unease sat like a rock in her stomach as she tugged at the cuffs, "At home, yes. This is a result of a different situation and a misunderstanding. It's taken care of." What else could she say? My daddy beat the shit out of me and I let him off scot-free? She wanted a *little* dignity to drag around with her.

He nodded, "Good. Just..." he focused on her throat, "take care of yourself and if you need help with anything, come see me or Captain Hunter."

"Yessir, I will. And thank you for reinstating me. I missed the job."

"I would take credit for it but it seems you have a benefactor working in the background. One phone call this morning put you on full duty again. I *will* say I hate having my best officers on the sidelines so welcome back. Go find some bad guys, Sergeant, and make me look good."

After leaving the major's office she headed to hers. Hunter sat behind her desk. "I'd guess this was the shortest suspension in the APD's hist… Good Lord, you can't stay out of trouble on or off the job. What happened?"

Before Josh, like Hoffman, began wondering about Ennis, Savannah explained, "Daddy had a little issue with me."

"I hope to hell you had him tossed in the pokey. Those look painful."

"One, they are painful and two, I didn't have him arrested."

"Why the hell not?"

"Because Lily did it for me."

"*Lily?*"

"Yes. Well, in a way, at least. She called 911 and circumstances worked out that the cops stopped him for speeding then arrested him for assaulting a cop."

Josh frowned, "The cop I'm talking to right now?"

"No, the one who pulled him over." Here it came. Another lecture from someone who didn't understand. "Please Josh, I did what I thought was best. He was angry yesterday. Had I pushed it with an assault charge, Ennis would need a new wife."

His brow sank. He didn't approve and put her on notice, "It's your choice *this* time. If he hurts you again, the rest of us get involved."

R.J. Prince could hold his own against a surprising number of opponents but a horde of angry cops descending on him? She winced at that thought.

"Hopefully he got it out of his system. So what's this about me having a benefactor? Would his name be Lee Morgan?"

"The one and only. Morgan called the chief, the chief called the zone commander and Hoffman informed me to call you. You showed up before I had a chance. Apparently, and I quote, 'Preston overreacted to a misperceived threat.'"

Savannah wasn't about to tell her boss that Preston hadn't entirely *misperceived* the threat. When the little bastard besmirched her mama's reputation, Savannah meant what she said at the time.

"Did I hear Sweeney riding you about Tucker's book?"

Josh approached the subject with kid gloves. She appreciated his effort. She heaved a resigned sigh, "Yeah, well, what do you expect from him? He's got to keep up appearances in front of his officers. It's nothing I can't handle."

She sifted through the paperwork and settled on John Mathis's request for vacation in three weeks. That meant trying to find a detective to fill in for him. Christine Clark came to mind. Christine was a good, hard-working detective that had transferred a year earlier. She wondered if her good friend might help her out for a few days. No time like the present to find out and catch up on current happenings so she reached for the phone, "Since I'm back at work, I'd better do some work."

"Before you make any other calls," Josh removed a slip of paper from his pocket, handed it to her, "take care of His Highness first. Morgan's called three times this morning. He wants to talk to you."

Oh great. One father kicked her butt, the other nagged her. She'd been trying to avoid both but apparently it wasn't working. She glanced at the note with Lee's cell number. She didn't have the heart to tell Josh she already had it. She wadded up the paper and chucked it in the trash, "What's that saying about people in Hell wanting ice water?"

"Call him, Savannah. I'm sick of him."

"Okay, I'll call him but while you're here, is it okay if I ask Christine to fill in for Mathis? He put in for a week's vacation three weeks from now."

He looked relieved when she agreed to call, "Yes, and I'll call Clark while you tend to that gazillionaire who's been tying up the lines and my morning. What dates should I tell Christine?"

"Starting the first."

"Done. One more thing. I hate to add more stress but I need you in uniform tomorrow. Taylor took emergency leave for a death in the family so I need you to be his rookie's FTO the next three days."

"Since when do I look or act like a field training officer? There's gotta be someone else who can change his Huggies for a while."

"There have been complaints on Graham. From other patrol units and Taylor himself. I need a sergeant to ride with him. Someone who's not shy about reeling him back in. Taylor's a little too lenient in my opinion."

"In other words a boss with three stripes and a big mouth."

"Someone with an official leash, yes. It's only for a couple of days and," he hesitated, "I need you to wear a body cam…"

She drew back, "Sergeants don't have to wear body cams."

"No, but consider this a personal favor. Hoffman and I need all the evidence we can get if we terminate this kid."

"In that case, consider your personal favor done." Savannah dialed Lee Morgan after Josh returned to his office. The voice answering the call sounded mighty happy for someone who should be wasting away in prison for rape. He offered the usual pleasantries then bulled into iffy territory, "I've been calling for a day or two and hoping to hear back. Everything alright?"

Was he kidding? "No. Everything's not alright." She tried to remove the utter contempt from her voice. The man had the clout to have her fired, after all. "I've been busy. Work, family, that sort of thing. And my little unplanned vacation didn't help my stress level but no one disparages my mother and gets away with it. You might give Preston that heads-up."

"What did he say about Charlene?"

She mentally rubbed her hands together. Finally. A chance to show Lee just how twisted his family was. Tucker wasn't the only malicious offspring in the clan. She explained hers and Preston's back and forth, including the fact he shoved a massive check at her to buy her off. By the time she finished, Lee's mood darkened, no matter how he tried hiding it. "I'll have a talk with him tonight. I apologize, Savannah. I had no idea. He won't speak ill of Charlene again, I can assure you."

"Thanks," was all she felt comfortable saying. He could promise anything he wanted. People like Preston Morgan used money and influence to back up their attitude and get their way. She'd prided herself on the fact she'd at least (hopefully) given him heartburn the day she walked out of his office without his check.

"Now that I have you on the phone, I'd like to meet for lunch so we can discuss a few things."

"What things?"

"I'd rather not get into it on the phone. Can you break loose around noon? I'll have our lunch brought in."

"I really can't today, sorry." And before you ask, "Or tomorrow either."

"Ah, I think I see where this is going." Papers shuffled in the background. He spoke to someone nearby, "Reschedule that meeting for four o'clock. I'll be out of the office until, say, two o'clock. I'll be at the police station on Maple Drive if you need me."

Holy shit, he's coming here! "Mr. Morgan," she called. He continued instructing his secretary, assistant or whoever stood by. She tried again, "Mr. Morgan, I'll be there shortly after noon. Don't–" *come here, damn it.* "Don't reschedule your day for me."

"Splendid." She heard the smile in his voice. He asked, "Are hamburgers okay with you?"

No. "Yes."

"Fine, fine. See you then."

"Goodbye," She left off the three words fighting for freedom. *You arrogant asshole.*

O O O

This counted as the fourth or fifth time in her life Savannah had been to the Morgan Tower. Most of the visits occurred during her uniform days and those revolved around security alarms or unruly visitors.

Besides four armed guards, the same two sharp-dressed men from her previous visit worked the reception desk. No one except a fool might try getting past the first floor muscle and firepower but she learned early in her career to never underestimate the audacity of a fool.

While other visitors received a critical sizing up by the guards and reception personnel, the six Morgan employees stood a tad straighter upon her approach and nodded a courteous *ma'am* to her. The men at the reception desk did not check their computer to verify her appointment. They seemed to already know she was expected. While one volunteered Lee Morgan's floor number to her, the other offered to escort her to the elevator.

Why was everyone kissing her backside? She turned down Morgan's security job. These guys had no reason to treat her any differently... Oh, I forgot, she rolled her eyes. *I'm the daughter. The One No One Talks About. Well, someone's doing some talking, aren't they?*

She saw the guy at the front desk grab the phone and forewarn the person on the other end, "Tell Mr. Morgan she's here and on her way up." What kind of ambush was waiting for her anyway? Things we need to discuss, he said. Discuss what, she wondered, that you raped my mother and I'm the result of that rape?

She allowed the second fellow to press the elevator button for her. He didn't follow her inside the elevator, she noticed, which suited her fine. Elevators usually drove her claustrophobia nuts but the Morgan elevator boasted room enough for two dozen people or more. Maple colored walls with gold trim and terra cotta colored tile floor gave the moving box a warm, sort of comfortable feel – if one didn't mind being locked in a moving box.

Savannah still spent the elevator trip battling claustrophobia but mostly anger. When the door opened she stepped out to a lounge (Savannah called it a waiting room) with dark wood décor and soft-cushioned gray easy chairs for guests. On one wall shiny gold script lettering spelled out "Morgan Industries". Modest, she thought. Not.

Two people waited to meet, she assumed, with Lee. The elevator ride tested her nerves enough she needed a moment to calm down before approaching Lee's secretary. When all eyes settled on her, she decided being on display was worse than the elevator so she moved along.

Lee's secretary rose from behind her cherrywood reception station. The young woman looked straight out of a magazine, beautiful and attired in the finest labels this side of Vera Wang. Her sugary sweet greeting made Savannah's teeth hurt. The woman continued, "Right this way, Sergeant. Mr. Morgan is waiting for you."

With high heels, she stood Savannah's natural height of five nine. Without them, Savannah estimated she stood shorter than Georgia's five six. The secretary led her down a hall, stopped at a door and knocked.

A beaming Lee opened the door decked out in, what else, Armani. "Savannah, please come in. I do appreciate you taking time for this meeting. Aubree, that will be all. Thank you."

"Yes, Mr. Morgan." Aubree bid them farewell.

Lee closed the door. A white sack, two drinks and a manila folder sat on the biggest, heaviest desk this side of Georgia's mahogany writing desk. Lee's loosely resembled the Resolute desk in the oval office. Savannah guessed it wasn't exactly an accident.

For his private domain he chose warm cream colored walls with dark wood trim. On one side of the room sat a large cream colored couch and against the adjoining wall he placed two matching armchairs and in front of those, a round polished wooden table.

She took in the paintings of (she guessed) his parents and another of him when he was younger. Those hung on the same wall separated by a few feet. He decorated the wall behind his desk with framed pictures of his family.

His hand settled at the small of her back, guiding her to the table. Savannah tensed at the touch. She thought of her mother, wondering if he'd done the same with her. *A light, testing touch to see if she stepped away or to see if she was receptive to it. I can tell you she wasn't receptive. She was Southern. Too Southern perhaps. Too polite to tell you to back off and she never got the chance to slap the shit out of you. Well, I'm not polite, Mr. Morgan. I go from zero to bitch in two seconds so get your hand off of me or you'll lose it. You and I have no past and you are not my father, no matter what you think or what a DNA test might say. I only see you as a rapist who got away with violating the sweetest lady ever born.*

She regrouped her thoughts. The meeting, whatever it was for, would go faster if she didn't speak her mind. Plus, she might stay out of jail too.

The aroma of juicy burgers and French fries tamed her urge for declaring war on Lee Morgan. He'd ordered take-out but had a proper place setting for their meal. Eating a hamburger and fries on expensive china. Why not?

Savannah debated over shucking her suit jacket. He results of R.J.'s temper fit were visible enough to catch plenty of attention as evidenced by Hoffman and Josh. What the hell, she decided, after what he did to Mama it's not like Mr. Captain of Industry can say much. She removed the jacket and draped it across the chair back.

Lee stood, ready to seat her. When she glanced back, he was staring at the red streaks. He never said a word. He'd seen the two stripes across her throat when she arrived but surprisingly kept quiet about that too.

He took the liberty of serving their meal, his vision on occasion shifting to the marks. Before sitting down he brought over two tumblers and a bottle of scotch. He poured a drink then paused when she shook her head, "None for me, thanks."

Lee sat the bottle aside with slight chagrin, "That's right." He turned back to the liquor cabinet, "Ethan said you prefer good old American whiskey. I'll remember next time, I promise."

Savannah declined. He poured anyway then scooted the tumbler closer, "A little nip won't hurt. You work hard. Indulge."

"I'm on duty."

He removed a slip of paper from his pants pocket and winked, "It'll be our secret."

That turn of phrase closed a fist in her gut. Had he stood over her shivering, violated mother and said those words with that same smirk? Or had he still been atop Charlene, in the process of destroying her faith in a man she trusted as her friend and boss, and whispered those words in her ear?

"Is something wrong?"

His question shattered the agonizing images and murderous

thoughts storming through her, "No, just thinking about a crime some jerk committed a long time ago." She shook out her napkin, placed it in her lap.

"May I ask what it involves?"

"Rape."

He placed his napkin in his lap, "You knew the victim?"

Unwrapping her burger, she nodded, "I knew her very well." *I have to be careful,* she reminded herself. *This man is on a first name basis with the mayor and police chief. He plays golf with the governor. Unfortunately, I can't help Mama but my family needs me to remain employed.*

Her veiled reference flew past him anyway. He sipped his scotch, "I hope the bastard who did it is behind bars."

"He's not." She stared at the whiskey. Tempting. Oh, so tempting. She tasted it on her tongue. Felt the warmth in her throat and stomach already. She worked her tongue once, twice... then picked up the Coke.

He smiled thoughtfully, "You're in safe company, dear. Feel free to drink. I guarantee you'll enjoy it. It's the finest America makes."

Savannah's vision fell to the glass. Safe company? Hardly. Enjoy it? Hell, yes she would – if she drank it. Her mouth literally watered at the prospect. Right now it became a tug-of-war to drink or don't drink and the former gained too much ground too fast. As for being the finest whiskey available? She had no doubt. "I'm okay but thanks."

"Suit yourself." He picked up his burger, nodded to hers, "On the phone I got the feeling you were, how shall I say it, put out. I'm hoping I'm not the cause."

You are. "Just a long week."

He stole a lingering glance at her throat and arms. His eyes tightened slightly, "I imagine those make it feel longer."

"They'll heal." She took a bite of her burger. It kept her mouth busy with a task guaranteed to keep herself out of trouble.

"You know, I still spend the majority of my time in Augusta. I've heard things over the years. People who abuse the children they raise–"

"Mr. Morgan." She stared at the whiskey harder now. Oh, *so* tempting... She forced her vision to his, "I didn't come here to discuss whether what you've heard back home is true or not."

Too much too quick, she read in his expression. Savannah watched him mentally retreat. The business world required bluntness more often than not, unless they were cutting a deal. Then fudging facts or gaining an ounce of leverage meant the difference between success or failure. He was leading up to one grand announcement, she could sense that. *You're my daughter – tried, true, a red, white and blue Morgan. Welcome to the family.* But he overplayed his hand by disparaging R.J. in a fast and loose manner. He let his temper slip and now he'd crapped on her daddy, or the man she knew as her daddy. Sometimes meaner than a striped snake, R.J. was still her daddy and she meant to tell Lee Morgan that. If anyone had the right to hold hard feelings, it was R.J.'s kids but the rest of the world better back off.

"I've overstepped and I apologize." The words rolled easily off his tongue. "I'll only say you bear the situation well as I'm sure you must. Remember that to me, you are the inquisitive, happy little girl running around my house with your sister trying so desperately to catch up with you." He referenced the slip of paper on the table, "The reason I asked for this meeting is in regards to my job offer. You make, what, around this much as a sergeant?" He sat his lunch down, slid the paper across to her.

Savannah grabbed her glasses from her purse, put them on and glanced at the number – then spontaneously gulped the food in one swallow. She chased the half-masticated lump with Coke. He quoted her salary to the very dollar and told him as much.

"You remember my offer? The salary?"

Good Lord, yes. The "Don't Worry, Be Happy" number that put the Ennis Rutherford family in a whole new tax bracket. Looking over her glasses, she nodded but held off taking another bite of her lunch. The first one nearly killed her going down. Besides, Lee Morgan hadn't touched his food yet.

He produced another piece of paper, "I've recalculated the salary. Here's the most I can offer for your services."

It's probably rock bottom now since I turned down his original offer… but why invite me here to have lunch and tell me that? Looked at the number. Instead of reducing his offer he increased it. Considerably. Before her mouth dropped open, Lee slid the manila folder over, opened it. A contract already filled out with her name in the appropriate places.

"All I need are the pertinent details such as social security number and so forth, you sign the contract," he flipped a page or two over to reveal the blank line awaiting her signature, "And you can start at your convenience."

This is how he trapped Mama. Showed her a huge number that would ease her family's financial burden then later on, well, she knew what happened then. The bump in the amount would pay off the house, cover Lily's college tuition (if she were college age) and still have enough left over to start on Anna's future.

"I'm hoping your silence is a good sign. You also have perks listed in here," he tapped the contract. "You golf and I heard your oldest girl, Lily, is a budding prodigy like you were back in the day. You'll enjoy memberships to the finest country clubs, your family will have access to the best medical care available, reservations at the finest restaurants and so much more. There are benefits to being in the Morgan fold. Valuable ones. Painless ones." His gaze dropped to the marks again.

Images of him with Charlene cut through the fog of luxury flitting through her mind. She could almost hear her mother's cries to stop. Curling up in tears each night, fearing that she'd get pregnant and the devastating reality when she discovered she was.

Savannah reached for the whiskey, downed it in one swallow. Anything to rid herself of her mama's agonizing cries and weeping.

Lee tipped the whiskey bottle to the glass in her hand, "One to celebrate our newfound relationship, perhaps?"

She let him pour another slug, not because she was climbing aboard the Morgan train but because her mother's tears kept flowing in her mind. "You never give up, do you?"

"I've learned in life that if you want something, keep working until you get it. For all the lies in Tucker's book, he got one thing right. I do run this business like the mafia. Successful people do."

"The mafia, huh? You got bodies buried in the end zone at Meadowlands after they discovered Jimmy Hoffa wasn't there?"

Lee Morgan didn't flinch. He did, however, pause half a second as if considering her question and how to answer. Then he winked, "I have more discreet locations for those. No, what I meant by the mafia comment was I have six rules I live by in business. One, learn to take a beating because not every decision will be a winner. Two, keep your friends close and your enemies closer. Know what the competition is up to. Three, be prepared to fight. There are times you should let something go and others you dig your heels in and fight for. Four, follow words with actions. A broken promise in business can ruin you and that goes for anything in life. Five, give people what they want and finally number six is why you and I are here eating hamburgers together and finalizing this deal – I hope. I'm keeping the business in the family. Nothing beats fierce loyalty. Unfortunately Tucker decided a tome of scathing lies was more important than family. You are loyal to your people, even to a man who has abused you all your life. From what I've seen and heard you're honest, smart, clever, and everything I want in a daughter and," he tapped the folder, "for this job."

14

Savannah sat outside the package store debating over a purchase. If she bought a bottle of Jack, her husband, sister and brother would pile on en masse and beat her into submission with guilt and lectures. If she didn't buy Uncle Jack, she'd lose sleep, constantly obsess over the shitty turn in her life and generally be a bitch. *How's that different from being drunk? You do all that when things go to hell anyway. Jack just helps you cope better.*

She pulled the slip of paper from her jacket pocket. She stared at the massive amount of dough Morgan earmarked for her salary. Earmarked for his new Chief Security Officer. No, her mind taunted, earmarked to *buy* a daughter *masquerading* as Chief Security Officer.

It was enough to cover bills, college, and provide absolute comfort for her little family – and she'd told him no. Lee Morgan rarely heard the word no, judging by his disappointment. He left the job offer open for her, he said, assuring that once she gave it "serious thought", she would reconsider. The only thing she'd reconsider was where to tell him to stick the offer – in his north end or south end. Hell would freeze before she worked for her mother's rapist.

The meeting stirred a deep, raging hatred in her when she envisioned what her mother endured. The trauma of enduring the sexual assault. The aftermath. The waiting. The pregnancy. Faces of rape victims appeared. The ones Savannah listened to, tried to reassure and held as they wept. Her mother's image evolved. The smile and laughter disappeared. Fear, devastation and depression replaced them. Instead of clear, sparkling green eyes, tears filled them, erasing any sign of the happiness once residing in Charlene's soul. How long had it taken before she recovered enough to be the gentle, trusting, loving woman Savannah remembered?

Savannah threw open the Charger's door and marched inside. She grabbed a bottle of Jack. She clutched the sweet relief in her fist, gave the familiar black and white label a glance. *Welcome back, old friend*, the whiskey coaxed. *I've missed you. You and I have lots of catching up to do. C'mon, grab another bottle for old times' sake. There's plenty as you can see and when you run low, you know where to find me. Go home, pour a glass and tell Uncle Jack your problems.*

She did. The second she got home, the purse and keys were laid aside, the gun stayed on her hip, but the bottle was opened. She poured a decent swallow, closed her eyes and threw it back. A trembling, satisfied sigh broke the silence. The kids weren't due out of school and daycare for a while yet. Plenty of time for her to knock the edge off and recover before picking them up. She was desperate but not entirely stupid. Driving drunk with her children in the car was a giant no-no, even in her unbalanced state of mind.

Before she drank another drop she had to make a quick call explaining to Josh that she felt sick.

"This sudden illness," he said. "Does it have anything to do with your father?"

Oh the irony of it. If it wasn't so sad it would be hilarious, "No."

"So those marks are your only injuries?"

"Yeah. I'm just not feeling well. I guess I didn't get over what I had earlier." How do you get over being the result of your mother's rape, she wondered.

For the next few minutes she stared at the open bottle. Stroked it. Swept her tongue over her lips. Mmm, she purred at the residual taste on them. Yes. Sweet relief indeed.

Yes, my good friend. You know me well. I dull heartaches, quiet troubled thoughts and anesthetize problems no matter the size. I can tell you're still feeling low. Let me help. I'm here for you, friend. How long have we known each other? Have I ever let you down?

The amber elixir poured smooth and easy into the glass. One more good swallow prepared her to crack open Tucker Morgan's bestseller to the index. She located the P's for Prince but thankfully the son of a bitch left a little doubt in readers' minds as to "Charlene's" identity so she flipped to the C's and stopped on Charlene. She thumbed to the first reference to her mother.

"Not long after Mrs. Powell's ugly departure, Dad hired Charlene, a beautiful woman who resided just across town. She was married to a local contractor who was known to be as ruthless in business as he was to his family. Her silken brown hair cascaded past her shoulders, her emerald green eyes sparkled when she smiled, and her luscious sultry voice was the making of any boy's fantasy. This woman, it turned out, was also Lee's first love and her employment not only reunited them but rekindled a romance that resulted in an affair and the first Morgan heir."

Okey dokey, bartender. Hit me again. Savannah poured another drink, basked in how the firewater burned until it hit bottom. Comfortably Numb she called it back in the day. That was her goal – but Comfortably Numb meant "not safe to drive" so that meant a call to Dane to pick up the kids. On second thought, Comfortably Numb could wait until evening and no one better argue with her indulgence. After all, their DNA was solidly imprinted. John Rutherford sired her formidable, hunky hubby and R.J. Prince fathered Seth and Georgia. *One of these things is not like the other,* she hummed the old Sesame Street song aloud while pouring herself an additional swallow. *One of these things just doesn't belong...* Yeah, she thought. Me. I don't belong.

With eyes closed, she knocked back the whiskey, relaxing as its heat coated her throat and slid into her stomach. The magic would kick in soon then who the hell cared who her daddy was?

O   O   O

Officer Graham, a decently handsome young man, stood her height, looked flawless in his uniform and dripped with conceit. Other officers might have mistaken it for confidence but Savannah recognized conceit as sure as she recognized a lie when her kids uttered one. They just had "that look", she told Georgia one time. And Officer Graham had an "I know it all" swagger about his demeanor. He looked smart enough to be a cop so what happened that she had to play nanny to the probationary officer? Upon reviewing his academy scores, she learned his grades were above the norm. Not to brag but she'd scored much higher in her academy days and also qualified as an expert marksman before graduation. He rated passable on shooting. The word grated on her. "Passable" meant he may or may not be able to protect himself and his partner while on patrol.

His biggest problem (besides conceit and his passable shooting scores) seemed to be aggressive behavior. He'd sassed his training officer enough Taylor brought it to Josh Hunter's attention. Probably why Taylor put in for vacation, she thought. The new kid was driving him nuts.

The moment she introduced herself as his temporary FTO, she understood Taylor's reasoning.

Graham flashed his pearly whites in a striking smile, "I thought since Taylor was gone I'd partner up with Wilson."

Graham's looks probably helped him gain popularity with the girls in high school but trying finesse the detective sergeant with his "charm" would end up wounding his ego. Instead of swooning over him, Savannah nearly laughed, "You thought that, did you? You figured the department would let two rookies partner up? That's like me letting my five-year-old drive my car. And since you're stuck with me as your FTO, your first job is to check over our unit. Don't forget to check the back seat and tire pressures and gas up the car if it needs it."

She might as well have assigned him to scrub the floors with a toothbrush. Grunt work, he mumbled.

"It's called necessary preparation," she corrected.

"Yes, Sergeant." He headed off to the patrol car.

"Graham, haven't you forgotten something?" she asked, lifting her bail out bag as a reminder.

He didn't appreciate that reminder in front of the other officers. "Oh. Yeah. I, um, didn't expect you to ride with me."

Yes. You assumed you made the rules and you don't. "Well, you've got me the next couple of days so let's make the best of it."

Since he suffered memory loss as well as a swelled ego, Savannah wanted to know, "You got extra forms for arrests and summonses in your clipboard?"

He rolled his eyes, "Yes, Sergeant. Taylor already drummed that into me."

"Extra ammo for pistols and long guns, first aid equipment, bottled water, granola bars or another type of snack?"

His open mouth closed as he considered her list. His brow furrowed, "Bottled water and granola bars?"

Huh, she thought, *how 'bout that? The old folks on the job have good ideas. Who'da thunk it?* "They come in handy when you're stuck at a scene. I've got enough for us today but tomorrow come prepared."

Their shift began uneventfully then at eight-thirty they were dispatched to a burglary call. They rolled up to the closed business surrounded by an eight foot high chain-link fence topped with razor wire.

Savannah and Graham walked around the perimeter – she at the back and he at the front. They saw nothing amiss and the doors and windows remained shut and intact. Savannah radioed in for an ETA on the owner. Twenty minutes. She asked dispatch to have the owner meet them out front so they could get inside the fence.

An antsy Graham, eager to expedite the call, waved Savannah off, "I can climb that fence easy."

She called him off but he'd already begun climbing, telling her, "We're wasting our time here. I'll check it out and we can leave."

By the time she told him they had to wait for the owner, he snagged his pant leg in the razor wire. Savannah shook her head. It was gonna be a long day at that rate. While he finagled his leg loose and cussed about ruining a new pair of slacks, she busied herself walking the front of the perimeter again then stopped.

Graham cranked up the cussing as his other pant leg caught in the razor wire. Frustration and embarrassment took over. He never asked for help and she never offered. She wanted to teach the arrogant kid a lesson and prayed it stuck tighter than his slacks had in the wire.

While he tried untangling himself, Savannah curbed a smile, "Hey, Spider-Man."

Red-faced and temper toeing a thin line, he snapped, "What is it, Sergeant?"

She fiddled with the lock, pulled the chain through and pushed the gate open, "You didn't check the lock."

Savannah heard him grumbling. The razor wire and fence rattled. She walked through and checked the doors and windows, finding them secure. She circled around to the front and found him leaned against the cruiser, checking the damage to his slacks. "After we're done here," she said, "we'll swing by the station and let you change."

She took some ribbing from the veteran officers about "taking their time" on a simple burglary call. When they saw Graham's pants and sour mood, they teased, "What happened to you? You get mauled by a tiger?"

She explained in a matter-of-fact way what happened, "I told him not to feel bad. That we learn new things every day on this job."

Detective Tierce, a new addition shortly after Hoffman arrived, sidled up to her. Except for his unfortunate hawk-like nose, she considered him nice looking. Two months into his detective's promotion, he acted eager to learn the ropes by asking advice from her, Ennis and sometimes Mathis – when John wasn't grouchy. He had the makings of a good detective and seemed like a solid cop which was more than she could say for Graham.

Tierce listened to Graham spout his egotistical diatribe then said, "Still got that attitude, doesn't he?"

"In spades," she replied in a grim tone.

Graham wheeled back to the small cluster of officers, "My father retired as an assistant chief in Trenton, New Jersey. He taught me everything I know and *I know what I'm doing*," he glared at Savannah, "if I was *allowed* to do it."

The cops dispersed, backing away from her. They knew her reputation. She'd not climbed the ladder being sweet nor the easiest person to get along with. And she possessed one hell of a temper when seriously provoked.

A veteran officer stepped closer with a covert, "Not telling you how to do your job, Sergeant, but this bird needs his wings clipped. Be careful out there."

She nodded. Unless Graham's attitude straightened up, she'd clip 'em alright. Right after she served her sentence as acting FTO.

The next day started on a tense note. They spent lunch at her favorite eatery. Neither said much. Shortly after returning to duty a call came in to pick up James Ward, a parolee wanted for robbery and assault on two police officers. His daunting description made her think twice about how to handle the arrest should they locate him, especially since he'd sent the last two cops to the hospital when they tried to slap cuffs on him.

An hour passed when they found him strolling down the sidewalk in an upscale residential area. The second he saw the patrol car, he took off running.

Savannah raced to cut him off, switched on her body cam, threw open the door with weapon drawn then ordered him on his knees. Ward stopped but did not kneel.

Graham took another approach – the wrong one. "Holster your weapon, Sergeant." He began talking to Ward, assuring him everything would be fine and that he was safe.

His command took a moment to sink in. "What did you just say to me?" she asked, still in disbelief and still pointing her gun at Ward.

"I told you to holster your weapon. My dad taught me how to handle these situations. First they have to feel safe, that their lives aren't in danger."

She barely contained her temper – and the only reason she did was the body cam clipped to her uniform. She wasn't losing her cool or her stripes over this clod. "*I* have to feel safe. He's already sent two cops to the hospital. I'm not taking any chances."

The parolee stood Ennis's height, a good five inches taller than her. He was built like him too. Broad in the shoulders and muscle all over, only Ennis never looked ready to launch himself at her and tackle her. This guy did. Savannah motioned with the Glock, "On your knees, Ward. This is your last warning."

"Sergeant Prince, put your gun away now!" Graham angrily shouted then stepped between her and the hulk of a man. He resumed reassuring Ward when the parolee bolted.

Muttering a few choice words, Savannah jammed the Glock in her holster and ran to the cruiser. She took off after Ward, leaving Graham behind and blaming her for Ward running "because he felt threatened". After reporting hers and the suspect's location, she radioed nearby units set up a containment area. Within two minutes, three patrol units cornered Ward. When she arrived on scene onlookers gathered on sidewalks to watch seven cops do the job of two. The fleet-footed parolee faced seven guns including her own and, like her, the officers brandishing those guns didn't buy Graham's bleeding-heart horseshit. They wanted to go home to their families. Ward dropped to his knees without a fight.

At the start of the pursuit, Savannah glanced in the rearview mirror to see Graham sprinting at top speed. The longer the chase progressed, the further back he dropped until she turned the corner, losing sight of him. The sweaty, egotistical rookie finally reached the knot of patrol units that boxed Ward in. He leaned on his knees heaving heavy breaths. "Why didn't you wait for me? You're not supposed to leave your partner behind. My dad told me–"

"Shut up, Graham," she barked, effectively rendering the rookie mute with shock. She fetched the handcuffed Ward and loaded him in the back of her cruiser, finishing, "You can serve him tea and give him his blankie when we get back to the station."

O   O   O

Josh Hunter's mouth dropped at her account of the day. She couldn't wait for the body cam footage to be reviewed. "What moron handed that idiot a badge and a gun?" she demanded to know. "Or did his ex-assistant chief father get him a free pass? You can't police with lollipops, teddy bears and therapy sessions to make perps feel 'okay' about being arrested."

"Calm down, Savannah. I told you the other day Graham was a problem child."

"He's a hazard and he'll get one of us killed if he stays on the job."

"Well, at least tomorrow is your last day."

"Yes, that's what I'm afraid of." She glanced at the clock, "I have paperwork to finish then my shift is over. I really need to see my family. Not even my kids drive me this insane."

She headed out to hear oohs and ahhs of officers around the desk sergeant's kiosk. Then she heard Graham's arrogant voice. She found him surrounded by officers, recounting his version of Ward's fouled-up arrest. Of course she took the brunt – no – *all* the blame. Savannah lost her patience with the brat. Josh trailed behind her to call Graham for his side of the story. Major Hoffman stood outside his office listening to the new officer's account. She didn't care if God stood by to hear this.

Savannah spun Graham by the shoulder, "What's my rank, Probationary Officer Graham?"

The other officers clammed up. Graham smirked, joking, "If I have to tell you…"

No one laughed. She stood face to face with him, "*What is my rank, Probationary Officer Graham?*"

He suddenly noticed the wide berth the others gave him and his livid FTO. He sobered up, "Sergeant."

"You're damn right and you'd better remember that tomorrow – and any other day we might cross paths." She turned and walked off.

15

Day three with probationary officer Graham started uneventfully. He rode beside her reserved and stiff as if he'd been reamed out by the bosses. Maybe after they got a look at the body cam footage, Hoffman and Hunter had a chat with him, she thought.

They stopped for lunch at a fast food restaurant. The meal was quiet. In the car afterward, Graham cleared his throat, "To save my job I'm supposed to obey any order you give, I'm not supposed to argue or have an opinion or solution, even if it's better than yours."

"It won't kill you to follow orders. We've been here longer, Graham. We know things that you still have to learn. We try to teach by experience. We are not the enemy, we are mentors if you'll let us be."

"My father is my mentor. He taught me what I need to know."

"This isn't Trenton, and *I'm* your boss. If you can't accept that, find another job. I didn't earn these sergeant's stripes by taking shit off other cops, new or otherwise."

A "shots fired" 10-13 call came over the radio with the address. "You know what to do," she told him. At least she hoped so. Perhaps Trenton, New Jersey followed the same protocol as the rest of the country.

She hit the lights, siren and gas as Graham acknowledged the call, telling dispatch they were two blocks away and responding.

"Your body cam on?" she asked. "Neither of us needs sixteen days suspension – or worse." The chief laid down the law. All officers below sergeant must wear a body camera and God help the cop who was caught not turning theirs on during calls. The first offense was sixteen days suspension. The second offense: termination. Last time Savannah patrolled the streets, body cameras weren't even considered for police officers but since she promised Hunter she'd wear one, she didn't want to forget to switch it on – or remind His Highness about his. After all, she was the FTO – and the twerp's mentor whether he liked it or not.

They screeched to a stop at the curb two houses away from the call. "Do not go charging into that house, Graham. I don't care what your daddy told you about cowboy policing but you won't do it on my watch, got it?"

He hesitated. His vision riveted to the cruiser parked down the way, the light bar still flashing. The neighborhood appeared deceptively quiet. Then Savannah saw them. Two uniform cops lying in the front yard. Neither appeared to be moving. "Do you hear me, Graham?" she asked the wide-eyed rookie.

"Yes, Sergeant." This time the know-it-all sobered at the sight. The cocky attitude finally gave way to the real rookie beneath, the one who trained for these situations but held misguided hope of never experiencing one, even in a large city.

"Stay with me, you understand? Whatever I do, you do unless I tell you otherwise."

He kept staring owl-eyed at the two cops in the yard. He nodded to them, "Are they dead? Are those cops dead?"

"*Graham*, pay attention. Every step I take, you take too. Got it?"

"Yes, Sergeant," his voice didn't sound right. Sure he was scared – so was she – but going into this thing required relying on training and experience. Graham had the former if he'd just use it.

She opened the door, Glock in hand and used the cruiser as cover to make her way to the three foot high brick wall lining the neighbor's driveway.

Graham moved in right behind her so tight she heard his rapid breaths and felt his hand on her belt. Both went to hands and knees as shots rang out, striking bricks and mortar mere inches from them.

Graham curled up tight behind her, "They see us! They're shooting at us! We can't move or we'll die too!"

"Stop panicking. We're going for that black Ford at the curb. Come on."

"No," he grabbed the back of her duty belt to hold her back, "don't go. Don't leave me here."

Savannah pulled his hand away and took off running. She counted four shots, all strafing the brick wall as she hightailed it to the Ford. Her heart bounded in her chest so hard she heard the frenetic beating in her ears, felt it in her hands and feet. Her breathing quickened to short, shallow breaths. She tried to calm herself. She'd made it.

She glanced behind her to check on Graham. She was alone.

"Sergeant!" Graham's pitiful wail sounded like Lily's on her first day of preschool when she whined for her mama not to leave her.

Savannah peeked around the fender to see the two officers,

Mandy Stewart and Marquis Thomas, in the yard. Stewart's chest rose and fell in quick, short breaths. Thomas lay a few feet away, motionless.

Marquis Thomas, a big burly black guy with a refreshing upbeat attitude toward police work, had been on the job six years, had a wife and kids around Lily and Anna's ages that he crowed about every chance he got. Stewart had been on the job just two years. She was astute, eager to learn and kind to everyone she met. She lived with her parents and was single (but still on the lookout for Mr. Right she'd told Savannah). Stewart squirmed on the lawn, her hand pressed at her stomach beneath the protective vest. Blood seeped between her fingers. Her pained, pale complexion said it all – *please hurry.*

Stewart warned, "Be careful, Sergeant. We were ambushed. Two are still in the house and they're armed. Marquis killed the third one."

"Sergeant!" Graham yelled. "Come back!"

Savannah ignored him, asking Stewart, "How bad are you hurt?"

"I caught one under the vest. I'll make it. They shot us from the front window and front door. Be careful."

Savannah turned back to Graham who peered around the wall. Savannah scowled, "Put a rush on that bus, Graham. Do *something* to help out."

To her anger, he froze. "Graham, call for the ambulance and tell 'em to floor it."

Nothing. She called it in herself followed by a Code 30 – officer needs emergency assistance.

"Sergeant Prince!" He wailed at the top of his lungs.

Shut up, she nearly said until gunfire broke out from the window.

Bullets struck the walls again. Graham scrambled safely behind the barrier like a turtle withdrawing in its shell.

Savannah asked Stewart, "What about Marquis?"

"They shot him in the head."

An image of Thomas's family flitted through her mind. Six short years on the job only to be gunned down and leave his family without a husband and father. And if she wasn't careful, she'd leave *her* family without a wife and mother. "Just stay still," she told Stewart. "Don't give 'em any reason to take aim on you." She radioed in, reiterating the urgency to get the ambulance there quick.

More shots fired from the window and door. Not assault rifles. Pistols. She stood a chance of running to the patrol car parked several feet in front of the Ford without getting nailed. If she made it, it gave her a better position to work her way toward the house. She cursed under her breath then, "Graham, snap out of it and back me up."

He peeked around the wall for a half a second. Did your daddy teach you that too, she wondered, because you pick a hell of a time to lose your balls, rookie.

The sun beat down on her dark blue uniform, turning it into an oven. She used her arm to wipe away the perspiration on her forehead. She took a deep breath to calm and reassure herself. She could do this. She'd done it before, right? Well, sort of. Not by herself, though. She glanced at Graham's hiding place. He wasn't there.

One step forward and she retreated when a tall, gangly black guy ran out with a gun in each hand, firing in her direction.

Shots zipped past her as he and his partner unloaded a barrage on her. A hail of bullets ricocheted off the fenders and hood. He charged around the corner as she warned him to get on the ground.

He turned and fired in reply. She repeated herself and tried taking aim while dodging bullets. The one at the window was also firing two guns at once, she finally decided, or Stewart got the number of shooters wrong.

One shot hit close enough she ducked and curled beside the wheel. She cursed between short, panting breaths. The shot came within inches of her head.

Sirens whined in the distance. Where had everyone been? Or had mere seconds passed since Graham wimped out and left her dangling alone?

The running suspect rounded the side of the house. He fired at her again. This time she fired back twice. One gun dropped from his hand and he grabbed his side.

"Get on the ground now!" she yelled.

He raised the other gun. Savannah fired three times. He dropped to all fours. She took a deep breath, braced herself and ran.

The suspect in the house fired repeatedly. She just kept running until safely blocked by the corner of the house. She kicked both suspect's guns away and cuffed him. A sound caught her attention. It came from around the corner. Footsteps.

"Sergeant, he's coming your way!" Mandy warned.

She cautiously glanced around the corner. He lifted the gun and fired. Bullet struck brick. Her heart practically leaped out of her mouth. The close call terrified and angered her. "You miserable son of a bitch, get on the ground!" she shouted between short precious breaths. "Get on the ground now!"

"His gun's pointed right at you. Be careful."

Savannah ducked lower, quickly peeked around again. The man, white and in his mid-twenties decided shooting Stewart was a better idea. He raised his 9mm at the wounded officer. Savannah fired three times. He went down in the grass mere feet from Mandy.

In many ways TV did no service to the truth about law enforcement. It led the public to believe cops were trigger happy and that one shot caused a person to instantly crumple when they were hit. She heard people say more than two shots was overkill. They didn't understand how adrenaline or drugs could affect a person. She'd heard of a cop and a murder suspect in a shootout because the suspect, though hit several times, stood there like the cop missed every shot. The suspect jumped in a car and drove half a mile down the road before succumbing to the wound. So no, in some instances one shot did not disable a hyped-up criminal and Savannah wanted to make damn sure this guy wasn't taking out another cop that day.

Two cruisers came to screeching halts in the street. Officers scattered in different directions, to the house, to the suspects and to the three cops in the front yard while Savannah raced to him and cuffed him. "Thanks for the warning," she told Stewart.

As she approached Thomas, she updated the uniforms that *finally* arrived and radioed in that two suspects were in custody. The sight of a fellow cop lying dead tested her stomach. Blood, tissue and bone littered the lawn. The right side of Marquis's face was gone. No handgun caused that, she thought. That's a shotgun blast. Savannah's knees went weak. What if they'd taken aim on her and pulled the trigger at just the right time? She and Marquis Thomas would both take a ride to the morgue. Suddenly she felt dizzy. Lord, she really needed to sit down.

Mandy strained to turn on her side. Savannah stopped her. No cop needed to see their partner mutilated. "He's dead, isn't he?" Mandy asked.

Savannah heard her choke up. She solemnly nodded, at a loss to say anything past *I'm sorry.*

She positioned herself between Mandy and Marquis to apply pressure to Mandy's wound.

A lieutenant approached Mandy and Savannah. Both gave their accounts of what happened. He surveyed the scene, amazed at what he saw, "Damn, Sergeant, we're nothing but a clean-up crew. Good work. Where's your partner?"

It embarrassed her to admit, "I don't know, sir. I'm a substitute training officer today and I guess I lost my rookie."

"His name?"

"Rodney Graham." She realized she'd grown so weak that she had to lock her knees to remain upright and a noticeable tremble developed in both hands that she concealed by holding on to her duty belt. All the blood went to her feet, it seemed, and between that and the gruesome memory of Marquis's face forced her to brace against a nearby elm tree before she collapsed.

"Lieutenant, she didn't lose him," Stewart volunteered. "He left her all alone. She kept asking him to help but he never did." She pointed a bloodied hand toward the brick wall, "He hid behind that wall the whole time."

O   O   O

They found Graham a block away sitting on a curb with a thousand-yard stare. Josh Hunter and Major Mike Hoffman arrived at the scene after officers cleared the house. The captain and major escorted Savannah to a cruiser to rest until an ambulance arrived for her. Protocol demanded she be evaluated and monitored for physical or emotional reactions that might require medical attention. At the same time, the staff would test for drugs and alcohol in her system to counter a defendant's attorney claiming impaired judgment on her part. The whole thing was routine but a complete pain to go through when she just wanted to go home.

Savannah felt exhausted and numb. She watched the crime scene techs count bullets, collect brass and take photographs, including one of her in her uniform to ensure she was immediately identifiable as a cop, a security measure against a defense lawyer accusing otherwise. During that time, Savannah overheard officers talking about the first suspect she'd shot. Paramedics who loaded him in the bus gave little hope of his survival. Savannah prayed he proved them wrong. With her life lately she'd hate to deal with killing a person too. Plus Internal Affairs, plus the grand jury, plus other cops' Monday morning quarterbacking regarding her actions.

She had no choice. With Stewart in harm's way and the two suspects throwing shots right and left at Savannah, it made her wonder how many guns they actually had. Those two weren't aiming to maim and neither was she.

Yes, she could have waited for backup but Stewart might have died alongside her parter. Savannah couldn't take that chance. If Stewart died due to Savannah's hesitation, well, she wasn't much of a cop, was she?

No, she did not regret her actions. She regretted being put in that position by a rookie cop who rabbited when the job got tough. For a know-it-all, he perfected the art of running away from danger, not the other way around.

Yes, she would regret the suspect dying (if he did) but he and his partners were criminals, and had shot two cops already and tried very hard to add a third and fourth to their tally.

If either suspect died, her life and her family's lives would change in a hundred different ways, none of them good. Not just trying to cope with killing another human being but the hellacious media scrutiny and public backlash. Most would happen anyway to some degree, but lately nothing set off public rage like a 'trigger-happy cop', a name given to officers doing their jobs.

Savannah leaned back and sighed. She'd already relinquished her body cam and duty weapon to Major Hoffman as per departmental rules. Zone commanders reviewed use-of-force incidents. She only prayed he saw the truth. She was alone and acted in defense of a fellow cop.

Stewart had already arrived at the hospital. The talk among the officers sounded optimistic. In that short span of time, Savannah had been assigned a union-appointed lawyer for her upcoming interview with

Internal Affairs and been informed by that lawyer to keep her mouth shut until she got there.

Josh asked if she wanted a companion officer just in case the suspect died. Her "companion" officer arrived a few minutes before Savannah's mandatory ambulance ride to the hospital.

Ennis rushed to the cruiser in a panic, "Are you okay? Why aren't you at the hospital being checked? Where the hell is Graham?"

She noticed Major Hoffman standing nearby. He gave them a moment while she explained, "One, yes, I'm shaken up pretty good. Two, that's my ride behind you and three, the rookie beat feet on me. The body cam footage will show that." At least, she thought, Graham won't be babysat by a sergeant anymore. He can spend his time finding another job.

Ennis's jaw clenched. His eyes narrowed, "That son of a bitch. When I get my hands on him—"

She put a shaking hand to his to shut him up. Hoffman moved closer. She cut her vision over her husband's shoulder, "I suspect Graham's days in this department are over, Ennis, so settle down."

"Why didn't you wait for backup?"

"Because Mandy Stewart was already injured and a sitting duck for those assholes. I couldn't live with myself if she died because I waited."

"Sergeant," Hoffman said. Ennis moved aside for him. The major proceeded, "Sorry to interrupt but your lawyer just arrived."

She thanked him. He replied, "From what Officer Stewart told me, you deserve a commendation. If the body cam footage confirms her statement, I'll make sure you get one."

o   o   o

By the time the hospital released her and she finished her interview with IA, both suspects still remained in surgery. After so many hours Savannah naturally assumed things looked dim for their future and hers. Ennis confirmed the first suspect, Chris Devers, hung on by a thread. The doctor offered more hope for the second suspect. She considered that a small silver lining. Ennis also forewarned her that the media not only aired the shootings but also a citizen's cell phone recording of the incident. He watched it on TV with their colleagues and said the shaky video was taken from several houses away. No one could identify faces but footage showed a male figure in uniform running from the scene, he said. The red banner beneath the video read "Coward Cop". The news ran a second portion of the video where numerous gunshots rang out with the female officer shouting *get on the ground* followed by more gunshots. Ennis didn't tell her what the banner read on that portion. Later she overheard two officers discussing the cell phone footage. One of them mentioned the title *Hero Cop or Overkill?*

Savannah pursed her lips. *So it's already started. They don't have anything but a shaky cell phone video from half a block away and they're already baiting the public against me.*

The atmosphere at the station however, held the complete opposite opinion of the news media. Savannah exited the IA interview to kudos from her colleagues. It was rumored that Major Hoffman already reviewed hers and Graham's body cam footage and had started preliminary paperwork for her commendation. At least she stood among friends – including Sergeant Sweeney who offered his support. She nearly fainted from shock. Despite the hoopla, all she truly wanted was a hot bath and to be with her family.

The moment she and Ennis stepped in the house, the girls greeted her with their bounding joy and enthusiasm while telling her about their day. Her eyes grew misty as she listened and wrapped both in a tight hug. She wanted to hold her babies in her arms and hug them and never let go. How close she came to never seeing these angels again, she thought. If she'd been hit by one or two of those shots, she'd have been in the morgue, not hugging her children, holding her baby boy or kissing her husband. In a fleeting instant of depleted adrenaline, complete exhaustion and emotional turmoil, she considered Morgan's offer, noting how sweeter it sounded by the second. Oh, how she wished she could accept that offer, especially after his "recalculated" salary combined with the luxury of rarely being shot at and always coming home to her sweetheart and three little darlings.

Before she lost her marbles and did something stupid like accept that job, she'd fortify herself to calm her shakes. Since the last pull of the trigger, the flashbacks began in horrific living color. Images of Marquis Thomas haunted her. Half his face. Gone. Just… gone. Mandy Stewart lying in the grass slowly bleeding out. She remembered every shot, every pounding heartbeat, every bead of sweat as she tried to save Stewart without dying herself.

It chilled her to recall Chris Devers's freakishly accurate aim as he ran for freedom. The metal report of bullets striking the patrol car. The sound of that one, single shot coming so close to her head that her heart pounded for minutes every time she relived it which she did quite often.

Her hand trembled as she tilted the Jack into a glass. The clinking of glass against glass forced her to hold the bottle with both hands. What if Chris Devers died? She'd never killed anyone before. How did a person cope with taking a life? According to her husband and colleagues, she'd saved Mandy Stewart's life and probably a few neighbors. As logical as it sounded, the same concerns cropped up in her mind. Number one – Thou shalt not kill. If Devers died, she'd broken one of the ten biggies in the Bible. How did God view that, she wondered? Did he give passes on killing someone if they protected others in the process? And if so, great, so now how do I live with myself and my actions, she asked. It was a burden she prayed she never carried.

I can help with your worries. I always have, Uncle Jack encouraged. *Pour a little more, friend. You need it.* She did.

"Hanging by a thread," Ennis had told her about Chris Devers. Kind of like her future if a grand jury chose Door Number Two – "Overkill" instead of "Hero Cop". Uncle Jack seemed to tip an invisible finger beneath the bottle and poured a shade more into the glass. *There you go, friend. Leave it to me.*

She ached to do just that but Ennis apparently disagreed. He busied himself ordering pizza for supper and but kept a keen eye on her drinking. She'd stop once the shakes subsided and the shock wore off and not a second sooner. Savannah tossed back the drink then fixed a bottle for Daniel who'd made his needs loud and clear. She tried changing his diaper and found herself wringing her hands to minimize the shaking long enough to finish the task. The diapering itself turned into a little nightmare of its own when the tabs refused to cooperate but she managed. And Daniel was such a patient child with her, bless his heart. It was as if he felt her stress. He even gifted her with a smile. She silently wept at his sweet gesture and thanked him while giving him a kiss.

Her cell phone rang during supper. Since her appetite abandoned ship it wasn't much of an interruption until she discovered who called. The Caller ID read Lee Morgan. This deserved another drink so she indulged in another swallow. Ennis's brow plunged.

"I heard what happened this afternoon and saw the news," Morgan said then asked if she was okay.

Forget the fact he sounded concerned. He knew she was the cop involved in the shooting and how did that happen? It was obvious to her that, "The media already has my name?"

"No, I know someone in the department. He told me. How are you?" he asked again.

"Managing is the best I can say," she dared another sip.

"What were you doing in uniform and why were you alone?"

"I was filling in for a patrol sergeant as field training officer, evaluating a rookie's progress." And lack thereof. "He discovered police work wasn't his calling and I discovered I could handle a tough situation alone." *And why am I telling him this? It's none of his business.*

Lee's frustration mounted, "This would never have happened if you were my chief security officer. The job is yours, Savannah, please just accept it."

"Mr. Morgan, I've already declined, plus I'm in no shape to discuss that job right now. I've still got follow-up interviews and possibly a grand jury to face."

"No, no, no, of course you're too busy right now but I was hoping you weren't too busy to meet for dinner later this week. I'd love to see you and meet your husband."

She reached for the Jack but decided against it when Ennis glared daggers at it. "Can we talk about this later? Ennis and I are still pretty rattled over today."

"Sure. I'll be checking on you from time to time. Take care and if you need anything, let me know."

I'd rather be tarred and feathered but to shut you up, "Will do."

She hung up. Ennis kept glaring. His disdain pricked her temper, "Is there a problem with my indulgence after what I've been through?"

He backed down but not too far, "I don't like it but I'd hoped you'd stop at one."

"After today we're lucky I don't drink half the bottle." She sighed with the realization any more Jack might inspire a hangover. The last thing she needed was the world seeing that.

Savannah pushed the bottle away to Ennis's relief. He offered her a heartfelt thank you.

"Anything for you, cowboy. By the way, as if our lives weren't complicated enough, Morgan just invited us to dinner this week."

He stared at her, unblinking. Then *he* reached for the Jack.

16

True to his word, Morgan called at least twice every day. He took the opportunity to nudge her about his dinner plans and upped the ante by expressing his desire to celebrate her heroic act with reservations at Canoe, an upscale restaurant tucked away on the banks of the Chattahoochee River. It was one of the country's most acclaimed restaurants and just so happened to be tops on Savannah's Bucket List. She'd dreamed of spending an evening basking in the rustic yet elegant atmosphere with the peaceful waterfront and beautiful green landscape right outside the window then taking a stroll through the carefully manicured gardens.

She planned for that evening to be spent with Ennis, not her pushy "pretend" father who insisted on invading their lives.

The day after the commendation ceremony (Lee attended that too, much to her aggravation and the family's disapproval), he called to tell her he made reservations at Canoe that evening. "Who doesn't enjoy dining there?" he asked. "And Ethan's asked to come along. He's anxious to meet Ennis as well."

She tried worming her way out of it but he checkmated every excuse. Finally she sighed and capitulated to shut him up and honestly he was right – who didn't enjoy dining at Canoe?

The dinner had gone well. No pressure and all easy conversation. She and Ennis received plenty of stares since they dined with Lee and Ethan Morgan. Either that or because they recognized her from the news. Thanks to the media, the public received plenty of chances to memorize her name and face. Since the shootings, she suffered a few vocal haters but that evening in her Bucket List posh restaurant with the Morgans, the patrons looked, recognized and returned to their meals.

As much as she appreciated Lee's attempt to celebrate her commendation, three things kept preying on her mind. One, the wounded suspect, Chris Devers, continued limping along on the critical list, two, she continually worried about public opinion regarding her actions and tried to be cautious when going outside, and three, the fact she hung out with a guy that kept introducing her as not only a hero police officer but his daughter too.

Savannah cringed each time he spoke to someone. She felt traitorous for not speaking up on R.J.'s behalf. *He* was her father. She couldn't exactly prove the DNA but he was her daddy, not Lee Morgan. She spent her childhood with a carpenter who owned a struggling construction company. He took his anger and frustration out on his kids but he also protected them with such ferocity it terrified anyone who messed with them. *That* was her life. Not being spoon-fed and pampered by the help and never seeing "Daddy" because he was off in London or Paris gobbling up the little guy's businesses or wheeling and dealing his way to another fifty million dollars.

Savannah awoke only a few times that night. When she did, her mind replayed one scene from dinner over and over. Lee grinning from ear to ear, placing a hand to her shoulder and telling anyone within earshot, "*This is my daughter Savannah…*"

O O O

The good news came three days after her award ceremony. The hospital upgraded Chris Devers from critical to serious. He'd spent most of the time in critical condition, long enough that she and her lawyer began preparing for the grand jury and a possible jury trial. But the promotion to serious encouraged her to the point she could breathe again. Savannah did more than breathe. After shift she headed to the bar for a few celebratory drinks.

She ended up having three nice, celebratory shots of Uncle Jack all courtesy of patrons who recognized her from the news.

Falling back into old habits wasn't so bad, Savannah thought. Except today, she always went home after shift, fed her brood and spent priceless time with them. She deserved a day for herself, and enjoyed every free drink she consumed and made sure to stay this side of legal in case some rookie pulled her over on the way home.

There was still time to get home and fix supper. She stepped out to thick humidity and a soft lilac and deep purple sky. She'd stayed later than she intended. Old habits, she snorted. Back then she was single and no kids. Now her family probably wondered where the hell she was and knowing Ennis, he'd ordered a pizza for them. He was a dear, priceless blessing.

Keys in hand and purse under her arm, she strolled toward the

Charger, still considering a quick call home to check in.

"Ma'am, could you help me please?"

Savannah turned. A petite woman with long blond hair and friendly face pointed to a couple of cars near the alley, "Do you know anything about changing a tire? I need to get back to the dorm but I've never changed a tire in my life."

"Sure. The silver Hyundai?"

The young woman nodded, "Yes, ma'am. Thank you so much. It's getting late and I hate being out at night."

Savannah went to the back of the car. No wonder the woman felt uneasy. She'd parked in the shadows between street lamps and the alley. Since it wasn't pitch black yet, it didn't bother Savannah. She'd been out in darker, uglier conditions – and in a worse part of town. "Pop the trunk, I'll get the jack," she told the girl.

Something solid pressed against Savannah's right shoulder blade. One, two, three then four men dressed in combat gear and masks converged on her. Each one held an AR-15 aimed straight her. They hadn't ambushed her. They flat-out sneaked up on her. She hadn't heard a sound, not their boots on the pavement, not a breath or a whisper. The one pressing the muzzle into her shoulder urge her forward, "Hands on the trunk and spread your legs. Take it easy, Princess, no sudden moves and you'll be just fine."

A gloved hand stripped her purse away. It retrieved her car keys, stuffed them in her clutch and tossed it to another armed man standing nearby. Everything moved with synchronized timing and perfection. Their posture and mannerisms... These were not average thugs with guns. Military – or ex-military, she told herself while staring down three assault rifles surrounding her. But why target her? And there was no question about it. She had been targeted.

The gunman's voice held an unspoken threat as he repeated his command and reinforced it with a nudge from the AR-15.

Since she knew the damage Seth could inflict being an ex-Army Ranger and knew she was far outnumbered by people, strength and training, she placed her hands on the trunk and shifted her feet apart. The one that took her purse searched her. He removed her phone then her snubnose, holster and all. Went through her pockets. Then she heard chains rattling behind her.

Savannah snapped around – Uncle Jack bolstered her courage enough to fight and shout for help. The leader grabbed her cocked wrist and twisted it behind her back. Before she could protest, another one lifted her pant leg and fastened what resembled a parolee's ankle bracelet on her. The guy who led this four man team – Savannah named him "Alpha Male" – promised her, "You try to scream again, that'll put you in your place. Now flat against the trunk." Leather-clad fingers wrapped around the back of her neck, clamped down and shoved her over the trunk until her cheek crashed against metal. An authoritative hardness crept into his voice (much like Seth when he got perturbed or angry), "I said relax and you won't get hurt."

"I'm a police officer–"

"I know what you are, Princess," he cut her short. "Now *shut up.*"

A waist chain fastened over her hips. Leg irons snapped on each ankle. Alpha Male fisted the back of her blouse and turned her to face him. She was immediately met with a barrel to her throat, "Just let it happen."

His buddy locked her wrists into the handcuffs connected to the waist chain.

Everything went black when a cloth hood slipped over her head. For her it might as well have been a plastic bag. Since childhood she suffered claustrophobia and now in an alley, bound and blinded and surrounded with armed men determined to... to do whatever they were going to do, the world closed around her like walls squeezing down on her. She couldn't see and could barely hear through her raging heartbeat. Panic set in. The fight or flight instinct kicked in. She thrashed against her captors, gasping for precious air through shriveling lungs. She bent over, trying to reach the hood with her bound hands in hopes of tearing the hood free. It took Alpha Male and another attacker to subdue her. Even then she struggled against their hold, "I can't breathe. I need air."

Alpha Male steadied her, "Relax and this will go easier for you. Come on, Princess. Let's go." His hand clamped around her arm, jerking her into an awkward, stumbling gait. *The alley. We're going down the alley.* She told herself to map their movement as best as possible for when (or if) she lived through this.

Small specks of light danced in front of her eyes. Her legs felt weak, perspiration moistened her skin and clothes. He yanked her along. Despite the ankle cuffs shortening her stride and hood restricting her air, Savannah kept pace, "I can't breathe and I can't walk. Don't expect me to run a race."

A car door opened. "Step up," he told her but mostly helped her inside himself. Someone belted her in. The car – or SUV, she suspected – rocked as others climbed in. Two sandwiched her in on both sides then the driver door closed followed by the passenger door.

"What do you want from me?" she asked between small, strained breaths. "I don't have money, I–"

A shock fired through every nerve in her leg and painfully contracted the muscles, pulling and drawing her ankle toward her thigh. She squirmed in the seat to combat the feeling of her bones vibrating. The Stun-Cuff on her ankle, a wireless device, delivered fifty thousand volts and could be delivered continually until the prisoner acquiesced, which she did whether she liked it or not.

"I want you to be quiet," Alpha Male replied calmly. "Think you can do that now?"

Son of a bitch. She heard the smile in his voice. If she hadn't been in the throes of panic made worse by that massive, unexpected shock, she'd have scorched him with expletives. Right now though, her efforts focused on trying to breathe. Making matters worse, she'd lost track of their approximate location as they drove. She was good and lost with no hope of orienting herself.

They took winding turns down side streets, entered the freeway and traveled. They'd left downtown but still remained in the city judging by the amount of passing traffic. Alpha Male kept driving until the sounds of the city disappeared. Then he stopped.

Two men helped her step down out of the SUV. Alpha Male leaned close, advising, "You might as well calm down. It'll be a lengthy wait."

"Wait for what?" She pulled at air that seemed to too thick and heavy to cooperate. "And can you take off this hood?"

"Get her inside and take it off."

The two men escorted her into a building. The door shutting behind them had a cavernous echo when it closed. She tried concentrating. A large building. A warehouse maybe?

Savannah barely kept up with their strides. The hood restricted her breathing and when she took a breath she sucked the hood in her mouth and nearly choked. Her face and hair were damp with sweat, her clothes stuck to her skin and she fought off a sudden chill from the cool room. During that trip to God-Knew-Where, she'd about lost her mind. The drinks she'd had soured her stomach. At the time, it seemed like a good idea because her life straightened out for a change. No dead suspects, jury trials, or outward public hate. Offers of free drinks rarely happened anyway so when those grateful citizens recognized her with thanks and drinks, she couldn't resist.

Now she wished she'd gone home. But if she had, Alpha Male and his cronies might have grabbed her there and threatened Ennis and the kids – or worse.

"Sit," another voice told her then pushed her into a metal chair. The hood came off. The masked figure laughed at her "whining" about being unable to breathe then uttered a lewd remark regarding her sweat covered features and flushed complexion.

After wearing the stifling hood, not to mention being abducted in the first place, he remarked, "I know a way to test your lung capacity, sweetheart," he accentuated his comments with a crotch hike then reached down to grab her arm. "Let's go see if you lose your breath then too."

Savannah put her anger to work by slamming both feet into his right knee.

He went down with a shout. Before giving him time to think or exact payback, she launched herself at him, leaving him fighting a crazy woman on top of him and cursing with female epithets usually reserved for porn flicks. He stopped cursing though, once she wrapped the leg chain around his throat.

"Thanks but I'll pass. I'm enjoying this more." She pulled and twisted her feet and legs, tightening the chain around his neck. "How's that lung capacity going for you, asshole?"

A handful of men laughed. Some cheered and rooted her on. No one tried to help him.

He choked and gagged as his fight soon escalated to frantic scrambling for oxygen. She clawed at his mask to see the bastard's face. It revealed a glimpse of his face before he yanked it down. Caucasian, mid-thirties, military cut dark hair, mustache. He had a jagged scar across his right cheek. If she lived through this, she would definitely remember that face.

The guy groped for a hold on the chain, flailed his arms to knock her loose but she held firm. He scrabbled for an item that fell from his pocket. The transmitter to the Stun-Cuff. She clenched her teeth, closed her eyes and bore down harder. Because of her bound hands, she stood a better chance of running a race than grabbing the transmitter so she used the only weapon she could – the chain binding her ankles.

A lightning bolt seized her with pain. The guy thumbed the button and refused to let up after she released her hold. She rolled and writhed as the shock continued. Her leg drew up tight until the muscles felt close to snapping.

The current finally stopped. She lay groaning as Alpha Male chewed Lightning Bolt out, "What the hell are you doing? You can't kill her."

"Why not? She tried to kill *me*," the man defended between short, desperate gasps and repeated rasping coughs.

Alpha snatched the transmitter from him then hoisted Savannah to her feet. Her legs wobbled like a newborn foal. Her right one buckled. The muscles fisted in her calf. Alpha steadied her and when she straightened, a battering ram unexpectedly buried itself in her gut, doubling her up in Alpha Male's hold. He easily bore the brunt of her weight while easing her back into the metal chair. He turned his ire on Lightning Bolt who stood, meagerly satisfied at his retribution.

Coldness crept into Alpha's voice, "Riggs, touch her again and you're dead. Got it?"

Savannah struggled for breath that didn't come. He'd practically knocked the wind from her. Nothing worked right, especially her stomach that felt as though the punch ejected it out her back.

She closed her eyes and drew a shallow breath and released a careful, shaky exhalation to prevent herself from puking.

"Savannah," a familiar voice summoned. "Are you alright?"

She cringed. What, exactly, about the last hour or so said she might be alright? Nothing was alright about anything, particularly after having had the shit shocked out of her and being hit by a freight train. She scanned the room, passing across several armed gunmen stood stationed around the room until her tear-blurred sight finally settled on the man who'd called her name.

Ethan sat about twelve feet to her right. He was restrained the same way and also wore a Stun-Cuff. A gunman stood behind him with an assault rifle. Ethan looked as scared as she felt the whole trip there. "Try to calm down," he told her. He glanced toward one of the captors, "What did you do to her? Do you realize she's a police officer? If anything happens to her–" he stiffened as if someone threw the switch on the Stun-Cuff.

"So you're our sister," another voice said. This one had the outright venom of Preston Morgan but also a heavy load of contemptuous sarcasm.

Like Ethan, Tucker sat restrained with his own ankle zapper and armed captor behind him. He scoffed, "The prodigal daughter returns after all these years. I finally come face to face with her just before I die. Perfect."

"Tucker, shut up," Ethan whimpered while trying to wear off the pain.

"I'm not your sister," she assured, too tired to get fanatical with a wordsmith who chose to use his talent to slice his family to ribbons. "I don't know why the hell I'm here or why this guy," she nodded to Alpha Male, "keeps calling me Princess." Something at the back of her head – the barrel of an assault rifle she assumed – nudged her. Thankfully it wasn't the creep who tried to kill her but this one possessed a don't-screw-with-me inflection when he told her to shut up. Fine, she thought. *I'm still trying to gather my marbles from that monster claustrophobia and that bastard's attack anyway.*

Meanwhile Alpha stared back at her. Another captor approached with her purse, mumbled something to him. Alpha reached in and withdrew the box containing her commendation. He opened it, tilted it toward the light to see it better then closed it and put it back.

Ethan saw the medal, "You know, Dad really wanted to come to the ceremony."

"He was there," she said. This got Alpha's attention for some reason. "I wish he hadn't because it put my family on edge the whole evening."

"Dad's your family too, Savannah."

That old saw got mighty old quick. She sighed, "No, Ethan, he's not. I'd only seen him a handful of times until a couple of weeks ago. If he was my father, he'd have told me and kept in touch more." She focused on the captor gutting her purse. Alpha Male removed her bottle of nitroglycerin pills. "Got a bum heart, Princess? We need you all alive, *especially* you," he pointed to her, "so don't go dying on us." He put it back and closed the clutch.

"Then keep Riggs away from me," she replied.

Alpha tsked and wagged a finger at her, "I'll take care of him. Your job is to be quiet and stay breathing."

"What's so special about her?" Tucker demanded to know. "She's the bastard of the family. Being a cop she can't even pay a ransom to save herself." Then he shifted into business mode, "Now I can pay you whatever you want if you'll let me go right now. How about five hundred thou–" Tucker yelped and writhed against the Stun-Cuff's current. He went limp and silent in the chair. The captor's message had been received.

"I don't care how much money you offer. If you don't keep quiet, I'll kill you. You're screwing with my payday, asshole. That bastard is worth ten times what you are."

Ethan chuckled, "Poor Tucker. He's been marked down."

Savannah busied herself trying to make sense of what she just heard. Worth ten times more? A figure of speech maybe but the guy made his point. She was the target along with Ethan. Apparently Tucker's ransom was just gravy.

"I have the resources to track you all down," Tucker threatened. "I'll find out who you are and–"

Shots echoed through the cavernous room. Savannah shied from the loud noise as Alpha fired several shots above Tucker's head. "I know where the next shots are going if you don't shut that hole of yours," the gunman threatened.

Savannah swallowed but her mouth had gone dry. At this rate Tucker would get them killed with his big mouth.

She looked past the armed men to where she was being held. She, Ethan and Tucker sat in a primarily empty warehouse. Cardboard boxes sparsely lined metal shelves at the far end and along one wall half a dozen larger, heavier cardboard boxes sat on pallets.

She centered on a sign at the far end of the room but it was too far away to read. Alpha stepped in her line of sight. Her gaze lifted to meet a pair of dark eyes staring back through the mask. "You're too inquisitive," he told her. "If you haven't noticed, you're not a cop right now. You're my meal ticket. Keep your head down, eyes closed and be quiet."

"Savannah," Ethan added softly, "let's just try to survive this."

Alpha smiled, "Your brother's smartening up, Princess. Take a lesson from him."

o   o   o

Georgia piled into her recliner with her mother's journal. Beside her in his own recliner, Dane shook his head as he switched on a football game, "You're gonna dog this until you find more dark, ugly secrets, you know. There's a reason they call 'em diaries. They're private. Leave it alone, darlin'. They're causing too much pain."

Yes, they were. But she wondered why their mother kept all the journals and stored them. Had she left them for the sake of family history or had she foreseen Lee Morgan contacting Savannah at some point and wanted the truth to be known? Lee wouldn't dare admit to rape, not even today, no man in his position would. Were Charlene's journals her last effort to set the story straight despite the pain it would undoubtedly cause?

Georgia began reading the entry about the time Charlene took her two daughters to the Morgan mansion. Christmas fast approached and the Morgans decorated on a scale comparable to Biltmore, transforming the estate's interior and exterior into a child's magical fantasy come true. Thousands of lights framed the mansion, draped from trees and hung like illuminated garland from the iron fence surrounding the property.

The interior decorations put the exterior ones to shame. An elegantly decorated Christmas tree occupied every room, each with its own color theme and motif. Miles of lighted garland draped stairway banisters and railings. To a child it was an awesome sight, Georgia recalled, like walking into Santa's private residence with the jolly fat man's butler giving her and Savannah a private tour of the enormous home.

Young, impressionable Savannah had taken the tour in wide-eyed wonder. Lee took over the tour at one point, taking the girls upstairs to see, in particular, one bedroom decorated in a beautiful pink and white theme. The huge room (huge to Georgia) had light pink walls, and white furniture including a queen size bed covered in a baby pink comforter. A room fit for a princess. At the time Georgia found it odd since Lee only had sons. He invited Savannah and Georgia, he added as an afterthought for visits anytime. He promised Mrs. Gardner's best desserts and the girls' favorite meals. Charlene balked at the idea. Georgia had seen a look pass between her mother and Lee that sent a little shiver down her back. He called the shots so shut up, his expression said.

Savannah wasn't as comfortable with Lee as she was the butler. She shied back to Charlene when Lee reached for her hand and offered to show her the room. He charmed and coaxed until she reluctantly took his hand. By the time the visit concluded – Charlene kept checking her watch – Savannah felt more at ease with Lee. Taking in the wondrous Christmas palace one last time, she asked if they could live there.

Georgia's hand fisted. She noticed Dane glanced at it from the corner of his eye. She was furious, "Oh, he's such a skank."

"Tell me something I don't know. Why don't you settle down and tell me what that outburst is about?"

She did, adding, "He had that house looking like Santa might pop out from the butler's quarters any moment. And that little girl's bedroom… That's creepy, especially for a man who never had a daughter. He set Savannah up to *want* to live there. And she did."

Dane's frustration surfaced, "You're more levelheaded than this, darlin'. Think about it. We don't know if his wife got pregnant with a girl and miscarried or if they had a girl and she died. Decorating a room for a girl he's never gonna raise doesn't make sense. Second, put those infernal books away. It's dredging up too much. Your mother didn't leave them behind for you or Savannah to suffer. I don't know why she did it but I sure wish she hadn't."

"I'm okay. I know you're worried about me and the baby."

"Yeah. Me and everyone else."

"I'll read another page or two and put it aside. Deal?"

He blew out a breath and a half-hearted okay. Dane wasn't stupid. He realized she'd plow through the book no matter what.

She began reading. *It's three weeks until Christmas. R.J.'s business is losing money. The materials aren't arriving at their destination in some cases and in others only half of what he's ordered is delivered. He wanted to change shipping companies but Lee won't release* him from his contract. No, Lee is punishing me for refusing to bring Savannah to see him and punishing R.J. for his temper which, I have to admit, is out of control. He's drinking more and when he comes home he's angry and violent because of Lee. Problem is he takes his anger out on Savannah. I try to protect her and try to talk R.J. out of his rage but nothing works. He's whipped Seth and Georgia for supposed disobedience but I worry most about Savannah. She's difficult anyway but he nitpicks everything she does or doesn't do, even simply talking at the table during meals so now she goes outside for hours after eating. She won't come inside until he goes to bed. Yesterday he gave her a whipping that left a few bloody marks for not washing her supper dishes. I tried to stop him. He pushed me away and I fell and hurt my arm. I've asked Seth and Georgia to look after her, to take her to her room – just anywhere he can't find her. And now Lee called today with his own threat. If I don't bring Savannah to see him, he said, Prince Construction will go under. Our lives depend on that business and with the shipments already affecting our income, I have no choice. I'll be taking Savannah over tomorrow but I'll have Georgia too so she'll feel more comfortable. I regret having to do it but it's either that or our family goes hungry and R.J. will not only hold Lee Morgan responsible but Savannah too. Neither Lee nor R.J. will get a paternity test. I can't prove who Savannah's father is but in my heart I know it's R.J. because she looks like him and, to a degree, acts like him. I just pray my baby girl doesn't suffer her whole life for what Lee did to me.

O O O

Savannah's backside went numb hours ago. Even the few bathroom trips they allowed never eased the soreness from sitting in the metal folding chairs or the tension in her back. Soreness and tension rated low on her scale of worries though. It was past time for her heart medicine but it was at home. The only thing in her purse was nitroglycerin. Since her heart attack she'd never skipped a dose of her meds. Today would be a first. She wondered what the kidnappers would do if she needed medical attention. They said they wanted her alive but did they mean it?

She checked her watch. Twelve hours passed. She figured Ennis long since called hospitals, neighboring police departments, the Georgia State Patrol, just anyone that might have seen her or her car. Last night he'd probably back-tracked her movements to the bar and questioned the bartender. Ennis would never give up searching for her.

"How much longer are you holding us here?" she asked Alpha.

"There's been a snag."

Snag or not, "I'm late with my heart medication."

He signaled another man. "Get the word out. Princess needs her heart meds pronto. Maybe that will get their attention."

She rolled her eyes. These people never listened. "If you're expecting the Morgans to pay a ransom for me, you've made a mistake. I'm not a Morgan."

"That's not what we've heard," he replied. "Might as well relax. Obviously, it's gonna be a while."

O O O

"Nothing? They've heard nothing about her?" Georgia panicked.

Ennis jerked the phone from his ear. Good Lord, Savannah's sister could raise the dead when she shouted.

"The only accounts are witnesses who place her at Garrison's Bar around six last night. Apparently customers were buying her drinks because they recognized her from the news. After that, she disappeared. Only her car was left behind." Ennis juggled two kids and an infant all night trying to keep them content while calling around for Savannah. No one had seen her after six forty-five.

He fed Daniel while talking to Georgia on speakerphone. Their baby seemed to sense something amiss and had been fussy all night. Morning wasn't shaping up to be any better.

That morning when Ennis opened the medicine cabinet for an aspirin, his vision centered on Savannah's heart meds. Her morning dose was five hours late.

Cloth over his shoulder, Ennis cradled Daniel to burp him. The baby came through with a whopper pretty quick. Ennis glanced from him to the TV. A "Breaking News" banner filled the screen. Three pictures filled the screen. Ethan and Tucker Morgan and one of Savannah. "Georgia, Channel 2 now." Ennis reached for the remote and turned up the volume.

The newscaster began reading from a page in her hand, "Earlier this morning, Channel 2 received a call from a person claiming to have kidnapped Tucker and Ethan Morgan, two of Lee Morgan's sons and Detective Sergeant Savannah Prince with the Atlanta Police. According to the caller, he contacted Lee Morgan's residence but said he was "getting the runaround" with the staff. The caller told Channel 2 that Sergeant Prince requires vital medication and wanted Lee Morgan to understand the "dire consequences of ignoring" his calls. When Channel 2 contacted the Morgan residence, we were told Lee Morgan is out of town at this time."

"Ennis," Georgia verged on tears, "what if she's having heart trouble? How do we get in touch with Lee? He needs to understand she's not in good health."

"I'll call him." When he tried contacting Lee, he suffered the same infuriating "runaround" the abductor had. So he made one thing perfectly clear to the lackey screening Lee's calls. "If anything happens to my wife, I'm holding him responsible so you'd better pray she comes home safe and sound."

O   O   O

Alpha marched in the room and called to his men, "It's done. Time to get rid of 'em."

Ice water flooded her heart. *Get rid of 'em.* In this case the phrase meant one thing. She knew this because of Alpha's response to Tucker's assumption, "Finally, we're going home."

Alpha laughed, "Yeah, right. Just keep thinking that, rich man." He cut his vision to Savannah, "She knows what's happening, don't you, Princess? No one goes home once the ransom is paid."

Tucker and Ethan protested in unison, their words and pleas

mixing into a muddled mush that faded to the background. She had to do something but what?

All three were yanked to their feet. Her guard slipped the hood from his pants pocket and he closed in. If they intended to kill her, what difference did it make what she saw before her execution? She charged him as best she could. He fell on his backside with a sailor-worthy curse and scrambled to his feet. He reached in his other pocket. In his hand – the Stun-Cuff transmitter.

A shock sent her flat to the cold floor. Her right leg drew up, heel against her bottom as the muscles spasm gripped hard and tight. Her yelp died to whimpers as her body yielded to the debilitating pain. The guard took the opportunity to slip the hood over her head. When the shock ended, it completely drained her strength and her fight. Ethan's repeated frantic pleas begged her to answer if she was okay. She finally managed a pained, weak *yes*.

A hand around her arm jerked her to her feet and hustled her out. That was the last she saw or heard from Ethan or Tucker.

Despite the warm night, a cold wave washed through her. Sweat crept to the surface. Her heart went crazy in her chest. Was this a heart attack or a massive case of nerves and dread?

Two men bookended her, both solid as stone and judging by the pressure at her sides, armed with handguns as well. The SUV took off and soon entered the highway. Even if she could reach across, open the door and leap out, she'd die from a gunshot, the impact or being run over by traffic.

Her brain flipped through a Rolodex of memories mixed with

possible escape tactics which was more folly than anything considering the physical restraints and number of armed men. Then she wondered if she'd scheduled Daniel's next appointment with the pediatrician. She didn't think so. And what about the casserole in the freezer? Ennis wouldn't know what temperature to set the oven or how long to heat it… Savannah tried shaking clarity back to the forefront. Did everyone conjure such strange, trivial questions when they saw the end nearing? Ennis was perfectly capable of scheduling an appointment for the baby and between Georgia, Katherine, and a crew of cops' wives, her family would be handsomely fed and cared for. She thanked God for all three families – her own, her neighbors and the law enforcement.

She noticed an oddity: her claustrophobia temporarily took a backseat. She wasn't calm by any means but her panic revolved around the next minutes and\or hours. It felt different when you thought you were going to die compared to the hard finality of knowing it. The irony would have been hilarious if it weren't so grave. So many brushes with death over the years and one greedy SOB cashing in on his family's dirty dealings would be her demise. Until DNA proved otherwise, she believed she was R.J.'s daughter but these people determined to end her life because they simply did not believe her.

They drove long enough she had time to reminisce about her past and think about her present life with her little family. Lily and Anna would remember her. Daniel would not. He would grow up hearing stories of his mother, not asking for her advice or hearing her cheer at his football games or meeting the woman he intended to marry.

Tears mingled with sweat. There had to be a way out of this, right? Had she lived to forty-one just to die and be a memory to people who loved her? "I can't even identify you," she told the men with her, "so why not let me go?"

The men remained silent. "Come on," she lashed out, "I have a family. An infant to take care of—"

"We know that too, Princess. We're just following orders," Alpha said.

The car stopped. Doors opened. She drew another short, labored breath in the stifling hood, pulling for what little it might allow.

A helping hand assisted her out of the SUV. It was quiet around them. Far in the distance she heard the late night hustle and bustle of Atlanta's traffic.

The hand on her arm tugged her along. "Walk," the voice said.

More car doors slammed behind her. Savannah's steps transitioned from pavement to grass. Her lungs shrank. The air somehow disappeared. She started feeling lightheaded. This was it, she supposed. *The last few moments of my life are spent gasping for air before I'm executed and why? Because I've been mistaken for a Morgan.*

"Savannah? Are you here?" Ethan asked from behind her.

"I'm here. Is Tucker with us?"

"I'm behind you," Tucker answered. He sounded as scared as she felt. He'd spent a good deal of time bargaining with the captors, especially after one got trigger happy with the Stun-Cuff. He offered more money than Savannah earned in her career or ever would.

They walked until the hand on her shoulder prompted her to stop. "Kneel."

Before she could argue he forced her to her knees then face down on the ground. The grass was damp and cool against her hands, just enough to elicit a shiver. The earthy hay-like smell of grass reminded her more of summertime than fall. It was early November. A time to enjoy autumn leaves, prepare for Thanksgiving, count blessings and celebrate family. Not bury people you love. As Ethan and Tucker took their places beside her, she thought of her family and the tragic fact this Thanksgiving a casket and funeral would replace roasted turkey, dressing, joy and laughter.

My precious family, she thought with tears in her eyes. They'll never know what happened to me until they find me, *if* they find me.

The muzzle of the assault rifle seated at the base of her skull. It pressed hard enough she squeezed her eyes shut, praying death came swift. She swallowed hard, hearing the other two begging for their lives. She'd already tried and failed. All that was left was a bullet and walking toward light at the end of the tunnel.

17

The doorbell rang after ten o'clock that night. Ennis finally coaxed Daniel to sleep and the girls seemed to drift off after he read two bedtime stories and kept assuring them Mama should be home soon. He hoped he hadn't lied.

He'd had a grand total of fifteen minutes to himself when the doorbell rang. He rushed to the door, entertaining outlandish, unlikely thoughts of her escaping her captors and thumbing a ride home. He could hope anyway. Once the door opened, hope disappeared.

Josh Hunter, a female uniform officer and the chaplain stood on the porch. Ennis's stomach dropped. His knees went weak. "No," was the only word he could find at first. "No, no, no," his voice cracked with emotion.

The trio stepped inside. Josh's voice sounded abnormally soft, "Ennis, listen–"

"No, she can't be..." his mouth refused to form *the* word. He swore his heart died in his chest but some mysterious force kept him upright and what apparently passed for conscious. A fog of disbelief descended on him, shrouding and numbing his mind in a surreal, mechanical limbo. If she was... *gone*, then certain things had to be done in a certain order. First and foremost, making an ID.

Hunter continued, "Since the kids know her, I brought Gabby Wilson to take care of them. Listen to me. Cobb County needs a list of Savannah's scars, tattoos and any distinguishing marks. They need an ID."

Josh's voice faded in the background as the words hit Ennis like a horse kicking him in the gut. *We need a positive ID.* Ennis had seen that sentence cripple grown men and sent parents and spouses to the floor in shock. How many times had he heard about needing *a positive ID* in reference to strangers? How many times had he and Savannah exchanged those words – We need a positive ID – about other people? Then there was The Family. We need to notify The Family, one of them would say. Ring the doorbell, wait for the poor unfortunate mother, father, wife or husband – or worse, one of the kids – to greet them. Savannah would introduce herself and Ennis then in her smooth, velvet voice say, *May we come in? We need a few minutes of your time.* Lead The Family to a chair or couch. *Please have a seat.* She always tried to bring the chaplain. She always handed them a list of important telephone numbers including her own, the coroner's office and grief hotline. Then she always wrote down what she called The Next Steps such as viewing their loved one and offering transportation to the viewing, when to expect the body's release so they could make funeral arrangements, etc. She never left The Family alone until someone arrived to be with them. That was Savannah, he thought as tears blurred his vision. Always thinking and ever compassionate. Now she was gone and someone else was telling *him* The Next Steps.

But Josh hadn't said *a positive ID*, had he? He said "an ID".

Ennis hoped it was an oversight on Hunter's part but his boss did not make those blatant mistakes. He'd heard Josh say "an ID" before. The victim had been mutilated so a facial ID was impossible.

Suddenly nothing worked right. Not his legs, his brain, mouth or stomach. Ennis thought about sitting then didn't. He thought about punching a wall but didn't want to wake the kids. Fate threw him into a situation he'd only seen from a cop's point of view. The roles had been reversed and he was the victim's family – and he had no clue how to cope. Some people physically collapsed. Others denied the news. Ennis was gonna puke. He swallowed back the roiling tide in his stomach just before he dared to ask, "Are you saying that's the *only* way she can be identified?"

"Just answer my question, Ennis," Josh prodded.

"No. You answer mine first."

"Then yes, that's what I'm saying. Now, tell me about her. I need any distinguishing marks and such from here down," his hand indicated chest level and below.

Sickness bolted up Ennis's throat. He'd never make it to the bathroom so he raced to the kitchen trash bin and threw up. He began shaking. Heaved again. Wiped his mouth with the back of his hand, "Her back... There are scars from R.J. and Jeffrey Holland." He drew a shaky breath, "And she's got a tiger tattoo at the small of her back about five or six inches wide. She got it to hide..." Ennis remembered when she told him the reason for the surprisingly artistic tattoo. It was their first trip to Texas together. He was massaging her back when he discovered it beneath her pajama top. She'd been embarrassed and reluctant for him to see R.J.'s abuse but finally relented and explained the tattoo was intended to minimize the scars. Ennis wasn't sure why he felt compelled to share that with their boss and on second thought, decided against it. Savannah was (or had been) a very private person and wouldn't want him blabbing it to the world. "Nevermind. How did she... What did this guy do to her?"

"First, we're not sure it's her, keep that in mind. I brought the chaplain in case it is. Second, you don't want to know what the kidnapper did." He sighed when Ennis tensed all over and clenched his jaw. Josh hesitated before saying, "Think Marquis Thomas."

Ennis hurled so hard he groaned. The face he fell instantly in lust with. Her stunning smile with those adorable dimples. Eyes the color of brilliant azure. Features that often garnered comparisons to Rita Hayworth. They were all gone now. "Where is she?"

"911 got a call about bodies found in a wooded area outside the city. There's enough similarity to the victims and Savannah and Ethan that Cobb County wanted the information."

It surpassed surreal five minutes ago. Now it was just insane. "The bastard left her in the weather with the insects, snakes and raccoons after he shot her?" Ennis looked up.

A subtle, palpable uneasiness crept into Josh's expression when he met the detective's gaze as if Hunter squared off with a wild dog contemplating attacking. Ennis did not dispel his fears, "I'm going with you. I want to see for myself what this son of a bitch did to my wife then I'm hunting him down."

"Daddy?" Lily yawned his name.

Ennis stopped cold. His little girl padded in the living room in her footed pajamas and clutching her Sleeping Beauty doll. She looked so much like her mother Ennis's eyes filled with fresh, hot tears. Gabby tried diverting Lily's attention, "Hello, Lily. Remember me? Gabby Wilson?"

Lily's balled fist rubbed her right eye as she nodded. She kept walking to her father, "What's wrong, Daddy?"

Ennis dropped to one knee and brought her into his arms. The adults averted their gazes as he broke down.

Still confused, Lily looked at Josh and the chaplain. "Why's Daddy crying? What happened?"

Josh answered, "Honey, I need to borrow him a while but Gabby's going to stay with you, Anna and Daniel while your daddy comes with us. He'll be back soon though."

Yes, Ennis thought. Unlike her mother, I'll be back.

O O O

A low level shiver vibrated through her already sore muscles. A cold sweat set in, chilling Savannah to the bone. Her heart squeezed and galloped inside her until dizziness made her head swim. She kept remembering the gun barrel pressed against the back of her head. How close she came – and still might – to losing her life.

The hairs on the back of her neck stood at attention with every noise. She did not move. Before walking away, Alpha Male stressed one important detail. Moving meant death. "Your daddy paid off like a slot machine. Take my advice and stay where you are. Any one of you moves in the next hour, you all die."

Tucker wanted to know, "How are we supposed to time–"

"Shut up, Tucker," Savannah and Ethan had warned in unison. Twice he'd practically gotten them killed with his runaway mouth. Three strikes and we're *all* out, she wanted to tell him.

Alpha chuckled at their berating, "You Morgans. It's a miracle you all haven't killed each other by now. To answer your question, when you want to move, assume one of us is still standing behind you..."

Savannah had heard boots brushing through the wild grass. Further and further until she heard only the sound of brittle leaves scraping together in the breeze.

Ethan asked, "Do you think it's safe yet?"

"I hope so because I'm dying in this hood. I have to get air." She heard the grass rustle as Ethan squirmed closer to her. No shots fired. She breathed a little easier.

"Hold on," he said. "I'm trying to crawl toward you."

Please hurry. Things didn't feel right in her chest or stomach but she put it off to a whole lot of claustrophobia and outright panic. She hoped that's all it was.

Hands inched their way up her arm until grasping the cloth at the back of her head. Ethan pulled off the hood.

Savannah sucked in several deep breaths then thanked him.

A blanket of black covered the sky. Only the moon's soft, ambient light glowed bright enough to barely illuminate the surroundings. The last time she checked her watch (which was forever ago) it read 8:34 p.m. The kidnappers held them over twenty-four hours – or, as her heart could attest, the equivalent of two missed doses of medication.

She rolled over and reciprocated by removing Ethan's hood. Once on their feet, they tried to assess their location. The gunmen left them in the boondocks with the city's skyline in the distance. She wanted to groan. She sighed instead, "This'll be a mighty long walk in these chains." Not to mention awkward and embarrassing with the Stun-Cuffs adding to their accessories. The three looked so much like prisoners on the lam they didn't stand a chance in hell of a catching a ride to town. "Because no one will pick us up looking like this." The thought of hoofing it miles upon miles a few inches at a time exhausted her just thinking about it.

She was busy looking around for the nearest road when Ethan mentioned, "Look. It's your purse and maybe your gun too."

He was right. Both lay several feet away in the grass. Now that's weird, she thought. What kidnapper was kind enough to return a person's belongings?

At that point she really didn't care. They were safe – or safer than they had been. She glanced past Ethan, "Looks like they left your billfold and phone too."

He shook his right ankle to reveal the Stun-Cuff still locked around it, "And left us these miserable things too."

She went to the purse and gun and asked Ethan to clip the holster on her belt. She picked up her purse, praying they left her phone behind as well. They had. She powered it up. While waiting she noticed they left everything in her purse as well. Nitroglycerin, wallet, and her keys with her latest birthday gift from the kids. A keyring that read *This Mommy Belongs To Lily, Anna & Daniel.*

"Hey," Tucker yelled, "what about me? Anyone gonna help me?"

Do I have to? They were damn lucky to survive this nightmare no thanks to his haughty jabbering. She saw Ethan debating a decision as well.

He begrudgingly started toward his brother, "Only because Dad'll kill me if I leave you here. We're just glad to be alive no thanks to you, you lousy, traitorous bum."

She dialed 911, gave her name and badge number and told the woman what happened and an approximate location to find them. "Use my phone's GPS to locate us and tell responding units to bring bolt cutters too. We're restrained like criminals out here."

Then she called Ennis's cell phone. He clicked on then blew his nose. When he spoke he sounded like he had a cold, "Is that you? *Is it really you?*"

She frowned, "Yes, why? You got another wife named Savannah?"

He started crying hard enough she could barely understand him, "We were on our way to identify your body. Someone called in saying they found bodies in a wooded area in Cobb County and one loosely matched your description."

"I don't feel a hundred percent but I'm sure not dead yet. Dispatch is tracking my GPS so they'll know our location pretty soon. It is a wooded area, an old nature walk I think." By the time she ended the call, Ethan had Tucker on his feet. "They leave your billfold and phone?" she asked Tucker.

He nodded, "Amazing but yeah."

Something hinky was going on. Gun, purse, billfolds and phones. They gave everything back but why? And why hadn't they killed the three of them? She was relieved but confused. Kidnappings rarely if ever ended this well.

And, "Why just us?" she asked. "I'm guessing whoever did this feels screwed by your father – probably because of that damn book," she scowled at Tucker, "and wanted a quick payday but why not round up Preston and Grady too?"

"Grady's out of town," Ethan said. "I don't know about Preston. Maybe they couldn't find him."

Once she got some rest and her mind glued back together from the claustrophobia and fear of dying, she'd try finding answers. Whatever was left of the evening would be dedicated to answering question from her colleagues. "Let's try to find the road they used. I think we're pointed the right direction."

Ethan's voice softened, "Forgive my nosiness but you seemed to have serious trouble breathing earlier and just before we left. I honestly thought you were having a heart attack."

"I have a problem with small spaces," was all she volunteered.

He relaxed, "Oh. Well, you're not alone about phobias. I freak out in forests."

Okay, that was a new one. "Forests?"

"Yeah. When I was a kid I got lost on one of our vacations in the

North Georgia Mountains. Stayed lost for three days."

"Alone?"

He nodded.

"Three days alone in the forest would make any kid phobic," she agreed.

Tucker caught up to them, griping, "He ruined the whole trip. We wasted days searching for him and found him–"

"Tucker," she tried thinking of a diplomatic way to say it then gave up, "shut up."

Ethan returned to his original question, " *Were* you having heart problems? I mean after being kidnapped then attacked by that guy... I mean those shocks couldn't have been good for you."

"I'm fine." Her muscles were sore and tense but she refused to worry about her heart right then simply because she couldn't do anything about it yet.

o o o

The cavalry arrived lights flashing and sirens wailing. Ambulances pulled in beside cruisers. Everyone converged on the three standing by the road. Cops busied themselves removing the restraints and Stun-Cuffs. That greatly eased Savannah's mind since no one within a hundred yards could activate the damn thing anymore.

Lee Morgan arrived seconds behind the ambulance. Three armed security guards filed out of the dark SUV and clustered close to Lee as if they anticipated trouble from any warm body at the scene. Lee went straight to Tucker. The security team stepped a respectable distance back but not too far. Lee spoke to Tucker who acted aloof and uninterested then moved to Ethan and Savannah who stood together. "Are you both alright?"

Ethan answered with a relieved yes. Savannah hated to be Debbie Downer but, "Depends on what you mean by *alright*. These last few weeks have been stressful enough, finding out my questionable paternity, that shoot-out and now this. I'm not really *alright* anymore but thanks for asking."

"She needs medical attention for her heart, Dad," Ethan tattled.

Savannah shot him a withering glare, "Stop acting like my sister, Ethan."

Lee immediately waved down a paramedic, "My daughter needs medical attention. It's her heart."

That sent her to the brink of losing it, "Wanna give me a heart attack? Keep calling me your daughter."

Lee sighed to the EMT, "Check her out please."

She capitulated only because she was concerned about her ticker too. She climbed in the ambulance but sat on the paramedic's bench, not the gurney as the paramedic indicated.

He gave a small resigned shrug but didn't argue. "Your name, ma'am?"

"Sergeant Savannah Prince, APD."

"And do you have a heart condition or are your symptoms new?"

"I had a heart attack a year ago July." Since Lee and Ethan hung out near the open doors, they heard every word. She thought Ethan's knees might loosen when he heard it. "FYI," she told the EMT, "unless you find some funky rhythm to my ticker, I'm going home, not to a hospital."

Before wiring her up, he closed the doors for privacy. She stopped him, "No, no. Tell *Daddy* I want to talk to him while you're doing your thing."

Considering the EMT heard hers and Lee's earlier exchange, he cautioned, "It's really not a good idea to introduce stress–" His mouth clapped shut at her frown then opened the door to tell Lee, "She wants her daddy. I assume that's you."

Lee climbed in beside her. He averted his gaze as she unbuttoned her blouse. Feh. Modesty. Big woo. After that night she felt lucky to *have* a heartbeat so who cared who witnessed her ECG? Besides, her angle on the bench prevented him from seeing anything anyway. "How much did you pay for the three of us?" she asked.

"It's nothing you should concern yourself with. As long as you're safe and your heart's okay I'll be thankful."

"Listen, I'm still wrapped pretty tight over this whole thing and I apologize for my outburst a minute ago. You really did an amazing thing for me and I appreciate it." *You're still a sick son of a bitch for raping my mother and I hate you more than you know – but thanks to you I can go back to my family tonight.*

He rubbed his brow with a frustrated, "I never expected someone to go after you. It has to be that tacky excuse for a book Tucker wrote."

"Have you had any threats to you or your kids since that book's been published?"

EMT decided the gurney was his new assigned seat and cautioned her to be quiet during the test. It was like being at her cardiologist's office. Bossy, bossy, bossy.

Meanwhile Lee contemplated her question. "I was concerned over Tucker. His hatred for me goes deeper than I expected and that's why I asked for official police protection in the first place. There are always threats to someone in my position because of what I do but I haven't noticed anything worse than normal. Mostly ex-employees threatening to sue. I'll ask the boys and compare notes." He glanced at the paramedic, "How's she doing?"

"Heart's running hard and fast but so far so good."

"You had a heart attack last year?" Lee asked.

She nodded.

The EMT finished the test and gave her a clean bill of health. Savannah buttoned her blouse and Lee faced her, "But you're so young."

"You can thank a serial killer for that heart attack. He literally drained enough blood to cause one."

The EMT shivered, "Jeffrey Holland."

Savannah nodded again, "He and I went around and around for years until someone killed him."

Lee ran his hand down his face, reminding her of Ennis when he got upset, "I remember him but I don't recall you getting hurt. July, you said." He thought back, "I was in Germany and Italy, that's why. Savannah, this is why we need to keep in touch. I want to be a part of your life, to know what's going on. It's important to me."

She refused to touch that one with a ten foot pole. "Now you've learned something new about me. It's my turn. How much ransom did you pay for us?"

"You're not giving this up, are you?"

"Nope."

He removed a pen and notepad from his jacket, scribbled, then showed it to her. It listed three numbers along with a name beside each one. He put Tucker first, then Ethan and lastly Savannah. Lee wrote the number and wrote beside it *for you* instead of her name.

Savannah's stomach clenched. She'd heard of people having this much money but to shell it out for a ransom? And her ransom... Whew. Hers rendered her speechless for a time. It was light years away from Tucker's and considerably more than Ethan's.

She tapped the EMT on the shoulder, "Hook me up again. This might cause a whopper."

Instead, he reached toward her stomach, prodded it gently, "I saw a bruise here. What happened?"

She flinched away from his hand, "Easy there, buddy. It's sore. One of them punched me after I attacked him."

"Hit you?" Lee fumed beside her. He removed a notepad and pen, "Give me a description of him."

"What, are you doing my job now?" she asked in jest. He did not smile. No, he was deadly serious and staring straight at her, waiting for her to comply. She'd not seen this side of Lee Morgan. It gave her a good idea how her mother must have shied from him before he attacked her. In his mood, she went ahead and gave the description, including the name Riggs. He'd never find the guy, she thought, so what was the harm in telling him?

O   O   O

Lee Morgan offered her a helping hand out of the ambulance. She heard someone calling her name. With Josh Hunter behind him, a panicked Ennis hurriedly wound his way through the maze of cops, crime scene techs and paramedics to get to her. He took her in his arms, "Are you alright?"

"I'm okay. I'm—"

He planted such a passionate kiss on her it would have driven the ECG off the charts and left the equipment smoking. He eased away from the kiss, saying, "I thought you were dead." His vision strayed beside her to Lee.

Savannah felt his body tense against hers. He went from grateful to homicidal in one second. He released his wife and advanced on Lee, "You. You're the reason our lives are upside down."

Savannah held an arm out effectively blocking her husband from flattening Morgan. They'd had enough drama lately. No need to add assault charges and arraignments to the mix. "Ennis, he paid a fortune to have me released unharmed."

"You wouldn't have been kidnapped at all if it weren't for him." He shoved his hands through his hair, "You nearly died *again*."

"Who's staying with the kids?" Better to change the subject than revisit her close calls with the Grim Reaper.

"Hunter brought Gabby Wilson to stay with them. Did you tell the paramedics about your heart?" Ennis asked her with an if-you-didn't-then-I-will inflection.

Lee answered for her, "Yes, she did and the ECG was fine."

Savannah discreetly nudged her husband when he aimed a murderous glare at Lee. He paid a fortune, she reminded under her breath. No, she was no fan of Lee Morgan either but he still paid for her freedom.

Lee kissed her cheek, "I'll give you both time to catch up but I'll be calling you tomorrow morning. I'm glad you're okay."

Savannah thought about leaning away from the kiss but decided against it. A little kiss was a small sacrifice for the ginormous amount of money he paid.

"Welcome back to the land of the living," Josh said as he approached. "You gave us quite a scare."

"Should have been in my shoes." She kept an eye to Ennis, "Are you gonna be okay?"

He leaned on his knees, "Not for a while, no."

Josh added, "I called Georgia to update her so get ready to be mothered tomorrow."

That's how Savannah knew Georgia was perfect mom material. In a crisis, her sister arrived like a one woman Red Cross team on steroids, rendering first aid while cooking, cleaning, and babysitting. There was a reason Savannah nicknamed her General Georgia when they were younger. The woman could organize anything from a yard sale to a military operation and not break a sweat. And she hadn't changed one bit.

18

By the time she finished answering detectives' questions, Savannah could barely think, much less perform her duties so she took the day off. The few hours of sleep slightly rejuvenated her enough she tried getting out of bed but discovered her muscles turned to concrete overnight. After a quick shower to loosen those, she'd be able to motivate and take care of the kids if Ennis wanted a half-day at work.

Savannah dreaded one thing like root canals without Novocain. Dealing with her daddy when he found out what happened because there was no if, it was when. And if she thought Riggs hit like a Mack truck, no one compared to R.J. Prince. Most of it depended on how the news media spun the kidnappings. Would they phrase her identity "Sergeant Savannah Prince" or the juicier way – "Lee Morgan's daughter Sergeant Savannah Prince"? For a minute she contemplated booking a cruise to Antarctica or Gilligan's Island. No one would find her there.

After her shower, she threw on her robe and opened the bedroom door to an abnormally quiet house. With three kids that meant they were asleep, gone or getting into trouble. She headed to the living room to scout the situation.

By the time she turned the corner she heard a woman's voice offer someone more goldfish. In Savannah's foggy state of mind it took a moment to realize she meant the crackers, not the actual swimming kind.

Georgia sat with the girls, keeping them quiet (which was a miracle) while they ate. She cradled a snoozing Daniel in her arms. Her sister was a miracle worker with babies.

"Hey, sis," Savannah greeted tiredly then made the rounds kissing her children. The girls' enthusiasm brimmed upon seeing their mother, so much that Georgia shushed them on the baby's behalf.

"What are you doing here?" she asked Georgia. "I was going to call you as soon as I got up."

They exchanged a kiss. Georgia motioned for her to sit down. "Ennis called me from the station last night. I came over so he could get back to work. He's determined to find the men that did this and I'll do anything to help him."

Georgia went to the kitchen and brought back a bowl of tomato soup. Lily and Anna scooted the box of goldfish crackers to her. Lily insisted they would make her feel better.

"I'm all for that," she said, shaking a few in the bowl. She looked to her sister who appraised her overall condition. She could save Georgia the trouble and say "shitty" but little pitchers had big ears and memories like elephants.

Georgia asked, "It's a silly question but how are you feeling?"

"Lucky to be here," she dunked her fish with the spoon. Stirred the soup slowly. "Lee paid a fortune for me, Georgia. Literally a fortune. My ransom was the highest of the three. I don't understand the individual amounts. It's never happened as far as I know."

The girls finished eating. Georgia smilingly shooed them to the living room to play then stared at the handcuff marks on Savannah's wrists. To maybe keep the questions at a minimum, Savannah asked, "How is the media reporting this? Am I Sergeant Prince or Lee's daughter?"

Georgia hesitated. Savannah groaned, "*Oh no*. Wait till Daddy hears, and it'll be all over the Chronicle for him to read." Her appetite vanished with that comment. She nudged a fish around in the soup then leaned back and sighed.

Georgia motioned to the bowl, "Eat. Daddy doesn't always read the paper."

To appease Georgia she took a bite. The soup and the goldfish tasted pretty good. "No, but he watches TV at the bar. This'll be the top story in Augusta."

"Savannah, stop. If he sees it, he sees it. Hopefully he'll realize you were a victim in both situations, the kidnapping and the assumption you're Morgan's daughter."

Before her sister harangued her to keep eating, she took another bite and chewed, "Yeah, because he's always been so understanding when it comes to me."

Georgia collected the girls' bowls and took them to the kitchen, "Ennis said they returned your gun and purse. Who does that?"

"That's my question. We all got our belongings back except my car but Ennis said they left it at the bar."

Georgia thought a moment, "Did you ever find out why Preston and Grady were left out? You'd think the kidnappers would aim for the full set of Morgan's kids."

"Ethan said Grady was out of town. And Preston? Who knows what he was doing. Shut away in a secret room counting his money like King Midas, probably."

"Not that I'm accusing but there's something about this, like someone wanted a handsome payday, or perhaps extra publicity for a book. Outlandish stunts to boost sales aren't unheard of. Gabriele d'Annunzio faked his own death for publicity purposes."

Savannah had no clue who the hell that was, "Didn't work. I've never heard of him. But I could believe Tucker set up the kidnappings except that guy really took a beating with the Stun-Cuff. I'm surprised he's still breathing. I'll find out who the ringleader is to this circus and God help 'em when I do."

Georgia pointed to the soup, "First you're going to recover then you can go full steam ahead. Eat."

To appease her, Savannah spooned up more soup. Her brow lifted, "Lily's right. The fish do make you feel better."

"It's the goofy smiles," her sister added with a tiny smile of her own.

O O O

Savannah closed her locker then headed to her office. She'd taken one day off to recuperate however the warm reception she received from uniforms and other colleagues made it feel like she returned from the dead. Sergeant Sweeney surprisingly sugarcoated his jibe – *It doesn't pay to be a Morgan but it pays to hold one for ransom* – with a semi-sincere *welcome back.*

She checked her desk for message slips and paperwork she'd left behind before the masked mauraders kidnapped her. She found a message from Detective Tierce dated that morning asking for a vacation day in five days. After checking the schedule, she called him into her office to okay the day off.

Tierce was an enigma in a way. The mid-twenties, clean cut rookie detective always showed up spit-shined, clean-shaven and not a hair out of place (hair that he combed carefully and precisely each time he stepped in from outside). That wasn't the enigma. That resided in his clothing. He looked fresh out of a nineteen sixties movie with his black suit, white shirt and black skinny tie. He dressed like a young Paul Newman in The Young Philadelphians which added a different panache to the detective squad but it also made her privately question if his closet consisted of twenty suits of same kind.

As always he arrived in his spiffy suit, not a hair out place and eager to please. Savannah okayed his vacation. He expressed his gratitude with a *thank you, ma'am.*

"Anything special planned for that day?" she asked in casual passing.

"My friend rented a place a couple of hours north of the city so we're going deer hunting."

Her cell phone rang. It was Mathis, "I'm calling as a courtesy."

What did that mean? "Thank you, I think."

"I'm at Lenox Park staring at a dead guy that looks like he was hit by sixteen trucks at the same time. He's beaten to a pulp. I'm sending you a picture of his driver's license now."

Savannah waited then check her mail. The face on the license sent a shockwave through her. Sixteen trucks at the same time, Mathis said. Beaten to a pulp. It was difficult to imagine this man in his mid-thirties with a mustache and short, dark military flat-top, and a jagged scar zig-zagging across his right cheek not being able to fight his way out of anything. God knew he leveled her so hard it left a bruise. James Riggs deserved a good back-alley beating and it sounded like he got a thorough one.

Her hand went to her stomach in remembrance of the powerful blow.

"You there?" Mathis asked.

"I'm here," she said, waving Tierce out the door.

"That the guy you nearly choked to death?"

"Yes."

"Thought so. I'll notify Hunter." He ended the call, leaving her stunned, concerned and a little uneasy. She'd given Lee Morgan Rigg's surname and description knowing the impossibility of locating him out of Atlanta's three million people. How the hell had he found him and had she, unwittingly, set Riggs up to be murdered? A shiver went down her back. Were the rumors true? Did Lee Morgan skirt the law and take matters into his own hands? Did he actually hire people to permanently fix problems?

19

Georgia pulled the Tahoe to a stop in front of the Morgan mansion. She remembered her mother parking the family Pontiac Catalina in the same spot when Charlene brought her and Savannah to visit many years earlier. At the time Georgia likened the huge, opulent house to a fairytale palace. Only certain people passed through the Morgan estate's sacred gates. Once inside, the staff treated the two young, wide-eyed sisters like royalty. She and Savannah need only mention cookies and milk or a slice of cake and someone fetched it for them. There was always someone available to fill a want or whim for either girl.

Georgia wore her nicest business suit to this meeting, intending to make a professional, no-nonsense impression on Lee Morgan and put him on notice. Leave Savannah alone. Her sister didn't need her to fight battles for her – in fact Savannah would blow her top if she found out about this meeting – but after reading Charlene's journals, Georgia felt she had no choice. She wanted answers then blood if Morgan refused to leave her sister alone.

First he violated Charlene then held the family's income hostage (no better than those creeps who kidnapped Savannah, she stormed to Dane) and threatened to destroy Prince Construction if Charlene refused to bend to his will. Now he and that twerp Tucker had the world thinking Savannah was his child, not R.J.'s. The backlash from the book plus Lee's continual insistence she was his daughter caused a tsunami of hell for her sister, Georgia told Dane who'd given up trying to calm her down. His only caution was *the baby. Think about our baby.*

She tried calming down but her mother's journal entry kept leaping to mind. *Lee told me in no uncertain terms 'I'm Savannah's father, we both know it, and I have rights. I demand to see my daughter in the next two weeks or I'll destroy Robert. I'll have him jailed if he lays a hand on her again. He's an abusive drunk and he's taking out his anger on my little girl. I won't have it.'*

Whatever Lee Morgan wanted, Lee Morgan got. And he wanted Savannah for his daughter. That circulated in Georgia's mind until stirring into a storm. She climbed the steps to the door. This was where she had to be careful. She did not want to make her sister's life harder but she wanted Morgan to understand the repercussions of his actions.

Lee answered the door in a white dress shirt, burgundy sweater vest and black slacks. With his styled silver hair and friendly smile, he presented a grandfatherly image more than a ruthless multimillionaire bent on destroying people.

He greeted Georgia with a warm, snug handshake that lingered a tad too long for her liking. His smile, meant to put her at ease, put her on edge instead. All her life she'd been told she was her mother's spitting image. That alone threw a guard up against Morgan after what happened to Charlene. He might think Charlene's spitting image was as soft-spoken and kind as she was. He'd be wrong.

She opted for one of three bronze colored easy chairs in the room instead of the matching sofa. Years ago Lee's wife decorated with floral patterns but now he replaced it with a more masculine wood, dark bronze and cream décor. She declined the offer of refreshments because she didn't intend to stay long. No, she didn't want to waste precious time on formalities when she only came to say one thing – leave my sister alone.

"I know your time is valuable, Mr. Morgan, so I'll get down to business. I'm not sure why you're so certain Savannah is your daughter but this constant upheaval is wearing on her. As you know she has a bad heart and that kidnapping could have easily triggered a heart attack. She's got three children who would like to grow up with their mother, not the memory of her so I'm asking, please back off this... this crusade to deem Savannah your child."

If her approach to the subject offended Lee, he concealed it well. "I regret my association with her is causing problems. The last thing I want is to hurt her. As you said, I am aware of her heart condition and what caused it. She told me about it that night in the ambulance. To be honest she handled the situation better than most people might. Maybe it's the law enforcement training, maybe it's how she grew up or perhaps it's just her nature but I was proud of her. I've always been proud of her, Georgia, I just never got a chance to show it when she was growing up. Now I can so I'm saying this respectfully. I will continue building a bond with my daughter. I've been denied too long and I'm too old to let anyone deny me now. If Savannah doesn't mind, why should you?"

"For one, since she's discovered you may be her father, she's drinking again. She had it under control until this started. Another reason is your presence in her life is affecting her relationship with our father and–" she stopped when his hand clenched in a fist.

He released the grip almost instantly, "Don't you agree she's not had much of a relationship with Robert? He mistreated her all her life, beat her, whipped her mercilessly. He also mistreated you and Seth but Savannah got the worst beatings, am I right? Have you seen her lately? What he did to her while he was in a drunken rage?"

"I've seen the marks, yes. He got angry because she met with you. He's got a black hatred for you, Mr. Morgan, and for good reason from what I understand. That's why I'm asking you to spare Savannah additional pain and suffering. Let her go. You don't even know if she's your child."

"Has a black hatred, does he?" The kind, grandfatherly persona disappeared as his voice hardened, "Then I guess we're even. He's the one abusing my child. I saw my girl once in this house, Georgia. Once. I had a legal right to see her but because of Robert, Charlene refused to bring her over or meet in public. I would have valued *any* time with Savannah but I got none."

She fought to keep her jaw from plummeting. This was incredible. The self-righteous bastard raped her mother and now felt perfectly justified vilifying her father. Her anger mounted. She wanted to strike out, to call him what he was. "Mama was too afraid to meet you, that's why."

"She was afraid of Robert. Afraid he'd beat *her* too." He'd moved to the edge of his seat now. He leaned forward, closer.

If he meant to intimidate her, he was about to find out she had her daddy's backbone – and his temper when provoke too far. "No. She was afraid to meet you because of what you did to her."

His brow dove into a frown, "What do you think I did to Charlene?"

For weeks she'd obsessed over the misery and pain Lee's attack caused her mother. She read the shame, embarrassment, anger and fear that consumed her mother. How she couldn't sleep, how she forced herself to eat for the baby's sake then barely kept the food down and how she withdrew from society just to try and cope with the assault.

An anger so fierce swept over Georgia, she let the truth fly on behalf of her mother who couldn't defend herself then or now. "Our mother wrote journals since her teenage years. Savannah and I found those journals. One included the year of Savannah's conception. Our mother detailed a horrifying account of sexual assault and you were the offender."

Lee's mouth set in a hard line. His eyes narrowed. He sat quietly a moment, his face evolved into an expression she'd never seen before. Absolute fury.

Georgia felt the urgent pull to leave. It grew by leaps and bounds the longer he remained silent. She squared her shoulders, showed no sign of the anxiety flowing through her veins or the uneasy flutter in her belly.

Finally he spoke. "I didn't realize I needed my lawyer present for this meeting. I loved Charlene, and she loved me too, believe it or not. She was unhappy at home and I admit we both succumbed to our desires that night. I may have been overly, shall I say, eager during that time but if she believed I was assaulting her, she would have said so or knocked me out with a lamp. If she wrote that I was harsh with her I rather expect it was to save face with Robert."

"Mama went to bed and stayed after what happened. She cried all the time. At first she refused to eat. That's not guilt from an affair, that's trying to deal with trauma."

"There was no trauma when Charlene and I created that beautiful girl. We shared a love she and Robert never had."

Oh, she itched to slap him. No, *hit* him, not slap him. She understood the rage her father harbored for this man, felt a burning need for vengeance – and justice – coursing through her. *He'll never admit he raped her. He can't. For one thing his ego won't let him. For another it would tarnish his reputation worse than Tucker has.*

She finally realized she lost focus. She let her emotions – and mouth – run wild so she reeled them in and returned to the reason for the visit. "I'm not here to right a wrong because it can't be done. I am here to ask nicely for you to leave Savannah alone. Our daddy is on the warpath because of this anyway. The more he hears about you, the meaner he is to Savannah."

"I intend to fix that–"

"How? You can't *fix* anything, especially the same way you planned to *fix* it the first time. You can't ruin Daddy's business anymore."

He bowed up at the threat, because it *was* a threat. "Fixing" something to Lee Morgan meant destroying someone else. She continued, "Mama detailed how you vowed to ruin his business and how shipments were delayed or halfway fulfilled."

"Why would I risk my reputation to *ruin* one small businessman who was losing money hand over fist in the first place? If a few shipments were misdelivered, that's life in the business world. No one's perfect. Robert wasn't cut out to run a business. Had you or Charlene ever thought of that?"

"I only know what Mama wrote in her journals. I believe her."

Leaning on his knees, invading her personal space, "Did she also write how dearly I missed seeing my little girl? How I tried many times to have her over with Savannah – I could have started legal proceedings to gain custody of her but I loved Charlene too much to steal our child from her mother. I told Charlene to bring you and your brother if it made her feel less clandestine. Robert was always jealous of mine and Charlene's past, Georgia. He always felt inferior and used his muscle to back his mouth while I used business sense and logic to back mine." His ice blue eyes bored into her, "After seeing Savannah's wounds from his last tirade, I'm using a different approach with him. I'm paying him a visit today and having a little chat with him."

Lee Morgan stood up and marched to the door, "Before this meeting becomes more adversarial, I suggest you leave. If you choose to spread your lies outside these walls, you'll hear from my lawyers. I can assure you anyone else would be removed from this premises by the sheriff so count yourself lucky that you're Charlene's daughter."

o o o

Savannah arrived at Georgia's bakery Pie In The Sky, bright and early Saturday. She helped out when her schedules at work and home allowed.

Today her home schedule would suffer – not as much housework would be done – but she needed this time with her sister. Or half-sister if one believed Lee and Tucker Morgan.

She sneered at the thought of the Morgans. Mathis ran a background on James Riggs. Divorced, one kid, ex-army and up until two years ago he was employed at the USP Atlanta as a prison guard. Then he landed a cushier, better paying job. The man who delivered a debilitating punch and punished her with a Stun-Cuff actually worked private security for Lee Morgan. In her opinion it gave credence to the theory that one of the Morgans set up the kidnappings. However Riggs's death continued to nag at her. The man truly was beaten to a pulp like Mathis said. For some reason Lee Morgan kept pinging at her brain. She remembered him standing outside the ambulance the night the kidnappers released her. He'd called someone and gave them Rigg's name and description with orders to *take care of it.* His tone made her shiver. When the body in Lenox Park was found, she figured she'd drastically underestimated his employees' abilities to hunt down a person. Later she found out Riggs worked on the Morgan family's security team and that both pissed her off and scared her. Did all of those men holding her, Ethan and Tucker work for Morgan?

Once donning her black apron with the bakery's pink logo, Savannah looked over Georgia's list of pies for the day (her sister changed the menu daily but baked the best sellers every day). Bourbon Pecan Pie topped the list. While Georgia prepared the mixers, Savannah took over measuring ingredients.

She collected the pecan pie ingredients and set them on the

counter. A flash of horror crossed Georgia's features at the sight of the bourbon bottle fisted in her sister's hand. She abandoned the industrial mixers to join Savannah, "I'll do the pecan pie. You can start preparing the crusts."

"Georgia, I can mix this filling without sneaking a slug of booze. Stop worrying."

"No, no. Honestly, I want to do this pie myself. This one and the," she paused a second, "lemon meringue. People love your pie crust more than mine anyway."

She gave Georgia credit. She concealed her initial shock of seeing the bottle in her hand well. Her spiel of wanting to prepare those specific pies was all bullshit and Savannah knew it but she surrendered the bottle anyway. She needed to stay busy. Nothing wrecked her day quicker than dwelling on her bastard status, whether it was true or not. "I use your recipe, Georgia. It doesn't taste any different." But her sister was sweet to consider her feelings.

She got busy measuring flour, sugar, salt and other ingredients. Soon her mind drifted from the current chaos in her life to not screwing up Georgia's business. She noticed her sister measured out the bourbon for two pies then went to the pantry to put the bottle away.

Savannah followed soon after for the butter and shortening, both chilled. Just as a passing glance, she noticed the bourbon missing from its usual place. She rolled her eyes. One mistake – one lousy screw-up – and the family started hiding the booze and probably planning an intervention. Gimme a break, she grumbled. *It's not every day a person discovers they supposedly share their DNA with a rapist.*

"Did you say something?"

Georgia stood behind her. She was fretting again, probably because her sister stared toward the vicinity of the unusually empty liquor shelf. "Just thinking out loud," Savannah replied. She retrieved more butter and shortening for the pie crusts. It eased her sister's worry lines.

She busied herself mixing, rolling and filling pie tins. She was in the middle of fluting the edges when she noticed Georgia staring at R.J.'s belt marks slashed across her arms. Self-consciousness set in. She'd worn long-sleeved blouses every day – except today, of course – to avoid that expression. She stopped working, "Something wrong?"

"Just wondering how those are healing."

"They're fine. My biggest regret is that the kids saw and heard the whole thing."

"I'm sorry Daddy did that. I wanted the journals, not you, and you suffered for my–"

"It's no big deal." *Just drop it already.*

"At least Lily had the presence of mind to call the police."

"Yes, how insane is that? She had to call the cops on her *grandpa*. Now she and Anna are terrified of him and I look as stupid as when Toby attacked me. A cop getting beat up off the job. I can only imagine what those uniforms think."

"Savannah, Daddy ambushed you."

"I could've fought back. In retrospect I probably should have. I just," she sighed. Waited to gather her thoughts. Why *had* she laid there and taken that abuse? To spare Georgia for one thing but she'd never tell her that. "I didn't want to hurt him. Crazy, right? I knew he'd play out.

He's older now and–"

"Still very strong." Georgia crossed her arms, "He could've done serious damage."

"I guess at that moment it was the most normal thing I'd had happen lately. Daddy gets angry, he takes it out on me. Now that sounds crazier than any of it." She needed to get busy so she resumed fluting the pie crusts and concentrated on not pinching the dough too hard. "Ennis filed a restraining order against him the day it happened. Explain how I can go back to Augusta and walk in that house without Daddy going nuts on me because of that too?"

Georgia went quiet. Anyone who knew her realized that was a bad sign. Fingers paused in mid-pinch, Savannah met her gaze, "Cat got your tongue? The answer is, I can't."

"Hon, I don't know how to tell you this." She pointed to a chair near her work desk, "Go sit down a minute. I need to tell you something."

Savannah balked, abandoning the pie altogether, "Considering my occupation I know how bad those 'you need to sit down' conversations get. Lay it on me. I can take it."

Georgia uneasily cleared her throat, "I went to Augusta yesterday. I dropped by a couple of places, one being the house. Daddy was flaming mad over your kidnapping but not for the reason you think. He, well… He saw you on TV with Lee and Ethan. It was shot from the scene where you three were left but it showed you and Lee exiting the back of the ambulance together. He held your hand to help you down."

"That's normally how it's done. Daddy's pissed over that? Lee was telling me how much money he paid for our ransom, not having me sign over my birthright."

"Did you realize Lee gave an interview shortly after that? I didn't know it until Daddy told me."

So far Savannah successfully ducked the media with their silly, invasive questions about the kidnapping. If a reporter pinned her down for an answer, she'd say *it happened* and leave it at that. They always twisted the truth with creative editing or manufactured their own spin so why bother volunteering information? It reminded her of the song "Dirty Laundry" in the eighties – ironically it was about the press.

> *Dirty little secrets, dirty little lies,*
> *We got our fingers in everybody's pie,*
> *Love to cut you down to size,*
> *We love dirty laundry.*

The fact Lee consented to an interview flummoxed Savannah. "Lee gave an interview at the scene?"

Georgia nodded uneasily, "He said he was grateful that his sons and daughter were released unharmed."

Savannah's knees and spine went MIA as she sank into the chair. "I'm mincemeat with Daddy. He'll kill me."

"That's what I'm afraid of, hon. Him losing control. Before you call him or go see him, you should know he banned you from the house. You and Ennis both."

It sounded so stupid she couldn't help but chuckle. The gravity of it hit when Georgia failed to join in. The chuckle faded to disbelief, "Oh, my God. You're serious. He *banned* us? I didn't give the interview, Morgan did. What, did he file a restraining order too?"

"No, he's using stronger measures than a piece of paper. That's why I'm forewarning you. He said he'll meet you at the door with Old Faithful. I don't think he'll use it but if he's drunk... Just stay away for a while. Eventually he'll calm down, I hope."

The news stunned Savannah. Old Faithful? He'd meet her at the door with his *shotgun*? Well, why not? Her life turned upside down so why not turn it inside out too? The song's chorus evidently applied to R.J. as well as the media:

Kick 'em when they're up, Kick 'em when their down,
Kick 'em where they sit, Kick 'em all around

She held her head in her hands, "This is incredible. I'm not welcome in my childhood home anymore. Life really is insane these last few weeks, you know? Now Daddy truly hates me, Morgan's shouting to the world that I'm his kid and neither one will take a DNA test to prove it."

"Well, it's not only that." Georgia hesitated. "I'm afraid I might have inadvertently stirred the pot myself but I was so angry about what had happened to Mama and to you."

She really wanted that bourbon now. It sat so close she could practically smell it and taste it. "What did you do, Georgia?"

The older sister shied from Savannah's expression. "I, um, went to see Lee yesterday."

Savannah's gaze narrowed. Inadvertently stirred the pot, her sister said. With what? Judging by her sister's expression she hadn't used a spoon to stir, she plunged a plane prop in the shit stew and gunned the engine. "Go on," was all she could manage.

"I kinda told him about Mama's journals and how she phrased their *encounter* together."

"You what!?" *Be careful, Savannah, she's pregnant. Remember Georgia's pregnant. No matter how much you want to strangle her, don't.*

Georgia cowered from the outburst, a rare reaction for her. Normally she stood up to her younger sister no matter what. This time she seemed to sense the rising poo she stood in. "I'm sorry, I'm sorry, I'm sorry. Look, I was trying to help. I wanted him to back off, to leave you alone. Only I made him mad. Really mad."

"Well, *yeah*. I mean, you do realize you accused a multimillionaire of rape, right?" She added, "We know what he did, he knows what he did but to say it to his face?"

"Actually he denies raping her. He said he loved her and that he might have been *eager* during their *time together* but if she believed he was assaulting her, she would have knocked him out with a lamp. Blah, blah, blah, the lying bastard."

"Hard to hit someone with a lamp when they've got you pinned down," Savannah said. Thanks to Toby Jackson she knew from personal experience how difficult it was to throw a guy – or disable one – that was hell-bent on raping a woman. Nothing about sexual assault surprised her anymore. Offenders used a plethora of excuses or cover-ups for their depravity. She nodded for Georgia to continue.

"He also denied trying to put Daddy out of business. Said he was already losing money and not cut out to run a business."

Her sister always had backbone but to exercise it with Lee Morgan? "Are you on a suicide mission? You're gonna have a kid, Georgia. If you keep stirring hornet's nests you might not, you know? Mess with Lee Morgan too much and you might lose more than a book contract or even your bakery. You could lose your *child* just from stress." Or your life if James Riggs' demise is any indication.

"I've done enough damage without intending to. I've been threatened with a lawsuit if I talk to anyone about Mama's journals plus, after Lee saw your arms, he said he was having a talk with Daddy about his abuse."

Savannah craved Uncle Jack now. She slumped in the seat and buried her face in her hands, "Can this *get* any worse?"

A hand went to her shoulder and squeezed. "'Fraid so, hon. I heard from Daddy this morning. Lee went to the house and braced him about those belt marks. About his general treatment of you all these years."

Savannah gulped then her mouth went cotton dry. "Lee confronted him? In person?"

Georgia hesitated, obviously uncomfortable about proceeding. "He, um, threatened Daddy if he touched you again he'd have a serious talk with Sheriff Donovan and the district attorney. He wants Daddy to serve the maximum time behind bars. Since Lee basically funded Donovan's election campaign and is friends with the DA, Daddy's toast."

Her heart sank, "Daddy *will* kill me if he sees me."

Georgia chose not to comment. She said, "I'm afraid he blames you for getting involved with Lee."

"Lee found me, not the other way around. I never asked for any of this."

"I know that. I tried explaining it. He's got to cool off a while before he listens to reason if he's going to. The confrontation brought back some powerful memories. All bad."

20

Savannah stayed at the bakery until after the lunch crowd thinned out. She dropped by the store on her way home to catch up on the grocery shopping. The second Lily and Anna spied her Charger pull into the driveway, they made a beeline to it from Katherine's house next door. Their enthusiastic greetings revived her weary bones and spirit. Police work tired a person but baking all morning could do it too.

Savannah waved to Katherine Collins who followed her in the house and put Daniel in his crib. "They were angels as usual and I don't think Daniel likes my Johnny Mathis rendition. I tried Elvis. *Love Me Tender* worked like a charm."

Usually anything by Johnny Mathis lulled Daniel to dreamland but according to Katherine, she lacked the panache to pull it off. Savannah took note that Elvis was a good backup. "Thanks, Katherine. I hate to impose so much lately. Good as they are, our kids can be a handful and I know it."

Katherine bobbed her brow, "Just let me borrow that juicy book about the Morgans when you're done. I can't get my hands on one for anything."

She hated to commit to it but did. Katherine probably heard about Savannah's paternity pickle anyway but at least she exercised the tact to keep quiet.

The neighbors parted ways and Savannah proceeded to unload the groceries from the car. A humorous smile curved her mouth at the thought of Katherine singing Elvis songs to Daniel.

She grabbed the heaviest bag last to haul into the house and closed the trunk, hearing car doors nearby. The few people who drove home for lunch were headed back to work. While they trekked back to their jobs, she mulled over what to serve for supper. They'd run through the usual meals for last few days so time to be creative, she thought.

Approaching the door, she heard Lily and Anna goofing around in the living room. She hurried to quieten them down for their brother's sake – and hers. She appreciated the fact Daniel liked Johnny Mathis tunes but Lord, singing them was getting old.

Running footfalls closed in behind her. She wheeled to confront the person. Lately nothing good came from people approaching her from behind so if they meant harm, she'd fling the grocery sack at them.

She had no chance to. A powerful blow sent her sideways and backwards. Her feet tripped over the threshold and she went down hard onto the tiled entry. The grocery bag crashed beside her, sending canned goods rolling across the floor.

Children's screams pierced the air. The baby began wailing. Savannah lay trying to protect herself from the next attack which already started. Pain slashed her arm, her side and back as R.J. threw back the hand holding a leather belt. He whipped it across her back, her front, legs, arms and head, swinging wildly at anything and everything. She grew up with these violent tirades and the older she got, the worse they hurt. The best way to survive them was hunker down and take what he gave. Not today. Not if she had anything to say about it.

"I oughta beat ya till ya bleed for what ya done an' that's what I'm gonna do!" R.J. shouted. The leather branded her shoulder blade on his foreswing and her throat on the backswing. Savannah curled, trying to minimize the frontal attack. The lashings concentrated across her back while she attempted to stand. She yelled for the girls to run to Mrs. Collins. Anything to get them out of the house and safe but the two stood walleyed at their enraged grandpa reading their mama the riot act while flogging her to pieces with a belt.

Savannah frantically pleaded with her children to *run to Mrs. Collins now.* Anna scurried to her room. Lily headed for the phone. In the back of Savannah's mind she swore to review a parent's basic rules with her daughters. Do As I Say *means* Do As I Say. There was no room for hesitation or disobedience in situations like this.

After deflecting his attacks long enough to stand, she grabbed the belt from him. She realized this was a dangerous thing to do since her father considered any interference flagrant defiance so she tried reasoning with him, "I didn't do anything, Daddy. I don't know what you're talking about."

His features evolved. Savannah swallowed hard but stood her ground. He was going to thrash her to pieces and like Humpty Dumpty, there would be no putting Savannah back together again. He jerked the belt from her grasp. The muscles in his arms flexed. His jaw clenched. Against her better judgment, she stayed still, "Daddy, let's talk about th–"

"Ya wanna fight me, do ya? Yer gettin' above yer raisin', girl, all 'cause of that son of a bitch Morgan and I'm gonna make sure ya don't forget where ya came from and what ya were taught." R.J. charged forward. She tried to sidestep but he anticipated the move. A brick wall rammed her backwards. She tripped, taking the brunt of his full-on shove that drove her ribs into the dining table's edge as she fell. The brutal pain stole her breath momentarily. It felt like a homerun hitter slammed a baseball bat into her side.

He stood over her, shouting, "You sicced that son of a bitch on me! He swore to see me in prison if I touched ya again! I'm here to show ya both I'll do what I damn well please with my kids!" He swung the belt. She barely shielded her face in time to feel the tip bite her ear. Another swing landed across her chest. The third wild swing lashed her right breast.

She pushed to one elbow then struggled to her feet while trying to protect her face and cradling her other arm against her ribs. "Daddy, I–" another lash, "I didn't sic anyo–" a harder one, "anyone on you, I swear!" She whimpered as the repeated hits finally began taking their toll.

"Stop hitting her!" Lily screamed and charged at him, phone in one hand, her other rolled in a fist.

"Lily, no!" Savannah tried to reach out and stop her.

In the throes of a drunken rage, R.J. backhanded Lily aside. She shrieked as she tumbled backwards. The phone dropped from her hand.

The sight sparked new life to Savannah's temper. She could take R.J.'s abuse as bad as it was but to attack her children? She doubled her fist and let her punch fly.

Either surprise or disbelief registered with R.J. just before her knuckles crashed into his jaw. She'd fought back when she was a kid but only to escape his rage. This was the first time she reciprocated with real violence.

A lingering flash of pain raced up her hand and arm when it collided with bone. The force and impact knocked him off balance and sent him sideways two steps. "I don't give a damn what you think I did!" she yelled. "Leave my kids out of it! Now get out of my house!" Savannah stopped herself before leveling an ultimatum – leave the kids alone or I'll make the beatings you've given me look like child's play.

She vaguely heard Lily crying. She was too busy watching her father work his jaw and push back his shoulders. The instant he lifted his vision to hers, her blood ran cold – but she positioned herself between him and the kids and intended to stay there at all costs. Judging by R.J.'s expression, the cost would be steep. "Lily, I mean it," she told her oldest. "You and Anna run to Mrs. Collins and tell her..." she stepped back once then twice as he advanced, "tell her to call the pol–"

His fist sank into her stomach, expelling every ounce of breath and triggering a heave that reached her toes. She sank to all fours, battling nausea, pain and desperately struggling to draw enough breath to spur the kids into action. She only managed strained groans resembling *Both of you go. Go.*

R.J. cocked his fist again, "Ya wanna hit me, girl? Yer own daddy? 'Cause make no mistake, ya little shit, *I am yer daddy*, and I aim to beat that respect back into ya."

Savannah had crouched, trying to get her diaphragm to release the vacuum on her lungs but the blows came too fast and furious. She couldn't stop him if she tried. Fighting back always deepened his rage and she committed the cardinal sin by hitting him. From the corner of her eye she saw Lily take Anna's hand and race out the door. *Thank you, Lord. Please let help come in time…*

21

The kids... I have to save the kids... she told herself. *Lily, Anna, go get help. Please...*

"She's waking up," a child exclaimed amid a clamor of unfamiliar voices.

Was that Anna? Were her children safe or was this a dream? Noises and voices sounded muffled. Her brain pounded in her skull – oh, how her head hurt...

"Mama, open your eyes. We're okay."

Lily. Definitely Lily. Something squeezed down on her right bicep. A stranger announced two numbers. She recognized them as a blood pressure reading and the number registered pretty high for her.

The faint smell of scotch and Old Spice still hung in the air. She opened her eyes to see uniform officers standing over her and paramedics crouched beside her. But the most beautiful sight was her kids. Daniel's distant, hysterical cries were music to her ears and though Lily and Anna looked scared out of their minds, they looked fine. Katherine Collins stood between the girls, holding their hands.

Savannah recognized Officers Sims and Olson from Lily's previous 911 call. She sensed two different feelings from the officers. Sims came across hopeful she might wise up and press charges against her father while his older, more seasoned partner left no question how he felt. His face read *here we go again*, a sentiment veteran cops (herself included) tended to develop on habitual domestic calls to an address.

Lily muscled between the paramedics. Her eyes swam with tears, "You wouldn't wake up. I was scared."

Savannah reached to touch her daughter's cheek and automatically jerked back when pain lanced her side. Everything ached. It hurt to move and it really hurt to breathe. "Don't be scared, baby. I'll be okay thanks to you."

"Sergeant," Olson called, "your daughter's an expert at calling 911 on your father."

Great. Just what she needed. More judgment. She wanted to tell him where to stick that comment but groaned instead.

He proudly announced (actually she considered it gloating), "Once we get him behind bars he's staying there. This time we got a witness willing to make a statement."

He pointed to a pallid Katherine who smoothed Lily's hair, "I couldn't believe my eyes. I ran in here and saw him beating you. I've never seen anything so vicious," she shuddered. "He left the moment he saw me but you were out like a light. You weren't responding to my voice or when I shook you."

Olson gave the go-ahead to the paramedics, "Let's get her to the hospital, guys. I want every bruise and injury photographed and documented ASAP. And I want a statement from you, Mrs. Rutherford."

Somewhere in the middle of this mess she'd apparently lost her title with Officer Olson. Instead of Sergeant Prince of the Atlanta Police Department she was now Mrs. Rutherford of 4886 Tilly Mill Road. Well, she didn't see any stripes on his uniform so, "I'm not giving anyone anything. I'm not going to the hospital either."

Katherine couldn't believe her ears, "Savannah, he beat you unconscious."

"Please go to the hospital," Lily pleaded with Anna backing her up loud enough to drive Savannah's headache deeper.

The neighbor assured, "I've informed Ennis of what happened and Edward can take care of Anna and Daniel while I bring Lily to the hospital. She's not letting you out of her sight."

Sims and Olson stepped outside. Katherine sent Lily to check on Daniel. Once she left, Katherine bent down to whisper, "R.J. was yelling about an *incident* regarding your mother years ago."

Oh great. Here it came. The One No One Talks About. Half the world already put two and two together but for R.J. to broadcast the information at top volume about finished her, "Did he mention names?" She didn't have to ask. Katherine's expression read "Lee Morgan" all over it.

Katherine nodded, "He was vehement about what Lee Morgan did back then, if you get my meaning." She glanced toward the cops outside, "Should I say anything to them?"

Savannah flinched while the paramedics rolled her to slide the backboard beneath her, "I'll tell them if they ask. I think the grumpy one's tired of dealing with me so maybe I won't have to."

"R.J. kept yelling about that and something about journals.

Savannah, I'm sorry. I sure never expected to hear what I did."

Savannah knew that feeling very well about a lot of things lately.

Katherine cut her vision to Lily, "I'm afraid Lily's been asking questions too. She's confused and wants to know who her grandpa is. I didn't know what to say."

Yay. One more problem. "Neither do I. Thanks for the forewarning, Katherine, and thanks for helping us out, especially the kids."

"Anytime. No offense but I hope they catch your father quick. I don't think you can survive another attack this brutal."

Neither did she. "They'll get him and when they do, Daddy will make me pay for that too." Savannah held a gentle hand to her ribs, "Katherine? One more favor?"

"Sure. Name it."

"Take Tucker's book. It's on the table beside my recliner. I don't want it anymore."

O O O

Doctors never listened. No matter her fussing, the emergency room doc insisted she spend the night in the hospital. Bruised ribs. Bruised kidneys. A mild concussion. High blood pressure. The list seemed endless – and the most visible wounds were the least dangerous. R.J.'s belt marks left the ugly, raised (and stinging) red marks on her arms, throat, chest and back. Ironically, he'd missed her ass every time.

She campaigned to leave the hospital, saying despite the test results and wounds, they were nothing she couldn't handle at home. His responding frown made her worry he'd admit her to the psych ward instead.

Savannah adjusted the flimsy hospital gown, making sure not to tangle the heart monitor's wires. The last thing she needed was to set off alarms and have the staff converge on her wielding a defibrillator. She pulled the Pepto-Bismol colored blanket over her hips and resigned herself to bad food, bad TV and a bad mood until being released the next day. She snorted her frustration.

Minutes later the usual crowd piled into her room. Ennis, Georgia, Dane, Seth and Lily trooped in single file, each one wearing a different expression. Joy, relief, concern, or shock.

As Ennis and Lily fawned over her, Georgia, arms crossed, braced her with an incredulous, "And you were afraid you'd hurt *him*?"

She realized how ridiculous she'd sounded the day before. "Guess I'm getting stupid in my middle age."

Ennis kissed her, careful to steer clear of the swelling on her bottom lip. "He's staying in jail for this, babe, I'm making sure of it."

"Great. Something else he'll blame me for." She groaned from the nagging headache she assumed might linger for days or weeks a lot like various Morgans had.

"What are you talking about?" Georgia asked.

Lily climbed onto the bed and snuggled beside her mother. Savannah hadn't the heart to tell her it was the side with bruised ribs. After all, the child saved her life. She eased her arm around her brave little girl, wincing as she did so. "He thinks I snitched and told Lee about that last whipping. As if the marks weren't obvious enough. Lee noticed them when we met for lunch. I never said a word but I got blamed for Morgan having a stern talk with him."

Seth rolled his eyes, "Ever since you two dug through Mama's journals our lives have been untenable."

"Thanks, big brother. I needed more guilt," Savannah shot back.

"Van, I didn't mean it that way. I'm so sick of the Morgans and that book's just a nuclear bomb of crap. I'm getting questions at work about Mama and Lee. They want to know if what Tucker wrote is true."

"The book is filled with lies except for the part about Charlene," a new voice vowed. Lee Morgan. He and Ethan entered the room, Lee in a business suit and Ethan in his casual attire of polo shirt and khaki Dockers.

Seth's hands fisted, "Well, well. If it isn't the bane of our mother's existence."

Savannah was too tired for another fight, "Mr. Morgan, I don't have the energy to deal with much more today."

"I called Lee," Georgia confessed. "I wanted him to see firsthand the results of his interference. You see, Mr. Morgan, Savannah paid the price. Again. She always has."

For the first time, she watched Lee Morgan's confidence wilt, "Savannah, I never meant for this to happen. You have to believe me. I was trying to protect you."

"It's true," Ethan agreed. "Dad never expected R.J. to hold you responsible for his visit."

How could she make them understand? Answer – she couldn't.

"No, but Daddy's always taken his anger out on me–" her mouth snapped shut and she did a mental facepalm. Damn concussion. It made her a jabbering half-wit.

Lee's back straightened. The self-assured, formidable businessman returned, "No one hurts my family and gets away with it. Your mother meant a lot to me no matter what's written or said, she was my first love and I never got over losing her. One way or another Robert Prince will learn his lesson about hurting my daughter – and you *are* mine."

Lily bailed out of bed. She ran to Lee, tilting back to meet the tall man's gaze. Savannah saw her daughter's barely restrained joy as she asked, "Mama, you mean Mr. Morgan's my grandpa?"

Lee bent eye level with her, "Yes, I am, sweetheart, and this is your Uncle Ethan."

Ethan shook her hand, "You must be Lily. It's a pleasure to meet you."

Lily nodded, wide-eyed with awe as her blue eyes volleyed between Ethan and Lee. Lee crowed, "You look so much like your mother did at that age. So beautiful."

"Mr. Morgan is not your grandpa," Savannah told her daughter. "Not until he gets a DNA test proving it."

The smiles on Lee's and Lily's faces diminished a shade. Lily countered with, "But he's nicer than Grandpa. He says I'm beautiful and he doesn't yell at you or hurt you."

Lee and Ethan exchanged glances then shifted their vision to Savannah. What could she say? It was true. Lee had called Lily beautiful and no, he hadn't yelled or hurt Lily's mama. But, "Until he gets that test and it says he's your grandpa, he is not your grandpa."

Lee cupped a hand around Lily's ear and whispered. Whatever he said inspired a giggle and a huge smile. He probably promised to buy her Disneyland, Savannah thought. He concluded with a kiss to Lily's cheek, "We have to wait until your mother feels better. I want her to have fun too."

Lily spun to her mother, "Mama, I don't care about stupid DNA. I want Mr. Morgan to be my grandpa."

Savannah nearly laughed. "And I want a normal life. Doesn't look good for either of us, kid. No DNA, no Gramps."

Lee heaved an exasperated sigh. Ethan shrugged, "She's as stubborn as you are, Dad."

"Yeah," he winced and rubbed his forehead. "I'm not having a DNA test and I'm fairly certain Robert won't either *but* if you can get him to agree to one, I will too. You're part of my family and I want to spend time with you and when I'm gone you will receive your rightful inheritance. You are the oldest of my children and should benefit as such."

Savannah argued, "If I'm so important to you, why didn't you keep in contact all these years? It's been over twenty years since Mama died and since then I've only seen you at police functions."

"I was there to see you receive your commendations," he said. "In your younger years I tried to see you. I even wrote letters that were apparently intercepted. Ethan and I both attended your golf tournaments. I always took your team to lunch after you won the championships because I wanted to share those special moments with you and get better acquainted. When I saw you at work a few weeks ago, I took that opportunity to make contact and try to build a relationship. I want to be more involved with all my children – and my grandchildren. I know Thanksgiving is weeks away but I'm inviting you and your family to supper. I expect Lily and Anna would love Mrs. Gardner's double chocolate pie."

Ethan rubbed his tummy and winked at Lily, "It's delicious. That and her cheesecake topped with chocolate sauce and strawberries."

Savannah saw Lily's eyes light up, "Ethan, you're not helping."

He shrugged, "We'd love to spend Thanksgiving together, the first one as a whole family, but I figure you're uncomfortable with Press and the others being there. Why don't you come by for dessert? The others barely stay for the meal so they'll be gone by the time you, Ennis and the kids get there. Just think about it."

Good old Ethan. The peacekeeper. She noticed Lee remained silent but raised a hopeful brow. He wasn't stupid. He relinquished the crusade to his son who employed persuasive charm, not a mallet. Meanwhile Lily let her opinion be known by whining *can we please go* as if her life depended on it.

Just to get temporary peace, Savannah looked to Ennis and sighed, "Okay, we'll think about it."

Lee beamed, "Excellent." He wrapped up the meeting with a professional flair. "I will be checking on you later, dear. Expect a call."

As the two exited, Ethan gleefully grinned, "Take care, sis."

O   O   O

This was insanity. Puredee ol' foolishness, Dane told himself. He'd heard pregnancy made women do weird things. He'd seen Savannah wolf down a whole box of Cocoa Puffs at one time when she was pregnant with Lily. Seen his sister-in-law Bobbi laugh, yell, and cry all within five minutes of each other. But this put a whole new spin on pregnancy quirks. He never expected his calm, levelheaded wife to risk life and limb for a dab of spit and a few hairs, yet here they were driving to Augusta to collect those items – from her daddy or more precisely, his belongings.

Still, if the stunt backfired, the world would implode on the two idiots racing around the two story house on Walton Way because if R.J. caught them, they'd be laid up in the hospital just like Savannah.

Georgia tried diplomacy by calling to ask for a DNA sample. R.J.'s reaction should have been a hint. Dane heard his refusal from across the room. Her father not only refused but added he and Charlene had three kids and he shouldn't have to prove it.

After her ears stopped ringing, she mentioned helping herself to his DNA on the sly. Dane about fainted. But like a good (and probably stupid) husband, he supported his wife's decision to swipe the samples. "I don't like this," Dane told his wife as he exited onto Walton Way. At least the light traffic along the street boded well in case they needed a quick getaway.

"So you've said. I wish you'd stop worrying. He should be at the bar right now so we'll be safe."

He wiped his brow. The weather turned cool for only the third time that November but he sweated like he sat in the summer Texas sun. He'd die of nerves or heatstroke, he was sure of it. "Darlin', look what he did to Peach. He could do that – or worse – to you. We shoulda brought Seth. It takes two men to pull him off someone, you know." He gripped the steering hard. He'd offered to come alone. When Georgia rejected the idea he mentioned calling Seth to accompany him. After all, the man had been an Army Ranger – no one screwed with those guys. Well, not normally, anyhow. When his wife remained quiet, he blew out a breath and headed to the Tahoe, resigned. He reminded, "One sign he's home and we're outta there, got it?"

"I want to help Savannah."

"I do too but I'm not sacrificing you or the baby for this. I'll drop you off at the church up ahead and handle things from there." It was the only reasonable option since they already passed the Peachtree Road turn off, the last one before coming to the house. If R.J.'s truck sat at the curb, Dane planned to drive past the house no matter what Georgia said. He shouldn't have been home at all. The whole mess could have been avoided had some mystery "benefactor" kept their cash in their pockets and not bailed R.J. out of jail. "Who the hell bailed him out anyway?"

"He's got a few friends around who might. One thing's for sure. None of us posted bail for him. And I'm going in with you. I don't want you arrested for assault. We have enough jailbirds with Daddy."

Dane wheeled the Tahoe into the church's parking lot anyway, "You're not going in, Georgia. I want to help Peach too but not at the cost of you or our child. He's too volatile."

She motioned him to drive, "Sooner we get there, the less likely he's home."

He wasn't home. Dane breathed a sigh of relief. The knot in his stomach, however, tightened and seemed to grow. He intended to race through that house faster than a prairie fire with a tail wind then they'd get the hell out of Dodge.

The second she unlocked the door they split ways, Dane heading for the downstairs bathroom and Georgia going for the cherrywood coffee table. She shook out a plastic bag and carefully dropped a shot glass in the bag then sealed it.

Dane emerged from the bathroom holding a comb, "Who's analyzing this DNA test? No matter where we go it'll look funny when we bring in these samples."

Georgia plucked several silver hairs from the comb and shook them into another plastic bag, "Daddy's not the only one with friends who do favors. Just leave it to me."

22

Her first day at work after R.J.'s tirade proved more painful than she expected. Between a headache, bruise on her jaw, a hitch in her back and simply trying to draw a deep breath (oh, how those ribs ached!), she wondered if her family had been right. She was nuts for returning so soon.

Heads turned when she walked into the station. Their expressions somehow confirmed that yes, she'd lost her ever-loving mind as Ennis so eloquently put it.

Always one to state the obvious, Sergeant Sweeney piped up, "You do realize 'go play in the freeway' is just a saying, right?"

She clamped her lips tight not only against the pain but the fiery retort scorching her tongue. She opted for, "Thanks for the newsflash."

Major Hoffman stood in the doorway to his office watching her walk gingerly by the sergeant's desk. "Sergeant Prince."

Savannah's shoulders slumped which caused a pang in her back and ribs, "Yes, Major?"

"Are you sure you're fit for duty? You seem… sore."

"Yessir, I'll be fine. Thank you."

"Prince," he crooked his finger at her.

She approached, still trying not to flinch when she walked.

Hoffman lowered his voice, "The building won't collapse if you take a sick day. I understand the hospital kept you overnight. Go home and take care of yourself a day or two."

"I appreciate your concern, Major, but I hate getting behind in my work and I'm a detective short with Tierce out tomorrow."

Savannah could tell he didn't approve. He nodded, "I'll say one thing for you. You're dedicated."

Until she responded to Mandy Stewart's distress call, she and the major seldom interacted. Hoffman had been highly impressed with his detective sergeant's actions, Josh said, and called her a valuable asset to the department.

Savannah had been called a lot of things but rarely a valuable asset. So why tarnish her newfound status by going home and resting despite it being her heart's desire?

She set her purse on the desk and pulled her holster off. Now for the test. Sitting without acting like she landed on a cactus. She tucked her left arm gently to her side to protect her ribs and, with a breath trapped behind pursed lips, eased into the chair. The breath released slow and shaky. She made it.

After locking her purse and holster up, she began reviewing paperwork. Off to the side sat Mathis's list of Morgan subsidiaries and a separate list of local properties. Savannah hadn't had a lot of time to look it over yet. After she made a few notes regarding the day's workload, she'd dive headfirst into the list.

Glasses on, pen in hand, she began jotting down her day's agenda. As usual when she got busy, her office phone rang. She answered it, "Sergeant Prince."

"Hello, Princess."

She fisted the pen in hand with the yearning to jam it in the caller's ear. The nerve, she thought. First he kidnapped her and held her at gunpoint for hours and now he had the audacity to call her. "*You.*" She abbreviated the phrase since *you son of a bitch* probably might get her in trouble somehow.

"Yeah, *me.* Wanna know who set up the abductions?"

"Why, are you turning yourself in?" Yeah, like that would ever happen.

"Only to you."

Uh-huh. And I've got a bridge to sell you... Savannah removed her glasses, "Only to me, huh? I go to an address and get jumped again only this time I don't go home alive. Sorry but I'm not that stupid. I have work to do. Bye." She reached to drop the phone in its cradle.

"Hey! Riggs is already dead and I'm probably next! I'm in danger here and listen close – I'm not the only one!"

She took a moment to explain, "That happens when you kidnap people, you know. No one likes a kidnapper." When she overheard him mumble *this was a waste of time,* Savannah lightened up on being the flaming cynical cop – sort of, "Okay, I'll bite. Besides you, who else is in danger?"

"I want a deal. I know I screwed up abducting a cop but I've got real information here. I need a guarantee – no prison time in exchange for me spilling the beans."

Yeah, right, "I can't promise you anything. Only a DA can make deals and I'm fresh out of those at the moment."

"That's right, Princess, play the smartass with me. For someone claiming you're not a Morgan, you're sure acting like one of them."

She blew out a sigh, "Let me call the DA. By the time I pick you up, she'll be here."

"Will you put in a good word for me? A real good one? I tried to take it easy on you and I stopped Riggs from killing you."

"I promise to do what I can to help you but this better not be another ambush or worse."

"It's not. Bring another cop with you but choose the one you trust the most. I'm in no position to do anything but save myself and the people I was hired to kill but time's running short since they took me off those jobs."

"The one I trust the most? You make it sound like cops are involved in this mess."

"Not every cop is true-blue, if you get my drift. One trusted cop and you. I'll be at Emerald Donuts two blocks from your station in twenty minutes. You'll see me when I know the coast is clear." He hung up.

An occasional officer strode by her doorway. Had any hesitated when they overheard her conversation? She hadn't noticed. Did Alpha Male mean uniform or detective? Because the last two months or so they received three new uniform officers plus one new detective, if that meant anything. And did he mean her station in particular or cops in general?

She didn't have time to analyze the cryptic conversation but she knew one thing for sure. One trusted cop? *No way, buddy. I'm bringing two.*

Savannah opened the desk drawer for her gun and holster. Her ribs argued when she equipped her belt with that and a set of handcuffs. She stopped by Ennis's door and knocked, "With me. I'll explain outside."

The two stopped by Mathis's door. "I need you with us," she told him. "We're going for donuts." And a felon – but she kept that to herself.

"You're talkin' my language, Sarge," Mathis grabbed his suit jacket and fell in behind his colleagues.

Once outside she confessed why she summoned them both then told Mathis, "You arrive first. We won't be far behind. This may be another setup so watch for an ambush. He said he'd be alone but let's face it – how many guys like this surrender peacefully?"

"But we *are* getting donuts, right?" Mathis wanted to clear up the "important" stuff first.

"Yes, John, go ahead and get donuts. But take your personal car, okay? If he sees two detective cars, I'm afraid it'll spook him."

Mathis was happy again, "Sure thing. Any special requests while I'm there?"

She knew what he meant but only cared about one thing. "Just don't let us get kidnapped or killed."

O   O   O

When Savannah and Ennis arrived at Emerald Donuts, Mathis already sat at a bistro table outside, two boxes of donuts in front of him and munching on a glazed donut. He took a bite, made brief eye contact with her then returned to his private eating orgy. Their colleague seemed engrossed in consuming his pastry but Savannah knew him. She'd been on enough stakeouts with him to realize Mathis could scarf down a meal while doing surveillance.

He'd positioned himself, back against the wall, in view of tables, the sidewalk and the businesses across the street. The morning rush for donuts subsided to a handful of customers who chose to enjoy their purchase outside before the day's heat set in.

Savannah and Ennis stood at the curb searching for anyone acting skittish or suspicious. After a glance at her watch, she realized how odd they looked standing on the sidewalk like tourists waiting to hail a cab. She might care more about that if her body turned down the misery level in her side and back. The car ride plus getting in and out of the car wasn't exactly pleasant.

"Should we sit?" Ennis asked. "You look uncomfortable."

Yes, the ribs ached anew from the exercise but sitting limited movement which made them more vulnerable. As appealing as sitting sounded, she'd tough it out with the comforting knowledge that her gun was in easy reach. "No. I want to be on my feet for this, just in case he brings friends." Savannah nonchalantly pulled her elbow in. On a good day when her daddy hadn't gone Muhammad Ali on her, she boasted a decent fast draw. Today, not so much. Despite the pain, her focus remained sharp, her eyes and ears on alert for sudden movements and any surprises.

Another glance at her watch. It would be a long two minutes.

After twelve more minutes, no one had shown. "I figured he was shining me on." She pointed to the car, "Let's go."

They started at a casual pace toward the car. Mathis rose from his chair, licked his fingers while keeping a covert eye to the couple. He hung back, stretching and looking at traffic passing by.

Savannah and Ennis kept ambling. They approached a tall hedgerow to her left. Her sixth sense said move closer to the curb to ensure their safety. Instead she placed her hand on her belly offset to the side near her .38 – just in case.

The nearer they got, the harder her heart pounded and the closer her hand edged to the .38. Something felt wrong about that hedgerow and wanted to be ready.

"Princess," a familiar voice called from behind the bush.

She instinctively grabbed the gun's handle, "I can draw my weapon in eight-tenths of a second," she warned. "Don't make me scare the public by shooting you. You better be alone and keep those hands in sight. Come on out slowly."

Ennis didn't screw around. He already pulled his .38.

"Who's your partner?" Alpha Male asked.

"My husband," she said.

"Does he moonlight anywhere?"

"No." She was irritated over his third degree, "now get out here."

"I got my hands up. Don't shoot." Another second passed when he stepped into view, hands raised as he'd said.

The man who had put an assault rifle to her head and advised her to *let it happen* looked like a mean son of a bitch who *would've* pulled the trigger if given the go-ahead. She motioned with her head, nodded to their detective sedan only feet away, "You know the routine."

He assumed the same position he forced on her that night near the alley. Hands on the car, legs spread apart. Ennis searched and cuffed him while she read the man his rights.

She opened his billfold. Caleb Franklin. "Mr. Franklin, I hope you have stupendous information for us because you're gonna need it to buy any break with the DA."

He looked over his shoulder at her, "For that to happen, I have to get there alive. Take me in the back door."

Ennis opened the back door for Franklin, "You're done making demands. Get in."

Franklin did. Ennis leaned in with a glare so deadly it she paused to ensure the glare was the only thing he gave him. It was.

"You kidnapped my wife," her livid spouse reminded their handcuffed suspect. "You deserve to rot in prison. I'll make sure you do." He slammed the door.

Savannah glanced back to see Mathis proudly toting the boxes of donuts to his car while devouring another glazed. She waved to him. He held the donut between his teeth and waved back. He was headed back to the station with his bounty.

She eased into the driver's seat and made eye contact with Franklin in the rear-view mirror, "Who are you afraid of at the station? Who might see you?"

He stared back in the mirror, "I'm scared of all cops right now but I figure it's better to take my chances with you than some other people I know. Just keep in mind I didn't have to surrender, Sergeant. I chose to because I'm not into killing. I want protection, I want a deal then I want a plane ticket to Timbuktu so no one finds me. Take me in the back door and get me that deal because if I go to prison, I'm not saying a word and you'll find a couple of bodies somewhere. And Sergeant, if you don't stop these murders, you'll never forgive yourself."

23

"This guy's a crackpot," Mathis hitched his thumb at Franklin sitting on the other side of the one way mirror. "He's certifiable. Probably watched too many *X-Files* over the years. He'll only talk to you and the DA together. The dumbass is demanding a free ride on kidnapping and terrorizing a cop."

Savannah paced in front of the mirror as she had the last half hour. The district attorney tried, along with Mathis, to pry the information from Franklin. The woman exhibited amazing patience after offering him a reduced sentence and even simple probation for his crimes. He'd refused to speak except to say he wanted Sergeant Prince in the room and the "fat guy" out of it. Now the DA's patience dwindled to the point she made noises about leaving. Savannah wasn't about to let that happen. She wanted to know what Franklin meant by *if you don't stop these murders, you'll never forgive yourself.* Her only obstacle: Josh Hunter. He'd ordered her to let Mathis handle questioning Franklin. Ordered. Not suggested. Not said "maybe it would be a good idea if..." He laid it out plain and simple, "Step in there and I'll double the last suspension. Stay out or else."

Savannah checked the hall for signs of her boss, telling Mathis, "You stand watch for Hunter and I'll sneak in there long enough to get answers from Franklin."

"That's a big risk, kid. The boss made it sound like Tibetan monks would be breakdancing at a disco before you got off suspension."

"You're simultaneously dating yourself and mixing decades. Come on," she left the observation room with a grumbling Mathis following behind.

"Okay," she capitulated. "I'll tell him he can trust you then I'll leave." She opened the interview room door.

Franklin's temper fired, "Where have you been? Did I not make myself clear? I only talk to you."

"Yeah, I got that loud and clear, but someone higher up the food chain banned me from doing it. Listen closely, Franklin. Detective Mathis has been my friend and trusted colleague for many years so you can talk to him. You did catch the word *trusted*, right? He's an honest cop. Answer his questions."

"I don't trust anyone but you and only because of what I know. You won't jeopardize lives. You can't afford to."

"What does that mean *I can't afford to?*"

"Sit down and get your DA here to give me immunity and I'll tell you."

"I just told you I cannot do that. I would if I could but I have people I answer to and they kinda control my career."

"Then I'm not talking."

What was he? Stupid? "Detective Mathis is honest. I trust him with my life. Talk to him." She turned to leave before Hunter caught her disobeying his order.

"You trust him with other peoples' lives? People you love?"

She wheeled with an expression that caused the DA to recoil. Savannah stalked to Franklin, braced her hands on the metal table and leaned in close, "What did you say?" Maybe she was nuts but it sounded like he threatened her family and no one got away with that.

Franklin did not shy from her, "Sorry, Princess. Go talk to those people who control your career. You have a choice to make – your job or people you love. Tick-tock, tick-tock, the clock's ticking. Someone's been contracted to do this dirty deed so you'd better hurry."

Mathis took her arm, "Remember what the boss said. Get outta here and let me do my job." He whispered to her, "I'll get info from him, one way or another." He opened the door and uttered a resigned, "Oh, boy."

"Sergeant Prince," a very disgruntled Josh Hunter summoned, "did I not order you to stay out of this interview room?"

She stared daggers at Franklin, "Yessir, you did but–"

"And you disobeyed that direct order. Do you happen to recall what I said would happen if you disobeyed a direct order?"

"Yessir, but I was trying–"

"Gun and shield, Sergeant. Now."

"Hey," Franklin argued, "she was telling me I could trust this guy. That's all."

Hunter took her by the arm and tugged her from the room while answering Franklin, "I don't need your input on how to manage my detectives. As of now she's suspended but she's right. Mathis can be trusted."

The captain closed the door and escorted her down the hall to his office. Trying to rein in her rising temper, she marched to his desk, plucked her badge from her belt and tossed it on top of his paperwork. She pulled the .38 from the holster, unloaded it and placed it alongside the badge.

Josh watched her carefully orchestrated movements then met her gaze for gaze as she faced him, hands clamped to her hips in silent defiance and outrage. He told her, "This little ritual is becoming a habit."

She spoke with barely restrained civility, "I was telling Franklin that Mathis was trustworthy. Otherwise he wasn't going to talk and still probably won't. Meanwhile according to Franklin, people I care about are going to die. Mathis has to get those names out of him. He has to."

Savannah nodded to her gun, "I'll bring my off duty gun after end of shift."

He tapped his desk, "Pick 'em up. You're not suspended."

Confusion parted the anger. Before she spoke he explained, "I saw everything from the observation room. He can't balk on talking to Mathis if you're not here so make yourself scarce by staying in your office."

O O O

She obsessed over Caleb Franklin's declaration. "You have a choice to make – your job or people you love. Tick-tock, tick-tock…"

To be safe she called the school. Only she, Ennis, Georgia and

Dane were allowed to pick them up. Once Lily and Anna were accounted for, Savannah instructed the school to keep the inside until she or Ennis arrived to take them home. Next she called the daycare to ensure Daniel was okay then called Georgia and Dane only to get voicemail. After leaving a message to stay home and telling them she'd explain later, she tried her daddy. As usual he was gone or ignoring the phone. She bet on the former since he stayed at the bar until after the local news. A call to Seth resulted in an annoyingly cavalier assurance that he and Leah would be fine and why was she so paranoid anyway? Savannah repeated what she left on Georgia and Dane's voicemails. She told her brother she'd explain later. The call ended with him questioning her mental health. By then she did too.

She spent thirty minutes pacing her office and fighting the urge to sneak into the observation room. She glanced at her watch. Thirty-one minutes. Tick-tock, tick-tock…

An hour passed. An hour and a half. She couldn't stand it anymore. Out the door and down the hall she went, determined to see the progress her colleague made with Franklin. She turned the corner and ran into Josh Hunter and John Mathis. Hunter's brow sank, "Going somewhere?"

"Restroom," she lied.

He directed her back to her office, "We need to talk."

For once that day she didn't mind following orders. Josh closed the door for privacy, "Ground rules first. I've assigned Mathis as lead on this case. You are a victim and a witness, understand? There will be severe repercussions if I find out you're snooping around behind his back and if you take it too far, you may end up in jail."

The mention of jail certainly got her attention. "Why would I end up in jail?"

Josh nodded to Mathis who in his own roundabout way began explaining, "Like Riggs, Franklin and his crew work security for Morgan. According to him, someone in the Morgan clan set up the kidnappings. And kid, you ain't gonna like this. There are cops on the Morgan security payroll."

She already knew that, she said. Franklin pretty much spelled it out on the phone. *Not every cop is true-blue.* Franklin's actions also indicated those not-so-true-blue cops might be working with her at Zone 2. He surrendered only to her. He demanded she bring one trusted cop with her. He asked if Ennis moonlighted after shift then told her to take him in the back door. Yep, that part all added up. "So which cops work here with us and moonlight for Morgan? I'm guessing they're working the eight-to-four with me since they spend their evenings terrorizing other cops."

For some reason Mathis seemed reluctant to answer. Then she found out why. "He sent us to his house for a thumb drive. Said it had that information and more on it but when we got there, the place had been ransacked and the drive was gone – if there was one to begin with."

The longer Mathis spoke, the deeper her frustration rooted in. Okay, someone found the thumb drive before Mathis did but that didn't mean Franklin couldn't cough up the names he dangled like carrots for the last few hours. The same ones giving her a simultaneous ulcer and nervous breakdown from worrying. She pushed her shoulders back, started toward the door, "Let me in there. I'll get those names outta him – and everything else. Whatever was on that thumb drive is in his head too."

She rankled when Josh blocked her exit. He took over, "He told us the names. Before you hear them though, do you enjoy being a sergeant?"

He had to be kidding. "Of course I do."

"Remember how hard you worked for it because there will be serious consequences if you disobey orders. One hint of interference can remove that title. That's from the zone commander himself."

Now she was confused again, "The zone commander? What's he got to do with this?"

He turned to Mathis, "Tell her."

He removed another slip of paper from his jacket. "How ya doin' lately, kid?"

Savannah detected the underlying meaning. *Are you still drinking like a fish?* She was drinking but thankfully relearned a valuable lesson with that nuclear hangover she'd had. "I'm fine, John. Really."

"This is the result of our other piece of business with Franklin. The hit list."

"There's a list?"

"The one on top is definite he said but the one under it depends on how the first one goes."

What? "What does that mean?"

Josh replied, "I think once you see it, it'll become clearer to you."

Mathis handed her the paper. She slipped her glasses on and

flipped open the note. The bottom dropped out of her stomach at the sight of the names. She shook her head, "No. No, no, no, this has to be a joke. A sick joke."

Josh pushed a chair behind her, "Sit down, Savannah."

She swallowed hard, willing the growing sickness to ebb. She did not sit for fear of needing to suddenly bolt for the bathroom. "Mathis, are you sure about this?"

"Franklin is," he replied in an uncharacteristic soft voice. "Initially he was the one contracted to do it. Now someone else has the job."

At the top of the list read Robert Prince. The second name listed: Georgia Prince Rutherford. She stared at the names, trying to wrap her mind around the bizarre turn of events. Someone put a hit on her father and sister the way John Gotti put a hit on Paul Castellano for control of the Gambino family. Just order it and it got done. The memory of Castellano's bloody, bullet-riddled body lying on the sidewalk outside Sparks Steakhouse raked a shiver down her, especially when she put her daddy or sister in his place. What happened if R.J. stepped out of his pickup outside the bar (Castellano simply went out for a steak that evening) and got mowed down? Or Georgia went shopping for a roast only to be gunned down in the parking lot?

Savannah snatched the phone off her belt, hurriedly accessed her contacts. She called R.J. but got the answering machine. She scrolled through her contacts until coming to the bar in Augusta that her daddy called his second home. The bartender hadn't seen him that day. A mild curse later, she tried Georgia at home. The answering machine picked up. She called her sister's cell phone only to hear Georgia's voicemail greeting. Savannah's next curse emerged hotter and coarser followed by, "Where the hell is everyone?"

She headed to the door. Josh blocked her exit, "Where are you going?"

"To wring more answers out of Franklin."

"Step one foot in that jail and you *will* be suspended," her boss warned. "And no bright ideas about going after the Morgans either. You'll not only lose your job but go to jail. Let Mathis handle the investigation. I'll assign a protection detail to Georgia – if she'll accept it – then I'll call Augusta and speak with the sheriff there about R.J."

o   o   o

A quick glance into the Hoffman's office showed Josh Hunter's more animated nature as he and the major discussed (rather loudly) Franklin's revelation. Hunter wanted Franklin moved out of their station and to a safer location, away from Morgan's lackeys *and* Savannah. While the two engaged in a spirited conversation, Savannah intended to pry more specifics from Caleb Franklin. Who, when, why and where and maybe even how she'd ask. And the bastard better cough up details or he'd realize *she* was the cop he should have feared all along. She wasn't about to sit on the sidelines while her family sat in the crosshairs.

The moment Charlie Sullivan – the officer in charge of the jail – saw her, he balked at her presence. She was aware Hunter gave him forewarning she'd likely show up. He also instructed Charlie to track him down if she did.   She tried her best to settle Sullivan down, promising not to murder Franklin. She didn't, however, promise not to maim him and even handed over her gun.

She headed to the cells where she found Franklin sitting on the cot, alert to every noise he heard.

"You're not supposed to be here," he halfway accused.

"I won't tell if you don't. Tell me which Morgan made that list."

"I don't know. It came from the Chief Security Officer which initially comes from Morgan himself."

"Who is supposed to kill my daddy and sister and when?"

"I don't know."

She grabbed the bars, "Who's going to kill my family, Franklin?"

"I told you I–"

"Don't tell me you don't know!" She gave the bars a hard shake then regretted it when an invisible horse kicked her left side. She held a hand to her throbbing ribs while slanting Franklin the evil eye. The frustration of a simple door separating her from learning the killer's name overwhelmed her. Just to pry those bars apart, climb in and beat the name out of him…

"Sergeant, you need to calm down."

Somehow during her haze of fury, Charlie Sullivan had approached her without her noticing. He stood a fair distance back though, giving her explosive mood a wide berth.

She leveled a look at Charlie that sent him back another step, "Unlock this door. I'm trying to save my daddy and my sister."

"I'm sorry, Sergeant. My orders are to leave his cell locked."

Franklin volunteered, "Your sister should be safe for now."

She wheeled back to face him, "*Should be?* I don't work on *should be*, I work on facts and the fact is her name is on that list." Despite the punishing pain, she rattled the door with all her strength, "Tell me who was assigned to kill my family!"

"Think. Cops on the payroll. Anyone around here been kissing your ass lately? Paying you more attention? There's a reason and it's because he's been told you're Lee Morgan's kid."

What the hell? She wanted answers, not a friggin' pop quiz. "I don't have time to waste, you son of a bitch. Tell me."

He stepped closer, just out of reach. Motioned for Charlie to scram. Franklin whispered, "Talk to your captain about providing me protection, getting me transferred, something so I'll be safe. You swear it?" After she nodded, he continued, "Don't go to your other boss because that's the person you're looking for."

She suddenly felt sick. A denial hung at the back of her throat. Hoffman? How was that possible? How could a cop agree to murder another person's family? A *cop's* family? Of course the answer led back to money, it always did. But a cop's family? Hoffman was an expert marksman. He proudly displayed the proof with awards hanging in his office.

Savannah grabbed the bars for another reason now. To brace herself from collapsing. She bore the ache in her side that seemed take a backseat to the fact her boss – the man who campaigned for her commendation, the one who sounded so concerned about her that morning – would be the one to kill her daddy and her sister. And which

Morgan benefitted from their deaths? Lee. He was the only one who insinuated himself into her life. Except Ethan, the others hated her and laidback Ethan minded his own business.

Franklin planted himself on the cot and sat back against the wall, "Before you ask, I don't know when, where or how but I'd assume it's very soon. As you know, your boss is a man of few words and hates procrastination. Isn't it ironic? If you accept the CSO job, you'll be Hoffman's superior because Lee Morgan wants you that much. Kinda makes you reconsider that offer, doesn't it, Princess?"

"I turned down that job."

"Doesn't matter. He wants you at all costs. Heard him say it myself."

She couldn't wrap her mind around this conversation even yet, "The cost of my family?"

He remained silent.

Well that explained Hoffman's "kissing her ass" as Franklin called it. First, Morgan told him she was his daughter and second that his daughter was considering the CSO job. What escaped her was who ordered the kidnappings and was Hoffman part of that crew? Was Lee that desperate to look like a hero that he arranged it? She didn't think so but she never thought he would rape her mother or resort to murder just to claim Savannah as his daughter either. "I'm sure Detective Mathis asked you this but I'm asking now. Who set up the kidnappings and was Hoffman part of your team?"

Franklin sighed, "Can't tell you who set up the kidnapping, but yeah, your boss was there. Even with the mask he was concerned you'd recognize him when he put the Stun-Cuff on you."

The nausea slowly crept upward. The radiating pain spread through her back and chest, forcing her to release her hold on the bars and cradled her side. Savannah felt stupid for leaping into Uncle Jack's Magic Juice. Had she abstained she might have avoided the kidnapping, "I shouldn't have had those drinks and maybe I would have recognized him."

"Sergeant, are you okay?" Charlie was on his feet and headed toward her.

"No, Charlie, I'm not but thanks for asking." She waved him off and got down to business with Franklin, "You said Georgia's safe for now?"

"Unless she starts making waves again, I understand she'll be fine. Try having a talk with her."

She'd do more than that. Savannah turned and on unstable legs, walked out and climbed the stairs. By the time she hit the landing, her misery skyrocketed so she popped a couple of Tylenol. She had to protect her daddy and Georgia and couldn't do it bogged down in pain. Both were stubborn as mules and R.J. still refused to see her but she'd do what she could.

Savannah went out the back door to her car. Technically Atlanta experienced autumn but only in name. Green, vibrant trees outnumbered the few others bearing signature orange, red and yellow leaves. Parks and front yards made the city look indecisive about the season, as if summer refused to surrender its grasp. The stifling heat and suffocating humidity gave testament to that and by the time she reached her Charger, she already broke a sweat. She dialed Dane's number. It too went to voicemail. She went ahead and left a message to call her back ASAP and added that it was critical he do so.

She dialed Georgia again and groaned in frustration when she received the voicemail prompt. Why did they both turn off their phones? Without fail, one always answered until today. She opted to leave the same message with Georgia.

Savannah took a deep breath. The next call was the hardest. R.J. may have banned her and Ennis from the house but he needed to know he was in danger. He'd blow it off, she knew that, but if he wouldn't allow her to protect him, the least she could do was tell him to duck and cover.

She dialed and waited. Again a machine picked up. Not surprising. R.J. refused to carry a cell phone and rarely stayed at the house past eating, sleeping and showering.

"Daddy, I know you're angry with me but you need to know…" she continued, giving a general explanation that he was in danger and to be extra careful everywhere he went and with everything he did. She ended it with, "Daddy, I love you and I want you safe."

While leaving her message she scanned the parking lot. The major's car was gone. Not an official APD vehicle but his own personal Volvo SUV that he raved about buying a few months back. Savannah had walked by his office while he bragged to Josh and the desk sergeant about the horsepower, front seat backrest massage, park assist pilot and premium sound system. Josh looked ready to puke. Now I know how he afforded that car, she reflected. By being Morgan's henchman.

She checked her watch. Quitting time. She'd drop by to see if Georgia was home.

She was on the highway to her sister's house when the phone rang. It was Dane, "Savannah?"

Savannah heard fear and something else in his voice. Anger? "What's happened?" she demanded, feeling a flood of adrenaline wash through her. Had Franklin been wrong? He'd said Georgia was supposed to be okay "for now".

"We're at Atlanta Medical's emergency – hold on."

She heard him ask *is she alright* then a mumbling voice replied. The voice sounded grim. Dane returned to their conversation. He wasn't angry anymore. He was frantic, "I gotta go," then hung up, leaving her confused, frustrated and on the verge of a panic attack.

"Dane! Dane!" she shouted into the phone then redialed the number. Voicemail. She exited the freeway and sped to the hospital instead. By the time she arrived, she worked herself into a frenzy of scenarios involving Hoffman and hit men.

She found a parking place so far away it felt like another county. She ran to the emergency entrance as fast as her ribs allowed. When the automatic doors slid open, her face glistened with sweat from exertion, pain and the infernal heat.

Several people sat in the waiting room. Few paid attention to the woman racing to the nurse's desk. "Where is Georgia Rutherford?" Savannah asked.

The nurse paused typing on a computer, "Your name, please?"

The question threw her but she decided not to waste time asking why she needed to know. "Savannah Rutherford. I'm her sister." She cringed when her side added a twinge to the radiating pain. It wrung her patience dry with the nurse who signaled someone across the room. She offered no information on Georgia.

Savannah tried not to let her anger show as she enunciated her sister's name again, "Georgia Rutherford. Where is she? I need to see her now."

"Ma'am?" a man called from behind her.

She spun to face him as memories of Morgan's thugs ambushing her entered her mind. It was only a security guard but a very big, intimidating one.

"Come with me, please."

Instead of heading toward the emergency room area, he strode toward the exit and waited for her to follow. "What's going on here?" she asked.

He motioned to the exit, "You're not allowed to see her."

Every head turned from the TV or looked up from their phones. The command surprised Savannah too but first, she didn't care what people thought and second, she was sick of being ordered around. And who the hell had the authority (and balls) to boot her from the hospital and prevent her from seeing her sister? "Who told you I wasn't allowed to see her?"

"Her husband Dane Rutherford." He motioned again, this time more sternly.

That deflated her anger. *Dane?* Why would he deny her seeing Georgia after letting her know where they were? "That's impossible," she countered. "He just called me to tell me she was here. This makes no sense." She noticed he assumed a slightly defensive posture as if expecting trouble completing his task so she added, "I want to see him."

"Ma'am," he reached for her arm but she sidestepped the attempt. His voice hardened, "You're not doing anything except leaving and don't try a different entrance. He provided security with your photo so we're all looking for you."

Savannah heard movement behind her. Two more guards arrived to "help" her out. She knew it wouldn't work but tried anyway. She pulled her badge and ID from her purse, "I'm a cop. I'm not exactly a threat, you know."

He glanced at the ID. The reaction was small but subtle, as if Dane forgot to tell him her occupation. The man stood his ground but toned down the attitude, "I'm sorry, Sergeant. I have my instructions."

She placed the wallet back in her purse, cringing when her side spasmed. The pain took a fair amount of fire out of her temper. "I've got no beef with you," she assured him, "but he just called me and..." She fought the rising emotion but still her voice wavered, "She's my sister and she's in trouble. I wanted to be with her." She turned to leave, telling the three, "Tell him I'm going home."

24

She didn't exactly go home from the hospital. She dropped off to buy an Uncle Jack. Today she didn't care how drunk she got. The world (most of it anyway) turned against her, including a man she considered a brother. Hurt, anger and betrayal sliced to the bone when she replayed the humiliating scene at the hospital. She and Dane always got along so what changed? Did he, like her daddy, hold her responsible for this shitstorm with Lee Morgan?

She obsessed over Georgia. How was she doing? Was she alive or... Savannah threw back a swallow of Jack to counter the "or". She wanted to know why Dane denied her giving Georgia support at this most critical time but he never answered his phone. It reminded her of Georgia's first marriage to Matthew Carlisle. Matthew despised Savannah and did everything in his power to separate the sisters, even kicking Savannah out of the house at one point. This was not Dane Rutherford's style. Something happened but what? She'd never know unless he called her.

She picked up the phone and debated over calling Seth. He and Leah left on a week-long vacation to California. Unless Dane called them, they were oblivious to Georgia's situation. Savannah sat the phone back on the dining table. Why panic them when she didn't know the details herself and was turned away at the entrance?

Did Georgia know Dane banned her from the hospital or did she expect to see her baby sis at her side and wondered why she'd abandoned her in her time of need? Savannah stared at the cell phone. Waited for it to ring. Willing it to. Two and a half hours passed since Dane's original call and every minute felt like another hour.

To block the images tormenting her, she threw back a healthy swallow of Jack. For some reason he failed her this time. All he managed to do was embolden her. She should be there, she told herself. No one should have the right to deny her seeing Georgia. Matthew tried it and she put the bastard in his place. Time for Dane to get a taste of that medicine too, she vowed while picking up her phone. *I'll show him. He won't have an ass by the time I'm done chewing on him. But first...* She poured another bracer and downed it. *There. That's better.*

On second thought, no, it's not. Her fist itched to teach Dane a valuable lesson but when she tensed, her ribs reminded her the only lessons being taught that day were how to kick Savannah to the curb. She put a gentle hand to her aching side.

She pushed the Jack away. Too much and she'd never get in that hospital – and, by God, she *was* getting in there. And she planned to have reinforcements with her. She called Ennis.

By the time she got ready to leave, Ennis walked in the door. He looked as angry as she did. Savannah grabbed her car keys. He stepped in her path, "You're not going anywhere."

She bowed up. One more slap in the face and she'd lose it. "I'm not drunk."

He braced her shoulders, "You're not going anywhere because it won't do any good. I tried to see Georgia and Dane told security to stop me too."

What the hell went wrong with her family? Had they decided to join their daddy in excommunicating her and Ennis? It sounded crazy but things like that happened in families. She just never expected it in hers.

A glance at her watch revealed a couple of hours before they picked up the kids. The kids. "Ennis, if this bizarre ban continues, how are the girls going to feel when they can't see Georgia or Dane anymore? They practically worship them."

He kissed her forehead, "Don't borrow trouble, babe. I don't know what's going on but you can bet I'll find out. Let me handle it."

As if wearing some outlandish version of a scarlet letter wasn't bad enough, "There's something else you need to know. About Franklin and our family – or what used to be our family."

"Hunter told me the targets but you can't protect R.J. without getting hurt or killed and as for Georgia, we both meant to warn her but Dane stopped us at the door."

Yes, exactly. She called to warn Georgia but good ol' Dane slammed the door on his well-meaning sister-in-law for whatever reason. Oh, she wanted to get her hands around his neck and squeeze till he squeaked *Uncle.*

She reached for her phone, "I'm calling again and if that twerp brother of yours deletes the message, I'm deleting *him.* He can't hide forever."

Ennis took her hand, "I left a message on their phones too. Dane's acting stupid right now but he loves Georgia and he'll protect her."

"If someone hasn't already tried to finish her off and at this rate, we'll never know." Savannah sank into the dining chair and began to weep, "I'm so worried about her and none of this makes sense. Dane's not vindictive or petty. Why keep us out? Did he know something we didn't? See something? Or is this mess with the Morgans affecting Georgia and the baby and he thinks separating us is the answer? I mean the last possibility sounds insane but we don't know what he's thinking." She tried drying her tears and ended up with a stuffed-up nose when she dialed Dane, "Please let us know how she's doing. It's killing me to stay away, Dane, so at least update us and tell her I love her. Please tell her that." By the end of the message she needed to wiped more tears and blow her nose. She did both.

Ennis moved behind her and rubbed her shoulders. Minutes passed in silence, Savannah battling tears and Ennis massaging the tension from her muscles. The last few weeks ran through her mind like a video stuck on fast forward, from Lee Morgan walking into her office to the three security guards standing outside the ER actually *watching* her drive off the property. She refused to tempt fate by asking how much worse her life could get.

"Franklin said you practically squeezed between the bars of his cell to get Hoffman's name."

She reached for the bottle of Jack. The last thing she wanted to talk about was Hoffman trying to kill her daddy and sister, especially if she couldn't keep them safe. She sighed when Ennis scooted the bottle away from her. "Yes. Would have maimed him too but he finally told me who the killer is – and now I can't protect either Daddy or Georgia." Savannah stared at the amber liquid, wishing for a top-up but her husband's fist remained clamped around Jack's neck. She settled for coaxing the last few drops from the glass. "Maybe they'll heed the warning if it's not too late."

They sat by the phone, waiting, hoping and praying for Dane to call. The longer the silence, the more she craved Jack for temporary relief however Ennis continued his vigilant effort of separating her from her favorite uncle. Every tick of the clock fell harder than a hammer blow. Each excruciating second reinforced her worst fears that Georgia... She reached for Jack. Her fingers wrapped around Ennis's grasp instead. Fine. If she couldn't drink, she'd storm the fortress. "I don't care if Dane's got the 101st Airborne Division guarding those doors. I'm getting in there."

Ennis hustled to catch her, "You've been drink–"

Her scowl cut him short. He grabbed the car keys from her. He did not apologize, "Well, you *have* been drinking. If you're dead set on doing this, I'll drive while you plan a way inside, Jane Bond."

They had climbed in the car when Ennis's cell phone rang. It was Dane. Ennis answered with a hot, blunt, "First, how is Georgia – if you think we're worthy enough to know and second, what the hell is this trend to ban us anyway?" He waited several seconds as Dane replied then, "Hell, yes. She's nearly crazy worrying and waiting for word on her sister and the baby. We both are." He punched the speakerphone button, "You're on speaker, Mein Führer."

"Georgia and the baby are fine," Dane assured.

Savannah felt the air and tension rush from her body. She could finally breathe again. She listened to Dane explain Georgia began cramping that afternoon and he'd taken her to the ER for safety's sake, "They were pretty powerful cramps and I was afraid, well, you know." He drew a shaky breath, "The doc ran a bunch of tests to make sure she and the baby aren't in any serious trouble then ordered bed-rest for a few days," he stopped a moment to compose himself.

Savannah heard him draw another shaky breath before he proceeded, "She just needs to take it easy. I dread telling her to back off the bakery hours but she'll have to. I want to apologize about today. It wasn't personal, Peach, I swear. I know you're both hurt and angry but I had to do something. R.J. was here until a few minutes ago. I didn't feel safe leaving him alone with her or I'd have called and explained earlier. I didn't want any confrontations and we know how he is. If he saw you or Ennis, I wasn't sure what would happen and I figured once I explained it you might understand. At least I hope you do. I was trying to protect Georgia from additional stress and she wouldn't let me ask him to leave. If you want to come on up, I'll meet you at the entrance."

o   o   o

The same security guards that blocked her way inside watched Dane embrace Savannah and shake Ennis's hand. She felt vindicated and less of a leper when they walked by the uniformed trio. Dane had told them why he needed Savannah and Ennis stopped, he said, and when they heard about R.J.'s temper, they took his request seriously.

The guard welcomed her back in a kinder tone which helped salve her wounded ego.

Ennis chose to get down to business and asked his brother, "How did R.J. find out about Georgia?"

Dane shook his head, "I don't know. I called Peach and that's as far as I got before the doc wanted to see me. R.J. just showed up, told the nurses he was Georgia Prince's daddy and demanded to see her. Apparently he forgets she's married but a very helpful nurse put two and two together and sent him right on in. Had I known he was coming, I'd have had him stopped, not y'all." He said this within earshot of the guards. Savannah appreciated it.

During the elevator ride, she tried to concentrate on Dane's voice rather than the claustrophobic sensation closing in on her. Ennis eased his arm around her. He realized how a simple elevator drove her nuts. Dane did his part by going ahead with his update, "Georgia knew you were standing on your head the whole time. She kept asking me to step out and call you but I wasn't about to leave her alone with him, not after what happened to you."

Her ribs smarted at the reminder. She resisted holding a hand to them, "You did the right thing, Dane. As you said, Georgia didn't need the extra stress. Do you have any idea why she started cramping?"

"She'll thump me for telling you this but she got a phone call yesterday evening telling her to stop harassing Lee Morgan."

Ennis tugged her closer after feeling her tense, "Did the person threaten her?"

"The caller left it unsaid but he spooked her pretty bad. She didn't get any sleep."

The doors slid back, allowing Savannah to relax. Sort of. Once she visited with Georgia and made sure she was settled in, someone on the Morgan payroll was about to lose a pulse.

Dane turned to face them, "Don't mention the call okay? She asked me not to tell you but this is personal. No one gets away with intimidating my wife. If I ever get my hands on the bastard who called–"

"We won't say a word, don't worry," she said, "and I'll take care of the bastard who called when I find him."

They approached the door. She eased inside followed by Ennis then Dane. The sight of her sister in a hospital bed jarred Savannah to the core. During the course of her life, Georgia had been hospitalized three times. Twice for allergic reactions to shellfish and the other when serial killer Jeffrey Holland tried to kill her several years ago. Savannah tried not to look away or react to Georgia's pallid complexion and the fact her eyes were closed. A cold hand closed around her heart, sending her back decades when Charlene lay dying in a hospital bed, so still and struggling for her last breath. Georgia looked so much like their mother but for some reason the sight brought back painful brought painful memories of Charlene's last days. Savannah shook free of those images. Her sister, unlike her mother, *would* be going home and hopefully be alright.

Georgia's green eyes opened slowly. They centered on Savannah's concerned expression. The younger sister noted the considerable effort it took to produce a tired smile. Georgia's greeting sounded jarringly frail as she joked, "I see you haven't killed Dane yet."

"Nah," Ennis tried for his own bit of humor, "you still need someone who'll haul the trash out and do the heavy lifting for next several months."

Savannah held her hand, kissed her cheek, "How are you, sweetie?"

"Truthfully, I'm exhausted. Daddy spent most of the afternoon here making me promise not to die, not to lose the baby and to stay home from the bakery. First time in his life he's told me to sit down and write a book."

Savannah nodded, "He's got my vote on it all."

Georgia frowned, "Not you too."

"Me three," Dane chimed in.

Ennis raised his hand, "Four."

"It's unanimous, sis." Her hand gently squeezed Georgia's, "You're staying home and dedicating yourself to penning another bestseller. People want to read your books. Give the people what they want."

"They want pies too," the older sister defended. A spark of Georgia's doggedness to Get Things Done come hell or high water flared, "Thanksgiving is only–"

Savannah held a hand up, stopping her. Now wasn't the time to argue with her sister so she softly advised, "Try not to worry about the bakery. You've got good employees and I'll do what I can to help."

"Savannah, I can't ask you to do that. You've got work, the

kids…"

"And I've got a sister who'll fret over her business like a good mother should. You can manage the place from home for awhile. I'll help with the physical labor. Geez, Georgia, for once in your life let *me* help *you*, okay?"

Georgia broke into a soft smile, "Thanks, hon."

Savannah greedily rubbed her hands together, "Tomorrow's specialty will be peach pie." She winked at Georgia, "And a few other kinds here and there. Maybe."

25

The next morning Lee Morgan denied everything when she braced him about the threatening call. Savannah expected nothing less. She'd been careful not to outright accuse him but she made it clear. Anyone who threatened or harmed her family wouldn't need an ambulance after she was done. They'd need a coroner so he might want to find out who ordered the hits and fix it before she did.

She went from Lee's penthouse to the hospital to see Georgia but took a side trip to the cafeteria for her sister's favorite "pregnant" food. A plate of mashed potatoes covered in hot sauce.

"Come again?" With one look, the middle aged black lady asked another question – *are you crazy?*

Savannah understood why because when she was pregnant with Lily, she bought up every Cocoa Puff in the city limits (it seemed) and every cashier gave her that same expression. She explained, "I'm bringing my sister her breakfast. She's pregnant and she craves mashed potatoes with Tabasco sauce. Lots of it. She'll put hot sauce on anything – mashed potatoes, fruit, cereal. I know it's a nutty request but can you throw that together this early in the morning?"

She nodded while gathering the oddball ingredients together. "She betta be havin' twins to put huhself through this. My sista ate ice cream on toast so theh's not much that suhprises me. 'Cept this. They sell Tums in the gift shop. Might pick up a box for huh. She gonna need it."

She should have bought the Tums for herself, Savannah thought, watching Georgia wolf down the concoction. The queasiness forced her to look away from the weird eating orgy. Dane flat-out left the room.

Savannah warded off a shiver, "I thought *my* cravings were strange."

Georgia held out a spoonful, "Here, try it. It's good."

Savannah's gut tried to leap out and make a run for it, "No, sweetie, I wouldn't deny you the pleasure of consuming that stuff but thanks anyway."

Georgia chuckled at her reaction, "I know it's a crazy combination but at least I'm not craving dirt. I've read some women do."

She stared at the TV hoping to distract herself from seeing Georgia dig in again. "Sis, that's one thing I'm grateful for. I'd hate to find you digging in your flower garden and wonder if you're planting annuals or just grabbing a quick snack."

Georgia chuckled again. The sound was music to Savannah's ears. Her sister was so happy to be pregnant that so far nothing dampened her spirits, not even indigestion from eating fiery foods. Savannah would hold off telling her what she could expect. Ankles and feet that swelled so big they resembled Oscar Meyer wieners on steroids, her cherished baby exercising their judo and gymnastics at inopportune times and made the mother's midsection look like something out of a horror movie. And the times while she was shopping and be thrown into a muscle cramp that tested the sternest Christian's tongue to let the most colorful language fly – in public – and not care one whit. No, she wouldn't tell Georgia these things because knowing her sister she would handle them with aplomb and class the way she always did. That was Georgia.

"How long are they keeping you here?" Savannah asked.

"Till this afternoon. My darling, overprotective husband says I'm going home and I'm only allowed to relax." She took another bite then asked, "How's Katherine Collins doing on Tucker's book?"

Savannah rolled her eyes, "I'm the talk of the block this week. She found the pictures and read all the references to me. For someone called 'The One No One Talks About', I'm sure mentioned a lot in that book. And I only remember a few times that Lee and I interacted. At his house, when he found me walking home from school, at the funeral home when Grandma Culberson died, and the times he treated the golf team to lunch when we won the State Championship." *And he spent most of his time chatting you up, not your teammates.* "Oh yes, and my commendation ceremonies. How could I forget that?"

Georgia cocked a brow, "You don't remember that he and Ethan attended Mama's funeral?"

"No. I was busy pulverizing our cousins for disparaging Daddy."

Georgia took another bite, "They sat right behind you at the funeral. At the time I considered it thoughtful for him to remember Mama but I guess he was also there to see you."

"He never approached me, did he?"

She nodded then swallowed. Savannah tried not to cringe at the sight while her sister explained, "Yes. He hugged you and offered to help any way he could. He told you to call if you needed him or wanted to talk. He extended the offer to me too but he spoke with you for several minutes."

Savannah tried to recall the memory but drew a blank. "Why don't I remember any of this? It's all a–" she stopped as the truth hit her, "Oh."

"Yes, you'd been drinking. You weren't drunk but you had enough apparently to get through the funeral."

The most amazing part of the situation was, "And Daddy let Morgan stay?"

Georgia's spoon paused midway to her lips, "I don't think he was sober enough to see two feet in front of him, much less notice who attended."

Savannah remembered R.J. wasn't so drunk that he couldn't separate her from her loudmouth cousins. She recalled his overwhelming strength as he, Seth and her cousin Bobby pried her away from her cousins skewering R.J. for being a bad husband and calling their father and a "useless, stinking" drunk.

She still felt the shame of her behavior. Her mother deserved better that day – from her extended family but most especially from her daughter. Before Savannah suffered the same shame about her daddy, she decided last night to heal the rift with him. No matter who caused the split, she wanted to reconcile for everyone's sakes. The guilt compounded daily. It kept her awake at night so she used the quiet time to think of a plan. Georgia wouldn't approve but she'd do it anyway. "I'm going to see Daddy after I leave here."

Georgia sat the plate aside much to Savannah's relief, "Do you think that's wise considering how he feels right now?"

"Well, having to separate us and Daddy to keep peace is silly and you don't need the stress."

"Don't do it for me. I'll be okay."

Savannah placed her hand on Georgia's belly, "I'm doing it for you, Dane, your little peanut and peace on earth, at least our version of it."

"What's your plan to mend fences?"

Savannah stayed awake trying to figure that one out. R.J. refused to speak to her, that much was obvious, and she risked life and limb if she showed up in person. There was only one thing he'd respond to and Georgia would balk at the idea.

"You *do* have a plan, right?" Georgia asked. "You can't show up and hope for the best. Daddy sounded livid enough to follow through on his threat."

"I'mbuyinghimabottleofJohnnieWalker." She ran it together, hoping to get it over with like bad medicine.

As Savannah expected, her sister was not happy, "Did I just hear you say Johnnie Walker?"

"Yes, and don't judge me. We both know that's the one thing that'll work. He's like a leprechaun with a big pot of gold and I'm his favorite kid for one afternoon. C'mon, Georgia, have a heart. I'm desperate here."

She thought a minute then sighed, "It does make him happy. Be careful though. You know how quickly his mood changes."

"Yeah," Savannah pointed to her black eye. For days she tried hiding it but makeup only concealed so much. "I learned that the hard way."

o o o

Savannah started out for Augusta. Though she hadn't expected him to thank her or even acknowledge her message yesterday, she needed him to take it seriously. That meant getting his attention. He loved Johnnie Walker even more than she loved Uncle Jack and no gift stood a chance of a truce like a bottle of her daddy's favorite scotch.

She exited I-20 and stopped for two bottles of Johnnie Walker Red at a package store not far from home. Before braving her daddy's presence, she took a notepad from her purse and wrote two notes. She'd considered her options the night before. If she wanted her daddy to heed her warning to be careful and why, there was only one way to make him listen and it was iffy at best. She'd take the blame for whatever he accused her of – from a distance, that was, because her ribs and stomach reminded her just how powerful her daddy's swing was.

I'm sorry for everything, Daddy. Please be careful because someone is trying to hurt you. I love you and want you to be OK. Love, Savannah.

She poked the note over the top of the bottle and slid it down the neck. She jotted another quick note, this one saying *I'm really sorry.*

Please forgive me. She slid the second note down the other bottle's neck and started for her childhood home.

R.J. usually returned from the bar about that time, whether for a nap or just something to eat then go back again but when she turned onto Walton Way not far from her house, his pickup was still gone. She passed homes built in the nineteen forties, fifties and early sixties shaded by large trees still clinging to their canopies of orange, red and crimson leaves. A huge majestic magnolia tree (her mama's pride and joy besides her flower garden) towered over her two story home and Savannah always looked forward to spring when the tree bloomed and filled the air with a lemony scent.

Savannah pulled to the curb, hopped out and ran the two bottles to the porch. She positioned them behind a bulky artificial arrangement Georgia stuck in the planter beneath the mailbox. R.J. always checked the mail when he came home so he'd see the scotch and their notes right away.

She turned and viewed the yard from the porch, remembering when Charlene spent hours in the flower beds dividing bulbs to give away to friends or rounding out holes for lilies, hyacinth and hibiscus.

The old neighborhood lacked the beauty and character it once had. People moved or passed away and the new owners never quite got in the spirit of keeping lawns or flowers as the previous owners had. The street still had a basic old Southern look and charm though, despite the years and many changes.

The walk to her car inspired more nostalgia when she recalled parking her Avenger beside her mother's Caprice. The days when she arrived home from golf practice to delicious aromas wafting from the kitchen. Her mama rivaled any chef and every time she came home, the first breath she took she swore she stepped into heaven.

Savannah shook off the memory because if her daddy caught her at the house, he'd blow his top then blow her to kingdom come since he sometimes carried Old Faithful in his truck. She got in the Charger and slowly crept down the street hoping to see her daddy's old truck round the corner from Lake Forest Drive. No such luck. She turned onto Highland and started for home when she passed by the burger place on Broad Street. The tempting, smoky smell of grilling burgers proved too much for her appetite so she pulled in.

Her cell phone rang shortly after she killed the engine. "You mean it?" the voice on the other end asked. For the first time in weeks her daddy sounded normal. Not angry, threatening or suspicious. Just *Daddy*. Despite not having done anything to instigate his attacks, she replied, "Yes, Daddy, I mean it. I never wanted to upset you or make you angry."

"Ya still in town?"

"Yes, I was about to grab a burger and fries."

"Make it two. I'll share my Johnnie Walker with ya or I got Wild Turkey, whichever ya want."

"I'll be there in a few."

The next several minutes were spent with a smile on her face. She called Georgia on the way to the house, "I think I'm in like Flynn. I apologized to Daddy and gave him a couple of Johnnie Walkers."

"You apologized? You did nothing wrong." Georgia replied then added, "But I understand. He never accepts the blame for anything so we always have to."

"I'm on my way over to eat a burger with him. At least he won't blast me in half with Old Faithful now."

"I'm glad you're on speaking terms again. Like I said, just be careful. He's an expert at taking offense at things you say."

Talking to her father had always been a minefield so she resolved herself to leaving gracefully, if possible, if his temper flared. Savannah turned onto Walton Way (named in honor of George Walton, a signer of the Declaration of Independence and one time governor of Georgia) and drove down the street, seeing her father's pickup sitting at the curb a block away. She gave the neighborhood another look, this time noting the changes since her teenage years. Back in the day the Denning house was painted white, the flower beds rivaled Charlene's and Mr. and Mrs. Denning drove a Ford Country Squire station wagon to accommodate their four kids, one of which had been Savannah's best friend in elementary school. Now the house sported powder blue siding, shrubs replaced the flowers and a sporty Lexus sat in the drive.

The Mitchells, Reeds and Fraziers all upgraded from a Cutlass, Corsica and Fairmont to Prius, Acadia and Escalade. Today, instead of Savannah and her friends playing outside, younger generations of those families played football and other games in the front yards. She and the children exchanged waves as she passed by. So many changes, she thought. Every time she came home she felt older somehow, as if time marched faster in Augusta than Atlanta.

She pulled into the driveway and parked. R.J. stood on the

porch, hands on hips. He'd been waiting for her. He stepped down as she got out with their meals. "Took ya long enough," he said. No sign of genuine impatience or hostility, only a matter-of-fact statement. She dared to breathe a small sigh of relief, saying, "I had to wait in line."

His hand lifted to her chin. She tried not to flinch as he examined her black eye, "You an' me come to an understandin'?"

"I hope so. I really hate making you mad." *But you come at my kids again and you'll be on the losing end of that fight...*

They started toward the porch. "Ya didn't get no onions on my sandwich did ya?" he asked.

"No onions, Daddy. I made sure of it." She checked it herself before leaving the shop.

"That's my baby."

A car sped up down the street. Her first thought: the kids down the block. She turned to see they'd edged closer to the street, curious about the car revving its engine and picking up speed, she assumed. She handed the bags to R.J., "Hold on, Daddy. I want to slow this guy down." She marched to the curb. The vehicle barreling down the street resembled a Denali. She held a hand up to slow down the driver who approached the Denning house.

"Get back in the yard, girl. He might run ya down if ya don't."

At least her daddy sounded concerned, not angry. She answered, "There are kids playing down the street." She pulled her badge from her belt and held it for the driver to see. The driver ignored her. The passenger window slid down.

"Damn it, Savannah, get back here. He's already past those kids.

He's a nut and I don't want ya run down by a–"

A gunshot split the air. Children screamed and scattered several doors down. Behind her, R.J. groaned. She wheeled to see her father lying on the ground. Burgers and fries spilled from the bag and scattered across the lawn. Savannah ran to her daddy, her clutch falling from her grasp.

Blood seeped from a wound in his leg. The SUV slowed down long enough she looked past the 9mm the gunman held. Both the passenger and driver wore masks but she assumed Hoffman drove the car instead of firing the gun or else she and her father would already be dead.

R.J. tried standing but his leg gave out, sending him flat to the grass. "Get yer ass inside where it's safe," he barked in a manner that normally forewarned violence. He added, "I'll be fine. It's just a graze."

She was already behind him, slipping her hands beneath his broad shoulders then locking her hands around his chest. Her daddy's wound wasn't *just a graze.* The shot hit him square in the calf. "No," she vowed, "we're getting *both* our asses inside."

Another two shots rang out. A sudden burning pain tore through her left shoulder and upper left arm. They weren't just shooting at R.J. Apparently the shooter wanted her dead too.

She began hauling R.J. up the porch steps and quickly discovered even at his age her daddy was all muscle and that muscle was damn heavy. He was nearly as tall as Ennis's six feet two, built like a brick shithouse and he made it clear he wasn't in the mood to be manhandled. "Leave me and get in the house, ya damn fool!"

"Not without you," she gritted her teeth against the ache in her shoulder and aching ribs. She wasn't making progress fast enough to get them both to safety, not with him fighting against her, "Come on, Daddy, push with your good foot. Push!"

Savannah pulled at the same time he braced his heel against the concrete and pushed. She kept an eye to the black Denali quickly closing in. Two more porch steps to climb and past one glass screen door and they could seek refuge inside.

R.J. groaned about his leg. His weight settled into her grasp like a load of lead. He pushed again but this effort lacked the strength of the last one.

Heartbeats fell in hammer blows inside her chest and ears while she struggled to gain a foothold up the steps. Savannah channeled her strength and pulled. R.J. complained. They climbed another step. She pulled again. Another slurred complaint, this one louder and laced with a threat for her to leave him or get an ass-kicking. Another step climbed. The Denali's driver pulled even with the Frazier house next door, slow, easy and unhurried as if they had all day to cut down the father and daughter fighting for their lives.

Savannah reached back, flung open the screen door and propped her foot against it, holding it open. The car casually stopped in front of her childhood home. Predator toying with prey. Watching, knowing at any moment they could end two lives in mere seconds with a few squeezes of a trigger.

Savannah pulled again, imploring her legs to move her father. R.J.'s weight strained at her back. Her arm ached from the pressure and began tingling. She was in good shape (she thought) and in the academy had to drag a one hundred sixty-five pound sand-filled dummy while being timed with a stopwatch but this was her *father* and he weighed more than that stupid dummy *and* she pulled him up stairs while battling a maniac determined to kill them.

The passenger fired twice. Savannah heard her father curse. He'd been hit but she couldn't see where.

The passenger swapped the handgun for an automatic rifle. She heaved herself and R.J. backward past the glass door an instant before the firing began. A cascade of glass rained down on them as she scrambled to pull him safely behind the wall. She slipped on loose glass then regained her footing by digging her heels in the carpet and giving one last solid push before collapsing behind R.J.

The gun kept firing. Bullets struck walls, splintered the entry table, and peppered the grandfather clock that voiced its displeasure with a low chime.

She gasped for breath with little success as she watched bullets riddle her childhood home. She remembered her parents scrimping and saving to afford those fine pieces of furniture and recalled their joy when they brought them home. Seeing their hard work reduced to kindling only added to Savannah's rage. She yanked her .38 from the holster. If Hoffman thought he'd do the same to her father, she'd empty her gun into the bastard, superior officer or not.

R.J. groaned above the loud gunfire, "Somethin's wrong. I'm dizzy."

She looked him over. One shot grazed his left side above the hip. Two caught him in the leg, one in his calf, the other in his thigh. The one in his thigh made her heart drop to her stomach. Blood quickly soaked his pant leg.

She moved beside him for a better view of the door then set the gun aside. She kept an ear and cautious eye tuned to the door in case they were ambushed. She unbuckled his belt and zipped it through the loops. "You'll be okay, just hold on 'cause this is gonna hurt." She slid the belt beneath his thigh and cinched it above the wound hard enough he made a lame attempt to shove her away. She held the tension with both hands. "I'm sorry, Daddy," she said. "I have no choice."

Three more shots and the shooting stopped. The Denali sped away. Savannah tried to catch her breath then grimaced at the blood staining her blouse. The shot in her shoulder and arm bled but not like her father's leg wound.

She reached for the cell phone on her belt, gritting her teeth against her injured arm's protests. She laid the phone on her leg and pressed 911 with a tingling index finger then hit speakerphone. Authorities and ambulances were already dispatched, the operator said.

She glanced at her father. Bits of glass sparkled on his clothes and in his hair. He was heavy-lidded but awake. She called his name. He turned to meet her gaze, "Ya done good, girl, but I'm still pissed at ya for not listenin' to me."

Heavy footfalls pounded up the porch stairs. She grabbed the .38 and aimed straight at the door. Those sirens were near but none had arrived yet. Whoever approached was about to get a rude, painful welcome.

"Vanna! Uncle R.J.! Are you in there? Are you okay?" The

strong, authoritative and *loud* voice belonged to her cousin Bobby Prince, the former Richmond County sheriff. She nearly broke into tears of relief.

He ran in at the same time she lowered her .38. Even the sight of help failed to lessen the tide of adrenaline surging through her. Her heart still pounded away in her chest and ears and now she began shaking – the latter she tried hiding from her cousin. It didn't work.

"They left less than a minute ago," she spoke between short, shallow breaths. At least she thought it was a minute ago. Her mouth felt like cotton. She pointed in the direction the car had been headed, "They drove a black Denali, tinted windows. Two guys in masks. They shot Daddy. They tried to kill him." She choked up on the last few words.

"Slow down, Vanna. Take a breath and try to calm down." He laid her purse aside and took over tending to R.J. In a surreal moment, it struck Savannah odd at the sight of the linebacker-sized man carrying a clutch purse. Bobby gave her trembling hand a reassuring squeeze, "You're safe now. The ambulance and sheriff are about here."

She nodded, still sucking in half-breaths and battling lightheadedness. "Daddy, how are you doing?"

He cringed, "Been better."

R.J. grabbed Bobby's wrist with a stern, "You catch this sunovabitch, Bobby. Ain't nobody gonna shoot at me and my baby and get away with it."

"The sheriff will do his job, Uncle R.J., but first we're getting you and Savannah to the hospital. Are you hit anywhere else besides the leg and side?"

"No, and I got that kid right there to thank for it," he motioned to Savannah. "If she hadn't drug me inside, I'd be dead."

Bobby turned to his cousin, pushed her sleeve up to inspect the wound on her arm then nudged her blouse's collar aside to check her wounded shoulder, "Can't tell but it looks like it'll be okay. Did you get hit anywhere else?"

She hadn't had time to take an inventory of herself and honestly she just wanted her daddy to survive. She answered as best she could, "I don't know. I don't think so." She wasn't sure how much time elapsed between the Denali speeding off and Bobby arriving but it seemed both a lifetime and a split second. "How did you know what happened?"

"One of the deputies called me after 911 received a 'shots fired' call from your next door neighbor."

Paramedics stuck their heads through the glass door's empty frame. Their mouths fell, agape as they surveyed the damage in the entry and living room – the ventilated grandfather clock, the toppled entry table and pieces of broken trinkets strewn across the floor. It was a complete mess.

After seeing the floor glittering with pieces of glass, they didn't know whether to open the door or walk through the void. They opted to open it.

One went to Savannah, the other to R.J. who shoved the EMT's hand away, "Check my baby first. She got shot too."

She countered, "I'm not bleeding like he is. He needs a hospital quick."

R.J. fussed under his breath. Glared at the EMT. Glared at her. Fussed again then cringed from pain, "Don't ya tell yer sister about this, hear me? She don't need the upset. I want that grandbaby born at all costs." Even in pain his hard look warned of dire consequences if she told Georgia.

"I won't tell her, Daddy. I want her and the baby to be okay too."

"Promise me, girl."

She managed to dodge death once and she had no plans to chance another brush with the Grim Reaper by tattling to Georgia. Her daddy meant what he said. Keep quiet. So she promised to keep quiet.

He zeroed in on Bobby, "No one better tell Georgia, that includes you. That girl's finally havin' a baby an' I'll kill whoever blabs this to her."

"My lip is zipped, Uncle R.J., don't worry."

o o o

R.J. and hospitals mixed like oil and water. The staff argued right back at the grouchy older man, telling him surgery was his only option – well, that or death. Savannah heard his boisterous protests from her own ER cubicle. After a point he settled down somewhat, making her wonder if they'd sedated him in preparation for surgery. A sheriff's department investigator hung around with Bobby, trying his best to get answers to his questions. She asked him to wait a moment to ensure her daddy didn't make a run for the exit even in his dire condition.

Once they wheeled him into surgery, she leaned back on the gurney, allowing the doctor and Investigator Harris to do their things. She told Bobby and Harris everything she knew which wasn't much. Harris listened and took notes until she mentioned Lee Morgan's name then he actually *laughed* and possessed the gall to pooh-pooh Lee's involvement in anything remotely illegal or immoral. He laughed again when she mentioned a Morgan being behind hers, Ethan's and Tucker's abductions. She wanted to punch him.

Instead, Savannah propped on her elbow to read him the riot act then fell back once her shoulder and ribs shot arrows through her. She gave in to the pain but *not* Harris, "My detective took a witness statement from one of the abductors. Boy, I really screwed up thinking you people might take this seriously."

Harris began to argue when she cut him off, "I know how powerful the Morgans are, but someone's turning that security team into a bunch of street thugs and my witness said it was a Morgan."

A passing nurse eyeballed Savannah then Bobby. Yes, she'd gotten loud. She was a Prince, after all, no matter what people thought and that meant being loud and stubborn. Bobby put a hand to hers and patted it, probably to shut her up. Good luck, she wanted to tell him. He stood a better chance of knocking sense into the oaf taking her statement.

Meanwhile Harris stared at her as if she'd lost her marbles, "You've got to admit those are wild accusations. I mean, Lee Morgan? He's a pillar of the community."

"Yes, yes," she rubbed the nagging ache in her temple, dreading the whopper that threatened if this guy didn't leave soon. "A pillar of the community and all that shit. My family is as important as the Morgans."

"I hear tell the Morgans are your family."

Savannah bolted to a sitting position ready to slap the smirk off his face. She'd reached the end of her fraying patience with the egotistical moron.

Bobby eased her back by her uninjured shoulder, "Let me handle this before you have a stroke." To Harris he said, "If you can't be objective, I'll talk to the sheriff. This was attempted murder, no matter how you slice it. Take her seriously or I'll have you thrown off the case."

"If it isn't Lee, it's someone else in that family. At least check them out," she said like there was no grain in his silo. Then she asked Bobby, "Can you get him outta here before I take a swing with my only good arm?"

o o o

While R.J. remained in surgery, she and Bobby sat in the waiting room. Savannah chose a corner chair, leaned back and drifted off to sleep, knowing her cousin was close by. The pain meds the doctor gave her kicked in and allowed her to descend into a deep sleep, one where she dreamed her family gathered for a picnic. Everyone brought a dish and they all spent the day eating, talking and laughing. She was horsing down a whole peach pie (with a side of ice cream, of course) when subdued voices floated in, drawing her from the wondrous, delicious dream.

She opened her eyes to Ennis, Georgia and Dane standing in front of her. She scrambled to a sitting position then regretted it when the sling yanked on her neck and made both it and her arm twinge. "Oh no," she groaned at the sight of her sister, "Daddy's gonna kill me." She'd called Ennis but told him to keep the incident to himself and reminded him of R.J.'s temper if he didn't. Apparently he had selective hearing.

"Daddy's not gonna kill you," Georgia assured. "Mrs. Frazier called me and told me what happened. She and her husband watched the house after the ambulance left." She eased into the chair beside her sister, took her hand, "How are you doing? Bobby said they did surgery."

"They mostly just plugged the holes and shoved a painkiller at me to shut me up." That wasn't exactly true but she squawked up a storm when the doctor hinted at keeping her overnight. He reluctantly relented. "How's Daddy? Is he out of surgery?"

Georgia gave her a gentle squeeze, "Yes, and he's doing pretty good for a man who was, and I quote, 'bleeding to death until my baby saved my life'."

"You're making a habit of being a superhero, Peach," Dane added. "You need a cape and a phone booth."

"No," she shook her head, "but I could sure use a twin. Make her carry part of the load around here."

Ennis kissed her, "R.J.'s telling anyone who'll listen how you pulled him up the porch steps, into the house and strapped that tourniquet on his leg."

Georgia nodded, "He's not happy about one thing though.

They're keeping him a few days."

Savannah laughed, muttering *they think they will.* "They'll be lucky if he doesn't hobble out of here tonight." He'd gimp to a package store or bar, get fortified then go home to sleep it off. Home. Painful images flashed in her mind of polished chips of wood flying from Charlene's entry table, the trinkets on top crashing to the floor. Of glass shattering and cascading in a wave over her and her father. Home. Yeah. What there was left of it. "Dear God the house is wrecked. So much was destroyed. Mama's entry table, the grandfather clock, the glass door, the–"

Georgia shushed her, "But you and Daddy are safe. We'll deal with the house later. Bobby's wife and daughter cleaned up the glass and have done what they can but we need you and Daddy on your feet again."

Savannah wanted that too. Her daddy for obvious reasons but her inspiration lay in getting back to Atlanta and confronting a certain major about his afternoon activities...

26

A knock on the bakery's back door at six in the morning gave Georgia pause. The employees scheduled for early morning already arrived so she approached the door with caution until a familiar knock followed up the first. Four raps, a pause, then two more raps. The knock repeated. Morse Code for *Hi.* She and Savannah created their own special knock as kids but re-employed it after Jeffrey Holland returned Michael Myers-like and tried to kill Savannah again.

Georgia wondered why her sister dropped by the bakery so early. Once she opened the door, she really questioned why. Savannah was dressed in casual clothes to help at the bakery. Georgia hugged her, careful to avoid the sling and wounded shoulder. "Hi, hon. What are you doing here? You need another day to rest and let your arm heal."

Anger swept over Savannah as her jaw clenched and eyes narrowed. At those times, Georgia reflected ruefully, her sister most resembled R.J. The swell of temper ebbed almost as fast as Savannah drew a deep breath. When she exhaled, her shoulders slumped, "I need to stay busy, sis. I'll take whatever job you think I can handle with this bum arm."

Georgia sensed more than an injured arm driving her sister. Her confidence and ego seemed to have taken a huge hit as well. She knew better than to push Savannah. History dictated that given time she would spill whatever bothered her if Georgia left her alone.

Her sister needed something meaningful to do so Georgia racked her brain for that something. She'd already checked her inventory of ingredients and drawn up a preliminary order to replenish them but maybe she'd missed one or two things. "I hate asking you to do inventory. It requires reaching–"

"I'll take it. Anything to help out and feel useful. I'll help serve and run the register today too."

The question *what's happened* lingered on Georgia's tongue but she resisted the urge to ask. She'd let her sister get busy in the pantry instead.

Fifteen minutes later Ennis called from the station, "Savannah make it there okay?"

Georgia answered yes. Even Ennis sounded tense that morning. She moved to a more secluded corner to avoid Savannah overhearing, "What's going on?"

"Nothing she can't fix if she'd keep her mouth shut around the bosses. I won't go into details because I need to get to work. Thanks for letting her help out today."

Ennis's reluctance to explain ignited her smoldering curiosity to a roaring need to know. Once they wrapped up the conversation, she dialed Josh Hunter but kept her voice low, "I assume she's been suspended again."

"Hoffman gave her two weeks. He debated about dismissing her entirely but decided this might give her time to think and, Georgia, she needs it."

Dismissed? Georgia sat down before her knees gave, whispering, "What did she do?"

"Accused him of attempted murder. She's going off the rails. I understand she's stressed but she was in his face. I'm the reason she still has a job. Georgia, I hope you can calm her down."

"I'll do my best. Thanks, Josh."

She hung up, stunned and confused. Why would Savannah accuse her boss of attempted murder? Had she been drinking and the alcohol loosened her tongue? Unfortunately like R.J., she tended to unload on people in harsh, verbal attacks when they imbibed too much.

Georgia peeked around the corner. Savannah probably hadn't heard the conversation over the dough mixers and the employees' conversations. She certainly acted engrossed checking bins and writing amounts on the clipboard propped against her stomach and gingerly clasped in her left hand.

Savannah also looked ready to kill. Georgia casually meandered closer, adding words of praise to the other ladies rolling out pie crusts, peeling fruit and chopping nuts. A covert glance toward the pantry revealed her sister mumbling to herself as she worked. Savannah stopped when she came across the Jack Daniel's.

Georgia's stomach dropped. She did a mental facepalm while internally berating herself for assigning Savannah inventory duty.

"I'm not touching it, Georgia," an annoyed Savannah assured over the loud mixers.

Georgia stepped in the pantry as her sister finished, "I saw you eyeballing me. You can relax."

She sounded defensive, as if the whole world wanted to pile on and take a swing at her. Georgia touched the trembling hand holding the pen, "Hon, let's sit down and talk."

"I need to stay busy."

"No, you need to talk and blow off steam."

"Who told you? Ennis?"

"No. He never said a word. I called Josh." She took Savannah's hand, "C'mon, sweetie, let's have a cup of coffee and go talk."

"I don't need lectures or advice. I got enough of those yesterday from Ennis, Josh and even Mathis."

"Savannah, what you did is serious–"

"I know that, Georgia," she snapped in a way suggesting Georgia was a few quarters short of a roll. A few long, silent moments passed when she apologized. "I couldn't sleep last night and Daniel kept fussing anyway so I just stayed up. I kept thinking *if I get dismissed there goes over half our income* but how do I keep Hoffman from murdering my family – and me – *if* he was even aiming at me? I mean a sergeant's death benefits aren't bad but I'd not exactly planned to kick off at forty-one either. I'd like to hang around and raise the kids, grow old with Ennis, have a grandkid or two, you know?"

"Hon, put that down and come talk to me. You look exhausted from the last few days."

She seemed to consider the offer. Georgia literally sweetened the deal, "If you do, I'll make an extra peach pie and it's all yours. A whole peach pie just for you."

Another pause. Savannah's anger waned enough the sleepless night's effects crept in. She yawned. She set the clipboard down, "You drive a hard bargain, sis. I'll finish this before you need to place your orders."

O   O   O

Since she arrived that morning heavenly aromas wafted from the kitchen. Various pies from chocolate to custard to apple and pumpkin filled the air and coaxed a painful rumble from Savannah's stomach. She'd skipped breakfast that morning and now wished she hadn't. The thought of a whole peach pie inspired another insistent hunger pain to roll through.

Georgia led her into the serving area away from the noisy kitchen then returned with a cup of hot coffee doctored just the way Savannah preferred with cream and a touch of sugar, plus a saucer holding an enticing slice of warm peach pie. Savannah nearly broke into tears.

Always thoughtful Georgia. A sympathetic ear, a perfect hostess and hell of a talented writer, cook and baker. The trade-off for the pie would be a difficult discussion (and likely result in a lecture) but resistance was futile as they said, because Georgia could "Southern Charm" her way into anyone's closest secrets just by being Georgia. She just had that knack.

When Georgia broached the incident with Hoffman, she used her well-honed skill to finesse her way through the minefield without stirring Savannah's temper. Without calling Savannah stupid, she tried gently setting her straight but misstepped by mentioning the whiskey.

Savannah sat her fork down, swallowed the bite she'd taken and surprisingly agreed, "I know booze makes me mouthy but I don't drink until after shift. I don't drive drunk either. I learned that one the hard way years ago. I was sober when I braced Hoffman. It's anger driving me. Pure anger. My life is in turmoil again and I can't find the eject button before I crash and burn, not without the Jack and as you can tell even that's iffy."

Georgia's vision settled on her sister's trembling hands. She took them in her own. They were warm and steady. A rock of stability whenever Savannah needed one and she truly needed one now. Before she could stop herself, she asked, "What do I do? I'm in such a mess."

Her smooth, calm voice reminded Savannah of their mother's, "I don't have the answers but I have a suggestion. When you see Major Hoffman again, consider offering an apology."

Savannah stiffened. Georgia continued, "I know you don't like it, sweetie, but consider it because as you said, that's more than half your income if he dismisses you. If you keep your job it will give you time to weigh your options."

Savannah's cold grasp tightened. She made solid eye contact with her sister who had always been their mother's spitting image and the older she got, gave sage advice reminiscent of Charlene. There was only one problem. "What about you and Daddy? How do I protect you?"

"Dane's with me most of the time except here and God love him, he'd stay here at the shop too if I asked. Daddy's stuck at home and fussing about the nurse that shows up every day. Plus, Bobby's keeping an eye on him."

Everyone wanted her to apologize to Hoffman just because he never left the station the day of the shooting. That didn't mean he wasn't involved but everyone reminded her she had no proof he was. They were right and that's partly what kept her awake the last two nights.

Georgia changed the subject, "Honey, you need time to relax. You're on edge because you're constantly blindsided. You and Ethan seem to get along. Didn't he mention playing a round of golf at Augusta National sometime? After your arm heals why don't you take him up on it?"

"Because somehow Daddy will find out and then I *will* end up dead. Besides I don't trust any of the Morgans. Ethan may be genuine but that doesn't keep him from having an ulterior motive."

"Has he given you any reason to distrust him?"

"His last name is enough for me."

Georgia frowned with a reminder, "Savannah, you enjoy golf. You've always wanted to play Augusta National. You grew up with that goal. Now is your chance. Ethan likes you and seems to admire you, at least from what I've seen."

"He's an eight-year-old in a man's body. He never grew up."

"Maybe playing golf with that eight-year-old is what you need. You could have fun and fulfill a lifelong dream. Daddy doesn't know anyone at the club. Chances are he'll never find out."

Savannah mulled it over. Rubbed her forehead. The argument with Hoffman caused such misery she'd gone to bed with a migraine. Her sister was probably right. It seemed Ethan meant well and he did, she hated to admit, treat her like an older sibling that he admired. But still, "So I should trust him, is that what you're saying?"

"I'm saying take him up on making one of your dreams come true. Precious few people get offered a round at Augusta National. I know you, sweetie. If you pass this up, every time you drive past the club, you'll regret not taking this opportunity."

O   O   O

Savannah stayed busy through the morning serving customers. The regular customers seemed surprised to see her and inquired about the sling. She blamed it on a "dust-up" at her day job which wasn't too far from the truth, she thought. The lunch hour crowd consisted of a mix of familiar faces and plenty of unfamiliar ones. Tourists found the shop since it had been included in "The Best of Atlanta" online and highlighted in plenty of tourist guides to the city.

Once the noon crowd thinned, Savannah took a moment to breathe. It was then she realized she hadn't once thought of Hoffman or the argument. She'd been happy serving the friendly folks who cared enough to inquire about her injured arm. She'd enjoyed hearing the different accents of the visitors from afar. Canadian, German, Swedish, and even a family from Texas. She truly enjoyed chatting with the Texans and mentioned Ennis was from Vega, a little town outside of Amarillo and two hours from Lubbock, the tourists' hometown. She and the family exchanged a few stories during a brief lull in the crowd.

Yes, working at Pie In The Sky could be fulfilling in its own way. If her days as a cop magically ended thanks to Hoffman, she'd consider it.

She'd need a second job though and Lee Morgan's offer (he stubbornly refused to take no for an answer) would weigh more on her mind if she overlooked his reprehensible behavior decades ago and the fact he decided to pull an O.J. on her family. She'd walk through hell to feed and care for her family but accepting his offer equaled to dealing with the devil. Personally she'd rather shovel shit until she died from the stench.

During lunch, she shrugged out of the sling and sat down to rest. She needed another adventure for Chester Chipmunk. As a child she tinkered with writing because Georgia enjoyed it. Anything good enough for Big Sis was good enough for her too. Until they stumbled across those old yellowing pages in the attic, Savannah forgot the fun of writing about Chester.

Lily found the stapled together storybook on her parent's dresser. The four lighthearted stories and rudimentary drawings of the jolly little rodent frolicking around the house and neighborhood in Augusta had enchanted her girls, prompting them both to ask for more. Considering she wasn't a creative soul – and was a tad busy trying to save her sister and daddy – she told the girls she'd try.

That day at the bakery, she'd had an idea. What if Chester hitched a ride to Atlanta and, like a tourist, explored the big city and visited familiar places to Lily and Anna? Between the zoo, amusement parks and dozens of other attractions, Savannah could cobble together several stories and, at the same time, throw in educational information to teach as well as entertain. She'd run it past Georgia for a litmus test.

After lunch, she left her arm free of the sling while filling take-out orders. Georgia sat at her desk engrossed in paperwork and Savannah hoped her sister had plenty to keep her busy because she needed respite from the sling's constant strain on her neck. The instant Georgia noticed its absence, she would harangue until Savannah put it on.

Sure enough, "Put that sling on. It's there for a reason," Georgia ordered in her best "Mama" voice. She stopped working and waited for her sister to comply.

Well, shit. She's not even given birth yet and she's already got eyes in the back of her head. Savannah gave the sling a baleful glare as it dangled around her neck, "Yeah, it's there to drive me nuts. Georgia, it's basically a flesh wound."

"Savannah Charlene, use that sling."

"Uh-oh," a different voice interjected from behind her, "she means business if she's using your first *and* middle names. Better listen, sis. She's right."

Savannah rolled her eyes as she turned to face Ethan. She guessed Georgia heard him use the nickname *sis* since she made it a point to get up and approach the counter.

Ethan stood, hands in his pockets, rocking back and forth on his heels, just as happy as a pig in poo. His attire of khaki Dockers and green polo shirt seemed more appropriate for the golf course – not a millionaire CEO of a Morgan subsidiary or five. Savannah glanced at Georgia as if to say *See? An overgrown kid.*

He reached over the display case to Georgia, "We met a long time ago but now I can officially say hello, I'm Savannah's brother Ethan Morgan." Savannah expected he added that "brother" bit to tweak his "new" sibling.

Unflappable Georgia took it in stride while shaking his hand, "Georgia Rutherford. Savannah's sister."

Ethan smiled easily, "Pleasure to meet you again, Georgia. I always liked that name. Just says elegance and beauty all over it and you fit that bill."

Georgia returned the smile, "Savannah, you didn't tell me Ethan was such a charmer."

Charmer was Georgia's diplomatic way of saying *bullshitter*, at least in this situation. Savannah could read her sister's expressions like a book. She may have liked Ethan – to a degree – but her eyes revealed what Savannah told her all along. Morgans did whatever necessary to get their way whether stroking an ego or, say, ordering someone's death. Ethan leaned toward the former but no matter what, Savannah reminded herself, he was still a Morgan.

Ethan waved it off, "Oh, pish. What morsel of charm I have is used to sway Mrs. Gardner to bake her lip-smacking fudge cake."

Savannah felt the need to remind her sister, "Mrs. Gardner is the–"

"I remember who Mrs. Gardner is," Georgia interrupted while still sizing Ethan up.

He pretended not to notice, "That's partly why I'm here. My sweet tooth, you know? It's been paining me for days for a piece of apple pie. Since your place is touted as one of the best, I wanted to see for myself. Hey," he pointed to Savannah's black and white apron, "looks good on you. Different from wearing a badge, I bet."

Her mouth tightened. Was that a dig? Had Hoffman bragged

how he'd humiliated her by sending her home "to think about" her employment and to "analyze whether she enjoyed being a cop"? "It is," she agreed. "A piece of apple you said?"

"Yup, and an extra large scoop of ice cream on top."

Georgia motioned to the sling, "Put that on now, hon. I have to call in my orders." She turned to the energetic Morgan across the way, "Ethan, it was nice meeting you – again."

"It was my pleasure, Georgia." He apparently had a brainstorm, "You know, we should have you all over for supper some night. Sound good? I know it's a drive to Augusta but we'd make it worth the trip." He bobbed his brow at Savannah, "Mrs. Gardner would for sure."

"My husband and I stay pretty busy in the evenings, but thanks for the offer." Georgia pointed to the sling which her sister handily ignored, "Now, hon."

Savannah rolled her eyes and slipped it back on. Ethan rounded the counter and helped her situate it. "There. Now both your siblings are happy."

"Goody." She busied herself preparing his order. He followed her everywhere she went. "Customers usually stay on the other side of the counter," she hinted.

"I wanted to see how you were doing and when you might be ready to hit the fairways with me. Obviously you can't golf until your arm heals but I wanted to reserve our date and tee times at Augusta. When do you think you'll be ready to play?"

Savannah automatically glanced at Georgia. Why did she smell her sister's involvement in this impromptu visit? Georgia, busy on the phone, peered over her reading glasses and shrugged innocent-like. Yep, guilty as charged, Savannah sneered then answered Ethan, "The doc said give it another couple of weeks."

Georgia cleared her throat. Liar, Savannah frowned at her sister. She wasn't on the phone with anyone.

"Okay," she amended, "he said a week or so and I'm free to do whatever I want as long as it's comfortable." She plunged the ice cream scoop deep. Extra large, he'd said, which in that shop meant two dollops. She scooped again, plopped it atop the pie then went for seconds.

Ethan slanted her a skeptical look, crossed his arms and leaned back against the counter, "I sense reluctance. Does it have anything to do with Caleb Franklin?"

The metal scoop slipped from Savannah's hand. The perfectly formed ball of vanilla ice cream splatted on the floor. She sighed. A young waitress named Sophia offered to clean it up but Ethan waved her off, "I caused it, the least I can do is clean it up."

Savannah didn't argue. She pointed to the paper towels. While he cleaned up the ice cream, he said, "Savannah, Dad's not Al Capone. He never ordered anyone hurt or killed. He did pay R.J. Prince a visit which, as you know, didn't turn out well, but c'mon, wanting someone dead? Dad's not like that."

"Then who called my sister and threatened her? Who shot up my house in Augusta, my daddy and me? Franklin forewarned me something would happen and it did."

He glanced up from scrubbing and smiled as if she'd slipped a cog, "I can't answer your questions because I don't know. Answer this."

He stood and grabbed the mop from the bucket and began swabbing the small area, "After finally making contact with his daughter, why would Dad try to kill her or risk alienating her by killing people she loved? It doesn't make sense."

He wanted to spar, did he? "I can't answer your question either but someone in your family ordered a hit on him and possibly my sister and I'll protect them both with my life."

"As well you should." The mop splooped back in the bucket. He stepped aside while she finished his order. "But right now let's concentrate on the fun part of life. The club opened a couple of weeks ago so let's reserve our tee times ASAP." He nudged her, "C'mon, big sis. What's say we make a date to square off on the greens? Savannah 'The Augusta Bomber' Rutherford versus Ethan 'The Hazard' Morgan."

She hated being blown off. Only she and R.J. seemed to treat the threat with due concern or credibility. Of course they would, wouldn't they? They were the ones who were shot. So Ethan's marquee match-up of the Augusta Bomber vs. The Hazard sounded like a hurry-up setup, especially after her earlier chat with Georgia. In Savannah's single days, her sister notoriously fixed her up on blind dates (there was a reason for that name, she told Georgia) so why not fix her up on a "golf date" with Ethan, the Morgan who reminded Savannah of Tom Hanks's character in the movie "Big".

One glance Georgia's way had her rolling her eyes. *Her* "big sis" kept a covert eye their way while waiting on hold with her supplier. Georgia gave a subtle nod saying "go ahead before he changes his mind".

Morgans never change their minds, she wanted to tell her

meddling sister but she did what any outranked younger sibling did. She capitulated. "Okay," she told Ethan then handed his apple pie to him. "But fair warning. I hate pimento cheese sandwiches."

27

Ethan called the following afternoon with good news. He'd managed to snag a tee time late the next week. Despite her earlier reluctance, a thrill ran through her at the thought of playing Augusta National. This was real, she told herself, not some fantasy or dream she'd wake up from only to feel disappointed. She actually had a tee time at Augusta National to play golf. And what perfect timing, she smiled. Fall decided to arrive the day before, bringing with it a crisp feel to the air and a gentle, cool breeze. Not only residents breathed a sigh of relief from the brutal heat and humidity but the trees perked up with the welcome reprieve and according to the weather forecast, autumn was here to stay.

Georgia noted the upswing in her sister's mood that morning, stating the spring in her step and the fact she stopping grousing when being reminded to wear the sling. She also dropped a comment on how she "didn't seem to mind golfing with a Morgan".

Sure Savannah hemmed and hawed at first. She had her pride, you know. But the desire to walk the manicured fairways and stand on the same challenging greens as her golfing heroes Arnold Palmer and Jack Nicklaus stirred her anticipation into an excitement rivaled by a child's on Christmas morning.

The hallowed gates of Augusta National teased her as a young girl aiming for professional glory. She watched the Masters every year on television. During the tournament when Charlene went grocery shopping and drove along Washington Road, Savannah saw smiling faces walking the sidewalks and lining up to go inside those hallowed gates – tourists from literally everywhere in the world lucky enough to score tickets to the event. She'd been so jealous she asked her mother if they could buy tickets from one of the people selling on the street – scalpers her daddy called them. *I'm sorry, honey,* her mother answered each year. *They're too expensive for us.* It hurt her mother to say those words. She realized how much Savannah yearned to attend the event even for one day. Charlene always added a caveat – maybe someday we can go.

"Someday" arrived next Friday when Savannah would pass through those sacred gates, not to *watch* a golf game but to swing her own clubs and putt for birdies on the same ground as the legends had. She'd have a chance to play the famed Amen Corner and conquer (if she could) one of the hardest holes on the course, the eighteenth hole named Holly.

But that was next week. Today she enjoyed working at the bakery. Well, when the customers weren't twerps, that was. Savannah busied herself clearing a table and wiping it down after a particularly persnickety customer left. He'd left a two dollar tip. Not bad considering he'd complained about the maple walnut pie being too "nutty", the coffee being too hot and the fact he had to wait for a refill of that "blistering" coffee while she took another customer's order. She only had two hands, she wanted to say, and in case he hadn't noticed, one of those was out of commission. Then she discovered he was from New Joi-

Zee. That explained it all and two bucks was a damn good tip just to restore her peace of mind.

By ten o'clock she'd done a fair morning's work serving regular patrons and tourists who had redeemed her faith in humanity by gushing compliments over the shop, the food and the service. Many left tips that put "Joi-Zee" to shame.

Her time and efforts paid off two ways. It kept Georgia off her feet and focused Savannah on serving smiling faces and not obsessing over nearly losing her job.

At eleven Georgia received a phone call that put a smile on *her* face as well. Pie In The Sky was to be honored as one of the city's best eateries and also receive recognition for its part in feeding the homeless. Every day Georgia sent whatever hadn't sold to the homeless shelter, plus she always seemed to bake a few extra pies that also found their way to the shelter. Now her hard work and generosity paid off.

While Savannah stayed busy serving customers, Georgia spent her time calling friends to tell them her good news. It thrilled Savannah to see her sister so happy. First the baby, now the ceremony. On her break she gladly added the event to her phone's calendar. She named it *Georgia's Big Day*.

At one o'clock the number of customers kept going strong like the employees making pies and manning the register while Savannah waited tables. Atlanta was called the New York of the South and at Thanksgiving and Christmas it lived up to its name, teeming with tourists and plenty of events to attend, sights to see and food to satisfy them. All the hustle and bustle tired Savannah by two o'clock and she took a brief break and a much needed pit stop so she headed to the restroom.

She was washing her hands when Georgia stepped in, "You have a visitor. Before you leave this room, remember how much you love your job. If you want to keep it, you'll think carefully before you speak during your conversation with him. "

"It's Hoffman."

"Yes. I'm serious, Savannah. I'd love nothing more than for you to work here full-time but I also know it would drive you nuts not being a cop."

Savannah dried her hands and gingerly slipped her arm back in the sling. She took a deep breath before venturing out to meet him.

Georgia already served him a cup of coffee when Savannah rounded the corner from the restroom. Hers and Hoffman's vision locked. The moment felt tense and adversarial like an Old West showdown only Hoffman's weapon equaled a cannon to her measly slingshot. When it came to careers she couldn't touch his but he could easily (and with great joy) destroy hers after their heated brouhaha the other day.

She approached the table with a stiff, "You wanted to see me," then added an afterthought, "sir."

His smile was more of a sneer as he motioned to the chair across from him, "Sit down, Prince."

She did. From the corner of her eye she saw Georgia monitoring the meeting from the cash register counter. Too far to hear anything but close enough to gauge moods.

"Hunter told me you'd be here." He looked down at his coffee cup bearing the black and pink Pie In The Sky logo, "I didn't realize you moonlight as a waitress."

"I'm mostly helping my sister. It's not against regulations and I enjoy the change of pace." Simmering anger knotted muscles anew, forcing her to remember Georgia's caution. *Think carefully before you speak.* She guessed that applied to her physical stance as well. If he saw or sensed her homicidal feelings, he might (oh dear) take offense to that too. So she consciously relaxed her shoulders from the wooden, defensive posture. It worked but not for long. It was difficult not to relive their blistering argument.

He sipped his coffee, then tossed a curveball at her, "Like it enough for full-time employment?"

Savannah tried not to bow up. Was that a snarky question or a threat? "Is the major forewarning me that I *will* be full-time here?"

"The major is forewarning the sergeant that one more incident of insubordination like the other day will drastically change her career direction – right to the unemployment office. I can't have my people disrespecting me and yelling in my face, Prince. It isn't happening without serious repercussions."

This was her cue, she supposed. The one step Ennis, Georgia, Mathis and Hunter advised her to take in hopes of salving wounds and retaining employment – at least until he threatened to fire her again. She'd rather have swallowed a Buick but went ahead anyway. "I was working on anger, adrenaline and information that you were involved. I overreacted and," she drew a deep breath to muster a convincing lie, "I apologize for my actions."

"I can see how difficult that apology was for you."

Yes, and according to his smirk he didn't care. Frankly, she didn't either. Her part ended with the apology, now it was up to him.

He indulged in another sip then leaned forward with a covert, "Let me set you straight on something. I *am* part of Lee Morgan's security team. I also know what Caleb Franklin told you and Mathis about my involvement in your kidnapping, James Riggs's death and everything else going on. He can't prove any of it."

"He has proof and told Mathis where to find it."

A smug smile replaced the smirk, "Yeah. Did Mathis actually find that USB drive? Have you asked him? You know, Prince, I think Franklin baited you and you fell for it. Ask Mathis if he's found anything connecting me or Lee Morgan to anything."

His cocksure attitude tweaked her temper. This was turning out to be a replay of her accusing him and him lording his power and position over her. Franklin wouldn't have reached out to her or turned himself in if he hadn't had a bargaining chip. He was too frightened to chance lying about it. Hoffman took a leisure sip of coffee but held steady eye contact, daring her to call him a liar – again. She stated as fact, "But you *were* there the night I was kidnapped."

Apparently sensing a turn in Savannah's mood, Georgia turned the register over to Sophia. She grabbed a broom and busied herself sweeping crumbs around a nearby table – no doubt to eavesdrop, Savannah figured. Georgia ventured a step closer then another, distracting Savannah to the point she warned her older sister off with a look.

Hoffman gave Georgia a casual glance then answered Savannah's accusation, "Again, prove it. All I know is Morgan was on TV announcing two of his sons and his only daughter were alive and well after being kidnapped."

.The cavalier reply tempted her to lash out. The stressful situation could have been fatal for her with her heart condition and claustrophobia. Judging by his attitude Hoffman only dropped by to tell her how screwed she was. That, and dangle her future in front of her. Play nice and you keep a badge. Don't play nice and wear an apron and serve pie and coffee until the end of time.

He leaned so close she saw the tiny brown flecks in his green eyes, "Here's another fact you should understand. Lee Morgan wants you. He wants you in his life and he's willing to pay an insane amount of money to get you any way he can, whether sitting at his dinner table or running his security. He's desperate but he's not desperate enough to put a hit on your family. Think about it, Prince. How stupid would that be?"

"How do you know for sure it wasn't Lee?" *Because Franklin said the hit list came from Chief Security Officer which initially comes from Morgan himself.*

"Because until you accept Lee's job offer, *I'm* Chief Security Officer. If you take the job I'll still be there but you'll be my superior officer. Now won't *that* be a fun arrangement? I'm in charge at the station and you're in charge after shift."

She smiled. She wouldn't be in charge only "after shift". She'd have the say twenty-four seven. One word from her and her "new daddy" would put Hoffman in his place at the station too. What fun indeed…

Anger hardened his features, "I see what you're thinking, Prince. If you want to assign me the crap jobs, you can. The guardhouse, walking the perimeter, staring at security cameras day and night, even walking his dogs. I don't really care what you do because the money I make gives me the freedom to buy what I need and want. But don't think for a minute you'll run roughshod over me at the station while you're there. That's my domain, not yours, no matter who the hell your father is."

His raised voice caused patrons to stop eating and turn to the pair squaring off. Georgia moved a shade closer. Both Savannah and Hoffman ignored her and all the blatant, nervous stares.

He stood up, threw a fifty dollar bill on the table. The sight took Savannah aback. He tapped the money, "*That's* the kind of tip I can leave for a cup of coffee. You could too if you take the job." He nodded to Georgia, "Nice place you've got here. I'll tell my wife about it." He looked back at Savannah, "By the way, Caleb Franklin made bail this morning. Just thought you'd want to know."

She stumbled for words until finally settling for a lame, "He didn't want bail. He wanted protection."

Hoffman shrugged, "Must have changed his mind."

"Who posted bail?"

"Don't know, don't care. You shouldn't either because you got more trouble than he's worth."

28

Ethan turned off Washington Road onto Magnolia Lane and stopped at the bright white guardhouse. A thrill of excitement raced through Savannah. She was officially on Augusta National property.

The security guard knew Ethan by sight and because she rode shotgun as a guest, they greeted her warmly as well. The magnificent drive down Magnolia Lane lined by old, established magnolia trees on each side inspired a childlike giddiness while she took in every detail and committed them to memory. She was *there*. Truly there. No more passing the gates and wondering what awaited golfers and guests inside the clubhouse. No more wishing she could swing her driver and watch the ball (hopefully) land far in the distance onto the emerald green, perfectly manicured fairway. "I'm here, Mama," she whispered. "I finally made it." Somehow she felt Charlene smile from above.

Ethan gave her a tour of the clubhouse, the Champion's Locker Room and the upstairs library where the Champion's Dinner was held. She stood speechless in the Trophy Room where shelves upon shelves displayed priceless items once owned by President Dwight D. Eisenhower and the club's founder Bobby Jones. In the main sitting room sat the Holy Grail of golf, an object which she took several minutes to admire.

Sitting on a four foot-wide base and weighing in at a hefty one hundred thirty-two pounds was the Masters Trophy. Made in England with over nine hundred separate pieces of silver, the perfect replica of the Clubhouse was ringed at the bottom with a nine foot, six inch silver band engraved with winners' names. The trophy remained in the Clubhouse at all times while Masters winners were given a smaller version approximately fourteen inches wide, seven inches tall and weighed twenty pounds.

Next, Ethan took her upstairs to see President Eisenhower's desk. She placed a hand on the chair's back then on the black rotary phone just to touch a piece of priceless history. She could only imagine the conversations that took place at that desk.

Ethan escorted her to the dining room, insisting they indulge in lunch. She did not refuse nor did she think twice of the staff's double-takes or the whispers rising from the other diners around the room.

She marveled at the hunter green and gold china customized with intricate images of the clubhouse. It seemed a shame to eat off such elegant dinnerware but when in Rome, as the saying went.

To her surprise, there were no menus on the tables. Instead, their waiter, an older black man, approached the table. Ethan more than happily introduced her to the waiter he knew by name then told him it was her first time at the club.

The man smiled and said, "Welcome to Augusta National, ma'am. It's a pleasure to meet you. If you're looking for a menu we don't use them. Tell me what you'd like to eat and we'll prepare it for you."

Ethan laughed at her stunned expression, saying, "Isn't this a marvelous place? And the food is spectacular as well. Come on, sis, live it up. Order your heart's desire. You'll love it."

Yes, but she would love it like a puppy she couldn't keep, enjoying it while she had it then reluctantly give it up and pine for it when it was gone. She ordered a light meal but caved to the ice cream and peach cobbler. After all, she didn't want to appear rude or ungrateful. They followed up by having a drink to celebrate their day together on the golf course. Somehow the Jack just tasted better at Augusta National.

The staff made Savannah feel at home, even like family in some cases. It was a member or two that caused her to squirm – or nearly squirm. While dining, one or two glanced their way to greet Ethan and Savannah although they couldn't place her name or face and made a point of whispering the fact to each other. One of the women sitting at a nearby table lifted a judging brow at Ethan's "guest", scrutinized her attire of black slacks and powder blue polo (which she apparently disapproved of) then returned to whispering to her companions. Not all the highfalutin muckety-mucks took her presence in stride.

What else could she wear on such a cool day? A skirt? Right… She volleyed her own disapproval back after giving the nosy bat's outfit a good sizing up. Savannah was here to play golf, not walk a runway wearing the latest fashions. Then she heard the woman mention Tucker Morgan's book. Ethan heard it too. He leaned closer, mumbling, "Bear with me a moment." He asked the gossiping gaggle of hens, "Ladies, this is my sister Savannah. Don't you think she favors Dad? Blue eyes and everything."

"Ethan," she shook her head. *Not* bearing with you, she tried to convey. She agreed to play golf at the most coveted and historic club next to St. Andrews, not be put on display like the Eisenhower bust upstairs.

To her surprise, Ethan ignored her apprehension and continued on his merry way, "If you've read Tucker's book then you already know Savannah deserves to play at this prestigious establishment. I'm proud to say you'll be seeing her frequently around here." He grinned at Savannah, "I finally have a golfing partner."

The women were shocked that Ethan braced their back-fence talk and like Savannah, they wormed a bit in their seats. To their credit, the staff went about their business and pretended not to hear his spiel.

"Ethan, stop," Savannah pressed while waving their waiter down.

He seemed to sense her unease regarding Ethan's gregarious behavior. "Yes, ma'am?"

She pointed to the empty whiskey glass and tried her best not to sound desperate, "A refill, please."

"Yes, ma'am." He walked away in a casual, professional gait. If he realized how desperate she was for that bracer, he'd run like the place was on fire. At this rate she'd keep him busy with those refills if Ethan refused to dummy up. So far he caused half the people in the room to recoil at least a little, including her.

The waiter returned with a generously poured refill of Uncle Jack. She thanked him. He nodded a knowing, "Yes, ma'am. Anything else you need, let me know."

Thank God for the staff. They were an answer to a newbie's

prayer. She nursed the drink but fought the urge to gulp it and another more down just to survive lunch. Two things stopped her. One, she sincerely wanted to play at Augusta (and wanted to play sober) and two, she could only imagine the next morning's headline in the Chronicle reading *Lee Morgan's Daughter Arrested For Drunk & Disorderly At Augusta National.* Not a good thing considering R.J. would see it, drive to Atlanta and beat the shit out of her again.

The murmuring continued two tables away. The women punctuated their secretive conversation with an occasional glance Savannah's way. They were still gossiping about Tucker's book, no doubt, and the mystery of why Lee Morgan slept with "the help" four decades ago. If they only knew the truth, Savannah thought ruefully.

"Satisfied now?" she asked Ethan. "They're still chattering away and it's not about their Louis Vuitton handbags."

He waved it off, mumbling, "Nosy hens. I didn't intend to embarrass you but I hate gossiping snobs." He motioned for her to finish her drink, "Time to tee up, sis."

She threw it back with a flinch as it burned its way down her throat. At this rate it would be a mighty long day and not because of golf. "Can you stop yourself from calling me your sister for five minutes please? There's no DNA proof we're related."

Ethan laughed loud enough to halt the women's gossip, "You're probably the only person who's fought against being in a wealthy family and why? We're not so bad."

One of you is. "I grew up the way I grew up. I'm not used to all the fuss and attention. I prefer a quiet existence which I haven't had since that book hit the shelves. Nothing personal but I like my middle class life. That said, today is fulfilling a dream I've had since childhood. I'm grateful I'm actually sitting here eating at Augusta National and I surely appreciate your invitation to play. I look forward to playing the course with you."

The diners had been listening. So had the staff but they had the decency not to show it.

Ethan rose to his feet, beaming at their audience, "Isn't she great? Honest and modest." He extended his hand to her, "Let's go live your dream, sis."

O   O   O

She scored a par on the first hole, Tea Olive. It not only impressed her, it surprised her considering the uphill shot ended on a challenging, undulating green. With a little body English on his putt, Ethan squeaked out a par as well. On the third hole, Flowering Peach, she scored a birdie while Ethan bogeyed. When they arrived at Amen Corner, Savannah paused to bask in the moment and immerse herself in her surroundings. Imagined the roar of the crowd as she and Ethan approached the thirteenth tee box. Today though a variety of birdsongs floated from trees bordering the fairway. A breeze gently stirred the branches of junipers, dogwoods and fir trees. People always claimed Augusta National was more gorgeous in person than on TV. Despite the absence of blooming red azaleas, yellow jasmine and pink camellia, in her opinion, the scenery rated this side of heaven.

Normally an aggressive player, Savannah opted to play number eleven, the par four White Dogwood, safe by hitting toward the right side of the green to avoid the pond. Her shot succeeded. Ethan wasn't so lucky.

Number twelve, the par three Golden Bell, presented its own challenges. Bunkers guarded the front and back of a narrow green and the renowned Rae's Creek waited to swallow any ball if the shot missed its target. Savannah and Ethan both landed in bunkers, the least damaging hazard of the two. Both took their misfortune in stride.

By the par five thirteenth, Azalea, Savannah felt daring enough to go for it. She let it fly on the tee shot, went a tad conservative on the second with a short iron then finessed it onto the touchy sloping green. She and Ethan enjoyed the round, keeping their sense of humor and their barbs good-natured. They laughed and joked together (another unexpected yet pleasant surprise that day), making Savannah hope they might play another round sometime.

They played on to the fourteenth hole. Ethan shook his head, amazed, after watching her drive sail down the fairway. "Now I see why they called you the Augusta Bomber. You can hit that ball farther than some men I know."

She really did like him. Georgia was right. She would have regretted bowing out of the golf round with Ethan. While she didn't believe he was her half-brother, she still felt remarkably comfortable around him. More comfortable than with her own brother, in fact.

He teed up and took his swing. Savannah figured it would hook to the left because his swing lacked the correct follow-through. Sure enough, the ball veered to the left and bounced through the Chinese Firs then landed somewhere in the pine straw below.

"Crud," Ethan sighed, staring at the mass of trees containing his errant ball. "I hate to ask but would you find the ball for me? That many trees will cause my phobia to kick in."

"Sure, I'll try to find it," she said. She recalled his phobia of forests but hardly considered a large stand of fir trees a forest. Phobias, though, transported a person back to the original trauma and for Ethan that meant being lost in a forest three long days as a kid. She couldn't imagine the fear in a child's mind. Tree trunks as far as the eye could see, a canopy of leaf-covered branches blocking the sky and no one answering his cries for help. It was no wonder Ethan developed a phobia of forests, she'd told Ennis.

"Thanks, sis. If you can't find it, I'll take the penalty and we'll move on."

The ball nestled itself between the two trees in such a way he'd need a genie lamp and all three wishes to save par. He opted for the one stroke penalty and still scored a double bogey.

Two front bunkers blocked easy access to the green on the seventeenth hole Nandina. The straightaway uphill par four looked like a cookie with a bite taken out of it since an ice storm destroyed the Eisenhower Tree years ago. A mere tree stump was all that remained of the loblolly pine that regularly plagued the president's drive.

After her tee shot, Savannah planned on a lofted shot onto the green depending on the length of her drive. She took a few practice swings with her driver.

"Wonder what this is about." Ethan nodded toward a golf cart headed in their direction.

Savannah rested a hand on her driver and waited, shrugging, as the cart stopped behind theirs. A spry elderly man in khakis and Augusta National kelly green polo hurried toward them, "Mr. Morgan, Mrs. Rutherford, I apologize for interrupting your game but your father called and asked you, ma'am, to call him immediately and asked you, sir, to call your brother Preston. There's been an emergency."

She and Ethan looked at each other, wordlessly wondering what emergency Lee spoke of. Ethan asked the man for more information but he shook his head, "Mr. Morgan only said an emergency," he turned to Savannah, "but was very insistent you call him ASAP, ma'am. *Very* insistent."

ASAP had to wait until they loaded their clubs and themselves into their own cart and drove to the clubhouse. They did so with their messenger following behind.

Once there she called Lee on her cell phone. He picked up on the first ring. It didn't sound like Lee at first because his voice sounded strained as if battling to retain his composure, "Savannah, I need you here as soon as possible. It's Tucker. He's..." the sentence caught in his throat. She thought she heard quiet weeping as he continued, "He's been murdered. Sabrina found him in his study."

Shock threw her into silence. It shouldn't have been a total surprise, she supposed, considering the enemies he'd made along the way but *dead?*

Lee called her name until she found her voice long enough to offer her condolences. Beside her Ethan collapsed on a bench, head in his hand. His complexion faded from rosy from physical exertion to ashen. "Say that again," he told Preston. "Tucker's what?"

Savannah put a hand to his shoulder. She couldn't imagine the devastating loss of either Seth or Georgia, especially to an act of violence.

Lee made no effort to hide his desperation, "Savannah, I need you with me. I need my children with me right now."

I am not your child, she thought but would go anyway. There was no choice since they brought Ethan's Porsche SUV. She wanted separate cars but he insisted on picking her up. "I don't know what support I can be but it'll take a couple of hours to get there. Ethan and I are in Augusta. Are you at Tucker's house?"

"Yes," he sounded genuinely relieved. "Thank you, sweetheart. I'll be looking for you both soon."

O O O

Sweetheart. A term of endearment her mama and sometimes Georgia and Ennis bestowed on her. Not a man she barely knew. Certainly not her father because one thing about R.J. Prince – he rarely expressed sentimentality with his kids. The closest he came was calling her "my *sweet* baby" and even those were in short supply. Georgia's nickname was "Sweets" and Seth was known as "my boy". No honey, sweetheart or dear for their daddy so when Lee addressed her as "sweetheart", it rang off-key with her for many reasons. If he turned out to be her father, she'd endure the nickname with grace then shiver in private.

For the last ten minutes silence hung between her and Ethan during the trip back to Atlanta. She'd offered to drive but he'd climbed behind the wheel as if he hadn't heard her.

Savannah remembered when her mother died. After the initial shock, memories seemed to drift in on the silence, as well as regrets, what-if's and whys. Ethan, it seemed, was no different. Even with the hell Tucker caused by publishing his book, they were still brothers. In her experience, a loved one's death either brought families together or widened the gap between them. One or the other always happened in families, she noticed, and more often than not, it was the latter.

"Hey," he glanced at her with a sad smile, "thanks for being there for me and Dad. I know he threw you in the deep end asking you to come with me but we really do appreciate you being there for us."

"Sure," she replied, "though Preston and the others won't be happy to see me." She'd heard the heated argument between Preston and Ethan on the phone. After breaking the news of Tucker's death, his and Ethan's conversation digressed into a near shouting match about her. Savannah busied herself unloading her locker and preparing to leave while Ethan unleashed an unexpectedly blistering temper on his brother – and his anger toward Preston had yet to subside. She hated that Preston allowed his petty insecurities to overshadow the tragic news but Ethan fought back, giving as good as he got and pulling Savannah into a firm one-armed embrace as if physically defending her.

Ethan white-knuckled the steering wheel at her mentioning Preston, "Press can be a difficult person to like, much less love. I'll handle him and if I can't, Dad will."

o o o

Tucker and Sabrina lived in the ultra rich Kingswood neighborhood in Buckhead where homes ranged from one to three million dollars. The quiet streets, beautiful homes and heavily manicured properties provided a lovely background for runners, among them Tucker's sprawling, two story ranch house with perfectly squared off hedges lining the walkway and tall leafy trees shading the house. Streets ended in cul-de-sacs so when Ethan began the turn onto Tucker's street and saw the fleet of news vans and gaggle of reporters, he eased the car to a stop in the intersection.

The crowd of nosy press clamoring for information turned in their direction and, recognizing the Porsche, the swarm dashed in a mad rush toward them. Savannah groaned. If her daddy found out she'd interacted with the Morgans again, she felt quite sure he'd put her in the hospital with more than injured ribs and bruises.

Ethan punched the accelerator and headed toward Tucker's alley entrance. He wheeled into the driveway and braked just short of a uniform officer signaling him to stop. Ethan sighed a long breath, "Now neither of us have to battle the media and R.J. won't see you on TV tonight."

Savannah breathed a sigh of relief, "Thank you, Ethan. Both were a dread."

"I got you covered, sis."

Two uniform officers approached the driver and passenger doors, ready to brace the newcomers for identification. They backed off when

Savannah climbed out followed by Ethan.

"I'm assuming you're taking charge of the scene, Sergeant?" The inflection the younger cop used told her he wondered if she'd take the place over just because she was "a Morgan".

She frowned at his inference, "You know what assuming does, right? I'm fully aware – as you and Sergeant Bailey are – of the conflict of interest where I'm concerned so no, I'm not taking charge." Yes, the desk sergeant would delight in her insinuating herself in the investigation only for Hunter or Hoffman to boot her out of it. Considering she was still on suspension, the whole idea of her taking over was ridiculous anyway but just in case the young cop missed her point, "Captain Hunter's in charge of this investigation. Is Detective Mathis here?"

"Yes, ma'am. Mathis is keeping the family in the living room or great room or whatever they called it. I'll take you."

She and Ethan followed the cop down a stone pathway that curved around a large nearby koi pond containing a variety of the species – some orange and white, others white with Dalmatian-like spots and one gold and black. On the opposite end of the yard stood a wall-like waterfall fountain that covered a large portion of the fence and was flanked with military-precision trimmed boxwood shrubs. Tucker and Sabrina liked their yard formal, not casual, she guessed.

The moment they stepped in the back door she heard a woman and little girl crying. Savannah and Ethan walked through the kitchen equipped with stainless steel appliances and white marble counters and hardwood floors. She followed the cop through the land of Spare No Expense into the living room, or lion's den as it were.

Preston and Lydia sat on a long, gray leather couch with Grady, Grady's wife Melinda, his young son Luke and younger daughter Belle. Sabrina and her two young children, a boy and girl huddled on a matching couch beneath a painting reminiscent of Renoir. Savannah figured it was the real McCoy because one never found knockoffs in a Kingswood home.

A weeping Sabrina hugged her daughter Tara who looked about Lily's age. Savannah guessed her son Jesse was around seven or eight. He unfortunately inherited his mother's severe, almost unkind features. He sat beside his mother arms crossed and staring daggers at crime scene techs as they roamed the house collecting evidence.

The instant Preston, Grady, Lydia and Sabrina laid eyes on Savannah, she felt as welcome as an IRS agent.

"What's she doing here?" a bawling Sabrina lashed out.

"Get her out of here, Ethan," Preston demanded. "This is for family only."

Ethan shook his head, "Now, Press–"

Tucker's son, still spoiling for a fight, launched off the couch and kicked Savannah's shin hard enough she winced. "Get outta here! You don't belong!" He threw in another kick for good measure. That made her mad.

She turned him by the shoulder to everyone's dismay (except Ethan's), grabbed the back of Jesse's collar and marched him to his seat, "Settle down, sonny, or you'll find yourself on the wrong end of my temper."

Grady's boy Luke came to his feet to defend his cousin. He was

younger than Tucker's son by a year or two but lacked no less chutzpah –
until Melinda, Grady's wife, pulled him back into her lap with a caution
not to get involved.

Ethan added, "Boys, Savannah's your aunt, treat her with
respect."

Embarrassment darkened Jesse's features. He huddled against his
mother using the only weapon he had left. Words. "She's not *my* aunt
and she doesn't deserve my respect!"

"I'll have none of this," a voice boomed from directly behind
Savannah, startling her. "Savannah is family," he slid his arm around her
waist, "and you will treat her like family." He aimed the next comment
at Jesse, "I'll deal with you later, young man. I know you're upset and
angry about what's happened but do not mistreat your aunt."

Savannah noticed the emphasis on "your aunt".

"She's not family until DNA says she's family," Lydia echoed
Savannah's hue and cry about DNA. "Bree's going through enough
without the stress of her being here too."

Savannah felt Lee draw her closer while putting the rest on
notice, "I've been more than tolerant of this family's tirades regarding
Savannah. Beginning now, you will treat her with respect and kindness.
Don't ask what will happen if you don't. We've lost a member of his
family, that should mean something to you. Except you, Sabrina. You
can dry your crocodile tears. You only married my son for his money, we
all know that, and I'm not entirely convinced you're not responsible for
his death."

The others' anger at Savannah switched to pure shock at Lee's accusation.   At the same time Sabrina released a howling sob and dissolved into another river of tears.   As for Savannah, she studied the woman's body language and demeanor.   Lee's zinger hit its mark and for some weird reason, his words rang truer than she expected.   Sabrina's tears *did* seem forced and the longer she "cried", the more tense and confining Lee's embrace grew.   Savannah was glad they weren't in the kitchen with the knives because he looked ready to go Ginsu on Sabrina.

"Sir," a familiar voice called from behind Lee. Hoffman.

Lee turned with his arm still around Savannah.   She and Hoffman locked gazes.   Her boss nodded a greeting, "Sergeant."

"Major."   She strove to sound businesslike and not on the verge of heading to the kitchen for her own knife.   Neither she nor Hoffman budged on their views of who ordered the hit on R.J. so she rode out the two week suspension as best she could.   There were four days left.

He addressed Lee, "I was in Chauncey visiting my sister when I got the call about Tucker.   I'm sorry for your loss, sir."

"I want to know who did this to my son, Mike," Lee demanded. "Anything you need, just ask.   Question Sabrina first.   Make it thorough but make no mistake – I want whoever killed Tucker taken care of.   You know what to d–"

Hoffman had pointedly glanced at Savannah then back to Lee before Lee finished his demand.   No one needed interpretation.   Lee demanded "eye for an eye" justice.

"We'll make sure to bring this person – or persons – to justice, sir," Hoffman's vision shifted back to his sergeant, an unspoken warning to keep that little conversation to herself.   He reinforced it with, "You have my word and Sergeant Prince's. Right, Sergeant?"

Oh, sure. Involve me. Thanks but no thanks. "I'm not part of this investigation or any of them for that matter."

Hoffman slanted her a deadly scowl, "You dug the hole you're in, Prince, not me." He looked at Lee, "I'll need to interview the whole family, not just Sabrina. It will be quick and painless. Let me know when it's convenient. I'll come to you."

Savannah sneered. *Well, how cozy. Most regular folks are told to come to the station for interviews but not the Morgans.*

"Sergeant," Hoffman drew her from her thoughts. "I'll interview you at the station."

M-hmm. Apparently not all Morgans get such cushy treatment.

"Mike," Lee said, "she and Ethan have been in Augusta all day. You can verify their whereabouts with Augusta National."

Hoffman lifted a brow at her, "Augusta National, huh?" Then he reverted to his role as loyal and faithful employee, "I'll be discreet with my inquiry, sir." He focused on Savannah, "Any objections to me taking charge of this investigation, Sergeant?"

Yeah, like what could she do? "No objections, Major."

He smirked as he stepped past her but Lee stopped him. He did not look happy with his CSO, "Before you leave, you and I are having a talk about that ridiculous suspension you imposed on my daughter."

Hoffman's smirk wilted as he headed toward the stairs. He took the steps two at a time – sort of the way he ran timesheets, she thought. Days ago Mathis called her about overhearing a conversation between Hunter and Hoffman. Hunter wanted to know why the major changed

Tierce's vacation day to on duty. Hunter reminded him Tierce wasn't there. Hoffman's gruff side emerged and told his captain Tierce was there and left it at that. According to Mathis, since their exchange, a thread of tension ran between the two commanding officers.

Loud voices upstairs caught everyone's attention. Moments later Mathis stomped down the staircase in one hell of a bad mood. When he entered the living room, the urge to step back nettled Savannah since her colleague appeared homicidal toward her. He wasted no time confronting her, "Did you kick me off this case?"

She stood her ground, "Think, Mathis. Have I ever kicked you off a case? Plus, I don't have the authority to remove a splinter from my finger without Hoffman suspending me so how could I have the authority to remove you from a case?"

His expression warned he did not want logic, he wanted to break heads. "So replacing me with Tierce wasn't your idea?" When she shook her head he calmed down – sort of. "That kid ain't got experience yet. He's too new."

True. Tierce arrived at Zone 2 shortly after Hoffman. They'd worked at Zone 1 together for two years so Savannah wondered how much pull Tierce had. It wasn't unheard of for bosses to bring along their friends or best officers to a new station. Still, assigning a greenhorn to a high profile case? What was Hoffman thinking? That as payment for reassigning Tierce to Zone 2, the new detective would toe the line on Lee's "eye for an eye" order? She wasn't sure. She only knew Mathis still looked close to a coronary. "Don't strangle me over something I didn't do, John. I only have stripes. The man upstairs has brass. Try to calm down."

"Yeah, you get booted off a case and see how you feel." He brushed his hands together, indicating he'd washed his hands of either the case or her. She refused to guess which.

She'd refrained from shooting back, "Try getting booted off the job for two weeks," because she preferred her head on her neck, not being bit off by a grouchy, middle-aged detective.

29

Lee Morgan proved capable of doing something beneficial for the world – well, her world anyway. He worked his millionaire magic, flexed his affluent muscle and got her back on the job. The next morning she sat at her desk, smiling at the mere idea of Lee tearing Hoffman a new one for suspending her in the first place. It paid to have a rich daddy, at least for five minutes.

Less than an hour into her shift, her desk phone rang. Still riding high on being back at work, Savannah answered with an upbeat *Detective Sergeant Prince* but stopped short of asking how she could help the caller. No need to tempt fate that early in the a.m. Expecting a colleague, a boss or forensics tech, she was taken aback by the waspish Lydia Morgan squawking in her ear, "If you have any common decency," the shrill voice said, "you'll stay away from Tucker's funeral. I know Lee practically begged you to attend but don't. Your presence will be too disruptive. If nothing else, think of Sabrina. She's just lost her husband."

Lydia was right about the begging. Lee almost embarrassed himself imploring Savannah to attend the funeral – as a personal favor if nothing else. Just to annoy Lydia she asked, "Lee doesn't think my presence would be disruptive. He wants me there so why shouldn't I attend?"

She smiled when Lydia floundered and sputtered. Finally she came up with, "I'm warning you, you vulture. If you enjoy having a job, you'll listen. You will not inherit when Lee dies so stop kissing his ass. If I see your face at the funeral, you'll pay." Lydia disconnected. It seemed she disconnected in more ways than one, Savannah thought while staring at the phone. And who did she think she was? Tucker died, not Preston, so what right did she have to dictate who attended the funeral?

Savannah chuckled. It was fun aggravating certain Morgans. Lydia probably knew a hundred higher-ups in the department though, and that sobered her amusement a tad. She hadn't planned to attend the funeral for several reasons and one of them still occasionally ached when she moved wrong or breathed too deeply. If R.J. found out she went to Tucker's funeral, he'd go ballistic and personally she wasn't too keen on dying just yet.

Less than thirty minutes later Sabrina called with the same basic threat to stay away or pay a price. Savannah let her rant then offered her condolences again before that Morgan hung up on her too. Interesting how the tears dried so quickly, she thought then remembered Lee's vehemence about Sabrina's involvement in Tucker's demise. After wondering on that a few minutes, she shrugged, telling herself it was Hoffman and Tierce's responsibility to locate the killer, not hers. She thanked God for it too. Answering to Hoffman was bad enough but answering to Lee Morgan? Uh-uh. No way.

Her phone jangled again. Odds were it was yet another Morgan chucking in their two cents about the funeral. Which one? Preston?

Grady? Grady's wife Melinda? Or that snotty little shit Jesse trying to make his mark with the family, kinda like the bruise his foot left on her shin? Preston, the president of her fan club, backed up his warning with one slight difference. "Unless you enjoy being humiliated on worldwide television, do not show up at Tucker's funeral. I've assigned our security team – including Mike Hoffman – to escort you out of the church or cemetery in full view of the media. Weigh that against how much you want to please my father."

"You're a little late, aren't you? Your minions got here first. That says something about a man when his wife fights his battles for him, Preston, and it isn't flattering. You must really be terrified of me."

Preston went silent. She heard what sounded like pages being fisted. He was seething. "I hope my father enjoyed those fifteen minutes of fame with your mother because it sure screwed up this family."

The urge to hit back with a comment about employers raping employees sprung to the tip of her tongue. She barely restrained herself from unleashing it, "You don't know what happened back then and you'd deny it if I told you. You can stop foaming at the mouth about the funeral because contrary to popular opinion, I have my own life and I've already told Lee I wouldn't be there so back off, Cujo." Then she hung up. At least she had the pleasure of slamming the phone down in its cradle. Cell phones didn't quite cut it when you wanted to make a point with someone.

She marched to Hoffman's office and knocked on the door. He turned from his computer. His mood appeared normal except maybe a little irritated at the interruption, "Yes, Sergeant?"

"For the sake of argument, what will happen if I attended Tucker's funeral?"

He leaned back and interlocked his fingers across his stomach, "For the sake of argument, I suggest you reconsider attending."

"Because you have orders to remove me if I show up?"

His expression remained inscrutable, "I'm paid to keep the family safe and to keep the peace."

"I thought you worked for Lee."

"He just lost his son. He's not thinking clearly at this point. The last thing he needs is a family ruckus during Tucker's eulogy."

"So Lee doesn't know about this arrangement you have with the family."

Hoffman slowly straightened in his seat, his hands clamped to the sides of his desk, "You thinking of telling him?"

Do I have "Stupid" written across my forehead? "No."

Her assurance did nothing to alleviate his aggressive posture, "Good because that would not be wise. C'mon, Prince, isn't there a kiddie recital or church event that needs your attention? Your husband might like a few hours with you too. Be more fun than standing at a grave of someone you never knew anyway, right?"

Despite wanting to shoot back with a snarky reply, she nodded, "I wasn't going but I don't appreciate Preston threatening me with public humiliation if I did attend."

He smiled a bit, "Preston doesn't know the word *subtle*. Never has."

Time to change the subject, "Why does Lee believe Sabrina is responsible for Tucker's murder?"

"Is that really any of your business?"

"Lee considers me his daughter so I think it is."

Hoffman sighed, "Lee believes she's a gold digger so I'm sure that fueled his accusation."

"He sounded pretty sure she had a hand in his death, not just his pocket."

"A knee-jerk reaction to the situation. Relax, Prince. I'm doing due diligence on the case."

"And how's Tierce handling it?"

"I know Mathis is upset about being replaced but how else is Tierce going to get experience? I'm mentoring him myself, helping him through the investigation. Takes some pressure off of you to oversee everything too."

Right. How kind of him to consider her workload and stress level. She played nice by thanking him anyway. "So how is the investigation going?"

"From the evidence we've recovered it looks like a junkie broke in and killed Tucker."

"A junkie? In Kingswood?" The land of Jaguars, Olympic-size swimming pools and state-of-the-art security systems? A junkie's desperation might have driven them to *try* and break in but usually the homeowner caught them or the security people called the cops. And no one would believe how fast a patrol unit could fly until a Kingswood resident was in trouble.

He seemed amused by her skepticism, "Well, they don't keep 'em locked up in the zoo so they are free to roam around town. I've seen the home's security footage. It's a junkie trolling for money and valuables. Tucker caught him and lost the fight."

It sounded too incredible. A junkie cherry-picking Tucker's house out of dozens in Kingswood.

Hoffman elaborated, "Maybe one of his old dope fiend pals paid him a visit. Not that I'm judging but Tucker was a problem child back in the day."

She knew that. Growing up in Augusta, Tucker fed the rumor mill often enough his antics got old. Age only emboldened him to pull more serious shenanigans that never seemed to land him in jail and in college his penchant for women earned him a rape allegation. Like father, like son, she thought. The drug problem wasn't new either but she'd forgotten about it and the fact he founded Crossroads rehab. "The drug problem, yeah," she said.

"Yes, not everyone hits the bottle, Prince." He let the pointed remark hang between them. "Once he got clean, or said he was clean, he created Crossroads to help other junkies and alkies kick the habit."

She tried to ignore the shamed flush reddening her complexion. How did he find out about her drinking? Neither Ennis nor Mathis would betray her confidence and she knew Georgia wouldn't tell Lee... would she? By trying to back Lee off, had she divulged that gem to him? If she had, no wonder Hoffman appeared smug when he mentioned it. Lee probably told him. "Does the security footage show the intruder clear enough for the public to identify him?"

He shook his head, "No. As usual he was wearing a hoodie.

Never got a good shot of him."

"Still might be worth a try."

"Why are you grilling me, Prince? I'm handling the case. Do you think I'm inept or something?"

Uh-oh… "No."

"Then maybe you should stick your nose in your own workload or I'll find more for you to do. How does that sound?"

Like a warning. "I'll get back to my paperwork. Thanks for the update."

"Yeah, about that. From now on, I'll decide if you need an update. You're dismissed, Sergeant."

She spent the trip to her office trying to walk a swaying tightrope of sanity and rage. She was shaking by the time she reached her desk. If she didn't calm down soon, she'd have a stroke. The nerve. The arrogance. The asshole. He not only slid in a backhanded insulted about her drinking but blew her off about Tucker's murder and treated her like a stupid, meddlesome rookie.

Her desk phone rang. Still on the cusp of blowing her top she answered with a curt, "Sergeant Prince."

"Princess, you gotta help me."

Caleb Franklin's voice capped off her already stellar crappy day. "Not you again. I tried to help you. You posted bail. You're on your own."

"I never wanted to be released. Someone else posted my bail. I even tried to decline. The cops just yanked me out and tossed me in the street. I'm in danger, Princess." He heaved between breaths making it sound more like an obscene phone call, not a call for help. "*Sergeant,* please. The cops said they never found that thumb drive with the files on it and they're lying because it's gone."

This day was trying her last nerve beyond belief, "What am I supposed to do about it?"

"I made a copy in case the wrong people got it. I have it here at the house. If you'll just come pick it up – you. No one else. I only trust you."

"Then we have a problem because I don't trust *you.*"

"I won't be here. As soon as I tell you where to find the SD card, I'm getting the hell out of Atlanta."

"Don't tell me that. I'll have to send uniforms to pick you up."

"No, you won't because you don't know which uniform cops you can trust. Listen, I stuffed the card in a Benjamin Moore paint can called 'True Blue'. It's in the garage on a shelf. The can's full of sand. Just pour it out and the card's in a plastic bag at the bottom. Come through the side gate. I'll leave it and the back door unlocked. One more thing. Remember the name Alex Davis. You got that? *Alex Davis.*"

"I got it but who is Al–" Franklin had already hung up. She pulled the phone from her ear and stared at it as if she held a strange foreign object. Who the hell was Alex Davis and how did he or she fit into the equation? First she needed that SD card. *Benjamin Moore's True Blue on a shelf in the garage.*

Hoffman's words came back to her. *Did Mathis actually find that USB drive?*

Neither she nor Mathis had found the USB drive Franklin told him about. It pissed them both off that it wasn't there. Mathis accused Franklin of running them in circles. Savannah figured one of the cops moonlighting as Morgan's security got there first. Well, they wouldn't this time. She'd take Mathis with her – or so she thought. When she went in search of him, she found a note on John's desk saying he and Ennis were chasing a lead on another case. Obtaining the SD card was up to her so she grabbed her car keys and snuck out the station's back door to avoid walking by Hoffman's office. It was 10:35.

o o o

Her phone rang halfway to Franklin's house. Caller ID read Ethan Morgan. She put it on speakerphone.

He asked if she planned to attend the funeral. He wouldn't like her answer but being manhandled and hauled away in front of the media *then* getting her ass kicked by R.J. again would do her in. "I decided not to. Your family doesn't need the circus of me showing up and I need time with *my* family."

"That and you're afraid of R.J., aren't you?"

"Yes. I only have so many ribs and I'd like to keep a few that aren't sore. I still have an infant that requires feeding and rocking to sleep and in my current shape, that can be a challenge. I'm making a donation to Crossroads instead of attending the funeral."

"I understand. I figure Press has been in touch too. He's been on a tirade about you again. Sorry he's a complete clod. On a happier note I'd like to set a tentative date for another round at Augusta since we never finished the last one."

"I'd like that but let's wait till things settle down in your family first."

"Sounds good. I'll let you go then. See ya around, sis."

Savannah started to tell him again she wasn't his sister but he'd already hung up.

She arrived at Franklin's house twelve minutes after pulling out of the station's parking lot. Traffic had been light that morning which meant maybe she could grab the SD card and get it to Mathis before noon.

Franklin lived in a neighborhood of smaller homes close to major highways, the airport and a variety of restaurants. Still, the neighborhood was quiet, at least when she climbed out of the car.

He kept his place nice, the lawn mowed and hedges lining the walkway to the door trimmed in rectangular shapes. The white two story traditional-style home with lap siding had a two car garage and looked like a storybook home for a couple with kids, which it had been until his wife divorced him. She'd left Caleb certainly not because of the lack of money, but because he spent all his time with Morgan's security team keeping Lee safe. That was the reason Savannah used to decline Lee Morgan's job offer for the hundredth time. She valued her family time more than the truckloads of cash she'd make.

Savannah strode to the side gate as Franklin instructed. A beautiful jade green lawn carpeted the back yard. She followed a narrow sidewalk past a couple of trees.

A few raps on the back door caused the door to squeak open

several inches. True to his word, Franklin beat it and was probably stuck in lunch hour traffic on his way out of town.

As a precaution she pulled her gun before stepping inside the dining area. She didn't trust him *that* much, not after being ambushed in an alley by him and his flunkies.

Beyond that was a shotgun kitchen furnished with black appliances, dark wood cabinetry and marble countertops, the last appeared so immaculate she wondered if he used them.

The living room was to her left. The place had hardwood floors and cream colored walls trimmed in white. His wife had decorated with what Savannah called classic furniture – not quite antique but not quite modern either. A fleeting thought came to mind. *Mama would've approved of this house, inside and out.*

The house sounded quiet save for the refrigerator cranking up. Time for roll call, "Franklin, it's Sergeant Prince. You here?"

Nothing. She tried again while moving toward the stairway. "I'm here for the SD card. If you're around, come on out." She passed by the fireplace where an antique clock ticked away on the mantle. It read 10:54.

I guess he meant it when he said he was leaving. She went upstairs to check the rest of the house and make sure he hadn't set her up for another ride in the Morgan rodeo. One abduction a month was about all she could take.

The house was empty so she headed to the garage. Like the house, everything had its place. Wrenches hung in graduating sizes on the wall along. Other tools, each outlined in white to show where each one went on the pegboard. On the opposite wall hung an often used mountain bike. Beside it, oil and antifreeze shared shelves with empty flower pots. On the shelf above sat a dozen pint size paint cans of various colors. She scooted them around until finding True Blue. Now for a tool to open it. She plucked a screwdriver from the pegboard, sat the can on the wooden workbench nearby and pried it open. The can brimmed with sand. She tilted it over the garbage bin sitting beside the workbench. Half the sand poured out when the corner of a plastic bag emerged. She pulled it out. The SD card sat safely inside. Yes, she whispered. The list of Morgan's security people. The plans for who was next on the hit list and who was assigned to carrying out the murders. And more, Franklin promised Mathis. Caleb somehow managed to assemble a goldmine of information.

Since he kept the place tidy she hated to mess things up so she she pocketed the SD card then used her fist to pop the lid back on the can and sat it back on the shelf. Time to leave and let Mathis know about her treasure.

Savannah wound her way back through the house and while heading to the back gate, she dialed Mathis who answered with an unusually upbeat, "What's up, Sarge?"

She felt like she won the lottery, "You won't believe what I'm bringing you. Remember that piece of evidence Franklin said he had?"

"Yeah, the lying dipshit. I still wanna knock him into next week. Why?"

"I got it. Meet me at the back door and I'll give it–" A sudden sound startled her. Movement behind her had her reaching for her gun but her fingers wrapped around a leather clad hand instead. A man's hand that jerked the .38 from the holster and flung it aside.

"Mathis, help–" she intended to say *I'm at Franklin's house* but a figure – a second attacker – struck like lightning, stripping the phone from her while the guy behind her locked one arm across her throat and the other across the back of her neck. He clamped down, effectively terminating the blood flow to her jugular veins. Between their speed and efficiency she stood no chance of successfully fighting back but she tried.

Heat flooded her face. Dizziness swept over her. Her legs loosened. Still she clawed, elbowed and struggled. Her brother's instruction and discipline gave way to wild panic. She was losing consciousness while Mathis shouted from her phone that lay useless in the second attacker's hand.

He disconnected the call then tossed the phone aside as if it were trash.

The world went gray. Her vision closed in.

"What do we do with her?" The voice behind her wavered further and further away in the distance.

"Tie her up and torch the house."

O   O   O

11:10 A.M.

Ennis heard John Mathis before he saw him. Not just by his huffing and puffing and feet tramping as he ran but by his urgent repeated shouted of, "Rutherford!" Mathis skidded by the doorway, his dress shoes refusing to cooperate when he applied his brakes. He hurried into Ennis's office, "Do you use that Find My Phone app?"

Ennis attempted to shift mental gears from witness statements to John's weird question, "Yes, why?"

"Track her phone. She's in trouble." He picked up Ennis's desk phone, "I'm calling a tech to locate her GPS as a backup."

Normally an empty donut box inspired the biggest reaction from Mathis. Today he freaked out over Savannah's whereabouts and that spurred Ennis into full-blown, five-alarm case of freaking out, "What happened? What was she doing?" He palmed his phone and tapped the app to open it. Once in the Cloud, he tapped Savannah's cell phone to track it. A compass appeared, shifting between left and right of north. Beneath the compass read *Locating*.

"She was picking up the thumb drive Franklin promised. I think the bastard lured her into another trap." He glanced at the phone's screen, "Hasn't it found her yet?"

The nondescript map displayed boxy gray squares and rectangles representing buildings and homes and a circle for the search radius and progress. The smaller the circle, the more accurate the location. The app zeroed in until the circle disappeared. The app was certain Savannah's phone was at a particular address in their patrol zone and around fifteen or twenty minutes away – a lifetime if she was in trouble. He was already on his feet, car keys in hand when Mathis mumbled under his breath, "That bastard Franklin. I'll break his neck."

"Not if I break it first."

They rushed out of the station with Ennis dialing her number then cursing when it went to voicemail.

When he slid into the passenger's seat of Mathis's detective sedan, he hadn't expected to need Dramamine. The old guy rivaled a Grand Prix driver the way he raced down streets and dodged traffic. He floored it through intersections, depending on Ennis to look right for traffic while he looked left. The lights and siren deterred most people from venturing in his way but the others quickly discovered how good or bad their reflexes and brakes were. Ennis lost count of how many times they were nearly T-boned.

Mathis merged onto the highway. The speedometer topped eight-five and on occasion teased ninety for whatever traffic allowed. Between John's driving and Ennis's nerves, the nausea percolating in his gut deepened but asking a maniac to pull over at that speed was suicide. He busied himself calling Savannah once, twice and three times. All went to voicemail. The definition of insanity may have been to keep doing the same over and over and expecting a different outcome but whoever said it apparently hadn't been trying to save his wife.

Through the light haze of smog Ennis saw a plume of smoke rising in the distance. It wasn't uncommon to see fires in the city but since they were headed in that general direction, he couldn't help but worry.

Mathis finally exited – more like flew – off the highway then slammed the brakes and swerved around a line of early rush hour traffic. The progress stopped one block later. They'd hit a traffic jam extending as far as Ennis could see.

Mathis inched up as cars began to move at a snail's pace. Several blocks away black smoke billowed into the sky. Franklin lives in that addition, Ennis panicked, and we're stuck in traffic. He glanced at his watch. 11:25. They approached a residential street, a through street if Ennis remembered correctly. "Hang a right here," he told Mathis while dialing Savannah's number.

"I'm trying, Rutherford, I'm trying."

Voicemail again. Ennis wanted to throw open the door and run like hell. Run like his wife's life depended on it because it did. Twenty-five minutes had now passed since her call was cut off.

The light turned green but traffic was at a complete standstill. A fact that infuriated Mathis who pounded the horn as he'd done several times during their trip. "C'mon! Move it! It's an emergency!" he shouted at the driver in front of them.

The Ford Focus moved just enough Mathis jerked the wheel to the right then forewarned Ennis to hold on. He gunned the engine, climbed the curb and squeaked so close between the Ford and a light pole that Ennis closed his eyes and leaned aside in case the light pole scraped the passenger door. Mathis bounced off the curb then hung a right on the through street.

Blocks away wind whipped the flames into a frenzy. The entire structure had to be consumed. Ennis's heart sank, "Mathis, is that fire anywhere near Franklin's house?"

"Yeah, it is," he swinging onto a connecting street. He drove two more blocks, turned onto Franklin's street and floored the accelerator. Fire engines clogged the street. Water jetted from hoses aimed at the blaze, sending clouds of steam and smoke churning in the air. Ennis saw Savannah's detective sedan parked in front of the fully engulfed house.

Mathis pulled to the curb across the street but Ennis had already jumped out and started running toward the house shouting her name.

Two firefighters held him back, "Go back across the street."

"My wife is in there! I have to get her out!"

"We'll take care of searching for her." He motioned to a nearby uniform officer.

Ennis tore away from the firefighter's hold. No one except God could prevent him from going in that house. He took off running again, this time heading to the side gate. Acrid, choking clouds of burning wood and plastic singed his nose and stung his eyes. He shouted her name over the roaring blaze. A ball of flame rolled from a broken window, forcing him sideways to avoid being consumed. His foot caught on something solid. Ennis went down hard on his shoulder.

Coughing, he pushed himself to his elbow to see what tripped him. A lifeless Caleb Franklin stared back.

O   O   O

11:28 A.M.

Before Ennis Arrived

Music slowly pulled Savannah to consciousness. A song played with repeated annoyance. Elvis. Yeah, that's who it was. The tinny, familiar sound of *A Little Less Conversation* drifted to her, bringing her from the depths of slumber. She finally realized it was her phone. Someone was calling her.

Baby, close your eyes and listen to the music

Drifting through a summer breeze...

Her hand closed in a fist thinking she'd found the singing cell phone. She grasped grass instead. And what was that God-awful smell? Had she left food in the oven and it was burning?

A little less conversation, a little more action please

All this aggravation ain't satisfactionin' me...

A series of racking coughs blasted her awake to face a nightmare of flames and stifling smoke only yards away. The phone call to Mathis and the terrifying encounter with her attackers raced back. She'd thrashed against the man's hold thinking it was her last few minutes as a living, breathing human being. And if she didn't do something quick it would be. Since she'd been unconscious, the house went from quiet, cozy and upscale to a hellacious inferno where fire reached from the roof to the sky, paint blistered on exterior walls and tendrils of smoke drifted from the slats. The window looked like the portal to hell itself with flames raging and threatening to consume anyone foolish enough to venture close.

Elvis reprised his song. It had to be Ennis calling her but she was a little tied up at the moment. Literally. Before they left, the men sealed her mouth shut with tape and zip cuffed her ankles together and hands behind her.

They hadn't left right away. The one behind her brought her down long enough to subdue her while the other guy primed the house with accelerant and threw a match to it. The two weren't finished with her. They stood watch over the fire's progress and shook their heads at her impotent attempts to free herself. The one who choked her within an inch of her life now braced a foot on her hip to keep her still, "Don't worry. We didn't leave you alone. Your pal is right beside you."

He rolled her to her back. Caleb Franklin's corpse lay several feet from her. He stared back at her with a glassy, thousand yard stare. White bone glared from his cleaved throat. Savannah swallowed hard.

The masked attacker towered over her, "You should have minded your own business." His tone developed a ring of finality, "Because now *we* get involved. Keep screwing around and here's what'll happen." He crouched beside her, "Pay close attention." He pulled out his phone, tapped a few buttons and showed her the screen.

A chill raked her. A photo showed a child about preschool age lying in a woman's arms – her mother's arms, Savannah presumed. The side of the child's head was gone as well as part of the mother's forehead. Blood and brain matter sprayed the walls behind them. The mother still had her arms around the child, trying to protect her while some son of a bitch murdered an innocent child then shot the mother.

The man palmed the phone, tapped another button. He smiled behind the ski mask, "Aww, now aren't these adorable? They're so cute playing together." He turned the screen to her again.

Now her heart stopped. It was video – or maybe a live shot – of Lily and Anna at school frolicking during recess. Lily always seemed to look after her sister the way Georgia had her own baby sis but no child could protect a sibling from this evil: A man so vile he murdered children.

Savannah looked past the images to the man's face. She prayed he read her expression loud and clear. Leave my kids alone.

He chuckled, "You can save the glare. Bottom line is your kids are safe as long as you behave." He reached in his pocket. Out came the small plastic bag containing the SD card, "This isn't any of your concern. Remember that because a lapse in memory will be fatal for these kids – and you." The was the last she heard or saw of the man before he rendered her unconscious a second time.

The phone rang again, bringing her out of the memory. Swirling smoke closed in, unleashing a storm of pain through her ribs when she coughed. Savannah wormed as far away as possible from the scorching inferno spitting bits of burning debris and hot ash at her. Voices at the street drew her attention. At some point fire trucks arrived. Through the fence slats she watched firefighters stretch hoses across the lawn while commanders shouted orders. The fully involved structure called for an external attack only, she knew that, so searching for survivors shifted to recovering the dead after they extinguished the fire. Since she couldn't alert them to her presence, she braced for the pain from her ribs and shoulder and rolled the last few feet beneath a tree and pushed herself upright enough to prop against the trunk.

Savannah eyed the closed gate, contemplating how to stand up, manipulate the latch and open the heavy wooden door to safety. Time ran out with every snap, crackle, pop and groan from the two story firestorm.

"Savannah!"

Ennis! It was Ennis. Not that he could hear her but she screamed behind the tape, hoping and praying he'd open the gate and see her. Through the slats she saw firefighters converge and stop him.

No! Let him through! Her scream died behind the tape. The firefighters waved at someone she couldn't see. Probably a cop. Ennis stood no chance of saving her now.

"My wife is in there!" he shouted at the fireman. "I have to get her out!"

"Buddy, it's too late," was the reply. "If she's in there, we'll find her later now go across the street."

"Like hell I will." Ennis took off shouting her name as he ran, this time toward the gate. He threw it open so hard it rocked the fence. As he ran he stared, transfixed in horrified disbelief at the massive ball of flames roiling from the window. Her name fell plaintively from his lips but he kept blindly running past her and straight toward Caleb Franklin's body. Savannah tried to scream for him to stop running but he snagged Franklin's shoulder and went ass over teakettle in the grass.

Ennis pushed to his knees, his vision focused on Franklin's severed throat. "Oh God," he looked up at the house. She could hear the hope leave his voice as he cried her name again. He still faced away from her, oblivious to her struggles to reach him. She tried screaming over the roaring fire. Anything to get his attention before he tried entering that inferno to search for her.

He stood up and stepped forward. There was only one way to stop him. She stretched her legs out as a voice from the front yard shouted for a withdrawal. The same voice called for a defensive attack on the fire and to focus on protecting the surrounding structures. They'd written off Franklin's house.

She fell onto her bad shoulder, releasing a yelp as she did so. Ennis turned. Relief and joy replaced utter panic and despair. He rushed to her, "*You're alive.*" His trembling hands cradled her face and he pressed a kiss to her forehead. Tears filled his eyes, "You're really alive."

She nodded frantically and waited for him to remove the tape. One deep breath later she said, "Let's get out of here. The house is too unstable. The roof's going to collapse."

There was no probably to it. Somewhere above them the burning rafters creaked and popped. More embers and sparks floated down. The outside wall groaned.

Ennis scooped his hands beneath her but she shook her head, telling him between coughs, "My gun and phone are by the cedar tree over there."

He grabbed them, and pocketed both then lifted her into his arms. A loud roar started deep within the house. Savannah burrowed against her husband who ran like Jesse Owens on a gold medal run. A thunderous roar behind them caused her to glance over his shoulder. An orange ball of flame and embers burst out the window as if the house purged Hell from its bowels.

Mathis met them across the street. He mopped his brow with his handkerchief, "Rutherford, I don't wanna hear anymore guff about how I cut through traffic or how I navigated between that Ford and the light pole on Piedmont. Judging by that stunt just now, you cut things a hell of a lot closer than I do." He waved an EMT over, "Hey, you. We need some oxygen over here for her and a tranquilizer for me." Then turned to Savannah, "You okay, kid?"

She managed a weak smile, "Thanks to my two heroes. I'd be toast if it weren't for you."

John retrieved a pocket knife and cut her ankles and wrists free. "Can I assume you don't have the SD card?"

"I *did* have it." She coughed again, "For two whole minutes until Morgan's goons struck again. This time they threatened Lily and Anna if I don't back off. They had someone watching them at the school and showed me video of them playing together." She pushed the offered oxygen mask aside.

Ennis took it from the paramedic and held it on her face. She frowned. He frowned back, "Don't argue. Just breathe."

Considering he saved her life, she did as she was told.

Ennis verbally fumed at the threat to their kids. He cited a colorful variety of reprisals that all ended with expediting Morgan to his Maker once and for all.

She grabbed his wrist and fought against his hold on the mask. When she realized the fruitlessness of her efforts she gave up, "Leave him alone, Ennis. This shit isn't worth losing our family." She hoped the warning penetrated his anger because she hadn't the strength to fight anyone anymore, not that day especially. She'd try getting answers from Lee since she didn't see him threatening his own grandchildren. As for Hoffman, he'd made his point with her. Her fight with him was over no matter how bad she wanted to wring his neck. And her husband better shelve his frontier justice ideas as well. She planned to plod along in her job, raise her kids with Ennis and hopefully retire to see a grandkid or two. Just the thought of Ennis trying to follow through on those threats made her weak.

"You're pale and shaking, kid. You need to lie down." Mathis nodded to the EMT who rolled a waiting gurney closer.

Again she didn't argue. Nothing like having your kids' fates in your hands. What happened if Hoffman (or whoever the hell he sent to steal the SD card) misinterpreted something she did as interference and her kids suffered as a result?

She overheard Ennis tell the EMT to "load her up and take her in". That was the last straw. No way was she headed to another damn hospital. She started to get up but Mathis pushed her flat again.

Mathis meant well. He treated her like an older brother would. Considering their ten year age difference, she kinda considered him one too. Today, however, she had one goal in mind and to ensure there'd be no misunderstanding, she lifted the mask, "I'm fine and I'm not going anywhere except to work."

Mathis leaned in, his voice secretive, "You ain't goin' nowhere but the hospital, kid. I know you're mad and I know who you're mad at but this is your future," he pointed to Ennis, "his future, and your kids' futures. There ain't nothin' worth risking those."

30

When she confronted Lee with the latest events, he blew his top and vowing to "take care" of the bad apples in his employ. He just needed help doing that, he said, then offered the CSO job *again*. She declined *again*. To say her answer frustrated him would have been the understatement of the century. For the first time, he vented his aggravation, "Why won't you accept it? It's a dream job to most people. Good money, basically flexible hours and still you refuse. Does it revolve around my involvement with Charlene? I promise you that Georgia's allegations are outlandish nonsense. They're simply not true and I resent being accused of such a deplorable act."

His hostility toward her sister cocked and primed her to fire back. Somehow she held her temper in check, "Mama wrote everything in her journals, that's how Georgia and I found out so don't blame my sister." The last three words surfaced as a firm "or else" caution.

Lee lifted his hands in surrender, "I apologize for speaking of her in that manner but you must understand how I felt being accused of such a heinous crime. I regret that Charlene considered my actions rough. Personally it was the most joyful day of my life and it *was* an act of love. The second most joyful day was finding out she was pregnant with my child. I loved your mother, Savannah. I loved her dearly. I'd never dream of violating her."

With each lie, sickness literally inched up her throat. She ran for the bathroom. Hot water filled her mouth while her stomach threatened a revolt – of what she didn't know. She'd left that morning without eating breakfast, drove to Augusta to face the man who paid a killer's salary. The more she reran Lee's little spiel about not hurting Charlene, the sicker she grew. He lied to her face and he despised Georgia for bringing his deeds to light.

Visions crashed in. Her mother fighting Lee, trying to free herself, to run, to scream for help, anything to stop the nightmare. Many years earlier Savannah found herself in the same position so putting herself in her mother's place was all too easy. The difference was Savannah barely but successfully fought Toby Jackson off. She couldn't imagine enduring the trauma of the rape then wondering whose child she carried, her husband's or the rapist's.

The lady resting in peace in Augusta's Westover Memorial Cemetery probably went to her grave thinking Savannah was Lee's daughter. For eighteen years, she'd lived with Lee's brutal attack yet raised Savannah with the love, patience and respect she gave Georgia and Seth and made her youngest daughter feel special while bearing the painful memories of the violent conception. The woman was a saint—

Four knocks on the door jarred her from her thoughts. "Savannah, are you okay?" Lee.

She offered a vague, "I'll be out in a minute."

"Oh no, is she sick?" Mrs. Gardner approached the door, "I'll fix you a cup of peppermint tea, dear. That'll fix you right up. Poor child, she's been through so much lately. It's no wonder she's feeling ill."

The tea helped but not as much as Lee leaving her to chat with Mrs. Gardner while he tended to "business" in another room. Savannah trembled to think what that "business" entailed... Before she left he tried one last time to foist the CSO job on her. She held a hand to her stomach to curtail the rumblings of more nausea while declining. Her life was complicated enough. Accepting the offer meant clashing with Hoffman off the job which would prove even more hazardous and frankly she wanted her old, stable routine life back. The one before Lee Morgan, before finding out about her mother's rape, before Hoffman – the life before her existence went to total shit.

Lee's job entailed too much uncertainty for her and too much volatility for Hoffman. She'd be questioning his decisions, investigating his existing employees and recommending termination for some of his crew. At that point he'd make her day job untenable, she felt pretty sure of it. Plus, being CSO demoted Hoffman to second banana and no one readily accepted that without holding a grudge – and she felt sure he played for keeps when it came to those.

She'd left Morgan unhappy but vowing to find her a place in the family employment ranks, whether in security or something else. Hearing that caused the nausea to plague her all morning.

At noon she walked into the station. She'd cleared the half-day with Hoffman who encouraged her to take a sick day but she wanted to clear the day's paperwork before she drowned in it. She planned to sneak by Hoffman's office but his office blinds and door were wide open. The major sat at his desk surveying the uniform officers and Sergeant Bailey assisting citizens at the sergeant's desk. With Hoffman, leaving his blinds open meant one thing. He watched and waited for someone. She only hoped it wasn't her.

She casually strode in, praying she rounded the corner before he saw her. Ten feet to go. Eight. Six.

"Sergeant Prince, in my office."

Shee-yet, she hissed under her breath. He'd practically shouted her name. Officers turned to her and citizens looked over their shoulders. She about-faced to his office. Hoffman motioned her to close the door. She did, dreading what came next.

"I heard about your eventful day yesterday."

"Yessir." A coughing fit caught her by surprise. She braced her ribs and cringed against the pain until it passed. The smoke inhalation, light as it was, nagged at her overnight and into the morning as Lee and Mrs. Gardner could attest.

"Got a call from your father. He wants you to take the day off and see a doctor. Said you refused when he saw you this morning."

"I'm fine, sir. The paramedics checked me out." They also recommended a hospital which she refused.

"Good." He leaned back in his chair, "In case you're wondering, I was here at the station all day yesterday. My wife packed my lunch so I didn't leave for my mealtime either. That's before you accuse me of killing Franklin, tying you up and torching the house."

"No, Major. I know you weren't there."

"I also heard about the threat to your children."

By his expression he'd done more than hear about it. He'd

ordered the two goons to extend the threat.

Hoffman's steady, piercing stare dared her to accuse him. When she did not, he continued, "Lee didn't mention it so I assume you chose not to tell him. Want some advice?"

Not from you, no. She nodded anyway.

"Whatever Franklin used to lure you to his house isn't worth pursuing if your children are in danger. You're a tenacious cop, Prince, but know when to quit. I put half a dozen case files on your desk this morning. They need a tenacious cop's attention. Choose one and get busy."

She nodded again, not trusting herself to speak.

He waved her out. The sting of his warning along with the lingering ache in her ribs and shoulder caused a wince that went to her soul. Something about his eyes triggered a new level of fear not felt since Jeffrey Holland stalked her. Hoffman wasn't human. He was a psychopath.

Savannah carefully removed her suit jacket and draped it around the back of her chair. Squirming and rolling on the ground the day before roused her ribs and shoulder to a constant dull ache so she vowed to take it easy.

Hoffman had excavated the unsolved homicide files until scrounging up the six oldest in Zone 2's history. She wondered how much dust he blew off the folders before depositing them strategically on the desk in front of a 5x7 with Ennis and the kids.

She trolled through the cold cases. One dated back twenty years. Hoffman *really* wanted her to stay busy.

She chose a case twenty years old. Leslie Rankin, 23. The Atlanta Fire Department responded to a fire at the Lenox Peachtree Apartments and after extinguishing the blaze, recovered Leslie's body. An unknown assailant tied her to the bed, sexually assaulted her then set her on fire. A neighbor reported seeing Rankin with a man she'd met a few days prior to the murder. There were no other leads except the neighbor's description of the suspect. A description, Savannah ruefully noted, that fit roughly half of North Atlanta.

She tried concentrating on the case but her vision kept drifting to the 5x7, stroked the faces beneath the glass. She meant what she told Ennis – this shit wasn't worth it. Let Morgan have his henchmen as long as he and those henchmen left her family alone.

Savannah went to the break room for coffee. She found Mathis hovering around the pot, waiting for it to finish brewing. "What are you busy with?" he asked.

"Hoffman has me going through cold cases."

"Cold cases?" He handed her a coffee cup then stepped aside, "Sounds like you'll need the caffeine more than me." He grabbed a glazed donut in the meantime, "How cold is cold?"

"Twenty years. Remember the Leslie Rankin case?"

Wide eyes peered over his reading glasses, "You really pissed in his Post Toasties, kid. That case ran Van Duren off the job and into therapy and he was only a coupla years older than you."

She remembered Van Duren. By the time he left the job he looked like he'd been put through a mental meat grinder. Then two years later he killed himself. "Thanks for the pep talk, John. I needed it."

"No joke. You better make like an ostrich till Hoffman gets over his snit. And don't go losing your mind or your life like Van Duren. I don't wanna lose you too."

She returned to her office. John's parting words inspired a smile. How far they'd come over the years when the name "kid" meant something less endearing and she retaliated by calling him the "Old Fart".

She sat down to get the day's paperwork under her belt then tackled reviewing Van Duren's notes on the Rankin case.

Two hours later the pull of a headache started. No wonder Van Duren ran himself in circles, she thought. Everyone he interviewed had a description of the suspect and none of them remotely matched. With a defeated sigh, she removed her glasses and pinched the bridge of her nose.

"Savannah Prince?"

The voice drew her from the brief, semi-relaxing break. A postal carrier stood in the doorway. He held an envelope in his hand. "Yes," she replied, thinking that fancy nameplate on her desk was for naught. "What can I do for you?"

"Certified Mail. It's Restricted Delivery so I'll need to see identification and get a signature."

She slid her reading glasses on and after retrieving her police ID, she hesitated. Whoever sent this gem paid a chunk to get it to her. With her life lately, she'd better ask a few questions before signing anything. "Do you guys scan these things for Anthrax and nuclear bombs before delivering the mail?"

He stared at her like she'd lost her mind. She explained, "I've had a really bad week and those are about the only two things that haven't happened to me yet."

Now he cautiously regarded the envelope in his hand. "It *should* be safe." He also couldn't get rid of it fast enough, urging, "Just your ID and signature please."

She obliged, "Sure. I understand. I wouldn't want to hang around me either. Lightning may strike."

He departed with a hurried, "Have a nice day."

She sneered. *Easy for him to say. He doesn't have to be at Ground Zero when this thing explodes.*

She examined the innocent looking piece of mail. Above her name the sender printed the words "Restricted Delivery" in red. She felt something small and not immediately detectable inside. Probably the bomb's detonator, she mused darkly.

Then she noticed the sender's name. Alex Davis. Caleb Franklin's words came back to her. *Remember the name Alex Davis. You got that? Alex Davis.*

She ripped into it. Tucked inside a folded piece of paper sat a micro SD card. She placed the card on her desk and read the note. "Sergeant, this is the only backup left. Make sure you protect it. C.F." Below his initials read, "P.S. Good luck, Princess. You'll need it."

Savannah folded the letter and pocketed it. She turned to pick up the micro SD.

"Morgan's really not happy that you keep declining his job."

She eased around to face Hoffman's smug features. He stood in the doorway, arms crossed. To be safe she stood in front of her desk to block his view of the tiny SD card. "Sorry but I'm happier with this job. I told him you were better equipped for the CSO job anyway."

The comment caught him off-guard. "How's that?"

"You're already in a leadership position. You have more experience than I do. I would be Chief Security Officer in name only. I would be relying on you to make the important decisions and in that case you might as well keep the position."

He considered her reasoning then nodded, "You make an interesting point. Still doesn't make him happy though. He's trying to fit you in somewhere in Morgan Industries. Even recruited Ethan to help."

"Won't do any good. I love law enforcement too much to leave it."

"That makes two of us. Bailey said you got a mail delivery. The carrier refused to let him sign for you. Said it was Restricted Delivery."

She scrambled for an excuse. "They're papers for me and Ennis."

"Papers? Something wrong in paradise?"

"No, just details regarding the orchards back home. No problems."

Her explanation appeared to suffice, "Glad to hear it. How's it coming on those cold cases?"

What was this? The inquisition? "Slow. I'm still reviewing the notes on the Leslie Rankin case."

He flinched, "You tackled the toughest one. I heard the last detective went bonkers trying to solve it."

"If three kids and my current life haven't driven me over the edge, this won't either. You're stuck with me, Major."

"Then I'll let you get back to work."

Savannah contemplated fastballing her paperweight at his head to expedite his departure. Instead she counted her blessings he bought the orchard lie and never pressed to see the letter. Now her legs felt wobbly and her heart tried to downshift from high gear. She let out a breath so long and deep she toyed with collapsing in the chair beside her. She didn't though. There were things to do and next on that list: Make sure to avoid Hoffman while delivering that precious SD card to Mathis.

31

After picking up the kids, Savannah rushed home to start supper. She threw together what she named Southwestern Casserole, a dish she created from scratch one weekend out of desperation. It consisted of macaroni, ground beef, a little onion, diced tomatoes, green chiles, Monterey Jack cheese and a diced jalapeño. Ennis and the girls loved it and she couldn't exactly call it a failure either.

While supper baked in the oven. Lily and Anna sat in the floor playing and coloring while Savannah fed Daniel. He was a good baby and quiet for the most part but at times fussed more than his sisters at that age. Her little boy loved exercising his lungs at the slightest noise and sounded off until her nerves frayed. When he slept, Daniel was the most beautiful baby she'd ever seen besides the girls, of course – but God love him, his protests could raise the dead.

Savannah burped him and sang to him. Some babies preferred "Hush, Little Baby" or "Rock-a Bye Baby" but their boy loved to hear the legendary silky-voiced crooner Johnny Mathis. They stumbled onto this gem one day she and Ennis tuned the radio to the oldies station. Their persnickety son calmed quickly upon hearing "Unforgettable" or "When I Fall In Love" so she made a point of buying Johnny's greatest hits CD. Singing his songs worked too for whatever reason which was why she sang "Unforgettable" until her eyes glazed over and she heard it in her sleep.

Daniel stared up at her and smiled as she sang and rocked him in her arms. He had Ennis's smile which meant she was doomed in years later when her boy flashed that grin asking for "just one more" cookie or, in his teen years, asked for the car keys.

But for now, he only wanted his mama's love and attention – and for her to sing his favorite songs so she gladly began "Unforgettable" for the third time.

His sweet expression made her think the angels whispered in his ear. Savannah delighted in these moments. They never lasted long enough. The girls were growing up too fast and soon their brother would join the ranks. Yes, getting up two or three times at night got old but once she settled her little one's upset, fed him or changed him, Daniel, as his sisters had, gifted her with a smile and adoring gaze that sent her heart soaring.

Lily darted into the living room, "Mama, have you got another–"

Savannah gently shushed her, "Use your quiet voice, sweetie. Your brother's nearly asleep. What did you need?"

Lily whispered, "Have you got another Chester Chipmunk I can read?"

She shook her head, "Not yet. I'm about finished with the latest one." She watched Lily's smile fade. The child really wanted another story. "Maybe by the weekend I can have it for you."

Considering a scant forty-eight hours stood between the weekend and Chester's new journey, the news brightened Lily's mood, "What's it about?"

It thrilled Savannah that Lily and Anna enjoyed her little stories following the cuddly adventurous rodent. "Chester gets lost in Atlanta then ends up at the zoo. He meets new friends and gets into some trouble along the way." *A little like me, I guess.*

She'd taken to weaving educational information, life lessons and history into Chester's inquisitive escapades – and to her surprise the girls still lapped them up.

Trying her hand at creative writing, Savannah gained a new respect for her sister's work. The challenge wasn't only putting her ideas on pages and trying to breathe life into them, those ideas had to come from somewhere. Strange as it sounded, being creative wore her out in a whole other way as opposed to her day job – but the girls' voracious appetite for her efforts and their smiles paid off like pure gold.

She checked the casserole's progress in the oven. Daniel finally settled down to sleep so she headed to the bedroom to place him in his crib. Halfway there the doorbell rang three times in quick succession. Daniel wiggled awake. Then he began crying. Savannah's shoulders fell. Well, there went *that* idea, she mumbled.

Savannah tried settling him down while Lily opened the front door. "It's Mr. Mathis!"

Too bad it's not Johnny Mathis the singer. We could use him right about now. "Let him in," she sighed, wishing for an encore of Daniel's sweet, angelic, *quiet*, disposition.

Mathis stepped in the door, scrubbed Lily's hair, "Hey, kiddo, where's your mom? I got something to show her."

Savannah stepped from the hallway, "Just follow the sound of the crying baby."

He winced, "He's got a set of lungs on him, don't he?"

"Yes." She tried handing him the baby, "Here. You sing to him and I'll look at whatever you brought."

Mathis recoiled as if she offered him a rattlesnake, "No, thanks. I've never been good with babies. I only make 'em cry more."

"Just hold him for me, John, and channel your namesake to hush him. He loves to hear Johnny Mathis."

He took Daniel awkwardly in his arms but seemed to settle in rather quick, "Not this Johnny Mathis, he don't. Babies hate my singing."

She grabbed her reading glasses, her tone dubious, "And you and your wife raised how many girls?"

"Enough I didn't want more." He bounced Daniel gently in his arms, "Reach in my right coat pocket. I got a coupla recordings I want you to hear."

She sat the glasses down and reached in his pocket instead. "Off the SD card?"

"Yeah," he cringed when Daniel squalled. "Hey, kid," he told the baby, "hold it down, eh? We're doin' business here." Then told Savannah, "I figured it was safer to bring it to you since Hoffman isn't lurking around every corner. The first recording is Lee Morgan's side of a phone call and the second is a meeting between him and, well, you'll see."

Daniel's displeasure increased in volume, forcing her to retreat to the bedroom to hear the recordings. She heard Mathis ask Lily if anything besides singing shut the baby up. She replied no. Mathis groaned. Just before Savannah hit Play, she heard a slightly off-tune voice coming from the living room.

She focused her attention on Lee's voice coming from the recorder. Wherever the recording device had been hidden, Lee's boisterous tirade came through loud and clear, "Who the hell shot my daughter and Robert Prince? I said I'd handle him, not kill him, and as for my daughter, whoever shot her will be dealt with either by you or me. Savannah's description of the car matches my security vehicles. Find whoever did this and take care of them today." The sharp rap of a phone slamming in its cradle jerked her hand away from her ear.

Savannah stared at the recorder. So Morgan *wasn't* responsible for the attack on her father. So who decided to mow her and R.J. down?

A thread of fear wound through her gut. Back to Square One meant anyone could be the culprit. She pictured each Morgan, hoping one image might trip a memory, phrase or expression she overlooked. They all hated her and probably never liked R.J. either and one of them took it a step too far but which one?

It took a while to calm down enough to brave the rest of the recording. Mathis resorted to impatient humming. She needed to hurry.

"The sister recognized my voice."

Savannah pressed Stop, rewound the recording and play it again. When she closed her eyes, she put a face to the familiar voice. Hoffman.

"Who are you talking about? Georgia?" Lee asked.

"Yeah. When I spoke to Prince at the bakery, the sister gave me a look. She knows who called her."

"She say anything?"

"No. She knows what could happen if she did."

She stopped the recording again. So Hoffman threatened Georgia. Savannah went from angry to homicidal in one heartbeat. She jabbed the Play button again, waiting for the next bombshell if there was one.

"To be sure, I want insurance. Find a way to get Charlene's journals," Lee told him. "Thanks to Tucker's book I've had enough scandal to last a lifetime. I won't risk those journals seeing daylight and I can't trust Georgia to stay quiet forever."

"I'll get 'em," Hoffman promised.

"Understand I don't want Georgia or her husband hurt. I just want the journals. Find a way in the house while they're gone."

"What if the sister doesn't have them? What if Prince does?"

"Same thing. I'll make sure she and her family have plans that day."

The recording abruptly cut off. Savannah cursed through clenched teeth. She wanted to punch them all, even Lee Morgan, so hard the entire bunch bounced off the moon and landed in another universe. Morgan raped her mother and tried somehow – God only knew how – to destroy her father. There was probably still a hit out on R.J. but thankfully Bobby and a few of his friends agreed to keep an eye on him. Her daddy couldn't drive yet but Savannah (against Georgia's wishes) had Bobby supply him with scotch. It seemed to tame her daddy enough he didn't cause too much trouble for the nurse who dropped by to check on him.

Her vision shifted to the nightstand. One of Charlene's journals sat right there begging Hoffman to steal it. Now she had to be wary about the house being unattended. It wouldn't be difficult to break in since she and Ennis worked days and the kids were either at school or stayed with Dane or Katherine. The biggest concern was Dane and Georgia. With her gone most of the day, that left Dane alone and Savannah didn't trust Hoffman to wait for the house to be unoccupied. If he abducted a fellow cop, what kept him from roughing up or killing a civilian merely to locate a few books?

Savannah thought a moment. They needed to hide the journals quick but where?

Mathis warbled an off-key rendition of *Mack the Knife*. Her nose wrinkled at not only his sour-note singing but his choice in lullabies. The longer she listened, the worse he sounded. Mathis! That's it! The thought practically made her giggle. Good ol' Mathis. Rotten singer but the answer to her prayers.

She returned to the living room to John's relief. "See?" he said, eagerly relinquishing custody of the screaming baby. "He don't like my singing."

"That's because the song is about a murderer," she teased.

He shrugged a shoulder, "Don't knock it. My youngest loved that song. Plus it's one of the few I know by heart."

She shushed her little boy and gently rocked him in her embrace while singing "A Certain Smile". Mathis stood by waiting to see if it worked. By the second stanza Daniel lost a few decibels on his fussing.

"What did you think of the recording?" he asked.

"I think Morgan's the skank Tucker portrayed him to be – but no one really doubted that."

With Caleb Franklin dead, Hoffman would concentrate on the journals to tie up that loose end for Lee Morgan. "I've still got my portion of Mama's journals. I hope Georgia still has hers. She hasn't mentioned missing them. I'll call her in a minute. I need a favor from you, John. If she has them, can you keep them somewhere safe?"

"Why not? I haven't had any excitement in my life lately. Might as well jump into your nightmare. Just don't ask me to babysit your son and we'll be okay. Speaking of nightmares, you're not going to Tucker's funeral, are you? You're just inviting trouble if you do."

She expelled an exaggerated sigh, "And I thought I got promoted to sergeant because I was halfway smart. Stop worrying, John. I told Ethan I'd send a donation to Crossroads instead of attending the funeral."

"That drug rehab Tucker created? Must be a cushy place. Junkies clean up in luxury."

"I've heard it's nicer than most but it's not a vacation at the Waldorf." Daniel quieted down enough they could talk without raising their voices. She mentioned Hoffman, "He's blaming a junkie for breaking in and killing Tucker but they didn't get a good look at the perp's face."

Mathis shrugged, "Could've been a junkie, I guess. I never got a chance to look at the footage. He's very secretive about the case."

"I noticed. Well, he's tarred and feathered me for the last time.

He can keep the Chief Security Officer job *and* Tucker's case."

The news buoyed John's mood, "Hey, you're not leaving us, after all. That's great." He winked, "See, kid? *That's* why you got promoted. You make good decisions – well, most of the time." He glanced at his watch, "Gotta get back before the commandant misses me. Good job calming the baby. You got a good singing voice. Tenor, right?"

How could a man who lived for anything associated with football, NASCAR, beer and pizza possibly know her vocal range? "What are you, a closet choir director?"

"I got a good education in high school choir. I never learned to sing but I had my pick of twenty girls who could. I could easily peg an alto from a tenor once I tested their vocal range in the football team's equipment shed – if you get my meaning." He bobbed his brow, "Ah, the good old days…"

After Mathis left she called Georgia asking about the journals. Thankfully she still had them but it took a truckload of assurances for her to agree to give them to John. Before committing, she asked one last question, "What if Hoffman realizes he has them?"

"John assured me he has a safe place. He's very resourceful when he has to be." Savannah hated to broach the subject but, "Why didn't you tell me you recognized Hoffman's voice that day at the bakery?"

"You were a gnat's eyelash from getting fired. Telling you certainly wouldn't have helped the situation."

Savannah understood but didn't like it. Between Lee Morgan and his henchmen security force, no one in her family was safe – and it was eating her alive.

She headed to the upper cabinet where she kept her stash of Uncle Jack. She'd nurse a glass while contemplating her next move. The sight of her favorite uncle brought relief. One drink, she promised. Not enough to get tanked, just enough to think.

You don't need a drink.

Her hand stopped partway toward the bottles. She looked around, afraid she'd been caught but that voice belonged to her dearly departed mother.

Savannah, stop. You don't need a drink and I should have taken a switch to Roy Carlson's backside for giving you that first taste. Throw the bottles away.

Roy Carlson, Savannah's high school boyfriend, introduced her to the warm bite of Uncle Jack's "magic potion". The night she learned her mother had terminal cancer he'd offered Savannah a drink to calm her down. Once her mother found out about the Jack, she'd threatened to horsewhip Roy but it was too late. Savannah learned about and liked whiskey's numbing effect. It was the first time in her life she understood why her father turned to the bottle. It softened life's devastating blows, at least for a while.

Mama, I know I'm disappointing you, she whispered, but I need a drink.

Charlene reminded her of the danger Lee posed. His ruthless business methods and the countless companies and individuals he'd ruined over a simple rejection or argument. *And sweetheart, look what happened to me,* her mother added – as if she had to. *I was a good, faithful employee doing my job and he took what he wanted because he could. No one is safe from Lee, not even you or your family. Think about it and think with a clear head.*

Charlene strongly urged Savannah to resist temptation – her mother had been doing this for weeks but Savannah kept making excuses why she needed a drink. To help her relax, to ease the emotional pain, to help her forget. Today she would listen to her mother and her own conscience.

She wrapped her hand around the black-labeled glass beauty, already mourning its loss. Uncle Jack proved his worth as a temporary salve to life's chaos. Okay, she used it as a crutch, she admitted it, so a moment of hesitancy and fear at losing that crutch seemed natural.

A week ago she would have called herself crazy for doing this. This week she'd call herself nuts if she didn't. Two lovely, *full* bottles filled with her magic elixir sat at the front. It about killed Ennis not to chuck them in the trash. He chose to lecture instead. That man's lectures put old Southern Baptist preachers to shame. Then lecturing got old so he stared. He enlisted the girls to stare. The kids' stares stirred entirely more guilt than his and went straight to her heart. Shame now washed over her just touching the bottles. She'd made a right fool of herself reaching for the Jack when things got tense or outright insane and she intended to remedy the problem. Next stop for the aged whiskey – the sink.

She pulled the two bottles from their hidey-hole and turned. Lily stood, arms crossed and glaring at her. Anna possessed quite an evil eye herself.

"Is there a problem?" Savannah inquired.

"Yes." Lily stabbed a finger at the offending bottles, "Those. Throw them out. Anna and I want you to stop drinking right now."

Anna stood in alliance with her sister and appeared perfectly willing to snatch both Uncle Jacks and smash them on the floor. To drive her point home, she shook her finger at Savannah, "Stop dwinking *now*."

Lily clasped Anna's hand as if realizing shaming their mother might incite her temper, not convince her to toss the booze out. "Mama, will you do it for us? We hate seeing you drunk."

The word hit harder than her daddy's fist. Drunk. Coming from her child it sounded worse than a sin. Her sister could preach and her husband could lecture but when her daughter backhanded her with that one single word *drunk*, it reached a part of her soul that deflated her posture and killed any reason or argument why she needed the booze. She averted her gaze to the floor. She couldn't look them in the eye after knowing she let them and Ennis down and *that*, in her opinion, was the worst sin of all.

Lily's tone softened, "Mama, we know it's stressful but you've had stress before and didn't drink. We're not being mean. We just want our mama back."

As a kid, Savannah wished for the day R.J. put down the bottle. She never braced him about it, of course, because she'd pay with pain and bruises. She hadn't gotten her wish but her children deserved better from her. Her entire family did.

Both girls embraced her. Anna begged, "Please, Mama."

Her children handled the intervention well for their ages. They touched nerves only children could. It hurt to pour out perfectly good Uncle Jack. It *really* hurt. But seeing the disappointment on her kids' faces hurt a hell of a lot more.

Savannah nodded to the stool Anna used as a booster, "Bring your stool to the sink. I want you both to watch."

Anna's jaw dropped, "You weally gonna do it?"

"I'm really gonna do it and you're both gonna help me." She'd never tell them she already decided to chuck the whiskey. At that moment the joy on their faces meant more to her than anything on earth.

Lily tightened her embrace, "Thanks, Mama. It means a lot to us."

"I know it does, honey." Before emptying the first bottle, she asked them, "I suppose I can depend on you both to tell Daddy and Aunt Georgia about this?"

The two happily piped up in unison, "Yes, ma'am!"

o o o

Tucker's funeral topped Wednesday's news both in print and on TV. Savannah figured her daddy – if he was still staying home like a good patient – scoured the crowd for her face. He'd be happy not to spot her in the mourners' midst but not as happy as her ribs would be. Nope, after shift, she and her family prepared to attend the Wednesday evening church service. She made a special effort to thank God for blessing Georgia with the sense to surrender the journals to Mathis.

For the first time in weeks neither Savannah nor Ennis were

called away from the church service. She thanked God for that too.

Only when they arrived home did the phone ring. Savannah wished God reserved one more blessing, this one to render their home phone mute, especially when it came to Lee Morgan.

"I'd hoped you might attend the funeral but I understand," he said with obvious disappointment. "Ethan said you bowed out because of Robert."

"Ethan should have told you I sent a donation to Crossroads in lieu of flowers, or getting skinned alive by Preston, Grady and their wives." She wanted to say "shrews" *in lieu of* "wives" but thought better of it. "I can recover from Daddy's bruises. Not so much unemployment and Preston just has a knack for acting on that threat."

"Ethan's right, isn't he? He told me you were pulling back from us. I didn't believe him but since you continue to decline the job offer and now skipped the funeral–"

"I didn't skip anything. My family needs me and I've been MIA lately. I intend to change that."

"Savannah, it's not in your nature to let anyone intimidate you. I can assure you the boys and their wives will treat you with respect once I'm finished with them."

She knew how too. Snip, snip and they're out of the will until they play nice. Now wouldn't *that* make her popular among the natives? She could almost hear them sharpening their knives – and claws. "You've got high hopes, don't you?"

"I have ways of persuading most people to do what I want. Except you, apparently. I won't keep you but I do have a question about

Tucker's case. Mike says you've been questioning his investigation. Why is that?"

Warning bells went off in her brain. She didn't believe Hoffman gave the investigation "due diligence" as he said but she wasn't about to tell Lee because, as *she* said, she hated being unemployed. "Simple curiosity. I asked some questions and he answered them, that's all."

"He believes you doubt his thoroughness."

"I have no reason to doubt the major. I'm sorry he took offense to my inquiries."

"I understand why you're saying this but I want the truth. Tucker put his life into Crossroads and made sure it helped everyone in need, not just the rich and elite. Mike wasn't fond of Tucker because of his past drug use. He's a good man and a loyal employee but I don't think he's giving this case his full attention. You would."

No thanks. "Hoffman wants this case, Lee, so I'm steering clear of it and him."

"Something's amiss and I trust you to find out what it is. First I want Sabrina investigated from stem to stern. He barely gave her a moment's notice." The longer he spoke the more agitated he grew, "He didn't check her alibi to my satisfaction then without informing me, eliminated her as a suspect. I know she had something to do with Tucker's death so be prepared to take over the investigation."

Yeah, right. "I can't wrestle a case from a major."

"But I can."

And that was only the beginning of her headache…

32

Hard leather soles clacked the tile floor. Savannah remembered the last time she heard such a steady cadence. Lee Morgan had just ripped Josh Hunter a new one about not receiving police protection.

She continued working at her computer that faced away from the door so foot traffic in the hall wouldn't distract her. Today, however, the foot traffic clomping down the hallway commanded her attention, particularly when the person entered her office without courtesy of knocking first.

A folder slapped onto her desk, startling her. She wheeled in the chair ready to give the person a piece of her mind until she came face to face with Major Hoffman who appeared one step away from exploding.

"The Tucker Morgan case," he said. "It's all yours. Have fun."

"Major, I never wanted–"

"Shut up, Prince."

Her mouth snapped closed from shock. Judging by his mood it took every ounce of control not to leap across her desk and throttle her so why chance it?

He thrust a finger at Tucker's file, "Evidently Morgan trusts a person he's known for five minutes more than he trusts his Chief Security Officer who's been with him for eight years. Don't expect any help from me and do not screw this up. But you'd better be prepared. Your daddy is a demanding bastard who will put you on a timer. Once you find the perp or someone who'll do as a scapegoat, he won't want them arrested. He will demand you handle it his way and guess what, Prince? I know you well enough I'd bet my pension you don't have the balls to follow through."

She kinda figured Lee might want the culprit handled "in-house" so to speak and to Hoffman's credit, he was right about her. She had balls but not the kind it took to kill on demand.

He marched to the door then turned back to her, "You got some nerve going to Morgan."

"I didn't say a word to him."

Hoffman stalked toward her desk again, "So out of the blue he gave his little girl a new toy to play with? He decided to hand over his son's murder investigation to a woman who couldn't care less if she was his child or not? Is that what you're telling me?"

Savannah began to answer but thought better of it when he leaned a shade closer to say, "I don't buy it. You told him I was full of shit, asked for the case and got it. I'll tell you one thing, Prince. Starting today, you better dot every i and cross every t because I'm going over your paperwork with a fine-tooth comb to make sure you don't step out of line. You can guess what happens if you do."

He stormed from her office, leaving her dumbfounded. How did these things happen to her, she wondered. Sitting there minding her own business and she got verbally flayed by her boss.

Just for kicks she checked the calendar. Nope, it wasn't Friday the 13th but Neptune was probably in Uranus or her Gemini moon was up Jupiter's nose. Whatever the problem, her life went to shit the last few weeks and she wanted it to stop.

She scowled at the file. After she called Lee Morgan to beg off this ridiculous (and obvious) attempt to reel her in, she'd return to her usual workload – and dot every i and cross every t. Geez, she thought, I can't stay out of the soup for a day.

O O O

At first blush it appeared Hoffman had been right. The security video not only lacked the quality and sound Savannah expected, but also a good shot of the killer's face. All she saw was a hoodie hiding a blurry image of the killer's face. Savannah brought Ennis and Mathis in to view the footage for their opinions. Both ended up like her. Nose inches from the screen, trying to identify any distinguishing features of the hoodie-clad intruder slinking around Tucker's million dollar home.

They found a split second when the figure glanced up enough the camera might have caught a glimpse of the face. Ennis voiced her thoughts, "Take it to forensics. I bet Billy Miller can refine that part into a useable image."

Savannah was already on the phone to Billy who shot down their great idea of making progress. "They're backed up because of the double homicide outside that nightclub day before yesterday," she told the men huddled around her computer.

Ennis sneered, "Unless Lee Morgan owns the crime lab, he'll have to wait with the rest of us."

She reached in a drawer for her steadily emptying bottle of Tums, "Yeah. Won't that be fun."

○ ○ ○

Major Hoffman made good on his promise. The next day she'd been at work less than five minutes when he summoned her to his office, motioned for her to close the door. "Why did Detective Rutherford require lost time yesterday?"

"A dental appointment. A filling fell out. Yesterday afternoon was the only time they could fit him in."

"He could've used chewing gum to plug the hole while he waited for a regular appointment. I've done it."

Somehow she doubted that. "Their earliest was two weeks. Major, he was in a lot of pain and wouldn't have been able to concentrate on his work during that time."

He scrutinized his computer screen again, "Sergeant, are you giving your husband preferential treatment? If so, I'll have him transferred. I've gone back and reviewed all your paperwork since your promotion and I don't like what I see. It seems Detective Rutherford's days off coincide with yours way too often."

"Sir, we're both on call if needed and Captain Hunter saw no problems with the scheduling or anything unsatisfactory about my work."

Hoffman tensed, his eyes narrowing as he squared off with her,

"Are you trying to get suspended, Prince? One more crack like that and I'll write you up for insubordination."

Savannah's stomach knotted. Insubordination? *He's spoiling for a fight and using one innocent, matter-of-fact comment to detonate my career.* "No sir, I'm not trying to get suspended."

"Who's the senior officer in the room?" he barked loud enough she fought the urge to recoil.

Heads turned outside his closed door. Hoffman really wanted to make a point, apparently, and wasn't above public humiliation. She answered calmly, evenly, "You are, sir."

"Damn right. It's my responsibility to keep Zone 2 working efficiently and productively and if that means making changes, I will, so I'll review your work, Rutherford's work, everyone's work and I'll make those changes as I view appropriate. Got that?"

"Yes, Major."

"Now, how's the investigation coming? Found Tucker's killer yet?"

"No, Major."

"Better hurry." He tapped his watch, "Your daddy's getting impatient."

This wasn't the time to correct him by saying Morgan wasn't her father. "Yes, Major, you forewarned me."

He thrust a finger toward the door, "You're dismissed, Sergeant. Get busy earning your paycheck or you won't have one."

33

Housed in the public safety annex along Donald Lee Hollowell Parkway, the crime lab was staffed by seven forensic examiners and technicians. Those seven handled evidence from murders in a city with a homicide/manslaughter rate of 17.7 per 100,000 people and analyzed everything from fingerprints and firearms to DNA and security footage. The worst part: they were backlogged beyond belief and Savannah was about to make things worse for one particular tech. She hated to nag people who could make or break a case but she needed progress on Tucker's case (Hoffman had been correct about Lee's impatience) and the security footage was the biggest key she had. Or maybe had.

Pressure was part of a forensic tech's job but having detectives breathing down their necks sure didn't add to the camaraderie. There was a noticeable difference in Detective Prince and Detective Sergeant Prince not just in title or salary. People treated her differently, including the crime lab techs. They, along with almost everyone else, felt more comfortable speaking to the former. When the latter walked through the door their guard went up and the formalities appeared. A boss, not a colleague, entered their midst.

She'd known Billy Miller for three years. He was one of the few in the forensics lab that actually understood her title may have changed but she had not. Upbeat, clean-cut and dressed in a dress shirt, slacks and loafers, he presented the image of a kid fresh out of college and ready to tackle the world – one homicide case at a time. No matter the stress or time crunch, he almost always spent a minute or two asking about her family. She knocked on the door facing, "Billy? Got a sec?"

A sigh rose from behind the computer screen along with a curt, "Hold your water." Squinting features appeared over the monitor. He resembled a prairie dog peeping out of its hole until he realized who she was, "Sorry, Sergeant. I thought you were Jarrett from Zone 6. She's made this a very long day."

She sympathized, "I've had one of those myself."

"I haven't had a chance to look at your security footage yet. I meant to get on that before she climbed on me this morning. I keep telling her I've only got two eyes, two hands and one computer."

Savannah realized his patience frayed with Jarrett's harping and now a sergeant checked up on his progress on another case. "I can tell you're feeling the pinch. If you could just give it a look before the weekend, I'd appreciate it." That gave him roughly thirty-six hours. Still a tight schedule but between Lee and Hoffman, Savannah's ass was in a vise too.

Billy shook his head, "No."

No? His vehemence took her aback. She hated to remind him that part of her job description was to solve murders and she needed evidence for that. Plus she would refrain from playing the "I'm the boss" card. She already had enough people hating her.

He tapped a few buttons, waited and crooked his finger at her,

"Jarrett can wait. What's the time stamp on the security footage you wanted?"

"3:14 p.m." Savannah halfway relaxed. If anyone stood a chance of enhancing that image, it was Billy. "Thanks for doing this, Billy. You have no idea how much I appreciate it."

He pulled up the footage, "I'm afraid I do. Dobbins received a call around seven this morning demanding this be first on my list. I was about to begin working on it when good old Jarrett stormed in."

Lee pulled out all the stops, not only notifying Hoffman but the crime lab director about the case. "Bet I know who contacted Dobbins."

"I'm guessing you do." Billy employed the mouse, used a pull-down menu on the screen and clicked. The image filled the screen. "Then Jarrett kept hounding me and since I have to work with her, I put her first just to shut her up. Sorry I put you on the back burner."

"No problem. Sorry you got hounded by Dobbins and Jarrett. I understand. I've got my own pit bull chasing me around about this case."

"Morgan?"

"Hoffman."

"Ouch." He accessed the pull-down menu again, clicked another selection. The picture focused pretty well. He kept working with the mouse and keyboard to sharpen the killer's image. "Mind if I ask you a personal question?"

"Depends on what it is, I guess. Shoot."

He brightened the image and fiddled with the focus again. "Is it true what they're saying? That Lee Morgan is your father?"

"Don't put money on it and don't believe what Tucker Morgan wrote. My mother did not have an affair with Lee."

He decided now was the time for eye contact, "But still, isn't this case a conflict of interest for you? Investigating Tucker's death when the popular consensus is you're his half-sister?"

She nodded, "I thought so but someone with more money and influence thought different."

Billy caught on, "Oh, I see. Dobbins *and* Hoffman received a call from You-Know-Who. Nothing like a nudge from high society to light a fire under a boss."

"Except this was a shove, and the case landed in my lap." He gave one last tweak to the image, "This is the best I can do on short notice. You'd think for a rich guy, Tucker would have sprung for better security equipment. This stuff is old school for today's technology."

She agreed while remembering the suspect's purposeful strides from the back door through the den to the stairway. He climbed the stairs like an athlete in training. The killer did not act like a desperate junkie. He appeared physically fit, focused and on a mission. She said as much, "You've seen the video. Doesn't he act like he's on a mission? Goes straight for Tucker, kills him but doesn't search for a billfold, a safe, or anything before leaving. I wish there was a better shot of his face but there's not."

"Let me keep working on it. For now, take this." He printed the image and handed it to her. "Dumb question but does he resemble any potential suspects you had in mind?"

She studied the photo. The hoodie still cast enough of a shadow over the killer's face that she shook her head, "To be honest I was handed Tucker's case yesterday so everything is new. Do you think facial recognition might work on this?"

He considered it. "It's pretty blurry for that but let me see what I can do. It could inundate you with a hundred thousand people to sort through."

Savannah gave a hopeless shrug, "At least it would eliminate two million, nine hundred thousand."

O   O   O

Savannah regretted tossing her Uncle Jack. She regretted it most when she walked into the station for the last few mornings. Hoffman lay in wait for her to come through the door then summoned her to his office. By the fourth day every uniform officer winced when he called her name when she stepped in the station. For fifteen minutes he questioned every keystroke of her previous day's work and grilled and berated her over the lack of progress on Tucker's case. The inquisitions became so intense not even Sgt. Sweeney badgered her when she walked past his desk. She kept her cool with Hoffman, clawed her way through shift after shift and continued spinning her wheels on Tucker's case. After work, she found herself driving to the package store where she spent ten minutes in her car debating whether to refill the liquor cabinet. Uncle Jack's persistent voice wore her down a little more each day. *See, you do need me, friend, and here I am waiting for you. Come on and take ol' Uncle Jack home. You know I can help. And stop using your kids as an excuse to ignore me. They're too young to understand your situation. Don't worry. Someday they'll realize how stressed out you were and they won't hold it against you. Trust me.*

On the fifth day of repeating the ridiculous routine (and praying the liquor store staff didn't sic the cops on her for loitering), Savannah climbed out of the car. She walked the walk of shame inside the store, grabbed a small bottle (for some reason it felt less like a failure) and paid out. When she got home, she couldn't open it. Her babies' faces – and their disappointment – consumed her. Lily and Anna were young but not so young they wouldn't remember Mama's betrayal. Technically she'd agreed (not *promised* because she wasn't *that* stupid) not to drink anymore. Before picking them up from Dane, she tucked the little bottle (her insurance policy) in an upper cabinet in the laundry room then camouflaged it with bottles of extra detergent and bleach. Then she asked her brother-in-law to keep the kids another hour while she took a good, long run.

On the sixth day, she endured Hoffman's interrogation once again. This time it lasted ten minutes. She prayed he bored of the ritual because that Jack looked mighty tempting about eight-thirty that morning but she'd be damned if she gave in during her shift. The last thing she needed was Hoffman smelling it on her and firing her.

So she delved into Tucker's case one more time. Perhaps she missed a pertinent clue the last thousand times she reviewed the scant evidence and even skimpier notes. Most of the neighbors weren't home at the time of the murder. The ones that were home never noticed anything out of the ordinary. And unicorns were more prevalent than useful fingerprints. After reviewing the video again, it was obvious the killer wore latex gloves. She had two clues. One, the video that showed the perp's trek through the house and his exit (he sprinted down the alley), and two, boot prints from a pair of men's Wolverine Durashocks size ten and a half. How many men in the area wore that size? With her luck, probably that hundred thousand Billy Miller mentioned the other day.

"I need to talk to you."

Savannah closed her eyes but curbed the groan at the back of her throat. She hadn't broken a mirror lately or let a black cat cross her path so what the hell was Lee Morgan doing there? Between him and Hoffman badgering her with their demands, she'd lose her mind.

Uncle Jack reminded, *I'm right here whenever you need me, don't forget that.*

As if she could. *I should have bought the big bottle. Two, maybe three of 'em*, she berated herself as she removed her glasses. She pinched the bridge of her nose. "Listen, Lee. Solving murders takes time. If you and Hoffman give me that time, I might stumble across a morsel of decent evidence but breathing down my neck like he is and now you?"

He waved it off with a curt, "I don't know what you're talking about. I haven't said a word to Mike about your progress. I do need your help though. Grady's been involved in a hit-and-run. He's undergoing emergency surgery for internal injuries. The driver mowed him down then drove off. At least two bystanders recorded it on their phones. They've offered the footage to the police. I want you to find this person, Savannah. I want you to find them and bring them to me."

Savannah refused to address his last few sentences so she offered her sympathies, "I'm sorry to hear that happened to Grady. Does the hospital know if he'll be okay?"

He grew increasingly agitated with each passing second, "They're optimistic, yes."

"Good. I'm happy to hear it. I can't take the investigation though. I'm busy trying to locate Tucker's killer murderer for you. Give Grady's case to Hoffman." *That'll give him something to do other than skewer me.*

Lee approached her desk, braced his hands on both sides as he leaned in, "Okay then. Hoffman it is *but* only if you agree to have my security team protect you. Someone's going after my children and I'd like to keep the rest of you alive if possible."

The conversation circled the drain of stupidity now. A bodyguard? For her? "Oh, for God's sake, I'm a cop. I don't need–"

"You're having a security detail and that's that. They're good so don't try to lose them. They will find you. Call me overcautious but I'll keep you safe any way I can."

The instant Lee Morgan blew out of the room, she slumped onto her desk, head in hands. *I will not drink, I will not drink, I will not drink...* She repeated the silent mantra to keep her sobriety and sanity in place, shaky as they both were.

A light knocking came at the door, "Hey."

Ennis. He carried half a dozen or so pages in his hands which meant either good news or more crap to entice Uncle Jack to whisper in her ear again. Concern etched her hubby's features as he closed the door and blinds. He crouched behind her desk, put a hand to her knee, "Are you okay, sugar? You look spent."

Spent? "I'm so spent I'm in debt. Hoffman won't take his foot off my neck and now because Grady Morgan got hit by a motorist, Lee thinks 'his kids' are in danger so guess who's getting a bodyguard courtesy of her brand new papa?"

Ennis stiffened, "First Tucker now Grady?   Babe, maybe Morgan's got a point. It can't hurt to have an extra set of eyes looking out for you."

"Don't you go to the dark side too. You know, it may sound stupid but I understand how Luke Skywalker felt when Darth Vader stormed into his life saying *I am your father.* Only I know – at least to the best of my ability – that my personal Darth isn't my father. Those kind of people just take over your life and not in a good way."

He stroked her arm, his voice honey smooth and sweet, "I've been meaning to tell you this for days."

She frowned. "Tell me what? You're leaving me because there are too many clowns in my circus?"

Ennis smiled a smile that calmed her and assured everything would be alright, "Not even close. I wanted to say you've handled this chaos like a champ without Uncle Jack. Morgan, Hoffman, home life, everything and I love you for it."

She cupped his face in her palms and pressed a kiss to his lips. His pep talk went straight to her heart. Hearing those words and seeing the love in his eyes reinforced her resolve to ignore Jack no matter how loud he shouted. Ennis was proud of her and that meant the world to her. "And I love you for being you."

He kissed her palm then her wrist, teasing, "You're just sayin' that to get me in the sack tonight and it'll work as long as we're both conscious."

His warm, velvet kisses stirred her in ways best left at home, "You'll be conscious if I have to poke you with a stick. Until then, what brought my white knight to see me?"

Ennis rose to his full six-two glory and picked up the papers he brought in, "Mathis printed a list of Morgan's employees for you. Thought you might want to glance through them. He ran the names and most are current and former law enforcement and former military."

"Retired cops?"

"Some but *former* fits them better. Let's just say these guys didn't play by the rules but made their own. Mathis put notes by the problem children."

She readjusted her reading glasses then skimmed down the list of several dozen names comprised of ex-army, former NYPD, Detroit and Atlanta cops. She centered on the ones highlighted by John's serial killer scrawls. The law enforcement bad apples had engaged in various activities such as tampering with physical evidence, abuse of official capacity, perjury and excessive force. She remembered two widely publicized incidents. Though her memory faltered recalling the ex-NYPD officers' faces, their actions vividly came to mind because of the fallout suffered by every cop in the nation, including Atlanta. Body camera footage brought their violent acts into living, undeniable proof some people should not be cops and the news regularly ran the footage on and off for months, reopening the wounds and reinforcing public distrust.

Kyle Henderson used a chokehold on a handcuffed suspect who later died from the officer's actions while Dominik Frankowski beat a suspect so brutally the man suffered bleeding on the brain. These two made a mockery of the job she loved and now they were protecting a man who spent his life doing no better, especially to Charlene. He may not have physically murdered her but he destroyed her in a way no woman could totally recover from.

Savannah blew out a breath. "And he wanted me for Chief Security Officer to supervise these goons." She meant it to sound incredulous. Instead it came out depressing.

Ennis put a hand to her shoulder, "Dodged another bullet, didn't you? Apparently Hoffman transferred the New York bad apples down here and ours up there. Lee has a whole nest of flunkies working for him in several locations."

She reached for the Tums in her desk drawer, "And the biggest one is in charge of my career."

34

The following morning Savannah didn't get two steps inside the station when she literally nearly ran into Hoffman. "In my office, Sergeant," he ordered.

Here we go again. She pushed her shoulders back to prevent them slumping from hopeless dread then followed him into his domain.

He closed the door but left the blinds wide open. Why the change, she wondered.

Hoffman rounded his desk and sat down. He did not offer her a seat. "First, your security detail. They are Shane Doherty and Jack Burke. They're both ex-NYPD. They were personally picked by me but Lee also approved them. Considering what happened to Tucker and now Grady, I strongly suggest you stick close to them and listen to them. That's a caution from Morgan's Chief Security Officer. Switching roles to your superior officer, I want to know what Tierce is working on."

He reviewed her work daily – with a microscope – so why was he asking her this? Her confusion must have shown since he confirmed, "I read your updates but I want to hear them from you."

She named the open cases that Detective Tierce plodded through slower than molasses. He was newly promoted but not so new he shouldn't have learned the ropes by now. He often needed a verbal kick in the ass to inspire him to work, at least for her. She kept that part to herself.

Hoffman nodded, "And Rutherford? Update me on his work."

She recited the two cases he toiled on and like most homicide cases, things went at a glacial pace except for one that had an unexpected breakthrough. He was currently out, she said, speaking with a new witness who said he had valuable information.

The major steepled his hands beneath his chin. "Good. That one's been a stubborn case lately. Now what about Mathis? Tell me what he's doing."

Savannah went through John's caseload, and confessed he'd hit a stumbling block on them all. Until she came to Mathis, her boss accepted each explanation with a nod. Now his expression evolved to one that nearly made her squirm. He said, "So if he's working so hard on those, explain why he accessed the database and ran backgrounds on my security team."

Her stomach went into freefall. He'd been checking up on her detectives – including her – as was his prerogative but the sting in his voice left no doubt. He was furious. She tried using logic, "He's working Caleb Franklin's case too. Why wouldn't he need backgrounds on the people he worked with?"

"Because we don't kill people, Prince, that's why. How did Mathis get that list anyway? I didn't hand him one and neither did Lee Morgan. Pretty sure Lee's boys didn't so how the hell did that list get in his possession?"

During these morning inquisitions, Hoffman's voice carried well outside his office. Today though, he jacked the volume where Ennis, Mathis, Josh Hunter and half of Alabama could've heard it if they listened halfway close.

From the corner of her eye, she noticed Sergeant Sweeney and his officers trying not to stare. The drama in Hoffman's office, however, captivated them like children watching a bully beat the stuffing out of a smaller, weaker child. In that time Savannah debated over telling Hoffman the truth. He'd find out somehow, she thought. He'd make her life impossible or outright fire her unless she confessed. "I got it from Franklin. He gave me a copy."

Hoffman's posture transformed from arrogant anger to a more aggressive one, "When did he…" He paused as the answer finally dawned on him, "The restricted delivery. You lied about what it was."

"I assumed you'd be angry if you found out about it. Considering what happened to Franklin that day at his house, I think you can understand why I had reservations about telling you, especially since the men who did it work for you."

Major Hoffman rose to his feet and rounded his desk, "Well, I *don't* understand, Prince, but *you'd* better understand this. The second Mathis steps foot in this station, you and he are going to hand over that list and anything else Franklin gave you. That includes an SD card, hard copies or anything else that has private information on it." He stood so close she felt his breath on her face and those fierce green eyes drilling into her. His voice developed a quiet, ominous quality, "Once I have everything, get out of my sight and start looking for another job because I've got some creative lying to do myself."

O O O

Hoffman lit into her and Mathis as if they'd stolen the nation's nuclear codes and threatened to publish them. When it was over he sentenced them to modified duty and docked them a week's pay. When Savannah defended John, Hoffman added another week to her penance. Mathis told her to shut up before she got fired. Little did he know…

They left his office madder than hornets. Again, Sergeant Sweeney kept his lip zipped when she stormed by his desk toward her office. She'd noticed Mathis handed over the SD card and list without a whit of argument, something she mentioned that once they reached the sanctity of her office. Mathis grinned like the cat that ate the canary. He looked strange wearing a smile that spanned ear to ear. The times she'd seen it, he was staring at an éclair or donut, not rebounding from losing a week's pay. He whispered, "I handed it over because I copied the files – well, half of them anyway. My kid called and cut me short. Her car broke down and she needed a ride to work but at least I got half the information."

Savannah sighed with relief. Half was better than nothing. "Thank God. Let's hope it's the right half. Who had the car trouble?"

"Number 4. Amy. She can't keep a car running to save her life."

A knock on the door cut their conversation short. She feared Hoffman forgot something to yell about and he wanted to end her day by outright firing her.

Two suit-clad men the size of wrestlers entered. They bulled in together, forcing Mathis back a step. While John protested the rude entrance, she nearly retreated a step as they approached her. Any miscreant would think twice of tangling with these two, she noted, as each extended a big, meaty hand and introduced themselves. No one could accuse them of possessing much charm considering Shane Doherty, the dark-haired one, spoke in a barely genial manner and Jack Burke, blond with a slightly crooked nose, nodded with a curt, "Ma'am."

For some reason their presence failed to make her feel safe. They didn't necessarily appear thuggish, only herculean, but as the employee list proved, Hoffman didn't hire squeaky clean security people. At least their names didn't sound familiar in a bad way. Of course after scanning the list of dozens and dozens of names, only a person with a photographic memory could remember them all and her photographic memory had faulty film.

Burke stood guard outside the door while Doherty took up residence in her office. She understood why but she realized having Hoffman's ally sitting in the same room came in handy for the major. His personal tattletales would shadow her at work, home and anywhere else she ventured. Not exactly how she envisioned living her life.

Later that afternoon Mathis lumbered in after giving both burly, armed statues a baleful glare. "Got a minute, Sarge?"

As a matter of fact, "Thanks to our boss I have a lot of them now. What's up?"

He centered on her grim "guest" Doherty who texted back and forth with someone for the last seventeen minutes. Savannah knew this because she counted them. "Hey, Laurel," Mathis barked at him,

"Hardy's waitin' for you in the hall. Why don't you join him?"

Doherty's vision lifted from the phone. He seared Mathis with a scowl that gave her goose flesh. She tried a more diplomatic, "It'll only be a few minutes."

Doherty left and closed the door behind him. Mathis hitched a thumb at the door, "That's gonna get old quick."

"It already has. What did you need, John?" She waved him around her desk and advised him to keep his voice down.

"You ain't gonna like this. Your abduction? Sabrina Morgan set it up. I can only guess it was a publicity stunt to hype book sales. The afternoon you, Ethan and Tucker were carted off, a judge dismissed Lee Morgan's lawsuit to block the book's sale. From what I gather, once the abductions hit the news, Tucker hit number nine on Amazon's bestseller list."

Savannah sat back in her seat, "Wow. Look who took the accelerated course *How to Act Like a Morgan*. I wonder if she paid Hoffman a tip to zap her hubby a few extra times because Tucker really took the brunt of that Stun-Cuff."

Mathis shrugged, "Dunno but that offshore account got really fat after Morgan paid those ransoms. Took forever to track it down too."

"I know how much Lee paid for my release and if Sabrina set the prices, her husband got the shaft. Like Ethan said, he got marked down. I'm curious why."

"Don't you watch TV? A few months ago he was caught with that floozy hotel heiress, you know, doing the horizontal tango. They had pictures of 'em in those tabloids at Kroger. I think Sabrina hired a private investigator to catch 'em. Since then it's been Ice City between her and Tucker."

Her mouth fell open. "John Mathis, you of all people? Reading scandal sheets?"

He shrugged again, "Why not? I gotta do something between football games."

Maybe he had a point about Sabrina. "If she had Tucker killed thinking she'd have another huge payday, she's in for a big surprise because according to Lee, he left most of his fortune to Crossroads and a portion to his kids. Nothing to her."

O   O   O

Before dressing for the Mission of Hope award ceremony, Georgia took a moment to admire Dane's progress on the baby's crib. He worked tirelessly to restore it to its former glory. Well, former to a point. Due to the crib's age, they couldn't find another cartoon lamb for the end panels, at least not an exact replica. That's okay, she told her husband. Preserve what you can, she said, because the original will give it character and keep the sentimental value. So the old, faded, frolicking lamb on the end panels stayed. Judging by Dane's efforts, Georgia discovered ranching wasn't her husband's only talent but carpentry and refurbishing rated a close second and third.

She laid a hand on her belly. Their baby girl. Sugar and spice and everything nice. A dream come true. She allowed herself a momentary vision into the future, wondering who their daughter might favor, what her interests might be, how they could protect her and still raise her to be strong and confident.

No longer just an aunt, Georgia was headed for the most important job a woman could have. Motherhood. And like Savannah when she first got pregnant, the road appeared foggy and uncertain. Years ago Georgia tried relieving her sister's worries about taking on the role of Mama. Georgia "just knew" she'd be a fine mother so why did she doubt her own abilities? She supposed every new mother did this but the tiny human growing inside her would rely on her for so much. Charlotte would come to her for help and advice – the person besides Daddy who was supposed to know "everything".

Now Savannah assumed the task of assuring *her* that motherhood would come as second nature. Second nature? Hardly. Being a good aunt did not qualify her to be a mom, she said but thanked her sister anyway.

Georgia closed her eyes as she ran her hand along the crib's smooth railing. Baby Charlotte's image evolved to Baby Savannah's, sending Georgia back to her childhood when the family welcomed a new addition. The newest addition to the Prince family wasn't raucous or terribly demanding, no more than any other baby Georgia had seen at the ripe old age of six years. She'd seen her share of Prince and Culberson babies that raised the roof and a person's blood pressure. Princes could split logs with their sharp, loud wails and Culbersons, well, they just cried *all... the... time.* Savannah, though, laid there wiggling her arms and legs sometimes smiling and overall seemingly happy by herself unless she needed changing or feeding. She really was a good baby, no matter what their father claimed. He hadn't expected another child six years after Georgia. Neither had Charlene. Georgia surely hadn't. She thought she was the baby of the family and yes, she resented losing that title – at first. No child loves giving up that coveted place in the fold. But she, along with Grandma Culberson, assumed caring for the baby while their father basically ignored Savannah and their mother descended into a deep depression and took to her bed. Grandma called it postpartum depression. At such a young age, Georgia didn't understand what that was. She only knew sometimes when her mama fed or held the baby, she cried the whole time. Georgia figured giving birth wore their mama out since during those nine months Savannah sent Charlene to bed with migraines, muscle cramps and bouts of crippling nausea. Once she had Savannah, their mama must have given out with that postpartum thing Grandma mentioned.

Charlene did what she could for the infant but often asked Georgia to look after her. That's where the bond between sisters began. After a point Georgia felt more like a mother to Savannah, not a sister. Once Charlene got on her feet again, Georgia was reluctant to surrender the role of surrogate mother but the bond held strong with Savannah from the day she was born. Giving up the title "baby of the family" paid off handsomely throughout Georgia's life. The sisters had been inseparable and still were, no matter whose DNA flowed through Savannah's veins. That's why the day's mail gave Georgia pause.

Savannah's DNA results arrived. In her heart Georgia knew R.J. fathered all three Prince children but that one seed of doubt – the "what if" – hung over the family. How would Savannah react if, by some bizarre hiccup in the universe, he *wasn't* her daddy?

In the few quiet moments that afternoon, she remembered Savannah diving back into the Jack Daniel's once learning Lee Morgan might be her father. Remembered decades ago when R.J. ignored the crying infant begging for his comfort. Only after Charlene and R.J. had a long, heated discussion did he begin warming up to Savannah and begin calling her *my baby.* All these years Georgia had assumed his resentment stemmed from the baby coming at a bad financial time in their lives. As a youngster and teen, Savannah received the worst beatings but anyone who knew her realized she hadn't been the easiest child to raise. As if she remembered his bitterness toward her as a baby, she defied him at every turn and paid for it. Then somehow, later in their lives, they called a silent semi-truce. He still went ballistic on her sometimes but he also depended on her a great deal. The older she got, the less she minded his calls or problems. So the sealed envelope sitting in Georgia's desk drawer could either be a balm to Savannah or a bomb detonating her life. Personally, Georgia would wait a bit longer before springing that on her sister. Maybe not the wisest idea but to be honest, she was scared to death of what it said.

Georgia trekked upstairs to dress for the ceremony. It took twenty minutes to decide what to wear simply because her clothes didn't fit quite right. She made a note to go shopping for larger slacks, at least. As it turned out she and Savannah chose nearly the same outfit, a black pantsuit with low heels, only Savannah chose a lilac colored blouse while Georgia chose a green one.

Calming her nerves was a joke. Why could she face a group of eager fans wanting her autograph in a book but not a crowd gathered to recognize her efforts for helping the homeless? The hum of conversations buzzed in the air like a beehive. Five hundred people. She couldn't remember being in front of five hundred people in her life yet here she was in the spotlight along with five other award recipients. Newspaper and TV reporters waited impatiently. Checked their watches. Cameras flashed in various spots in the crowd. Georgia prayed for the night to get underway before she passed out from nerves. Grief, she scolded herself, you've seen your share of reporters and cameras flashing before, mostly when your newest book is released so why are you so nervous now?

Because having a prestigious organization such as Misson of Hope solely recognize *her* for Pie In The Sky's efforts to feed the homeless made her uncomfortable. She, Dane, Savannah, the employees and patrons made the business a success which allowed her to help the city's less fortunate. While Mission of Hope sang her praises, she would sing the praises of "her partners in success."

The start had been delayed ten minutes for some reason. That ramped up her nervousness. She caught herself fidgeting and glanced at her family. Dane, Seth, Leah, Savannah and Ennis sat in the audience along with a few employees who came to support her. Ennis sat with his arm around Savannah and she leaned into his embrace, the couple an embodiment of true, endearing love. Georgia caught Savannah's eye. Her sister's overjoyed smile and wink settled her down. She was blessed beyond words. Between her family's encouragement and Dane crowing to strangers about his wife's successes and how proud he was of her,

Georgia realized how blessed she was and thanked God for such a loving, supportive family.

Watching her sister chat with Dane and hearing her laugh at one of his jokes, Georgia saw a woman who managed to balance marriage, children, work, and now an endeavor into creative writing. Lily and Anna fell in love with Chester Chipmunk in his green plaid jacket and stylish fedora. The small collection of stapled notebook pages hidden away for thirty-some-odd years captivated them so completely they begged their mama to write more – and like a good mother Savannah tried.

From what Georgia read of the newer stories, her sister possessed real potential. At Savannah's request, Georgia proofread and suggested minor refinements. Once Savannah made the changes, Georgia encouraged her to send it to a publisher. The world needed more children's stories and, in her opinion, Chester Chipmunk would make a fine addition. Her sister hemmed and hawed, thanked her for the compliment then told her, "I'm glad you enjoy them but you're the writer in the family, Georgia. I'm just a cop. I'll never have the talent it takes to be published."

Georgia doubted that and to prove it, she shipped a copy of the stories to her agent Avery Dean and publisher Blake Crenshaw. She'd heard from Avery three days ago. He liked them. He really, really liked them. That made Georgia all the more anxious to hear from Blake. Publishers took their time, of course, but waiting for his opinion compared to waiting to tell Savannah, Ennis, Seth and Leah that she and Dane were not only having a girl but naming her Charlotte. They decided to tell their family before the ceremony which brought a special joy to the night for everyone.

A thoughtful smile crossed Georgia's lips at the memory of Savannah's reaction. "Not only a girl, but already a name," she'd gushed with a giddiness Georgia hadn't seen in ages. "And what a beautiful name it is. It has class, elegance and beauty, just like her mama."

Georgia looked at her family gathered to celebrate her success. Once more she settled on her sister. *Oh yes, losing the title "baby of the family" was a blessing because I gained a bigger blessing in my life. My baby sister.*

○ ○ ○

Savannah beamed at her sister, listening to her thank her family, employees and patrons for making Pie In The Sky a success in business and the community.

Georgia proudly held the plaque, occasionally glancing down at it, as if to ensure both it and the moment were real. If anyone deserved recognition it was Georgia and Savannah hoped she basked in memories of this evening forever. She vowed to continue efforts to feed the less fortunate in their fine city and challenged other eating establishments to do the same. As Georgia's speech shifted toward Mission of Hope's goals, Savannah's memory rewound to an hour earlier when her sister revealed The Big News. She and Dane were having a girl. Not only that but they'd already chosen a name. Charlotte. The second she heard it, Savannah envisioned the child with her sister's meadow green eyes, wavy chestnut hair and her mother's stunning beauty. She imagined the girl having Dane's sense of humor and love for nature and her sister's gentle soul full of kindness and generosity and the steady pull to either write spellbinding stories or get her hands dirty planting grand, colorful flowerbeds like her mama and grandmother.

Georgia wrapped up her speech by once again thanking everyone in her life and most of all God. Savannah stood to applaud. Dane, Ennis and the others followed suit. When the host began introductions for next recipient, they took their seats again. Savannah noticed Doherty hadn't moved an inch since choosing the seat directly behind her. The presence of her two shadows, Doherty and Burke, at first threw a wet blanket over her enjoyment that evening. Thankfully she completely forgot about them when Georgia took the stage but now the same nettling *someone's staring at me* sensation returned. This bodyguard thing wore thin real quick.

Her phone vibrated. She excused herself to answer it. Georgia, seated on stage, offered a sympathetic frown. Savannah felt fortunate to stay as long as she had. Being a cop had plenty of downsides, this being one. Private evenings or family get-togethers were frequently interrupted.

The call came from a Captain Erickson whose name sounded familiar but not enough to bring a face to mind. There'd been a report of a body in an alleyway in the northern end of Zone 2. She wrote down the address and returned to her seat long enough to tell Ennis and the family she had to leave. Then she looked to the stage. Georgia mouthed, "Leaving?"

She answered with a disappointed nod. Staying for the whole

event would have been a miracle anyway but this was Georgia's shining moment. Proof that she not only wrote bestsellers but could whip out a successful business known far and wide. "I'm sorry," she mouthed back then put a hand to her heart with a silent, "I love you."

"Love you too," Georgia replied.

Savannah made a quick exit and headed to her car. Thankfully she'd found a parking place two rows from the entrance. She climbed in, dreading the trip. Over the years the area, as her daddy might say, had gone to the dogs. When she patrolled there as a uniform cop, apartments, a bar, restaurant and a small farm-to-table grocer used to call the block home. In the last decade, family businesses closed, leaving the bar in competition with a strip club and a hole-in-the-wall gambling venue. The riff-raff soon followed and families moved away to newer areas with more wholesome surroundings including outdoor malls nearby. Lately even the strip club, bar and gambling abandoned the area, leaving only the riff-raff behind. Riff-raff that loved using and dealing drugs and worst of all, hated cops.

The passenger door opened. She reached for her gun then realized who intended to join her on the trip across town. "Take your own car," she told Doherty. "You can follow me to the scene."

"My job is to keep you safe. Can't do that if I'm in another car. Just pretend I'm not here."

If only. She cranked the engine and took off. During the trip Doherty regaled her with tales of his days with the NYPD as if Atlanta hadn't seen a true crime since its inception. This rambling was the most he'd spoken in her presence since introducing himself. When he finished, she thanked God he finally shut up.

She turned the corner and saw one car parked at the end of block. No car or foot traffic, she thought. No patrol units, no uniform cops, no one milling around. Even Doherty appeared confused. She eased the Charger closer then stopped. Something didn't quite feel right about this call. Lately they'd had a couple of instances where cops were called to a bad part of town only to be ambushed and nearly killed. For the first time since meeting Doherty, she was glad he was there.

"I'm calling dispatch," she told him. "Someone must have given them the wrong address or it's a prank or set-up."

"Go ahead and pull up. We'll check it out then you can call."

"It's a waste of time. There's been a mix-up or it was a prank call." *Guess they don't have those in the NYPD...* "Doherty, I'd like to get back to congratulate my sister." She inched the car a few feet forward.

The glow from the street lights across the way failed to illuminate the alley. That didn't set well with Doherty. He glanced in the rearview mirror as a car pulled up behind her. Burke's SUV. "Burke's here. He can help me. Park it and we'll take a look. Where's your flashlight?"

Where most flashlights are, she wanted to say but sighed instead. At this rate she'd never get back to see Georgia. To appease him, she shifted into Park, "In the glove compartment." She checked the time. A quarter to eight. If they hurried she might be able to see Georgia before the ceremony concluded.

Doherty grabbed the flashlight and bailed out while calling out to Burke to help him. Savannah retrieved her phone to text Ennis. Might as well let him know it would be at least thirty minutes before she'd be back.

The driver door suddenly opened, startling her. Phone in one hand, she reached for her gun with the other. Burke shoved the barrel of his .45 against her temple, "Kill the engine, give me the key then put both hands on the wheel."

While moving the phone to her lap, Savannah slowly withdrew her right hand from her gun, hoping to divert his attention to that movement instead of what her left hand was doing – dialing 911. Hopefully the operator would grasp the gravity of the situation and track the phone's GPS.

The 911 operator answered. Savannah spoke clearly, "Burke, you realize you're pointing a gun at a cop, right? Not just a cop but Lee Morgan's daughter." She hadn't thought twice about tossing the "Lee Morgan's daughter" hint out there, especially if it saved her life.

"Kill the engine, hand me the key and put your hands on the wheel."

The operator went silent. "Okay, okay, don't shoot," Savannah shut off the engine and pulled the key.

Burke grabbed it from her and while he pocketed it, she sat the phone in the floorboard then placed her hands on the steering wheel.

The passenger door opened. Doherty reached across, removed her gun from the holster then retrieved a pair of zip cuffs. She tried to give 911 more information, "Burke, you and Doherty haven't thought this through because once Lee Morgan finds out two of his security guys kidnapped his own flesh and blood, you're both goners."

"That's the beauty of it," Burke replied. "He'll never know who did it and they're never going to find what's left of you. Now shut up and get out."

She got help with the last part. Burke dug his fingers into her elbow and jerked her out. He forced her over the hood hard enough to stir up her ribs and that made her mad. She wrestled herself straight, turned and punched him hard enough he let go. Then she ran. If they planned to kill her, she wasn't sitting by and letting them have their way about it. She'd make it a challenge and maybe catch a break. The faint whine of sirens registered. If she could hide, run or just live long enough for the uniforms to see her...

A shot rang out. Savannah kept running. One of them fired a warning shot for her to stop – or they were just inept with a gun. She bet on the former. Footsteps pounded behind her. A hand shoved her forward. She stumbled, knowing she was going down but tried to angle away from a wrecked sedan parked at the curb. She fell against it while reaching out to cushion her descent. A cry spilled from her lips as the impact compressed sore ribs and pain ripped through her right arm. She'd fallen against the abandoned sedan and sliced her forearm on a jagged piece of fender.

She stilled at the steady pressure at the back of her head. Doherty heaved for breath, "You move and I'll fire. I don't care what our orders are."

The siren she heard multiplied into a symphony of four-wheeled saviors coming to a fellow cop's rescue.

Burke approached, he too still tried to catch his breath. He ran through his repertoire of cuss words and settled on a few X-rated ones to describe the woman who'd clocked him. The men pulled her to her feet and took her back to her Charger. Burke returned to his Land Cruiser. He brought back ankle cuffs. Doherty pushed her over the hood. Savannah braced before her face collided with it. Blood trickled from her arm onto the shiny finish of her prized Dodge until Burke cuffed her hands behind her. He crouched down to apply the ankle cuffs. Doherty yanked her upright as Burke asked, "Do you hear that?"

Doherty cocked his ear, "Yeah, I do." He pointed to her car, "It's coming from in there."

Unfortunately Savannah heard it too. The tinny sound of a 911 operator's voice coming from her phone. A voice telling Sergeant Prince help was on the way. Was she okay, the woman asked. "I heard a gunshot, Sergeant. Can you answer me? Are you there?"

Doherty spun Savannah to face him.

A battering ram crashed into her jaw. The painful collision knocked her off-kilter, sending her sideways against Burke. Her ears rang. A deep nausea stirred in her gut and she heaved. Nothing came up.

Doherty fisted her hair, brought her upright while Burke presented her with an item guaranteed to finish her off. She thrashed against their grasp while screaming *no*. She begged them to stop then screamed for help when they ignored her. A swift punch in the gut silenced her screams to a loud grunt and groan. She squirmed for leverage but Doherty braced her over the Charger's hood, hands on her shoulders and pressing himself against her to hold her still. Burke slipped the black hood over her head and cinched the drawstring.

"Hey!" A voice called from across the street. "Let her go!"

Savannah screamed for the man to help. "I'm a police offi–" her cry was cut short by another brutal punch, this one to her back. Two shots rang out as hands clamped on her arms and forced her toward to Burke's SUV.

"What do we do now?" Burke asked.

"Ask Hoffman," Doherty said.

35

Ennis gave Georgia a hug and shook Dane's hand before heading home. He'd not seen them this happy since their wedding. Their lives came together with little Charlotte and an added bonus – Georgia's business venture gained recognition not only as a top eatery in Atlanta but helping feed the homeless. He left them in good company, chatting with other award recipients and their families.

He stepped into the cool, humid evening. Laughter drifted from inside the auditorium, prompting him to smile. It marked the first time in several weeks the whole family – minus R.J. – gathered together and everyone had a great time. Life seemed to be smoothing out for a change. Georgia and Dane were happy and Savannah stopped drinking. Now if they could get Hoffman off her back, they'd be golden.

Ennis was on his way to his truck when his phone rang. He halfway expected it to be his wife since she usually took a moment to update him on when she might be home. He clicked on without looking at Caller ID, "Hey, babe, how's the–"

"Ennis, it's Josh. Dispatch notified me that Savannah dialed 911 a few minutes ago. I'm on my way to her last GPS coordinates. Can you tell me why she went to that location? I thought she was going to Georgia's award ceremony."

His heart soared into his throat and lodged into a throbbing lump. She called 911 and he'd been laughing and celebrating, completely clueless that she needed help. "She got called away to a crime scene." He raced to his truck on unsteady legs. Seconds meant the difference between life or death and half the city stood between him and his wife.

"Ennis, she's not there. The supervisor at dispatch put out a Code 30 on her."

An iceberg slid into his stomach. The world stopped. Code 30. Officer Emergency – Possibly Dead. That code sent a tsunami of uniforms and detectives to the scene. It also sent out an SOS to off duty cops who dropped what they were doing to go help a fellow cop in danger. He'd responded to a Code 30 before but never in his wildest dreams expected to respond to one for Savannah. Ennis swallowed hard while trying to fight off images of his worst fears. "What's the GPS location?"

Josh told him. During the trip, he repeatedly dialed her cell, praying for her to answer. Then he flew mad at Doherty and Burke. What good did those two "bodyguards" serve? They helicoptered around her day and night and still couldn't protect her when things went to hell? Something was wrong with that scenario. In Mathis's research on Lee's security officers, he hadn't flagged either ex-NYPD cop for misdeeds or corruption. So Ennis stupidly assumed they might actually protect her.

Ennis announced his arrival by pulling to a loud, abrupt stop at the curb. Police cruisers blocked the scene, their blue and red flashing lights reflected off the surrounding buildings. Crime scene techs had already arrived and set up portable lights to illuminate the area around Savannah's Charger. Uniform officers and detectives swarmed the area, the former cordoning off the area with crime scene tape, the latter converging on the lone Charger parked at the curb near the alley entrance. Equipped with gloves and flashlights, detectives had opened the trunk and doors of Savannah's car in their search for evidence and clues. One leaned in the driver's door, another in the passenger side.

More flashlight beams darted around the alley until two more detectives emerged from the alleyway shaking their heads, their faces grim.

Ennis jumped out of the truck and ran for the car, ducking under the tape until he approached a line of yellow evidence markers dotting the asphalt. As he approached, he slowed down. The trail started at her car and ended twenty feet away, close to where he stood. The portable lights revealed spots of blood at every marker. He headed for her car at a dead run.

Josh Hunter saw the frantic detective racing to the Charger. He started toward him while cutting short his conversation with an officer, "And tell him I want it now." He barely caught Ennis before he reached the car, reiterating the fact, "She's not here, Ennis. We don't know where she is but she's not here."

"Have you found her phone?"

"Detectives already have it. It was on the floorboard. She managed to call 911 before–"

"Have you heard the call? Was she able to say anything?"

"Yes and yes."

"I want to hear it."

"No. I can't have you running around town like a madman looking for her. Just answer this. Those guys shadowing her all the time. Morgan's bodyguards. What are their names?"

The mention of them turned him homicidal, "*They* took her, didn't they?"

"Ennis, answer the question."

"Shane Doherty and Jack Burke. Both ex-NYPD."

Josh waved two detectives over and updated them. Ennis impatiently waited until finally demanding, "I want to hear that call."

"I said no. Let these detectives handle this."

Ennis faced Hunter. For a moment he considered slugging him, "She's my wife. I have a right to hear it."

Hunter stood his ground, "Step back, Ennis. I'm cutting you a lot of slack considering the situation and the stress you and Savannah have been under but that ends if you don't get out of my face."

His rigid posture slackened and he retreated that step while shoving a hand through his hair, "Do you know what's going through my head right now? First Tucker died then Grady was hit by a car now Savannah's lured to this location, kidnapped and maybe killed. These people – whoever they are – are picking off Lee's kids and she's not even one of 'em."

A detective approached Josh with Savannah's phone, "She received a call from Captain Erickson at seven thirteen but dispatch doesn't have a record of anyone reporting a problem at this location."

Josh looked confused. "Erickson retired two months ago."

"This was a setup," Ennis told the detective, "John Mathis has a list of Morgan's security personnel. Check with him and see if Erickson is on it. He probably is." His vision locked on the blood-smeared hood, "That's her blood."

"At this point we can't prove it's hers." He put a hand to Ennis's shoulder, "We'll find her, Ennis. Right now you need to talk to the detectives and tell them everything you know."

A uniform approached Hunter, "Captain, dispatch got a call from Lee Morgan. Ethan Morgan is missing too."

Josh swore under his breath. "Where was he?"

"He was scheduled for a meeting with his father at seven. He never arrived. They found his car at home. It was running, the driver door was open and his cell phone was in the car. Sounds exactly like what happened to Sergeant Prince." He tore a page from his notepad and handed it to Josh, "Ethan Morgan's address. Lee Morgan's going to check the security video." The officer lifted a brow adding a sarcastic, "Said he'd let you know what he finds."

According to Josh's expression, Lee Morgan stepped on his last nerve. He fisted the note in his hand, "One handsome donation to the widows and orphans fund and he thinks he runs this department. Get Lee Morgan's phone number for me. I'll make the decisions on who checks what."

Ennis retrieved his phone, "I have Lee's number right here. I'll trade you that for the 911 call."

The two squared off until Josh capitulated, "Fine but I'm warning you, Ennis. Do not go rogue trying to find Savannah or I will assign you hospital patrol detail for the rest of your career – if you even have a career after this."

O   O   O

Had it been an hour? Two hours? Half the night? She stopped trying to track the time when panic sapped the last of her strength. She struggled for every breath, hoping for more air but finding little. The snug drawstring felt like a boa constrictor around her neck. For the longest she fought her own warm, moist breath and the hood determined to choke her while she fought for each breath.

The evening seemed to be a replay of the first kidnapping except this time the car never stopped and the longer they drove, the faster hope faded and morbid finality set in. She would not be going home alive.

During the drive the air turned colder, thinner. Savannah first attributed it to nerves. Now she unsuccessfully fought off a bout of shivering and wondered if they hadn't driven to a much higher altitude.

The hum of the tires wound down as the car slowed and turned off the highway. The terrain changed from smooth road to a rough ride. The Land Cruiser rocked and dipped. Tires crunched over small rocks and snapped small branches for what seemed like half an hour or more until finally coming to a stop. Burke and Doherty climbed out. The smell of damp earth and pine trees drifted in on cold, humid air that sank to the bones and raked her with tremors.

"You're late," a female voice complained.

Burke unlatched Savannah's seat belt then yanked her out of the

SUV. She lashed out at Burke for the rough handling then turned her anger on the "mastermind" of this plan, "I figured it might be you, Lydia. You or Sabrina." The inability to draw a good breath cut her rant short.

The strong scent of musk and vanilla wafted thru the hood when Lydia stepped closer, boasting, "Once Mike has your mother's journals, Preston and I will have Lee right where we want him. With you, Ethan, Tucker and Grady out of the way, he doesn't have a choice but leave the business and inheritance to Preston."

"Preston's part of this too?" Ethan asked.

"Ethan?" Savannah was surprised but happy to hear his voice. At least she wasn't alone.

"Right here, sis," he replied. "I guess you and I drew the unlucky straws today."

"Preston hasn't a clue about this," Lydia said. "He's done Lee's bidding for years, made fortunes to last his daddy ten lifetimes yet my husband can't see he's losing his birthright. So if I get rid of the firstborn," she pushed Savannah backward until she stumbled against Ethan, "Preston's next in line but if you're all gone, everything is his when Lee dies."

When, huh? "I guess you've made a date for Lee's demise too?" Savannah asked.

Lydia chuckled, "I have everything planned, including when to divorce dear Preston. After he has Lee's fortune, I leave him and Mike and I can live comfortably, or who knows, I may let Mike kill him too." She addressed her brother-in-law, "Ethan, you might remember these woods. God knows I've heard the story ad nauseum. Sad little Ethan lost in the woods, couldn't find his way out." She turned to Savannah, "It took three days to find him and by then he was raving mad. Burke, Doherty, get them out there and have your fun. Just make sure they don't come back."

Fingers squeezed around Savannah's arm, urged her to start walking.

She traversed each treacherous step with care until Burke's impatience kicked in. He tightened his grip on her bicep and tugged her along at a faster pace. The cold, thin air made it impossible to breathe. If they were in the North Georgia Mountains, the wilderness areas alone spanned an area of nearly half a million acres. Perfect for killing and waiting for the wildlife, including feral hogs, to clean up most of the evidence.

Burke and Doherty hustled them along. Her lungs and heart strained to keep up while her mind raced to find a way to save Ethan and herself. They had to fight back somehow. Despite being restrained and blind to their surroundings, they needed to try – except once Lydia mentioned the past, Ethan quickly lost his composure and calming him down worked as well as calming herself after the hood went on.

The lengthy hike became its own form of torture at the higher altitude. The thinner air and colder temperatures made her think Rabun Bald or Brasstown Bald, the highest peaks in the state. For a girl who grew up at an elevation of one hundred thirty-six feet above sea level, a nearly five thousand foot increase in elevation made a considerable and more agonizing difference, especially for someone with a compromised heart.

The uneven terrain caused both she and Ethan to stumble often and sometimes fall. They helped each other to their feet since neither Doherty nor Burke offered. Throughout their march, her mind searched for solutions and inevitably came up empty. When they were told to stop, panic surged to the forefront, shoving logic out the window and settling for flat-out fighting, for all the good it might do.

She and Ethan pushed their captors, charging them, kicking them when they could. Both paid the price for trying to save themselves and each other, she with a battering ram to her gut that expelled a cry that died in the dense woods and Ethan released his own yelp of pain for his efforts.

A gun to her head guided her where Burke wanted her. By the end of the trek, she and Ethan met shoulder to shoulder, both kneeling on the damp ground and shivering from cold and dread of what came next.

Savannah tried to reason with the two ex-cops, "There's no need to kill us. Just walk away. You can still get your money from Lydia and leave town."

"Stay still," Doherty told her.

A hand clamped around her ankle. Surprisingly he unlocked the ankle cuffs and did the same with Ethan. In a moment of folly, she wondered if Doherty had a change of heart, then quickly dismissed it when he told her, "We're supposed to leave you here anyway, Prince, but here's a going away present for you."

She closed her eyes and tensed for a gunshot. Something thunked beside her on the ground. Doherty chuckled, "You'll be needing it. You both will because it's gonna get a lot colder out here tonight."

Footsteps padded away on damp pine straw and leaves. "One more thing," Doherty called out before leaving. "Watch out for bears and hunters."

O O O

Ennis thumbed tears from his eyes. Her terrified screams. Her hysterical pleading. All alone against two men doing... Oh God, what he imagined them doing. Those kind of screams were reserved for the vilest, most devastating acts a woman could suffer and Ennis's mind went straight to it. He recognized Doherty's and Burke's voices on the 911 call but couldn't discern exactly what was happening because her screams (*those horrible, haunting screams*) drowned out everything the two assholes said. He only knew Doherty and Burke were dead men once he got hold of them.

He shoved his hands through his hair and closed his fingers. No matter what he did, nothing dulled the sounds of those screams and images of what she'd gone through – and probably still suffered. Doherty and Burke committed that reprehensible act and what? This shitty neighborhood just sat back and watched? Unconscionable. The neighborhood had no soul left with gangs taking over and the whores and drunks hanging out where they could but ignoring a woman's cries for help?

He forced himself to listen to the recording again then nearly retched when he heard the last two gunshots. No, he kept assuring himself. She was still alive and screaming after the gunshots. Then he wondered if that was a good thing or not if they'd carted her away only to continue violating her before killing her.

"I'm sorry, Ennis," Josh said softly. "I know what you're thinking and that's why I didn't want you to hear it."

"When I find them, and I *will* find them, I'm gonna make 'em suffer before I end them. I'll find whatever it takes to cause them as much pain as they've inflicted on her." He glared at Hunter, "And no one's stopping me."

Josh did not argue, "I imagine there will be a line of people waiting their turn, including me. I might as well tell you. Forensics ran both the blood on the hood and in the street against Savannah's records. It's a match."

Ennis's legs lost their strength. His butt crashed onto his Ram's back bumper, rocking the vehicle. He braced his hands on his knees.

"On a slightly more positive note, Lee Morgan is offering an enormous reward for hers and Ethan's safe return. He also offered us any assistance he can so we had him fax over Doherty's and Burke's information. Mathis is busy reviewing it."

Yeah. That was a real bright spot in his night. Lee Morgan trying to help. "Add Hoffman to that list."

Josh's brow sank, "Hoffman? Why?"

Ennis gave him a brief rundown of all that had happened, including Franklin's recorded conversations between Lee and Hoffman.

"That SD card had tons of information on it. Hoffman was the one who threatened Georgia but we still don't know who shot R.J. and Savannah. Franklin got plenty of dirt to bury Hoffman, and probably Lee, but we never got a chance. Hoffman took the SD card before we could see it all." He said it with such venom, Josh's jaw tightened. Yes, Ennis was pissed off. They had evidence and at the time Hunter made it clear. Investigating Hoffman was off-limits. Ennis didn't give a diddly shit how angry his boss was, Josh shouldered plenty of blame for that night's fiasco. And while he had Hunter's attention, "Who's to say he's not behind Savannah's disappearance? He already agreed to steal Charlene's journals on the pretext no one gets hurt but do you really believe he cares if anyone does – or even dies in the process of retrieving them?" His expression dared Hunter to defend him again.

"I get it, Ennis. You blame me but *you* try launching an investigation against a superior officer, especially one with the connections Hoffman has, and see how far you get. I didn't sit on my ass, you know. I poked around Hoffman's activities too. Know what I got? A stern warning from the deputy chief to let him handle it. You see what happened? Nothing. I didn't leave you, Savannah, or Mathis hanging. I don't do that to my friends. Let me call Lee Morgan and get Hoffman's records from him." He'd already reached for his phone.

Ennis straightened, "Can you track Doherty's or Burke's phones?"

"Tried and failed. They turned them off." Josh greeted Lee Morgan as he answered the call.

Ennis took that time to look around. Twenty or thirty people gathered behind the crime scene tape. Most belonged to the Black Disciples, a gang ran by a ruthless twenty-something bastard named Acquon Scott. Ennis saw no whores or drunks but never expected to. They knew to retreat when Acquon's bunch assembled. Since Ennis arrived, the group constantly tossed derogatory taunts that lately became the norm for law enforcement. That, flipping them the bird, and anything else they could get by with. He expected no better treatment and certainly no help but he had to try. Sometimes one person hung at the back of a crowd like a shy kid choosing to sit in the back row in class.

With Josh busy talking with Lee, he pushed to his feet and started toward the hostile gathering. He recognized Davontae Brown, Acquon's right hand man, standing front and center. Ennis looked past him in search of a particular expression of interest, a subtle nod, any silent sign meant to get a cop's attention. As he approached the rowdy crowd, one of the more vocal gang members spit. Davontae's contribution splattered inches from Ennis's shoes. Another derogatory remark spurred more hate from the majority of onlookers.

"Anyone see what happened here tonight?" Ennis asked.

Emboldened by his audience, Davontae taunted, "I heard one of y'all, how y'all say it? DRT."

Ennis kept his cool amid the rousing cheers. DRT. Dead Right There. A deep breath later, he continued, "Brown, if you don't have information, get outta here. Anyone else? If you heard anything, saw anything, recorded anything–"

Uproarious laughter cut his comment short. "If we recorded anything, we'd post it on YouTube," said another who sported the same dreads and gang tattoos across his chest. "We ain't helpin' you wit nuttin' 'cept outta dis neighbahood. You trespassin'."

Most of the big mouths held cell phones in their hands aimed right at him as they taunted. He knew he'd end up on YouTube anyway, no matter what happened.

One pointed to Savannah's Charger, "Not unless that car's thrown in as a *ree*ward. That and about a billion dollars!"

More raucous laughter, nods and fist bumps. Ennis fought the urge to fist his hand and ram it down the bastard's throat until his knuckles hit Brown's toenails. He kept his cool because of the cell phones pointed at him like weapons but he waited for the laughter to die down before continuing, "Laugh all you want but there *is* a substantial reward for the detective's safe return."

Oinking noises arose from the back of the crowd then *Sooey! Soo-soo-sooey!*

Davontae found it knee-slapping funny, "Little piggy, come out, come out wherever you are!"

"Ennis," Hunter waved him closer. "What the hell were you thinking asking them for help?"

That perhaps one of them loved money more than they hated cops. "I'm desperate, Josh. I want her back."

The gathered mob hurled more insults and taunts as Ennis walked away. He shook his head at how parts of society treated cops these days. He halfway feared one of them might pull a gun and shoot just to have something to post on the internet.

"Hey, pig! *Is* that car part of that *substantial reward* you talkin' 'bout?"

He stopped and turned to face Davontae's lackey, "Don't be stupid."

Hunter gave his detective a parental frown, "Stop taking the bait, Ennis. Welch just told me we have a witness to her kidnapping and he wants to talk to you."

A witness out of this rabble after what he just saw? Sure. And the moon was made of green cheese. "Oh, fine. Which one of those yahoos is gonna string me along now?"

"I'm pretty sure it's not a *yahoo*. Go. He's standing in the doorway of that boarded-up strip club by your truck. He doesn't want to be seen and will *only* speak to you. Welch already searched him for weapons."

Hope tried renewing in his heart but his brain warned against getting too excited, especially after the last few minutes. In these neighborhoods "information" rarely panned out when it involved cops. It was just another way to waste law enforcement resources and make fools out of them.

Still he couldn't help but pray this time was different. He approached the dark doorway with caution. A shadowy figure pressed against the brick wall, out of sight. Their helpful citizen reeked of whiskey. Ennis's heart sank. *And my wife's life depends on him.* He purged a sigh, "I'm Detective Rutherford. You have information?"

"Yeah, but crouch down, man. I'm using the truck as cover so those animals don't get curious."

Ennis partially crouched behind his truck. The man peeked out momentarily and Ennis got the feeling he sized him up. Meanwhile, Ennis reciprocated. The man appeared to be in his late fifties but his bloodshot blue eyes, haggard face and long, unkempt beard gave him an older appearance. The man scratched his beard with a shaky hand. That's when Ennis noticed an old crutch propped beneath his left arm. The guy settled his weight against it but slumped as far down as possible to stay out of Davontae's line of sight.

Though he seemed lucid enough, Ennis doubted his credibility since, at some point, he'd basically soaked in a barrel of Southern Comfort. "What's your name? What did you see?"

"Allen Lamar. How much is the reward?"

He felt positive Lee offered a small fortune. "Enough to keep you in booze for years." He regretted it as soon as it left his lips – but not as much as Allen Lamar resented it.

"Hey man, don't judge me. I'm a vet who fell on hard times and I got my own way of dealing with it. You don't want my help, fine."

If he could've felt shittier, he wasn't sure how. Lamar started out of the doorway but Ennis blocked him, "I apologize. It's been a bad night because I know the detective involved."

"She your partner?"

Ennis would've considered the *she* validation the guy saw something but with all the cops milling around, the guy could've overheard the missing detective's gender. "Yes, she is."

Lamar leaned slightly forward so Ennis barely saw his face, "I'm guessing by your behavior, she's more than that." He zeroed in on Ennis's wedding ring. "She's your wife, isn't she?"

For the guy to make that leap he was either clairvoyant or Ennis somehow telegraphed it to the world. He let a little more hope into his heart, "Yessir, she is."

"Sorry this is happening to you, man. It's gotta be rough. I don't know how long they'd been here because I was a block away when I heard the gunshot..."

Ennis listened to the man recount exactly what the 911 call entailed. He took a few notes, trying hard to see his writing in virtual darkness and halfway stooped over.

"...when I rounded that corner I saw two men forcing her over the Dodge's hood. Her hands were tied behind her so she couldn't even fight back." He winced, "She was screaming something awful so I thought... well, you know what I thought they were planning to do. When a woman screams like that..."

Ennis closed his eyes, telling himself he could do this. He could listen to Lamar's account without losing his mind and obsessing over worst case scenarios. When he opened them again, his pen was bearing down so hard on the notepad it tore the page.

"Sorry," Lamar apologized. "It just got to me is all. When I called out for them to let her go she started screamed something – in retrospect I believe she tried to tell me she was a police officer – but then he punched her in the back. They put a hood over her head then shoved her into a Land Cruiser."

"You didn't see them, you know..." the word stuck in his throat and swelled until he felt sick.

Lamar said it for him, "No, man, they didn't rape her when I saw

them. They tied her up, put the hood on, threw her in the car and left."
He waited for Ennis to release his pent-up breath before continuing, "I
got the license number of that Land Cruiser if you want it."

Ennis couldn't believe his luck. A witness. A real witness. Not
only had Lamar reassured him Savannah hadn't been sexually assaulted
(at least at that point), he had the presence of mind to memorize the
Land Cruiser's license plate number. If nothing else it proved Lamar
wasn't as drunk as Ennis originally thought.

"I tried to help your wife but with my bum leg, I can only move
so fast. I got good eyes and a shitty leg. When those guys saw me
coming they shot over my head to scare me off but I kept on truckin'
toward 'em. I heard one of 'em ask *what do we do now* and the other
one said *ask Hoffman.*"

A bum leg but good eyes and ears too. "You're sure that's the
name he mentioned?"

He held up his right hand, "I'd swear to it in court. I was close
enough to hear it. Why? Does that name ring any bells with you?"

"It sure does. Come with me. I want you to tell my captain what
you told me."

"Hold on, buddy. It may not be much but this is where I live.
I'll have a target on my back twenty-four seven if those guys," he
motioned to the mob out front, "see me helping you."

For the first time in over two hours, Ennis smiled with hope,
"Mr. Lamar, after what you just told me, I doubt you'll ever spend
another night in this neighborhood. If we can get my wife and her friend
back alive and well, you'll be rolling in dough."

36

After a few acrobatics to help each other up, Savannah and Ethan focused on removing the zip cuffs. Ethan thankfully carried a pocket knife with his credit cards and cash. The trick (and it was a trick) was Savannah fishing for the knife while they stood nearly back to back. Once they freed themselves of the cuffs, they removed the hoods. The more spacious surroundings began calming Savannah down but the clumps of towering trees around them ramped Ethan's panic into high gear.

Surrounding them were towering loblolly pines and thick gray-barked white pines with long, sharp, painful looking needles. Ethan hurriedly circled the immediate area, searching for a trail leading out. "There's nothing. *Nothing.* How did they get out of here? Where did they go? I can't even find their footsteps because it's so dark."

The steadily rising pitch of his voice and lightning fast speech forewarned her of a long, complicated night with her companion. She needed to calm him down somehow, "That's why we need to stay here right now. We can't see where we're going." With scarce light and unpredictable terrain, one wrong step they'd buy the farm. Just what Lydia wanted.

She glanced down to see what Doherty left behind. A bottle of Jack Daniel's. The symbolic dig at her drinking problem infuriated her until she redirected her attention to Ethan who kept chattering, sometimes nonsensically. For a moment she contemplated offering Ethan a slug to settle his nerves but doing so would lower his core body temperature and neither of them needed that along with everything else.

She wrapped her arms around her for warmth. Even with a blazer the cold humidity slipped deep past her bones straight to the marrow. A November night in the forest was not only damn cold (at least that night) but the most dangerous time of day. If they moved at all, she cautioned, they needed to be careful.

Ethan stared at the trees as if they were loaded cannons aimed straight at him then rushed toward her, eyes wide and his speech shifting into Warp 9, "We gotta get outta here. Let's start walking and see where it leads. Come on." He grabbed her hand and tried tugging her along but she held her ground.

"Ethan, I know you're scared but listen. Nighttime isn't safe to go hiking for a trail. We need to find the way leading downhill but we don't want to find it the hard way. When we do search, keep listening for running water. If we find a stream, we'll follow it but from a distance." She decided not to explain why. He already freaked out so telling him that some wild animals hung around the water at night wouldn't exactly settle his nerves. "We need shelter but it's not safe to traipse off and find it right now." By his reaction, she'd sentenced him to death. His breathing digressed into a tempo destined for hyperventilation. He teetered close to losing his composure entirely. He needed a task to divert his attention so, "For now, help me find the moon."

"The moon?" He might as well have called her insane. "I'm going nuts and all you care about is the *moon?*"

"Moonlight is reflected sunlight so the bright side of the moon faces the sun and the dark side faces away. It'll give us a general direction from east to west." *Thank you, Seth, my dear mountain-hiking obsessed brother.* Funny what a person gleaned when that person's brother received a new compass on Christmas Day.

She breathed a sigh relief. Finally. Ethan stopped a moment to think. His stride slowed as he walked around the small clearing, staring up through the canopy of towering loblolly pines in search of their elusive, celestial ally. It surprised her when he jabbed a finger upward as if accusing it of intentionally hiding, "There it is."

Savannah stepped closer. A crescent moon, barely visible through the abundant pines, gave her another small surge of hope. Seth taught her and Georgia survival tips that he'd learned either in the army or when he was in the mountains for a weekend getaway with his buddies. She'd filed most of his information in File 13. She'd never need them, she'd said, so what was the point? Now she thanked her brother for those "useless" tips. He told them if they ever got lost to remember the survival mnemonic "STOP". Number one was *Stop*, he said, and stay where you are and don't panic. Two, *Think.* What do you know about your situation and location? Don't move until you have specific reason to. Three, *Observe.* Gather information to figure out where you are. Use a map or compass or use the sun, moon or stars to navigate. Last, *Plan.* Consider possible courses of action and choose one. If you're injured or night is falling, it might be best to stay where you are.

Savannah lined up the moon's two horns then extended the line to where the horizon should be. Now they had an approximation of due north but should they continue since it was nighttime? She rubbed her arms for warmth, debating what to do. It would only get colder and they had no shelter. "Do you see anything we could use for a makeshift shelter?" she asked.

He wheeled to her, "I'm not staying out here. Forget it."

She explained her thoughts but he bowed up with fear and anger, "I can't stay out here! I'll be crazy by morning, don't you understand? Do you know what that feels like?"

"You can stop yelling now." Savannah bit her tongue to avoid snapping at him but reminded, "Yes, I understand what going crazy feels like. I wore that stifling hood for hours being driven from Atlanta to wherever the hell this is. I still think we should shelter in place for the–"

A gun fired. The shot struck the tree nearest them. Ethan seized her wrist, "Bet that changed your mind," then launched into a sprint so fast it left her stumbling to maintain her footing.

She shouted at the hunter firing at them, "Stop shooting! We're lost and need help!"

Another shot rang out. Small chunks of bark exploded from a tree close to Ethan's head. The near miss spurred him into a faster, more frantic pace while tightening his hold on her hand.

"I don't think he cares," Ethan told her. "Hurry."

Yeah. Right. *Hurry* he barked at the heart patient racing for her life at an altitude only experienced by space shuttles, satellites and alien spacecraft. Her lungs strained for air, her heart galloped wildly as she fought to stay upright. Considering his frame of mind, if she tripped and fell, he'd end up dragging her through the forest. "Ethan, watch your step," she warned when her ankle nearly turned on the ground's uneven terrain.

He answered by squeezing her wrist so tight her hand went numb while he continued towing her along. He zigzagged between pine branches that slammed back into her, piercing her with needles from shoulders to knees while she barely succeeded in shielding her face. Between dodging bullets and those damn hurtful trees, *plus* keeping up with his aimless mad dash and fighting the altitude, she quickly grew so winded she struggled to speak.

Savannah stumbled at the same time a third shot rang out. In her condition, she wasn't sure if she'd been hit or not. *Watch out for bears and hunters*, Doherty said. He neglected to mention she and Ethan were the prey.

Ethan wound them deeper into the dense maze of trees. Her chest suddenly tightened as if an anvil landed on it. The world around her tilted askew. "Can't breathe," she strained for air so he'd hear her.

"Breathe later, sis. I see something up ahead. Let's go."

As if she had a choice. They bobbed and weaved several more yards through the forest when the ground dropped from under them, sending them into freefall several feet into a black void. Her feet met solid rock, slid sideways and turned the right knee until a twinge shot up her thigh and down her calf. Beside her, Ethan cursed about his ankle.

Savannah shushed him then realized the stupidity of it. If nothing else, their heavy breathing would alert their pursuer to their presence. She listened for movement above them but the world fell eerily quiet. The pause gave her a chance to try and regain her composure. After several minutes and no one closed in to finish the job, she wondered why they waited. She and Ethan were sitting ducks for Lydia's flunkies – and Savannah bet ol' Preston's wife sprung for night vision equipment for them too. There was no reason to delay the inevitable unless the hunters chose to run them to death.

Ethan wigged out for a whole different reason as he stared at her greedily gasping for air. "You really *can't* breathe. You're not having a heart attack, are you?"

Why did he sound so surprised? He dragged her through the woods at the speed of light then wondered if she was going down for the count? She shook her head, "Don't think so. Thin air," she said between breaths, "and exertion."

"Is there anything you can do to calm down?"

Well, since he asked, "Stop running for my life would be nice."

o o o

After a point, they dared to forge ahead. She fully expected to be dropped faster than a deer on opening day of hunting season but not a shot was fired during their journey – they were, however, being watched and followed. Savannah had no proof except an uneasy feeling and a nettling at the back of her neck.

The two came across a small log cabin tucked in a clearing. Darkness prevented her from reading her watch but her body told the tale. They'd been walking miles (if she listened to her knees and aching leg), traversing uneven terrain of hills and valleys. They'd wound their way around and through stands of prickly white pines that left her itching from needle pricks. By the time they found the cabin, they were both chilled, shivering and exhausted. No one answered their knock so Ethan shouldered the door open.

Though unoccupied, the place showed signs of recent use. When they approached the cabin, she envisioned them tangling in cobwebs, righting toppled old (probably broken) chairs and tables, and using newspapers dating back thirty years for kindling – if bird nests weren't clogging the chimney. Switching on a lantern inside the door revealed a clean, one room interior with minimal dust, rustic furniture crafted from logs including a bed, table and chairs that required no righting and the only newspaper she found dated only two weeks earlier. The North Georgia News. A small banner above the two page paper's name touted "Land of Lakes, Mountains, Scenic Beauty and Friendly People". Beneath, in bold red ink, proclaimed it the "Hometown Newspaper of Blairsville, Suches and Union County". So maybe they were near Brasstown Bald after all, she thought. The question was exactly how far away from civilization were they?

The aged cabin tucked into the pines was someone's private getaway, she assumed, and considering the kitchen cabinets contained basic food staples and bottles of liquor and water, she wondered if they meant to return soon. Further rummaging produced a welcome and needed item – a half-stocked first aid kit. Once she built a fire for them, she'd tend to Ethan's ankle and the cut along her forearm.

Luckily the former occupant left plenty of cut wood in a rack outside the back door. She collected that and some kindling. It wasn't until she stepped back inside that Ethan presented her with the biggest gift of all. A bolt action rifle. She smiled with relief. Maybe this little gem helped even the playing field for them – if it worked. Either way, it gave her hope. "It pays to leave you alone for two minutes, doesn't it?"

"I won't use it, though. Golf was always my thing. Dad, Grady and Press are the hunters. I don't like guns anyway and I'll end up shooting myself – or you – in the foot so the rifle is your responsibility. Plus, it's kinda dusty. I'm not sure it'll fire."

Unlike the furniture, a thin skim of dust coated the old Remington. She wiped it down and brought it over to the lantern to examine it closer. Savannah opened the plate for the magazine but found no ammunition. She worked the action to remove any chambered rounds. There were none. When she pulled the trigger, it made a metal snapping click. Her heart sank. She sighed, "Oh well, it was a nice thought."

"Won't work?"

"No. The firing pin is broken and somehow I doubt in this hunter's paradise we'll find a spare one or else he'd have already fixed it." She looked it over. It may not fire but it could still be used as a weapon. She laid it on the dining table. "Let's get warm, eat then rest," she said. "Tomorrow's going to be a long day."

Ethan opened a cupboard. He wrinkled his nose, "Ugh. Sardines?" He scrounged deeper, "Granola bars, peanut butter, crackers, nuts. Not bad."

They ate a modest snack and took advantage of the bottled water. A yawn crept up on her. She hadn't realized how tired she was until having food in her stomach and a warm fire to snuggle close to.

Ethan offered her the bed for the night while he sat watch but she declined. After shaking out the blankets, they split them up, one for her, one for him, then Ethan climbed in bed. Savannah opted for the chair with the blanket draped over her and the rifle across her lap.

Sometime in the night a noise outside brought her to her feet, rifle in hand. She fingered the curtain aside but saw no one – however someone left a calling card on the porch. The bottle of Jack that Doherty left behind. It didn't surprise her that Lydia's gunmen found them, not with the smoke signals their cozy fire sent up. It surprised her that they hadn't already stormed the cabin.

Around sunrise a different noise snapped her to full awareness. The fire burned down to glowing embers in the fireplace but the radiating heat had lulled her halfway to sleep. The sound of boots stepping onto the porch supplanted drowsiness and tired, aching muscles. She took the rifle in hand, laid the blanket aside and got to her feet about the time Ethan roused from a sound sleep. "What's going on?" he asked.

She shushed him, pointed to the door that began opening. Whoever invaded their temporary residence was about to receive an unexpectedly rude welcome. She stood behind the door slowly creaking open. The moment the intruder came into view, they lifted their rifle straight toward the bed. Eyes wide centered on the gun aimed at him, Ethan scrambled out of bed at the same time Savannah swung the rifle butt into the trespasser's knee.

He collapsed on the floor, releasing the rifle in favor of holding his injured knee. Ethan snatched the rifle from beside the guy and aimed at him. For someone who claimed to dislike using guns, he sure looked ready to shoot their bold, unsolicited guest. Savannah guessed having a weapon aimed at him temporarily changed his mind about the benefits of holding one.

Savannah questioned Lydia's henchman while searching him. He remained silent but her efforts produced a holstered 9mm automatic, extra ammo and zip cuffs but no phone or identification. She stripped him of his shoes and socks. The last two she employed from an earlier incident in the spring when her family visited Ennis's family in Texas. A gang of escaped convicts held the whole family hostage during a blizzard. Thanks to her brother-in-law Joe Bob, a career ranch hand, she'd learned the art of hogtying so she utilized the intruder's supply of zip cuffs to subdue him so tight he couldn't twitch. Joe Bob would be proud.

Savannah grasped the ski mask, "Now let's see who this mute bastard is." When the mask came off, she halted, shocked at the face staring back. She halfway expected Doherty or Burke but not, "Tierce?"

Her new detective looked away. She grabbed his jaw and forced his vision to hers, "How much is she paying you? How much to gun down two innocent people?"

"Someone else shot at you, Sergeant. I didn't. I just put the booze on the porch."

Ethan stalked closer, the rifle still seated against his shoulder, "So what were you gonna do if Savannah hadn't stopped you? Serve us tea and crumpets?" He looked to her, "Who is this guy?"

"One of my detectives." Tierce. The cowardly twerp wasn't even listed on Lee's security payroll and here he was, gun in hand, paid to kill a fellow cop and an innocent citizen. The idea was out-of-this-word surreal but so were the last several weeks. Her life turned into a parallel universe where right was wrong and wrong was right. Police killing witnesses and those same cops then turning their weapons on other cops. Between Lydia and Hoffman, she and Ethan barely stood a chance of surviving, a lot like the day she and her daddy were shot. Oh yeah. Those two made quite a team. Lydia put a hit on Lee's heirs while Hoffman bumped off Caleb Franklin and had his toadies intimidate Savannah. Lydia had the money, Hoffman had the badge and employees to make it happen, all while he lorded his power over Savannah, threatened Georgia, altered timesheets… Wait. Time sheets. Vacation. *Tierce's vacation.* It wasn't a vacation at all. It was a cover story.

Logic parted her anger like the Red Sea. Hoffman's private meetings with Tierce. Altering the time sheets so it showed Tierce was at work the day she and R.J. were shot. Tierce had avoided eye contact with her since the shooting. He left the room or immediate area when R.J. was mentioned and always had a lame reason to excuse himself. She lacked solid proof Tierce shot them but there were enough coincidences that were *not* coincidences, at least according to her gut. "It was you that day in Augusta. You shot my daddy. You tried to kill him."

Again he averted his gaze, "No. It wasn't me. I was at the station. The timesheets say so."

"Because Hoffman changed them. You wanted that day off, I approved it. Hunter noticed the timesheets had been changed and brought it to Hoffman's attention. Only three people could authorize that. Me, Hunter and Hoffman. I didn't do it, I know Hunter didn't because he found the change. That leaves Hoffman." Rage and adrenaline flooded her until she trembled with unspent rage. "My daddy nearly died, you sorry bastard!"

"How do you know it was him?" Ethan asked.

She refused to go into details of Hoffman's penchant for altering timesheets and other reasons she believed Tierce pulled the trigger that day. Ethan would dismiss it as coincidence and to her, Tierce's reaction served as an admission of guilt. "I'm not telling you. He will." She fisted her hand in Tierce's jacket, "Confession's good for the soul – and your life expectancy– so get with it, asshole."

He frantically shook his head, "I didn't do it."

She grabbed the 9mm and pressed the muzzle against Tierce's thigh, "How about I show you what my daddy went through? How it feels to bleed out from an artery, except no one will help *you* stanch the bleeding."

Both men launched into a heated protest, Tierce begging for his life and Ethan aghast that she'd threatened such a violent act. Savannah hoped Tierce believed she *would* pull the trigger because Ethan realized how serious she was. He turned white watching the scene unfold. She advised, "Turn away, Ethan. You don't need to see this."

He swallowed hard, "Savannah, think this through–"

"*Turn away*," she ordered but he seemed rooted to the spot, mortified at her actions. She addressed Tierce who begged her not to shoot, "C'mon, you were so hellbent on killing Daddy that you accidentally shot me – at least I think it was an accident – and you destroyed parts of my childhood home. Let's see how you handle a taste of your own medicine."

Tierce's face shined with sweat as he watched her finger tighten on the trigger, "No, God, no! Please stop!"

"Savannah–" Ethan sounded sick.

"Ethan, shut up and look away." She pressed down until Tierce flinched, "This pain's nothing compared to bleeding out. Take it from me. I know and because of you so does my daddy. Who sent you to kill him? Mathis copied that SD card Franklin sent. John's going through it file by file. My answer's on it but I want to hear it from you." She had no clue if the SD card contained that information. The important thing was, as far as she knew, neither did Tierce.

"Hoffman destroyed the card. You can't possibly–"

"Mathis copied it before handing it over, Tierce." Her bluff appeared to be working. Maybe. "Save yourself a painful death. Tell me who sent you to kill Daddy."

When he hesitated, she jammed the gun deeper into the muscle, "Now!"

His face contorted as he whimpered, "It was Hoffman."

"Who ordered Hoffman to kill him and intimidate my sister?"

Tierce kept staring at her trigger finger, "Lee Morgan wanted Prince to pay for abusing you. He never wanted him shot or dead. Hoffman's the one. He assigned me to kill him. Hoffman resented Lee offering you the CSO position so he figured if Prince ended up dead, you'd blame Lee."

"And Georgia? Did Hoffman want her dead too?"

"No. He listened to Lee about her. Lee only wanted Mike to scare your sister, that's all. To silence her accusations so she wouldn't go public with them. Whatever happened to her is on Hoffman. He did it."

"If killing my daddy was so important, why didn't Hoffman do it? Why trust you with it? Who the hell are you to him, anyway?"

Tierce finally made eye contact, "I – I'm his nephew."

37

At daybreak, they stepped outside into an icy, damp blanket that wrapped around them and caused a constant shiver to vibrate through her. She gathered her blazer tighter around her, estimating the temperature about twenty degrees colder than Atlanta's cool but moderate morning temperatures. These foreign, glacial conditions felt just this side of Antarctica.

Faint morning sun filtered through the mixed pine and deciduous tree canopy but a thick, low-hanging fog obscured the view afar, providing perfect cover for Lydia's snipers.

Once Savannah and Ethan ventured outside, she wanted to move along and fast. It was harder to hit a moving target. Now they'd test that theory in the forest – if he managed to stay calm. He showed promise and good judgment when he grabbed a handful of granola bars and stuffed them in his pockets, gathered the first aid kit then handed her Tierce's rifle. Maybe there was hope for him after all.

She picked up Tierce's 9mm and extra ammo and left Hoffman's nephew tied up with the assurance they'd send help – if they didn't die first. Before they walked out Ethan asked Tierce how many gunmen Lydia hired. Tierce replied two, himself and one other. Ethan was relieved. Savannah knew he lied.

Besides surviving, her plan was to listen for streams and rivers along the way. That was the plan last night. This morning, however, Savannah realized how deluded she'd been to think Ethan could step outside and keep his wits. He nervously paced the porch, his breathing short and shallow and his rounded eyes stared at the trees as if they advanced on him like something out of Lord of the Rings. The hike down the mountain depended on her now, she supposed, while combating not only Ethan's fears and Lydia's lackeys but her own physical frailties. For that, she needed superhuman strength and truthfully after last night, she felt fresh out.

She urged him off the porch and felt him pull away. The beginnings of panic rooted deeper as he surveyed his surroundings. She clasped his hand. It was ice cold. "You can do this," she encouraged. "Focus on finding a stream. Listen for running water. And try to remember where your family went on vacation that year." If nothing else it gave him something to think about other than the trees. She tried getting their location from Tierce but he refused to tell her and worse, Ethan stopped her from going medieval on him, stating he feared she might drop of a heart attack. Well, staying lost in the mountains wasn't condusive to good heart health either, she told him, and neither was dying. "Close your eyes and concentrate," she continued. "Lydia said the story's been told for years. That was a Blairsville newspaper in the cabin so I'm guessing we're near or already partway up Brasstown Bald."

He shrugged, "I only remember Press never forgave me for ruining the trip and anytime the subject comes up at holidays I leave the room. So what do we do now?"

Beat Tierce into submission, she thought, because Ethan's wild eyes shouted he quickly lost his composure. She pushed her sleeves back and turned to the cabin door. Ethan blocked her, "No, sis. He won't tell you and if you have a heart attack, I don't know how to save you, not out here. Let's go. Listen for running water, right?"

"Yes, and watch for signs of people. Old campsites, litter, voices, church bells, any sign of civilization. And Ethan? Remember, you're not alone this time. I'm with you and somehow we'll find a way home."

o o o

Back at the station, Ennis waved off another offer of coffee. He didn't require caffeine to stay awake. Worry worked just fine. He checked his watch. Savannah needed her heart medication hours ago. All night he fought images of her lying dead in alleys, streets, ditches, abandoned buildings, anywhere a killer might dispose of a body. Every conceivable indignity and manner of death tormented him so no, he wasn't sleeping for a damn long time.

He, along with every law enforcement agency and officer, chased dead-end leads throughout the night. When Doherty and Burke abducted her, they seemed to disappear and each passing hour slowly sealed her fate – if, his brain hatefully reminded, she wasn't already dead. He constantly pushed away thoughts of funerals, memorials and raising the kids alone because thinking about it gave it credence and somehow made it real. Each passing hour it taunted and nagged, telling him it wasn't a possibility anymore. It was a probability.

Ennis's phone rang. He glanced at Caller ID, still hoping to see Savannah's name. It was forensic tech Billy Miller. "Any word on Sergeant Prince?"

"Nothing yet," he was sorry to say.

Billy's voice reflected his disappointment, "Well, it's not exactly a priority right now but I analyzed the video from the Tucker Morgan murder. I have a name."

Ennis waved Josh Hunter over, "Forensics put a name to Tucker's murderer. Who is it, Billy?"

"You might want to sit down for this. There was a split second when the camera caught a shot of his face. I've been up for hours watching this thing and finally found it. I'm sending you a photo."

Ennis waited. When the photo arrived, he clicked on it. He and Josh Hunter stared at the screen, speechless. For one insane moment, Ennis entertained throwing the phone against the wall. Of all the faces, he hadn't expected this one to pop up on his screen but there it was in living color. Billy Miller captured the most distinctive feature of their killer and thank God he had because no one past Toucan Sam possessed a schnoz that prominent. He ground the name between clenched teeth, "Lance Tierce. That son of a bitch."

Josh made a call, "Find Lance Tierce now. Arrest him for murder and bring him to our station." He clicked off, telling Ennis, "This place is going to get crowded soon. They picked up Captain Erickson fifteen minutes ago. He's on Morgan's employee list and he did make the call luring her to the location." He watched Ennis bow up and continued, "And no, you're not getting your hands on him. Try to leave *someone* for the district attorney to prosecute, okay?"

Ennis's phone rang again. He answered without looking at Caller ID. It was Detective Christine Clark. "Ennis, we got Hoffman. He broke in and went straight for the journals. We're bringing him to your station. I've already called Mathis and told him. He wanted me to tell you he's connected Hoffman to the Riggs murder too. Something about an SD card."

Finally some good news. Savannah asked Christine and a uniform officer to stay at the house the evening Georgia received her award. She and Ennis figured Hoffman might use the occasion to steal Charlene's journals. When they questioned him they could begin delving into his other extracurricular activities for Morgan, especially the ones missing on the SD card.

Ennis cracked his knuckles. Mike Hoffman would talk. He would make damn sure of it and once he was finished with the major, the DA could put what was left of the bastard behind bars.

o   o   o

Ennis wanted Christine Clark back at Zone 2. He'd beg, wheedle or outright demand she return to their fold because she'd proven to be not only a good detective but a trusted friend, unlike her replacement Lance Tierce.

At Ennis and John's behest, Hunter reluctantly allowed Mathis in the same room with Hoffman. They needed someone who knew Savannah in there, they said, someone who would fight to get answers,

not a cop who knew her only by name. Josh soon realized his mistake
when forced to physically wrestle Mathis from the interview room for
trying to dislocate Hoffman's jaw. During his scathing dressing down, he
told Mathis, "I didn't expect 'fight to get answers' to actually involve
fists."

Hunter then called Christine up to bat. While Mathis tried to go
Muhammad Ali on Hoffman, she'd boned up on the case with Ennis's
help. When she stepped in the interview room, it didn't take long for her
to draw blood a different way. She mentioned incriminating text
messages on Hoffman's cell phone, these from Lydia the night before
telling him she waited on Doherty, Burke and the others to "dispose of
the problems". Hoffman refused to talk about Lydia and the texts but
Christine worked methodically through his phone's messages, reading
texts verbatim that revealed his affair with Lydia and their plans to make
Preston the sole heir to Lee Morgan's estate. Lydia's texts expressed the
arrogance of the ultra-rich who believe they were above the law and could
say whatever they pleased without repercussions. Hoffman's replies,
while more subdued and cryptic, would still be considered incriminating
to a fine district attorney. That and with what Mathis copied from the
SD card would hopefully seal the major's fate. And once Lee discovered
who conspired against him and his kids, Ennis doubted he'd spring for a
lawyer for his Chief Security Officer. In fact, he'd bet his next month's
pay Lee Morgan might cherry-pick the DA to bury Hoffman under the
prison, perhaps literally.

Christine asked forensics to trace Lydia's texts from the previous
evening. Two pinged off a cell towers close to the North Georgia

mountains within an hour of Savannah's abduction. Christine issued a BOLO on Lydia Morgan and her Jaguar.

Less than an hour passed when Lydia Morgan wore a pair of silver bracelets fashioned by Smith & Wesson and not Tiffany's as she was accustomed. Once back at the station, the only thing she confessed to was wanting a lawyer. After receiving a call from his lawyer about Lydia's arrest, Preston burst through the station doors at ten that morning shouting Lydia's innocence and threatening the "incompetents with badges" with unemployment.

Ennis marched down the hall determined to square the bastard away once and for all – except Christine, like his wife, seemed to possess a sixth sense and detoured him to the locker room to "cool his jets", she said. By the time Christine stopped blocking the door to let him leave, Preston was nowhere to be seen – or heard.

His mind raced. Where could Savannah and Ethan be? Why would Lydia go to the North Georgia Mountains? To escape? Paris or Milan were more her style, not roughing it or cabin living. Would she retreat there to hide *because* no one expected her to? Maybe. It was a perfect place to burrow up. The region, part of the Blue Ridge chain, spanned the whole north portion of the state. It was best known for the resort areas but there were probably hundreds of square miles dotted with small, isolated cabins for hunters and fishermen. A perfect place for Lydia to hide out, if she had a mind to. But Mrs. Preston Morgan turned her nose up at places without spas and room service. Ennis knew even as desperate as she was, unless a place offered luxury accommodations, she wouldn't step foot inside. So why would someone

with her money and influence head to the mountains, unless it was to
meet someone – say, someone hired to kill a couple of people standing in
her way of a fortune?

Ennis sprinted down the hall in search of Preston. He raced past
Josh's office then Savannah's where he pulled to an abrupt stop. Dressed
in Gucci, Armani or whatever the hell stupidly rich people wore these
days, Preston stood behind her desk studying a framed photo of Ennis,
Savannah and their three children. Morgan casually glanced up when he
heard Ennis step in, "Thought I'd check out my sister's office while I wait
to speak with your captain." The words *my sister* surfaced less venomous
than in past weeks. Not exactly warm and fuzzy either but not
acrimonious. "I guess I have to accept her in polite company, but I still
believe–"

"I don't care what you believe." Ennis had it up to his eyes with
the Morgans. They could go to hell once he got Savannah back – *if* he
got her back. "All I want is an exact location. Where did Ethan get lost
in the woods? Tell me where that was." If Savannah and Ethan were
anywhere near Rabun Bald or Brasstown Bald they spent the night in
humid, thirty-six degree weather – at an altitude that was sure to stress
her already vulnerable heart.

"Why?"

"If you care about your brother, you'll tell me."

Preston smirked. Ennis came thisclose to slapping that smirk
into the next county. He clenched his fist but held his temper – for now,
"Listen, Morgan, you may not like the fact Savannah might be your sister
but she's a police officer. If you delay her rescue and she dies, I'll make

sure you join your wife, Mike Hoffman and a bunch of others who are charged with murder."

Preston glanced down at the framed five by seven in his hand. The smirk disappeared yet he remained oddly silent.

Ennis stepped closer. His hand ached from clenching it so tight. "Do you hate her so much you'd sacrifice your brother to see her dead? To ensure she won't inherit? She doesn't want Lee's money and she sure as hell never wanted to be a Morgan."

Preston kept staring at her photo. What did he expect to find, Ennis wondered. A family resemblance? An ulterior motive behind her gorgeous smile? Or was his hate so pure and profound that he secretly hoped they found her dead? Every wasted second lent credence to that last theory so Ennis reached for his cell phone, "I'm calling Lee. I know he'll help."

"Most men want sons," Preston finally spoke. "My father had four and yet she was his obsession. For years I heard about Savannah, grew up in her shadow, heard about how R.J. Prince would pay for abusing her. My father could have ruined him financially. Only his feelings for Charlene and Savannah stopped him."

He didn't have time for a rich boy's pity party, "I couldn't care less about–"

"But you care about Savannah and you want that location so you'll listen. It was also Dad's feelings for her and Charlene that drove my mother to an early grave. When Charlene worked for him, he and Mother separated. She knew their history. Only when Charlene quit did my mother return but their marriage was never the same. It drove her crazy when he maintained Savannah was his daughter. Mother died soon after she, Georgia and Charlene visited. It was Christmas. I've hated Christmas ever since. I blame Dad, Charlene and Savannah despite the fact Savannah was a pawn in this ridiculous power play. Fact is she's the firstborn and Dad's determined to include her in everything now. She's always been in his will, she just never knew it but he's determined to include her in the family and the business and for me that's pretty hard to swallow, having to live in her shadow *and* work with her too. I can't stop him though. I tried talking to him and when that failed, I offered Savannah money – an enormous amount of money – to refuse Dad's wishes and she would not take it." He shook his head in amazement, "Who does that? I've never had that happen. People always want money but not her. She basically told me where to stick the check then stormed out of my office."

Poor little Preston, Ennis thought. The sniveling shit. Wallowing in self-pity *and* piles of money while his brother and Savannah fought to survive – if they weren't already dead. Interesting how he neglected to mention how he dredged Charlene's reputation through the mud while offering that "enormous amount of money" to Savannah. Ennis knew exactly how *he'd* react to a stranger attacking his mother's character and also realized Preston got off easy with Savannah telling him to shove it then simply walking out. "That should tell you what kind of person she is. Integrity means more than money to her. Now give me–"

"It won't matter what kind of person she is. Dad gets what he wants. He wants her. She is a Morgan, with or without a DNA test. He buried himself in work for years but I guarantee she wasn't far from his thoughts. Tucker's book renewed his obsession with her. He filed injunctions for several reasons, one being Tucker revealed his and Charlene's affair and the fact my brother basically called Savannah the bastard child. Dad loses it when anyone refers to her that way.

"Before that rotten book, we had a peaceful existence. It was nice. For the record, I regret my wife went to these lengths to ensure I inherited Dad's fortune. I've lost one brother, nearly lost another and now the other is missing. I hope he and Savannah are found alive and well because Ethan doesn't do well in forests, if that's where they are." He finally made eye contact, "Do you have a map of the Brasstown Bald area?"

O O O

A fair walk behind the cabin ran a small stream. The discovery temporarily dialed down Ethan's panic when she mentioned the probability of finding fishermen along the way. It was still morning, she said, and a good time to see them out. At least she hoped so. After such a cold night, it might be too cold for fish to be active but she refused to tell Ethan this. He was already hyped-up on adrenaline so she told him to look for people – those with fishing rods and good intentions and others with rifles and orders to kill two wandering Morgan heirs.

They traveled an hour downstream where the water picked up speed. During their journey she observed their surroundings. Eerie silence encompassed the area as if the canopy above shut out the world beyond. The soft, weak glow of morning sun revealed carpets of brilliant green fern in the few clearings they passed. They followed alongside the babbling pebble-lined stream, breathing in the smell of damp earth, musty wood and fragrant pine. A picture perfect experience for adventurous hikers wanting a vacation from the hustle and bustle of the city but a nightmare for two people trying to survive armed killers.

Lydia's men had time, incentive and weapons on their side. They also had plenty of allies to aid in their quest, ones that clawed and sank their teeth into flesh. She kept a cautious eye out for bears and bobcats but especially wild hogs. Some of the largest wild hogs in America roamed the North Georgia Mountains. People believed Hogzilla was a myth. It wasn't and she and Ethan had enough trouble surviving a gang of gunmen, much less being charged and gored by a giant piece of pork.

After another hour of walking, they opted to rest a few minutes. They found a small clearing and sat down behind a rocky embankment beside the stream. Facing the water and the area's openness eased Ethan's anxiety but his breathing, like hers, sounded short and erratic from stress and exertion. His hands trembled from a combination of cold and fear, she assumed, so she wrapped hers around his left one and held it, hoping to calm him down.

He offered an apologetic smile, "Bet you never expected to find yourself in this kind of mess. It's not always dangerous to be a Morgan, I promise."

"Once Lydia, Hoffman and some others are behind bars, it will definitely be safer for a lot of people." Drawing in thin mountain air made every effort feel like she breathed through a straw. She really wanted off that mountain and there were only two ways to do it. Hike down the big bastard or be carried off in a body bag.

"You're sure optimistic that we'll get out of here alive." Ethan's expression wanted to believe it but his voice fell far short.

With her free hand, she hugged her knees to her chest to conserve warmth and help the settle her own shivering. "Ennis and my boss have the whole department – probably all law enforcement in the state – looking for us. So I have hope, yes." She strained at the air again, looked away to her hide her distress. "You ready to go?"

Her pep talk inspired a lift in his spirits. He kissed her cheek, "I'm ready, sis."

The Morgan clan's bank accounts bulged at the seams but most of them were morally bankrupt. Except Ethan. If she was a Morgan (which she still doubted), he was her kind of brother. If not, he was her kind of friend.

He pushed to his feet and started helping her up. A shot rang out. Ethan jerked and twisted. His hand raced to his bicep. After a quick glance, he appeared incredulous, "I've been shot. I've never been–" A second shot fired. Ethan stood there, stunned.

Savannah heard the shot hit him. She grabbed his hand and pulled him to the ground as the gunman fired again. The shot buried in the ground behind them. "Where are you hurt?" she wanted to know. "Your arm and where else?"

Ethan rolled to his side to assess the wound. Blood slowly spread above his right hip. He verbally shrugged it off, "It can't be that bad. It doesn't hurt like I imagined it would."

She reached for the first aid kit. She'd heard it before. People had been known to go home to their normal routine without realizing they'd been shot. Ethan, though, would eventually feel the effects whether pain or blood loss. Right now adrenaline and fear fueled his mind and body.

She ducked flat on the ground when another shot fired and landed in the embankment. Wildness flared in his eyes and he began struggling again. His vision darted nowhere in particular and focused on nothing. His muscles tensed. He was going to bolt.

"Don't move, Ethan," she warned him. "It is *not* safe to move."

"No. Let's go now. We can make it." Ethan held a hand to the wound while struggling to stand but froze at the sight of the trees surrounding them on three sides.

His panic crested again, creating a difficult dilemma for her – how to keep him from getting killed while trying to track the shooter. Savannah wrestled him to keep him flat, "I said stop. You're making it worse."

He tried shoving her away. When that failed, his trembling grasp pried at hers until he finally begged her to let go, "I need out of here. If I'm dying, it'll be running for my life, not suffocating in this forest."

"Think, Ethan. You won't get two feet before he cuts you down and kills you."

He verged on tears, shouting, "I don't care! I don't want to die here, not in this hell around me!" He thrashed to free himself, forcing her to carefully position herself half on and half off of him to pin him. His eyes seemed to center only on the trees around them, not the openness the stream provided. Ethan clawed at the ground to pull himself from beneath her, "They're closing in, don't you understand? The trees, the *trees…*" He cried, "Let me go, Savannah. I need out of here now. Away from all these trees or I'll go crazy."

"Close your eyes. At least you won't see them." She tried keeping an ear tuned around them in case the gunman crept up to finish them off however Ethan's crying made it nearly impossible.

He closed his eyes, waited two seconds then squirmed beneath her, his breaths growing shorter and more ragged, "It's not working."

"Ethan," she tried to redirect his attention, "listen to me. Take a deep breath and slowly let it out." He did. She continued, "Concentrate on breathing. Remember that guy out there is waiting for us to panic so he can kill us. There are two of us and one of him. We have guns and ammo and can defend ourselves. We can get out of this alive but we both have to focus on that, not on *where* we are right now. You can do this."

"I can't! I can't!" One massive shove threw her back against the rocks.

She frantically scrabbled to catch him but he already pushed to his feet and sprinted into the forest that frightened him so. "Ethan, get down!" she yelled.

Another shot fired. In the time, the gunman repositioned so he had a clearer shot at her. Savannah grabbed Tierce's 9mm, aimed in the attacker's general direction and pulled the trigger. With the automatic in one hand and the rifle and first aid kit in the other, she sprang to her feet and sprinted into the grouping of loblolly pines, trying to catch up to

Ethan. She had to find him before he hurt himself, got lost or killed.

The gunman fired as she ducked behind a tree and kept running, watchful of tree roots and fallen limbs that might trip her. If the shot hit her, she never felt it. She turned and fired. Up ahead she heard swift footfalls on damp pine straw. Little by little she gained on Ethan to the point she saw his bright green polo in the thick, misty fog.

Her lungs gasped for air to no avail. The intense stress and heavy running took a toll, forcing her to stop and brace her back against a tree to catch her breath and combat her brain's swaying motion. *In through the nose, out through the mouth. I need more air or I'll faint. Fainting means dying. C'mon Savannah, in through the nose, out through the mouth...*

The gunman bounded through the woods toward her. Savannah chanced a quick peek around the tree. A shot zipped past her head. She returned fire, forcing him to retreat behind a tree for cover. Her heart pounded so hard and loud in her ears, she felt certain he heard it too.

The toe of the shooter's boot inched into view from behind the tree trunk. Savannah dropped the rifle and first aid kit. She used both hands to steady the 9mm as she aimed. The foot gradually inched further into view. She fired at his ankle. The gunman went down.

She hurried to him and kicked the gun from his grasp. Her aim may have wavered from the cold but it held steady enough he thought twice about fighting her when she searched him. Like Tierce, she collected a 9mm, a rifle then pocketed the extra ammo he carried. She grabbed the zip cuffs from his belt, warning, "You give me trouble and I'll perforate your liver."

He decided against a perforated liver but it didn't stop him from calling her a few X-rated names. Once Savannah cuffed his hands and feet, she removed his mask. She wasn't exactly surprised to see Burke staring daggers at her. He spat an embittered, "I wish I'd killed you earlier despite what Doherty said."

"Yeah, well, life can be disappointing like that. Have fun communing with nature, asshole." She headed back to retrieve the first aid kit and Tierce's rifle then hopefully she could track down Ethan. She prayed he was still alive.

Several minutes later Savannah found him lounging against a moss-covered, rocky embankment, his hand pressed to his wounded hip. He appeared calmer, at least enough to watch the burbling stream flow around and over rocks. Without looking away, he stated, "This is a nice spot."

Fatigue weighed down his voice. Before she could answer, he struggled to his feet. Blood seeped between his fingers and stained his slacks. He pointed downstream, "I bet we're getting close to civilization. The water's running faster."

Before he collapsed she told him to lie down but like every Morgan she'd ever met, he refused to listen. Even when he slightly wobbled off balance, he insisted, "Nope. We need to keep moving and judging by the sudden quiet around here I'm guessing we can?"

Savannah saw his knees loosen. She hurried to catch him, dropping the guns and the first aid kit to reach out for him. It felt like a boulder landed in her arms. For his physique, Ethan was solid and heavy. She eased him to the ground, removed her suit jacket, folded it and placed it behind his head, "I took care of the problem, yes, but you need to stay still. Please don't move, Ethan. Promise me."

"Why?" He grabbed her hand, held it hard, "You're not leaving, are you? Don't leave me, sis, please. If I'm dying, I don't want to die alone…"

He needed immediate medical attention but not applying constant pressure to the wound sentenced him to certain death. "I'm not leaving and you're not dying," she pulled the first aid kit closer, removed gauze and bandages and placed them on the wound. "I have to press hard on this to slow the bleeding and it's going to hurt. It's *really* gonna hurt. Try to brace for it." There was no way he could, she thought, not with the pressure she'd have to use.

She cringed when he cried out. It was the first time she heard Ethan curse like a sailor – but thankfully not at her. His cursing ended on a whimpering, "Holy shit, when you said hard, I didn't think you meant push my guts in the ground." His hands fisted beside him, probably to avoid grabbing her by the throat.

Sweat shined on his face. His cheeks grew pale. Warm blood saturated the bandages and coated her hand. She ripped open fresh packets of gauze with her teeth and replaced the soaked ones. There weren't enough bandages or gauze to stop the bleeding, only stanch it long enough for… Yes, for what exactly? She couldn't leave him. There were no signs of fishermen, hunters or anyone other than Lydia's armed idiots and none of them had phones. She could only pray someone good and decent found them before Ethan bled to death.

She apologized while replacing the wet bandages, "I'm sorry it hurts but I have to do it.”

"I know." He spoke in a strained, "You’re just one very strong lady." He waited a moment before asking, "Can I ask you a question?"

Still ripping open packets of gauze, she nodded.

"Do you know what Georgia accused Dad of doing?"

Savannah stopped mid-rip, shocked that he’d asked *that* question of all things. Of course she opened Pandora’s Box by asking Tierce who bullied Georgia in the first place, hadn’t she?

Ethan’s casual approach to the subject forewarned her he was oblivious to the entire situation. Telling him now, especially in his condition, was out of the question. Instead she resumed her work, "Don’t worry about it. You need to focus on staying still and calm." Though she avoided eye contact, she felt him staring at her as she added more gauze. He wasn’t dropping the subject.

"I know what it was. Dad told me when I asked him about Georgia’s visit."

Her vision snapped to his as she held her hand firmly on the wound. Will Rogers once said, "Never miss a good chance to shut up." So she remained quiet. Ethan really didn’t need or want to know her feelings about his daddy but judging by his expression, he already knew.

He said, "For what it’s worth, he said he never meant to hurt your mother."

Words were cheap. How many times had she heard rapists or murderers utter the same, exact words? So many that it fell on deaf ears, "What’s done is done. Can we change the subject?" *Before I say something I shouldn’t?*

"I honestly believe he loved her and I know he loves you." He winced as she kept the pressure firm and steady. "As for me, I'm truly glad you're my sister."

She prayed her smile didn't appear forced. Ethan's kindness meant a lot but it didn't change Lee's unconscionable behavior. She'd never forgive Lee Morgan, no matter if she was his biological child or not.

Movement in the distance caught her eye. For a few costly moments, she'd let her guard down. The stream camouflaged any noises the person made and the morning fog obscured figures in the distance so she guessed whoever skulked toward them found a good position for firing and for cover. Ethan's yelp probably drew him to their location since it carried for miles in the quiet surroundings – or she feared it had. She moved the rifles within easy reach and grabbed the 9mm for protection.

Ethan's eyes widened, "What did you see?"

"Someone's out there."

Ethan tried sitting up then flopped back down. "Thought I could help," he winced.

"Your job is to stay alive." Every moment that passed without help stole a little of Ethan's life. She tried not to think about his pallid cheeks or how his gradually weakening voice. *Her* job was to protect them and get him help. Number one on that list was locating the bastard slinking behind those trees.

"I should've listened to you but I panicked. Now look at me. I'm sorry my craziness put us in this mess." He touched her arm, "I'm glad I'm with you though."

She glanced down at him and tried bolstering him with a tense yet genuine smile, "I'm glad we're together too, Ethan. We'll get home and reschedule that round of golf at Augusta."

He mustered a small pained smile in response, "Savannah 'The Augusta Bomber' Rutherford and Ethan 'The Hazard' Morgan. The Rematch."

She prayed they lived to play that game. Hell, she prayed they lived to see nightfall, forget the game at Augusta. She wanted to see her family again and wanted Ethan (the only decent Morgan) to live. Their only hope would be to concentrate on removing Lydia's threats, not chatting about things in the past.

Twigs snapped. She turned toward the noise, leveled the 9mm in that direction, "Who's there? Come out with your hands up or I'm shooting till I take you down."

"Sergeant Prince, this is the Union County Sheriff's Department," a voice shouted from the fog obscured trees. "Are you or Ethan Morgan hurt?"

Ethan blew out a shaky, relieved breath, "Thank God. Help." He called back, "I've been shot!"

Savannah shushed him. His mouth gaped in disbelief. His voice put words to his desperation, "Why? We finally get help and you want me to shut up? Savannah, they're cops."

"So are Hoffman and Tierce." She turned to the shooter's position to put him on notice, "Come out from behind those trees and keep your hands where I can see them."

He fired at her. She ducked but saw a shadowy figure running through the dense stand of white pines. She squeezed off a shot, cursing the intense cold for tightening her muscles and skewing her aim.

The gunman darted behind another tree. She fired again. A blistering curse rose from somewhere in the mist. He ran again, gradually moving to her right to get a clearer shot.

Ethan's trembling hand touched her arm, "Hand me your gun and you take the rifle. Maybe I can help."

A valiant offer and a wonderful idea but he was too weak. She squinted into the distance to try to find the shooter. It sounded like she'd hit him so had he gone down or not? "Stay still and awake. That's how you can help."

He groaned, "It really hurts. Can't you let up a little?"

Her heart broke for Ethan. He'd not only been hunted down and shot but she added to his misery by "pushing his guts in the ground". She apologized, "I'm sorry. I know it hurts but I have to do it."

Quick footfalls pounded over twigs and wet pine straw. From the corner of her eye, a man in a beige uniform dashed toward them, his right arm hanging limply at his side and in his left hand, an awkwardly aimed 9mm. She turned and fired once, bringing him down.

He collapsed to his knees and abandoned the gun. Instead he pressing a hand above his navel, cussing and calling her a name Ennis would gladly knock him into next week for saying.

"Sticks and stones, you son of a bitch," she kept low in case the shooting drew more of Lydia's men to join the fun. "Now toss that gun over here. Try anything and I'll give you something worse to cuss about."

His feeble effort flung it halfway between him and Savannah. It would have to suffice. She pointed the gun at his duty belt, "Take those cuffs and cuff your hands behind your back." When he hesitated she shrugged, "Fine. I'll just put a bullet in each arm. That'll fix you."

He promptly cuffed his hands behind him, "You can't stop all of us. Whoever kills you receives a hefty bonus."

"If that's the case, bring me that fancy 9mm you flung over there. A word of caution though. Move the wrong way and you'll receive a bonus you don't want."

"My hands are cuffed behind me. I can't bring you anything."

"If you're clever enough to hunt us down, you're clever enough to find a way to bring me that gun. Go on."

He scowled at her but shuffled forward on his knees and reached back. He fumbled groped for the handgun and finally grasped it by the handle. Savannah kept steady aim on him while he started toward her. A little too eagerly, she noticed. He intended to collect on Lydia's bonus offer.

She volleyed his glare back at him, "When you turn around that hand better be on the barrel and not the handle or trigger."

He lost his nerve and tossed it near her feet. She nodded to the small clearing in front of them, "Go wait out there for your buddies – on your belly."

He waddled on his knees toward the clearing. Before lying down he offered a happy reminder that, "You're both dead. When the others catch up to me, you won't have enough guns or ammo to survive."

Problem was he was right. Even Ethan acknowledged the fact, "Savannah, he's right. You can't hold off a gang of them."

She begged to differ. She beat the odds more than once with Jeffrey Holland so she sure as hell wasn't letting some greedy rich bitch have her way, no matter how many armed minions roamed the forest. She met his vision to state an unyielding, "Don't give up on us yet. You and I have a date to square off on the golf course. I don't intend to break that date, do you?"

The corners of his mouth lifted into a shaky attempt at a smile, "No, sis, I don't."

"This is the Union County Sheriff's Office!" A heavy Georgia accent bellowed from the fog shrouded trees. "Put down your weapons and come out with your hands up!"

Union County Sheriff's Office. Yeah, right. She'd heard that one before. Savannah thought about saying those very words until noticing numerous indistinct shadows passing between trees. Each figure moved in military precision and took up a defensive position for battle. She counted. Four, five, six. Her heart sank when more appeared. Eight. Nine. Ten. Eleven. The "others" arrived en masse and they meant to collect Lydia's bonus.

The handcuffed deputy lying in the clearing was right. They were not only outnumbered in people and weapons but also trapped.

Mounting inner panic and the high altitude air squeezed her lungs in a large, invisible fist. She struggled to retain her composure, to appear in control of the situation which she felt fairly sure she wasn't anymore. How could she focus when she couldn't even breathe?

Ethan put his hand to hers. They exchanged a look. "It's okay, sis. Up to now you've done the impossible. Why not do it again?" He said it with a confidence she wished she felt.

He followed his pep talk with a bolstering squeeze on her wrist. She noticed he didn't try to pull her hand away from the wound. He just wanted to show his support. The man was bleeding internally and still believed in her. She couldn't – *wouldn't* – let him down. She mustered the commanding ring back to her voice, "We're not sticking our heads up so you can shoot 'em off. Drop *your* weapons and put *your* hands up then we'll talk."

There was a long pause before, "We're looking for Sergeant Savannah Prince of the Atlanta Police Department and Ethan Morgan–"

"I'll bet you are," she called back, defiant. "I'll tell you what I told your buddy right there. Step out from behind those trees – all of you – and keep your hands where I can see them. You start shooting like that guy did and you'll end up like him, only worse."

Tense silence followed. Savannah tightened her grip on the gun. Warm blood seeped between her fingers, reinforcing the importance of a speedy rescue, something which seemed improbable now. She pressed down harder on the blood-soaked bandages until a trickle of blood oozed down Ethan's hip. His loud protest drew their unwelcome visitor's attention, "Sounds like he's in bad shape."

"No thanks to your colleagues." She pointed to the handcuffed deputy in the clearing, "That guy's lucky I didn't kill him."

"Ma'am, I have forty deputies and I could pick each one out of a crowd by sight. I don't know who that fella is or how he got that uniform but he's not ours. Now let us get you and Morgan some help."

He actually expected her to fall for *that*? Contrary to what he thought, she wasn't a few feathers short of a full duck. "I said show yourselves and keep your hands in view. You don't and I'll start firing. I may not get all of you but I'll get enough of you."

He waited a few seconds before answering, "My deputies are staying where they are. I'll come out unarmed."

He gradually emerged from the opaque curtain of mist, no gun in his holster and hands lifted to his shoulders. She guessed his age around mid-fifties with silver hair and matching mustache. On the surface he looked like everyone's best friend. He wore no jacket (Savannah assumed he handed it off) and walked out in black uniform slacks hiking boots and a white uniform shirt that stretched over a small paunch.

He tramped over the thick blanket of green fern, passed the handcuffed thug dressed as a deputy then stopped several yards from her position. "Ma'am, I'm Sheriff John Maddox, and I understand why you're nervous about us. I got a call from the Atlanta Police this morning. They said you'd be skittish when we found you."

"*Who* from the Atlanta Police called you? I want names."

"Captain Joshua Hunter and a Detective Ennis Rutherford," he cautiously replied as if hoping the names guaranteed his safety.

"I don't believe you." It was a trick. Odds were Hoffman instructed the sheriff to mention Ennis and for good measure, throw in Josh's name too. Anything to lure her and Ethan out of hiding.

He pointed to his duty belt, "Let me call them." He retrieved his phone and dialed. She heard him speaking to someone but the stream's rippling flow drowned out the words. Maddox punched a button and held the phone out, "It's on speakerphone, ma'am."

"Savannah?" Ennis's anxious voice came through loud and clear. "Savannah, are you there? Are you and Ethan okay?"

For the first time in several long, difficult hours, hope filled her heart. It truly was Ennis. A voice she never expected to hear again. She'd trudged miles in the wilderness, fought off Tierce and battled a small army of determined men paid to kill her and Ethan. She did it all keeping Ennis and their children firmly at the forefront of her mind, vowing to return to them alive and well.

"Savannah?" Ennis called again. "Are you there? Can you hear me?"

Yes, she could hear him. And maybe that was the point. It's a trick, her skeptical side cautioned again, to lure you out. Don't fall for it.

"Ennis! It's Ethan! We're not moving until we know if these are the good guys!"

"They are," he replied. "We checked them out. Savannah, you and Ethan can trust them."

Her shoulders slumped as she sat the gun aside. Safe. Last night it seemed like a far-out, implausible concept. She was truly going home. *Home to the people she loved.*

The urge to break down and cry overwhelmed her. After such a long, harrowing night all she wanted was to go home, get warm in her husband's secure, tender embrace and sleep for two days straight while surrounded by her family. She scarcely swallowed back tears, "I'm so glad to hear your voice. I was so afraid I'd never–"

"Me too, babe, but you can relax now. You and Ethan are safe. How are you both doing?"

I've been better, she wanted to say, but Ennis worried worse than a mother about her. With a healthy dose of oxygen, she would easily recover but Ethan's survival was still in question. "I'm okay," she told her husband, "but Ethan needs to be airlifted to a hospital quick."

"You don't sound so good yourself, babe. The second paramedics arrive, let 'em check your heart."

Maddox handed her the phone then used his radio to call for a helicopter. He waved his deputies into the clearing and began assigning tasks. Two deputies converged on Ethan with first aid kits. They took over from Savannah who, at first, refused to surrendered her position beside Ethan. Only when the deputies assured her they had paramedic training did she move out of their way. She had to trust them, she told herself. Trust. A word so foreign in her vernacular she doubted she'd ever use it again except with family and very close friends, including Ethan.

She worried about his pale complexion and the blood loss. His trembling hand clutched for hers. She knelt beside him, out of the way. Her hands enfolded his and held it close to warm it and comfort him, "Help's on the way, Ethan. It won't be long now."

Tears glistened in his eyes. At that moment he reminded her of a scared boy, not a wealthy CEO of a major company. Whatever battles he fought in life, whether physical or in the boardroom, nothing compared to this one. Struggling for every breath, willing the heart to keep beating, fighting to retain consciousness. She'd been in Ethan's position when

Jeffrey Holland left her to bleed out. Knew what his body was going through, maybe even what he was thinking. He was as terrified as she'd been and just as desperate to live. His grasp tightened on her hand, "You're staying with me, right? You're not gonna leave me."

She gave his hand a tender squeeze, promising, "I'll be right by your side."

He braved a smile, "Thanks, sis." In his unwavering gaze Savannah *thought* she saw the one thing Georgia mentioned weeks ago. Admiration. Tears slipped from his eyes, "I'm so glad you're my sister."

Whether related by blood or a series of life's crazy situations, over the last several weeks she developed a bond with him that just *felt* like family. She couldn't explain it but she honestly liked it. "Me too, Ethan. Me too."

38

A WEEK LATER

Lee Morgan stood at a podium facing a crowd of reporters from local TV stations and a couple of national networks. Behind him were a wheelchair-bound Grady who arrived in a tan Ralph Lauren robe and a cobalt blue blanket covering his lap. His wife spent countless minutes fussing over his hair and blanket until Grady shooed her away and shook his head hopelessly at Preston who eye-rolled his brother's frustration. Grady's wife needed to loosen up, even Savannah had to agree. She complained the whole time about her husband appearing in public during his convalescence but Lee had insisted his children attend the press conference – with the exception of Ethan who still called the hospital home.

"Hmmph," Preston scoffed to Savannah, "Grady thinks having a helicopter wife is a pain in the ass? Try being married to a criminal."

Savannah wasn't sure what to say so she nodded. With Lydia behind bars and Preston filing for divorce, she supposed Grady's aggravation toward his wife's hovering did grate on his brother's nerves.

Neither Grady nor Preston appeared thrilled to attend their daddy's impromptu press conference but Preston made the most of it by arriving in GQ style wearing an Armani suit. That left Savannah who felt like a third thumb even being there anyway, no matter what she wore. She'd spent an hour trying on outfits until settling – out of frustration – on what she called a Macy's Special – an affordable navy skirt suit set with a white blouse and mid-heels usually reserved for Sunday morning services. She tinkered with classing up the outfit with high heels but decided against it. She'd have stood two inches taller than Preston who already suffered an inferiority complex around his taller brothers.

At first it galled her to show up at Lee's little press event until he told her why she and Ennis should attend – and Ennis planned to until he'd been called to a crime scene thirty minutes before the press conference. Lee had scheduled the meeting to update the world on Ethan and Grady's progress, to publicly thank Savannah for saving Ethan's life (he'd already done this but seemed to conveniently forget) *and* he wanted to honor one special person. That "one special person" changed her mind.

Looking more like an executive at Lee's company than a man who'd previously called the street his home, Allen Lamar stood humbly beside Lee. He wore a suit *not* purchased at Macy's, of that Savannah would bet her next paycheck. Lee made sure to spare no expense for the hero who'd helped Ennis the night Burke and Doherty kidnapped her. Yes, for Allen Lamar she'd swallow her disdain for Lee and acknowledge the army veteran's sacrifice for his country and for her.

Lamar endured the lengthy speech with grace but anyone with two good eyes noticed he constantly fought the urge to fidget and tug at his collar. Savannah sympathized. He was a private man thrust into the media spotlight and with that came microscopic scrutiny of his life. They already dredged up his drinking problem and if he sneezed wrong in his past, they'd probably publish that too. He may have been a hero but that didn't keep the jackals at bay, not when it came to reporters.

Lee commended the man who'd stepped up to help Savannah and rewarded him handsomely with a six figure check and an offer of free room and board at Tucker's Crossroads rehab center to shake his booze addiction. Allen gratefully accepted and shook his hand, thanking him.

Lee also used the opportunity to update the masses on his sons' progress. Grady was recovering nicely and was expected to recover to his "normal, vivacious self". Ethan was touch and go at first but thanks to the speedy, competent medical professionals, soon would be "up and around but very sore". As for Savannah, she'd been thoroughly checked (he wasn't kidding either) and was "fit as a fiddle". He made a point to thank his "daughter", saying her efforts saved Ethan's life and that he would always be indebted to her.

Savannah saw Preston flinch at the word "daughter". Lee's oldest son treated her much kinder than ever before, probably because Lee took him aside and warned him to. After the cameras switched off and the reporters dispersed, she and Preston hung back while Grady's wife bundled up her hubby and exited the place like someone shouted *fire*. Grady barely had an opportunity to wave goodbye to Preston before being whisked away.

Preston watched his brother being wheeled out, mumbling, "I wonder if she breathes for him too." He shook his head as if ridding himself of the image. "I'm glad this is over. I hate meeting press these days. I'm always fielding questions about the divorce and Lydia's part in this whole fiasco."

The jackals pounced on him – or tried to – after Lee concluded his update. The reporters hounded Preston for answers about Lydia, rapid-firing questions and shouting over each other until Lee put a stop to it. During the chaos, Savannah occasionally glanced at a stoic Preston. He perfected a poker face that no one, not even she, could read however she figured betrayal was betrayal, no matter who suffered the dirty end of it. Lydia paid to have Tucker killed and nearly succeeded with Grady, Ethan and "the bastard" as Lydia labeled her. Savannah replied, "You handled it well this evening, Preston, and I've no doubt you're capable of handling the media in the future. No matter what happens, at least you have your kids, Lee, Grady and Ethan."

"And you too apparently." He said the last part in a matter-of-fact manner with no obvious resentment. Savannah told herself to mark it on the calendar.

He turned to her, "Thank you for saving Ethan. He told me what you did and I couldn't have done that, at least not successfully. No matter my feelings or our past, I do appreciate your efforts."

Wow. Pigs were flying somewhere nearby. She'd not just mark this on her calendar, she'd stick a gold star on it too. Preston Morgan appreciated her–

"Ma'am?" Allen Lamar had approached without either of them noticing.

Savannah's face split into a wide grin, "Lieutenant, I'm glad

you're here. We didn't have time to talk earlier. Maybe we can now."
They'd spoken only briefly prior to the ceremony when Lee spirited him
away for photos and introduced Lamar to anyone with a pulse. She and
Allen had a twinkling of time to chat that amounted to exchanging hellos
and a thank you from her.

Lamar seemed surprised and pleased she addressed him by his
army rank. His chest seemed to broaden a shade and his shoulders
straightened. Someone remembered his life before he fell on hard times.

"I'll let you two talk," Preston began walking away.

"Sir," Lamar called, "I'd like you to stay if you have time."

He checked his watch, "Sure."

In front of the cameras, Lamar was a shy man. Savannah put it
off to stage fright but he was indeed a reserved soul who struggled to
make eye contact at times. He lifted his gaze to meet both of theirs, "I
wanted to thank you and your family for your generosity. Your father
has me set up in that fancy hotel and now I've got all this money and,
well… This is so overwhelming for me… I can't find the right words
except thank you, thank you all." Lamar shook Preston's hand then gave
Savannah a two-handed handshake, "I'm sure grateful you're okay,
ma'am."

The lieutenant was a fine, gracious man. She prayed he kicked
the alcohol and stayed sober. He certainly deserved a good life. "I'm just
fine thanks to you. The world needs more people like you, Lieutenant."

After her compliment, he glanced away, tugged at his collar for
the hundredth time.

She thought she saw Preston curtail a full blown smile, "Take off the tie. I hate those things too."

While Allen removed the tie and slipped it in his suit pocket, Savannah opened her clutch and handed him her business card. "I'm afraid my show of gratitude can't measure up to Lee's but I do want you to have this. My cell number's on the back. If you need anything, call me day or night."

Lamar studied it. When he glanced up, his chin was trembling, "Thank you. You've all been so kind."

"There you are," Lee called to Allen. "I've been looking for you." Lamar and Savannah exchanged nods and smiles as Lee led him away to meet another of his friends.

Preston shook his head at her, chuckling, "You are one hard person to dislike. Day or night? You really mean that?"

"I really mean that. I also have something for you." She retrieved an envelope from her clutch, "Take a look at this."

He read the return address listing the testing company Georgia used. "A DNA test? But Dad–"

"It's not Lee's DNA. It compares mine to Robert Prince."

His shoulders tensed. When he looked at her, she knew he searched her expression for a hint of what awaited him but she too wielded a mean poker face.

Georgia gave her the envelope days ago. Her sister stood on one foot then the other, waiting for Savannah to slice it open and remove the coveted results. Both their jaws dropped.

Preston removed the enclosed page, shook it out. He looked it over as intently as a legal contract. His brow sank. "I don't recognize the lab's name. How do I know these are real?"

"Easy enough to find on your phone's map application." She pointed to the phone number at the top of the page, amazed that he overlooked the obvious, "Or you could just call them."

He gave her a sidelong frown. Still the skeptic. "How did you get his DNA? He and Dad were adamant they weren't having this done."

"My sister did it on the sly. He never knew."

A hint of a smile lifted his mouth, "So this is it. The truth after all these years."

"Yes. I'm a true blue Prince, not a Morgan."

"Are you showing this to Dad anytime soon?"

They both looked at Lee whose hand was on Allen Lamar's shoulder and he beamed from ear to ear. A few reporters remained, asking questions to both Allen and Lee.

"I can show him before we leave if you prefer," she offered.

Preston stared a moment at his father then handed the paper to her, "He's riding pretty high after yours and Ethan's safe return. Why don't you wait a day or two?"

She folded it and placed it in her purse, "Whatever you want."

He laughed, "I'm surprised you're giving me a choice."

Savannah shrugged with a humorous, "Must be a blue moon tonight."

O O O

For the next few weeks, anyone associated with the Morgans discovered how bright the media spotlight burned and how unsympathetic the public was to their plight. If anything, reporters dug deeper than ever into their past, hoping to dredge up more fodder for their next editions. Savannah certainly wasn't spared this indignity. They trolled information and interviewed people until she felt as exposed as she did for a check-up at the gynecologist's office. The press laid bare past events in her career, revealed what they knew about her present life, and for the first time in several months, Jeffrey Holland's photo reappeared in the paper along with a recap of her ordeal with him.

Preston and Lee suffered the brunt of the media's invasive wrath. They dogged Preston about Lydia and threw in questions about Tucker's wife Sabrina. They hounded Lee over Hoffman and every conceivable charge brought against his family and employees. Big bold headlines accompanied by photos featuring the two wives, Hoffman, Tierce and other security personnel dressed in orange jumpsuits and transport restraints graced the front pages of Atlanta Journal Constitution and Augusta Chronicle. News networks carried the torch by airing video of the jailbirds and the innocent relatives left behind (including Savannah despite her denials of being related) then compared the Morgans to modern day Sopranos. Savannah went to bed with a migraine over that one.

It was not a good few weeks for Morgan Industries stock when investors frowned on the bad publicity, nor was it a stellar time for anyone associated with the family. In one week Ennis and Savannah chased more reporters off their property than they shooed stray cats in the years they'd lived there. The day the media tried snapping a picture of the kids playing in the yard, Savannah traipsed out the door with handcuffs dangling from her hand. She wore jeans and a blue t-shirt that just happened to read *I Can't Fix Stupid But I Can Cuff It*. The next morning her picture on page two of the AJC – pointing at the photographer with a steely-eyed Make My Day glare and holding those cuffs – made it clear: this was one Soprano you didn't screw with. Georgia clipped it for posterity, calling the image "priceless" then threatened to frame it and hang it in the bakery. Savannah promised to break it over her knee if she followed through.

She thought the paternity test might force the Morgan tornado to spit her out and leave her alone. She tried to force Lee into making the results public but he refused, saying the family suffered enough lately without adding a bald-faced lie to the craziness. The meeting resulted in her storming out of his office and her revealing the results to the world only the world didn't care. The press rejected the truth because being Robert Jefferson Prince's daughter didn't raise ratings or sell papers but being Lee Morgan's daughter did.

In the meantime sales of Tucker's book Bad Blood soared to the top of the New York Times Best Seller List and shot straight to number one at Amazon. This nightmare, she decided, would last forever. She contemplated buying space in the AJC to publicize the DNA results but why waste the money? No one wanted the truth. They wanted scandal. Gossip. Innuendo. A real life soap opera and the Morgan family provided better entertainment than HBO or a street brawl. The rich brought to their knees by murder, mayhem, and disgrace.

Once word spread she worked part-time at Georgia's bakery, business picked up considerably. Savannah chose to work in the back preparing pie fillings as opposed to her regular waitressing gig. Georgia was happy to see the uptick in patrons, telling Savannah, "This is giving us widespread publicity. You're making us famous."

"So would a listeria outbreak but you don't want *that*, do you?" Okay, so she was a killjoy. She would have said *so sue me* but with her luck lately, someone would have.

She spent so much time saying "no comment" she heard it in her sleep. She skimmed over the morning paper for the newest headlines in the ongoing melodrama and praying she wasn't mentioned. Sabrina confessed to setting up the earlier kidnappings to get her "fair share" before Lee rewrote his will to include Savannah. Evidently she missed the newsflash. Savannah was already there and had been since birth. Sabrina also admitted that Tucker's kidnapping was punishment for screwing the hotel heiress on the side.

As for Lydia, she confessed to hers and Mike Hoffman's affair. With evidence plus Burke, Doherty and others making deals with authorities, she finally admitted she wanted to pad Preston's monetary worth by knocking off Lee's heirs – but swore that Mike Hoffman had the idea first. Either way, she and Hoffman were destined for a long stay in prison.

The news brought a rare smile to Savannah's face. Now perhaps her life might settle down and the reporters could hound politicians over broken promises or write about the pothole situation around town.

As usual she'd been wrong. Reporters likened Lee to Tony

Soprano but it turned out he was a real life John Gotti. A true Teflon Don. No matter his crimes (the precious few that could be proven), no one in power, from the police chief to congressmen and the governor, wanted him prosecuted. The hardest part came when Lee's part in stealing Charlene's journals came to light. The police chief, mayor and those other "higher authorities" decided to overlook his "lapse in judgment", as they called it.

The mayor called her to his office – with the police chief, a congressman and the governor present – to speak with her about the decision. She voiced her disapproval as vehemently as she dared without losing employment. "It figures," she'd stormed. "My mother gets screwed again. He can't be tried for rape but he needs to be prosecuted for theft. There's proof he ordered Hoffman to steal her journals. I heard it myself."

Both waved her argument away, citing the greater good and what Morgan Industries provided to the state and the world, blah, blah blah… The bullshit piled so high it practically choked her.

By the time the powers that be agreed not to throw Lee in jail, she knew his portion of the SD card involving Charlene's journals – and everything else had been conveniently erased. So, like Bobby Ewing's death on Dallas, the whole thing never happened, except there was no cheesy shower scene to wake Savannah from her nightmare.

She left the chief's office so angry she dared not go back to the station or go home. She passed by a dozen package stores and never slowed down. She stopped at a park for an hour to calm down. Had she not been dressed for work she'd have taken the longest run of her life. As it were, she settled for walking off her rage until the urge to hit something became so overwhelming she clenched her fists then cocked her arm back at a tall, mature oak tree. A sudden ping in her ribs killed the idea. Just as well. The media might accuse Lee Morgan's daughter of decking an innocent, elderly citizen.

She pulled the gold badge from her belt and studied it. Stroked the eagle along the top. Cops risked their lives every day to find, arrest and put away criminals. They shed blood, sweat and tears to build their cases with evidence and witness statements. Then they handed them off to the DA, hoping that somewhere along the way justice might be served. But when ego-bloated bureaucrats stepped in and magically freed them, it made a mockery of law enforcement. She'd worked hard for so many years, faithfully adhering to her oath as a police officer, only to be screwed by the people who signed her paychecks and had control over her career in one way or another.

This wasn't the first time she became dissatisfied or thoroughly disillusioned with her job but this one hit the hardest. It wasn't her that got the shaft. It was her mother and that was unconscionable. No doubt Lee contributed a hefty sum to certain campaigns (and probably plenty of certain bank accounts too) to buy his pass on prosecution. If the police chief began tooling around in a Jaguar or toting a Rolex on his wrist, she'd know. *She would know.*

This job. This job she loved for so long. Protect and Serve. Helping others in need. First on scene. She couldn't remember every victim's face but the abused kids and rape victims? Yes, she recalled them. Their names too. Some stayed right in the forefront of her mind and on occasion they appeared on long, sleepless nights. Certain words or phrases or their desperation, their tears, their pleas to her for justice. She'd fought for them, thinking *what if this happened to my mother, my sister or my daughter?* And it *had* happened to her mother. And her mother lay in her grave after a lifetime bearing those horrific memories and never saying a word about it. And Lee Morgan got off scot free then and now. A point she tried to make with those crooked, baby-kissing snake oil salesmen that afternoon. Four decades ago, Lee raped a good, God-fearing, church-going woman who'd trusted him. A woman working to make ends meet, to put food on the table and clothes on her children's backs. She had to do this because Lee Morgan held grudges against this woman's husband. In fact Morgan hated him for "stealing her from him" in a manner of speaking, so Lee used his money and influence to nearly ruin this man financially. Meanwhile this good, God-fearing, church-going woman believed she was pregnant from Lee's brutal attack. For everything done to her family, Savannah told them, Lee Morgan should spend his life in prison. She yearned to recite it to those spineless politicians who protected Morgan from prosecution. She wanted to shout it to the world but no one seemed to listen or care.

She cursed under her breath. She and Ennis were spinning their wheels at this job. Justice was a joke. In a moment of folly she fantasized about walking into Morgan's office and blowing the bastard away. Now *that* was justice. Then she realized *she* would be arrested, convicted and sent to prison and take up residence beside Lydia Morgan's cell. Oh boy, she lamented. That little scenario sounded like one of Dante's nine circles of hell.

Blowing out a frustrated sigh, she jammed the badge back on her belt. She worked hard for that badge and if the sergeant's salary hadn't paid what it did, Savannah would've seriously contemplated chucking the thing for a different job. But what exactly compared to a sergeant's salary for paying mortgages, insurance and baby formula? The subject needed more thought and also input from Ennis. She'd love a job with less stress, semi-normal hours and no interaction with people who lied for a living.

She walked to her car and started for home. On the way she passed a Barnes & Noble advertising Tucker's poisonous tome *Bad Blood*. In large, bold lettering the placard announced "In Stock Now – 25% Off". Ethan's remark during Sabrina's trumped up kidnapping came to mind. "Poor Tucker. He's been marked down." And he truly had been – again.

She went home and changed clothes, intending to clean the house to a spotless, sparkling condition and if she pooped out before she finished, well that was just too bad. That's why God created pizza delivery. She only needed enough energy to pick up the kids later then she'd wait for Ennis to get home and discuss finances and the fantasy of changing jobs.

At three o'clock Ennis surprised her by arriving early with the kids. He toted Daniel in his arms and, like the wise father he was, let the girls converge on their mother with hugs and kisses before he dared try muscling in. Lily, Anna and Ennis smothered her in cheerful greetings, tight hugs and plenty of kisses. The extraordinary degree of attention surprised her and inspired a fair amount of regret for contemplating murder. How could she live without her babies and her dear, loving husband? Being separated from them comprised *all nine* circles of hell.

Ennis planted a quick kiss to her lips, "I heard about Morgan. I'm sorry, babe."

Savannah shrugged it off, "I guess I halfway expected it. Money talks."

He placed Daniel in the crib. "Doesn't make it any easier though."

"No, it doesn't. What brings you home so early?"

His arms encircled her waist and drew her against him, "You. Josh approved my time off and I'll make it up tomorrow. Put your Sunday-go-to-meetin' clothes on, Mrs. Rutherford, cause I'm taking you to dinner at a place with an actual dress code, one that's stricter than a ruler-wielding nun teaching a roomful of kids." He bobbed his brow, "It's Date Night."

Butterflies took flight in Savannah's stomach. Date Night. In the olden, golden days before they had kids, Date Night involved, well, dinner and some fill-in-the-blank activity like a movie, trip to a museum or a show at the Fox Theatre (the last one they reserved special Date Nights like anniversaries). But the evening always, *always* ended in the bedroom for the grand finale.

She couldn't remember exactly when they last indulged in Date Night. Sure, they'd had nights out together since then but to actually invoke the sacred term "Date Night"? This man had a super special evening planned and she hoped it ended with them in bed getting randy with each other. Though she felt sure he'd covered the bases, she asked,

"And our rugrats?"

"Covered. I called Seth and he and Leah are babysitting for us. We'll be all alone, the whole evening to ourselves." He reclaimed her lips in a kiss so passionate it sang through her veins.

She put her arms around his neck, luxuriating in the velvet caress of his lips. Mmm… So soft, so warm, so inviting. Moments like these made the last several weeks bearable. She broke the kiss, lilting seductively, "I'm beginning to like this idea."

"Babe, you don't know the half of it." He dove in for another kiss – a long, slow one that left her breathless and sent spirals of desire through her. His lips seared a path down her throat where he lingered at her quickening pulse. He smiled against her skin, "Hmm. You do like this idea."

"Ugh. That's gross." Lily stood, arms crossed and frowning.

The youngster's sudden berating startled Savannah. Hadn't she seen both girls leave the room? She was sure of it – at first – but now she couldn't remember, not after being lovingly waylaid by her romantic, *very* persuasive husband. Savannah hadn't intended on teaching her daughter the facts of life (or the beginnings of them) in a personal demonstration, but there Lily was, watching them and looking none too impressed at Mama's and Daddy's antics.

Ennis sighed at Lily, "You're supposed to be getting ready to head to Uncle Seth's house."

"I was but I wanna wear my Olaf shirt."

Savannah cleared the lust from her voice before answering, "It's in your middle dresser drawer, sweetie."

"Now run along," Ennis prompted.

Lily stayed put for several seconds, probably waiting for her parents to break their embrace but they didn't. "Okaaay, but you both better behave." She walked off shaking her head and huffing her disgruntlement like a frustrated parent, "I can't leave you two alone anymore."

Ennis and Savannah laughed. The moment Lily was out of sight, Savannah inquired, "Where are we going tonight, Casanova?"

"Prepare yourself. We are dining at Nikolai's Roof in one hour and fifteen minutes. We will ride the elevator to the top of the Hilton and you will choose a three, four or six course meal and we will dine with an awesome view of Atlanta's skyline."

His arms tightened as her knees grew weak. The butterflies went wild in her stomach. Her heartbeat skyrocketed. Nikolai's Roof. One of the top restaurants in the country. Not the city, the entire U. S. of A. It received the four diamond restaurant award for the chef, menu and ambiance. It took real influence to grab a table at Nikolai's and she wasn't about to ask how he snagged a table. Nope, no way, no how. She was along for the ride and would let her hubby treat her to one of the rarest, most sought-after evenings any woman could dream of.

"That's not all," he teased. "After supper, we'll go to a movie, take a carriage ride, or–"

"Misbehave while Little Mama's away," she cut her vision toward Lily's bedroom.

He broke into a dazzling smile, "I was hoping you'd opt for that one."

39

The doorbell rang. The visitor followed up with four solid knocks that rattled the door. The last week tested Savannah's patience to the hilt. Today's bold visitor snapped the final thread. Besides fending off that nightmare media blitz plus keeping semi-regular work hours, she'd spent the last few evenings preparing and freezing dishes for Thanksgiving the following week. Every year Georgia cooked the turkey and made pies. This year was no different despite Savannah's strong suggestion she leave the bird to her this time. Georgia remained steadfast. Thanksgiving would stay the same. The two sisters would slice the turkey and prepare the dressing together and everyone would proceed with the meal's customary menu. That meant Savannah's contribution were cakes and half of the side dishes (their sister-in-law Leah prepared the other half). Savannah checked off each dish the way convicts marked off days behind bars. Cranberry chutney, sweet potato casserole, macaroni and cheese. That left two cakes which the family would choose at this weekend's get-together. A lot of work in a short time that took serious wrangling to fit it all into her schedule. A cinnamon apple cake baked in the oven for that night's dessert and while it finished up, Savannah tackled supper.

Between the hectic cooking and baking schedule, Lily required pointers on her golf practice, something Savannah normally enjoyed but lately felt the pinch of time. She powered through however, since the child showed real passion for the game and Savannah hated to dampen her enthusiasm by turning her down. Then Anna's teacher informed her and Ennis that the girl needed help on fundamentals of math. Little Anna Rose was her mother's daughter in that respect so Savannah and Ennis split tutoring duties and taking care of Daniel.

With everything going on recently, Savannah's temper ran pretty short and hot, especially when some clod beat on her front door the way SWAT did before breaking it down.

The visitor caught her chopping fresh basil for supper (Chicken Parmesan), a meal which already ran late. She laid the knife aside, checked the cake in the oven then grabbed a dish cloth to wipe her hands. The person beating on her front door was about to get a refresher course on manners. She headed to the door, slinging the cloth over her shoulder as she went because she'd need both mitts to strangle the persistent idiot. God help them if they were selling anything because she'd give them something for free. A good, loud lecture on manners.

Lily ran to answer it but Savannah lifted a hand in a "stop" gesture. Anyone willing to beat on their door deserved to face an adult, not a child.

She made sure Lily stood a safe distance from the door before she jerked it open, her mouth cocked and primed to give someone the what-for. It took one second for her brain to analyze the danger in bitching out the surprise visitor and one more second to evaluate his mood and stance. Thankfully she saw no sign of aggression. Just the sight of him threw her busy mind into total confusion, "Daddy? What are you doing here?"

Lily dashed to the bedroom. Probably not a bad idea, Savannah supposed, at least until she discovered his reason for being there. Only when Lily announced *I'm calling 911!* did she protest, "No, sweetie, don't." She nearly said *not yet* but thought better of it.

Dressed in his usual tan khakis and white t-shirt, R.J. cradled a bottle of Jack Daniel's in one arm as he helped himself inside. Old Spice wafted past as she stepped aside for him. He'd cleaned up that morning, fresh clothes, clean-shaven and topped off with her mother's favorite cologne for him. The one smell not registering with Savannah: scotch. This was a treat. A sober R.J. in her midst.

Lily vehemently protested his presence and provided a stinging reminder about "what happened before". Savannah shushed her daughter before the girl sparked his anger.

Oh yes, no matter how he dressed or groomed himself, he looked imposing enough to take on a small army and flatten half of them. He stood six feet with plenty of muscle left on his bones, and his shoulders and jaw perpetually set in a way daring anyone to take him on. Today his blue eyes narrowed just enough to bring a low-level ache to her ribs. She prayed she hadn't screwed up by allowing him inside.

"Sweets said ya tried making Morgan tell the world you were mine and not his," he began. No *hello, how's it going* for R.J. Prince. He always got down to business.

Savannah felt an uncertain twinge in her gut, particularly about that topic. Why *had* he made this trip? He still hadn't answered that question and it bothered her. Oh sure, he held an Uncle Jack – which normally served as a peace offering – but he could just as easily decide to break it over her head. "I tried but he refused. He won't accept the truth."

"Ya tried though. That's what counts." He plunked the Jack on the table with a bit too much force, "My question is where'd ya get my DNA and did I ever say it was okay to take it?"

She swallowed hard. The lump that instantly formed stayed put. How could she signal Lily to call the cops if she couldn't speak? Her vision shot to the hallway. Lily looked on, phone in hand. Thank God, she thought, because I *will* need an ambulance after this, maybe even the coroner. Now to answer his question. She'd never rat out Georgia or Dane. To protect them she needed to confess to the deed herself. The words stumbled onto her tongue just as R.J. put a heavy hand to her shoulder, saying, "Settle down, girl. Point is, ya proved what we all knew. I'm yer daddy, not that son of a bitch."

She nodded while trying to calm her heart from the sprint it started a moment earlier. His hand stayed on her shoulder, giving it a squeeze. She tried not to wince. The only thing that came to mind was, "Yes, so hopefully he'll leave me alone." Fat chance but it sounded good anyway.

"That's not the only reason I came to see ya." He released her but she kept a covert eye to that hand, remembering the power of his punch and the damage it caused. He asked, "Sweets tell ya she's havin' a little girl?"

Savannah nodded again. The knot in her throat finally dislodged. Her father's visit went well so far but she wouldn't count her

chickens too soon…

"She's namin' her Charlotte. Beautiful name, ain't it?" He turned toward a standoffish Lily, "like Lily."

"Yes, Daddy, they are pretty names."

He put hands to hips, sighing, "Well, that Nazi nurse finally let me outta that house. I tell ya, yer sister can find the meanest people in healthcare I ever seen. I'm cleared to drive again so I brought ya that." He pointed to the bottle on the table. She thanked him then picked up the heavy bottle with an impressive nod. He'd bought the biggest they made which translated to the grandest apology he'd offer. Weeks ago the whiskey would have put her over the moon. Now she wondered if it was too uncouth to re-gift it to someone.

Without glancing up, Savannah felt Lily's scathing disapproval from across the room. Her daughter would have to learn that refusing the liquor might incite a riot with R.J. and no one wanted that.

R.J. said, "It's a gift for what ya done for me that day at the house. Ya done good, girl."

She set it on the kitchen counter, "I love you, Daddy, and I want you safe."

"Yep. Same goes for me. So, ya interested in celebrating yer sister's news with that?" Before she answered, he turned back to Lily. "I come in peace, girl," he said loud enough the child backed up a step. "Yer mama and I have our disagreements but we're still family and I'm still yer grandpa. Don't ya forget it and don't let anyone tell ya otherwise."

From the corner of her eye, Savannah saw her daughter

completely withdraw behind the wall and assured R.J., "She won't forget."

He started toward the hallway. Lily raced to her bedroom. The door slammed. "Come back here!" he yelled.

Savannah tensed. Maybe today *wasn't* a good day to interact. She waited to see if Lily obeyed. She didn't. Savannah prepared to revert to Mama Bear mode since R.J. wasn't accustomed to his commands being ignored. She was surprised to see him reach in his pocket for a package of Skittles.

He handed it over, "I brought her these since she likes 'em." He summoned Lily again, "I brought ya something. Come on out here."

No sign of Lily. Or Anna for that matter.

Savannah slowly released the breath she'd been holding, "I'll give them to her, Daddy. Thank you."

"Sure." He retrieved another package, "This'n is for Anna. Didn't get the boy anything since he's too young."

"That's fine." She nodded to the dining table. "Have a seat," she said, trying to block images of the last time he stepped foot in her house. She'd slammed so hard into the table it nearly broke a rib.

He settled into Ennis's usual chair. "What's in the oven? Smells good."

"Cinnamon sugar apple cake. It's about done. Want a piece?"

"If yer offerin'. You and Sweets sure took after yer mama. Never a dull meal or dessert." He nodded to the whiskey, "Crack 'er open. We'll toast to Charlotte."

Savannah glanced toward the hallway. After fleeing her grandpa

and shutting the bedroom door, Lily magically reappeared again. She, like Georgia, possessed owl ears. Lily peered around the corner, those piercing blue eyes centering on her mother. R.J. wasn't the only one capable of freezing a person with a glare. Lily proved to be an expert.

The five-year-old shot up to an impressive four feet tall and at times displayed an eerily convincing maternal frown. Today that frown was seasoned with a hint of R.J.'s squinting judgmental stare that always produced an uneasy feeling in Savannah's gut. Don't even think of taking a drink, that look said – and it was not a suggestion. It was a warning.

Savannah had no intention of drinking. The second R.J. left, she'd pour the liquor out and have "Mama" Lily witness the act. "I'll pour you a drink, Daddy, but I'd like to save mine for later if that's okay. How about a piece of cake to toast Charlotte?"

"Fine by me."

She pulled the cake from the oven and a few minutes later, brought a slice apiece plus a small glass of Jack for her father and a glass of milk for herself. She scooted the milk into Lily's viewing range to ensure her kid understood the strongest thing her Mama drank was whole milk. Lily smiled and retreated behind the wall again.

R.J. did the honors, raising his glass, "To Charlotte and Sweets. Hope she has two or three more, includin' a coupla boys. This family could do with more of 'em."

Savannah clinked her milk glass to his whiskey. "To Charlotte, Georgia *and* Dane," she amended. After all, Dane hit the winning home run, so to speak.

R.J. dug into the cake. One bite and he lapsed into a blissful smile, "Mmm-hmm. Just like yer mama's." He glanced in the kitchen and spied the chopped basil on the counter, "What ya having for supper?"

"Chicken Parmesan."

"That stuff with the red sauce?"

His palate lacked adventure but he did enjoy Chicken Parm as she recalled. "Seasoned tomato sauce, yes. Want to stay and eat? We'll have plenty."

He forked another bite into his mouth, chewed, then chased it with whiskey after he swallowed, "Wish I could but the Nazi's comin' back at five. Rain check?"

She nodded, "Collect anytime." She sampled the cake. Not bad. Not as good as her mother's despite what he said, but not bad at all.

"How 'bout you an' me have lunch this week? Maybe the battleaxe'll let me out for that."

She smiled, "I'd love to have lunch together, Daddy."

"You buying?"

Was there any other way? "Yes, I'm buying."

Now *he* smiled, a true rarity if one knew R.J. Prince. "Lemme know when and I'll pull a jailbreak."

O O O

Georgia set two pink and black Pie In The Sky coffee cups on the bistro table farthest from the steady noise of the dough mixers. One cup of black coffee for herself, the other with cream and a touch of sugar for Savannah.   She and her sister spent the Stupid-o-clock hours (as Savannah called them) rolling out pie crusts and mixing fillings to prepare for the day.   When other employees began arriving for work, Georgia decided she and Savannah deserved a break.

Savannah slid two maple walnut pies in the oven and loaded pumpkin pies on the other racks.   The bakery soon filled with the warm spicy smells of cinnamon, nutmeg, ginger and maple, all the delectable aromas of Thanksgiving.   This week they dedicated to preparing for the holiday and last minute flood of orders for pumpkin pie.   With autumn in full swing and Thanksgiving a few days away, the usual staples of apple, cherry and blueberry remained popular but nothing outsold the tried and true pumpkin pie so Georgia made a surplus.   Special orders began rolling in over a month earlier.

Without fail every year, starting a month before Turkey Day, customers began placing their orders for pumpkin pies and Georgia, Savannah and the staff at Pie In The Sky baked enough pumpkin pies to fill over three quarters of the pie storage. The day before Thanksgiving, Georgia made sure to stock a few extra for last minute dinner-goers but it didn't stop the phone from ringing off the wall with desperate people searching for the last pumpkin pie in Atlanta.

Savannah dabbed perspiration from her forehead.   Who said baking wasn't hard work? Anyone with that misconception should try working all day measuring, rolling, fluting, and mixing the pies *then* working a steady carousel of moving pies in and out of an oven.   But it paid off with the joy, smiles and laughter of patrons.   When they opened the door and caught the first hint of delicious smells lingering in the air, something magical happened. The decadent aromas pushed their troubles to the background long enough for an uncomplicated moment of pure childlike delight to spring forth. It stirred memories of long ago when life was simpler, happier. Savannah had seen nostalgic smiles curve the lips of both men and women then heard the remark "this reminds me of Mother's" after taking a bite. Baking pies was tiring work and a vast contrast to her day job – but a good one and uplifting for the soul.

She washed her hands and joined her sister in the seating area, grateful for the break. A glance at the clock revealed an hour until opening time. The place filled in a hurry the closer it got to Thanksgiving so she'd have an abbreviated break and try to convince Georgia to sit out the rest of the morning because she looked exhausted. She knew the likelihood of success rated around zero but she'd try anyway. Georgia never sat by and watched people work. Her guilt trips went both ways – she gave them (and with astounding effectiveness) but never hesitated to impose one on herself either. It was her business, she told Savannah and the dedicated employees, so she should do more than wipe down countertops and do paperwork. If Savannah had her way, her sister would do a shade more than that. It required no strenuous activity and would take five seconds of her time.

Savannah noticed it when she stepped through the back door that morning and decided Georgia was either deaf or liked pushing people's buttons, "You hung that lousy picture after I threatened to break it over my knee."

Adding insult to injury, Georgia curbed a chuckle, "It's a fantastic shot. The look on your face is priceless. If you notice, I hung it in my desk area. The customers won't ever see it."

"It's hideous. I look maniacal." She rolled her eyes, "And that shirt…"

"That's the best part. *I Can't Fix Stupid But I Can Cuff It* – and you're holding handcuffs. I love it and you'd better leave it alone." Georgia leaned back in the chair, "Speaking of irritating subjects, have you heard from Lee lately?"

Savannah sipped her coffee. She closed her eyes on a groan. Between that and the aroma of fresh baked pies, it was pure bliss. "He's still expecting me, Ennis and the kids over at Thanksgiving for dessert. The man has no conscience so to answer your question yes, I've heard from him." She leaned across the table mumbling, "I still want to kill the bastard."

Georgia's mouth pressed into a line. She knew better than to argue because she felt the same way. "But orange isn't your best color and you can't kiss your family through plexiglass barriers so you won't kill him. Home is much nicer than prison." She waited a moment before furthering the conversation, "I don't suppose he'll ever accept the fact you're not his."

"Nope. He told me I'm staying in his will. I can already hear his family sharpening their knives and grinding their axes. Except Ethan, of course."

Lifting the cup to her lips, Georgia smirked at the dark humor, "Just a wild guess but you don't want to be in Lee's will?"

"About as much as I want to go bungee jumping without a

bungee. But then I figured why not? Not about the bungee jump but the will. It would be infinitesimal repayment for what he did to Daddy's business back when. Nothing could repay what he did to Mama, of course, but I could use the money to help Daddy if he's still alive." She half-shrugged, "And since you confronted Lee with Mama's journals, the promised 'inheritance' is probably a payoff to keep me quiet."

Georgia didn't contest her sister's logic. "He certainly won't admit what he did, I found that out."

"Nor will he ever give up trying to hire me apparently. Since many of his security detail are behind bars, he offered me the Chief Security Officer job for the millionth time." She proudly added, "And I told him no for the millionth time."

Georgia shook her head, "He is one stubborn man." She reached in her apron pocket, handed Savannah a folded sheet of old, yellowing paper. "This explains how stubborn he really is."

Savannah unfolded it. It was an official paper from a lab in Atlanta dated when Savannah was six years old. It had three columns, one with only rows of numbers, then two others labeled "Child" and "Alleged Father". If Charlene hadn't written "Savannah" beside "Child" and "R.J." beside "Alleged Father" Savannah would have never known who'd been tested. Each row of numbers, when read left to right, gave the sample result, then Savannah's then beside hers, R.J.'s. A match was indicated by a checkmark. Beneath the three columns was a Probability of Paternity that spelled it out in bold numbers. R. J. Prince fathered Savannah.

The start of a smile played at the corners of Georgia's mouth,

"That paternity test is ninety percent accurate because all they had back then was HLA, ABO and serological testing. I'd say ninety percent was more than enough proof you were Daddy's even back then."

Savannah marveled at the page she couldn't make complete sense of. She just saw a lot of checkmarks and checkmarks were good for her and R.J. She didn't know an HLA or ABO from an M-I-C-K-E-Y or an M-O-U-S-E but ninety percent way back in the middle ages of paternity testing? Damn good enough for her. "Where did you find this?"

"Tucked between the pages of another journal. Mama's entry says she showed it to Lee and he denied it was real. Even then he refused to accept the truth."

A sudden wave of emotion washed over Savannah. Tears of happiness blurred her vision. If she didn't rein in the urge to cry, they'd have a flood on their hands but the news was better than winning the lottery. It meant Charlene knew the truth long before she died. She knew while raising her youngest daughter that R.J. fathered the child.

Just like their mama and grandmother, Georgia magically produced a fresh tissue from her apron pocket then handed it to her sister who dabbed away tears, "So Mama *didn't* die thinking I was Lee Morgan's kid." For weeks and weeks Savannah obsessed that she had.

"No, she didn't. Now you can rest easy. We all can." She reached across and gave Savannah's hand a tender squeeze. She watched Savannah gradually overcome her tears and waited until her sister straightened her face before inquiring, "How are the Chester Chipmunk stories coming along?"

She shrugged, "Okay, I guess. Don't get much time to work on them. Lily and Anna seem to enjoy them when I *can* finish one."

"They're not the only ones who like them."

She blew her nose then chuckled an incredulous, "Don't tell me you and Dane are Chester fans. I'm not *that* good."

She lifted a brow, "You're better than you think."

She waved off the compliment, "Oh, please. My kids' demands for more just means they're easily entertained."

Georgia's smile evolved into a tentative one. Why the change in mood, Savannah wondered. Her sister always spoke her mind, well, at least most of the time. Only when something went really wrong did she hesitate. That realization forced two words (spoken way too often lately) to fall from Savannah's lips, "What's wrong?"

"Nothing's wrong."

But Savannah heard the under-the-breath *yet*. Nothing's wrong *yet*. Georgia expounded with a nervous, "I just hope I didn't *do* something wrong." She reached in her other apron pocket and removed a piece of paper, "I took the liberty of transcribing your original written stories onto the computer."

"Okaay," she cautiously dragged out the word. "So far so good. They needed to be easier to read anyway." She waited for Georgia to fire the next round at her. It wasn't over, the older sister's expression warned. And the next shot would be a whopper. She noticed Georgia grew antsier by the second, squirming in the seat, fiddling with that little piece of paper she held and obviously contemplating what to say next.

How bad was this news, anyway? It couldn't be devastating. They were stories, for God's sakes. "Georgia, just tell me. Whatever you did, it's fine."

"I sent them to Blake."

Except that. She sent them to Blake *her publisher?* No wonder Georgia looked ready to run for the hills. Just to be clear, "You sent Chester to *Blake Crenshaw, your publisher in New York?*"

Georgia flinchingly nodded like she'd lit the fuse to a bomb and suddenly found herself trapped for the blast.

Savannah shrank back in the chair, battling shock and humiliation. She could only imagine the hysterical laughter in Blake's office while he plodded through the simplistic, silly tales of a rodent's travels around Augusta, Georgia.

Her face suddenly felt hot enough to pop off like Aunt Emma's pressure cooker lid when it blew and plastered potatoes all over the ceiling. She buried her face in her hands to hide the crippling mortification. She never, never, *never* considered handing those silly stories to anyone except Lily and Anna. Now they sat in the hands of a big name publisher waiting to be rejected, of course, because all writers were rejected, weren't they? But she *wasn't a writer.* She was a cop.

She should have been furious with Georgia but was too busy trying to avoid testing the spontaneous human combustion theory. How could her sister embarrass her this way? She'd never be able to look Blake Crenshaw in the eyes again. She shook her head, begging to know, "Why? Those were meant for the kids. He probably laughed himself stupid."

"I took a chance because I thought they had promise." She tugged Savannah's hands away. Georgia was grinning at her, "He liked them, Savannah. He wants to publish them with Bluebird Books, the company's children's imprint. He said the stories need more work and I can help with that then he'll line up an artist for illustrations and Avery said he'd be happy to sign on as your agent…" Her spiel wound down to silence when she noticed Savannah lacked the same enthusiasm. It was Georgia's turn to ask, "What's wrong?"

Savannah felt the blood suddenly abandon her cheeks. She swallowed and held a hand to her stomach. Was this real? Could this possibly be happening? To *her*? Had she gone from cop and part-time baker to maybe adding published author to her resumé? She'd gained a publisher and agent in less than five minutes – if she wanted them. Only a fool declined such a lucrative offer. As a girl she wanted to be just like Georgia most of all. Her sister always tinkered with words and on occasion created cute little bedtime stories for Savannah. That's when Savannah came up with Chester. If her sister wrote stories, she would too, and when Georgia sold her first book to a publisher, that also became Savannah's goal. Now, decades later, that dream came true if she chose to accept it.

It wasn't a bad idea. If she penned stories to supplement her day job, perhaps becoming a bonafide author wasn't so far-fetched. But Chester's competition played in the major league – they had a tried and true fan base and had for generations. In the world of Pooh Bear, Berenstain Bears, Cat in the Hat, pigs, dogs, turtles and caterpillars and a ton of other animal characters, was there room for her inquisitive chipmunk? "I don't know, Georgia. Chester's got a fight on his hands with all the competition plus I've got my family and job. I can barely find time to write those things as it is. I'd love to be published but I don't think my life will allow it."

The reply failed to slow the full-steam-ahead runaway train known as General Georgia, the woman who Got Things Done. Once she set her mind to something, people either stepped aside or got flattened. "Savannah, they know you have a hectic life but Blake assured me that the earlier stories plus what you've penned lately, he's got a few years' worth of publishing material. Except for the kids demanding new stories, you wouldn't have to write a thing for a long time, hon. As for competition, do you think Blake would offer a contract if he thought Chester wouldn't sell?"

Georgia really wanted this, Savannah thought. She'd not seen her sister this excited since... well, since that day in the attic when she revealed she was pregnant.

The older sister placed the piece of paper on the table and slid it across to her, "They both want to hear from you."

Savannah stared wordlessly at the names and phone numbers. She came to the bakery that morning to help out and spend time with Georgia. She'd go home with more options than she ever thought possible. A published author? Nah, not her. That was Georgia's bailiwick. The devil on her shoulder agreed. *You're not good enough. You'll have a contract. Deadlines – and you already have too many of those at work. And what happens when the well runs dry on ideas or worse – your books don't sell? Then what do you do?*

The angel on her other shoulder reminded her, as Georgia had, that Blake Crenshaw never frivolously gambled with his company's earnings so she *must* have a morsel of talent, at least.

For the heck of it she envisioned her name on a book cover – Savannah Rutherford? S.C. Rutherford? Or perhaps go Georgia's route of first, maiden then married name. She tried it on for size. Savannah Prince Rutherford. Yeah, she liked that. She liked it a lot.

Holding the piece of paper, she reviewed what Georgia said. No writing deadlines for more than a year. That helped. And with Georgia's help on revision and editing, she could do it and simultaneously learn about the art of creative writing. A spiffy book cover came to mind. One with bright, happy colors and a professionally drawn Chester Chipmunk in his dashing fedora and green plaid blazer. And gracing the cover in all its glory: the name Savannah Prince Rutherford. Hmm, she hemmed and hawed. On second thought, Savannah Rutherford sounded just right.

A smile slowly inched across her face. Across the table, Georgia's nervous hopefulness gave way to a cautious sly grin, "Is that a yes?"

"It's a yes – for now. Once I talk to Ennis and the kids and contact Blake and Avery, I think I'd like to give Chester a chance in the big world of publishing. Who knows," she winked, "maybe there's an adventure in it for him." Savannah folded the paper, pocketed it. She and Ennis would discuss the opportunity at length but she knew his answer. He wanted her to be happy and right now, the thought of seeing her work on bookstore shelves and entertaining children with a furry little friend was right up her alley. The endeavor into writing also allowed her to leave something of herself behind, not only for her children but her grandchildren. Proof that Grandma didn't just toss bad guys in jail but penned adventures of an inquisitive, often times mischievous chipmunk.

Before making that final decision, she and her family needed to talk but for now she'd bask in the opportunity to fulfill a lifelong dream. She'd test drive the idea of becoming a published author and if she liked the feel of it and the ride didn't cost too much, she'd happily sign on the dotted line and drive that idea home.

Georgia raised her cup, toasting, "To Savannah and Chester. May they stay in enough trouble it keeps them both busy for many years."

J.L. Lemon lives in Texas surrounded by a loving and supportive family, two adorable and devoted puppies, and hordes of garden gnomes.

Before 2002, J.L. Lemon wrote opinions and product reviews for an online consumer guide. When fellow reviewers cited the author's knack for humor, she decided to return to writing fiction. Along with the standalone title Second Chances, she's published 14 books in the Savannah Stories Series.

www.ingramcontent.com/pod-product-compliance
Lightning Source LLC
Chambersburg PA
CBHW030743030726
47497CB00001B/106